CROSSING POINT

JAMES GLICKMAN

A Vireo Book | Rare Bird Books
Los Angeles, Calif.

This is a Genuine Vireo Book

A Vireo Book | Rare Bird Books
453 South Spring Street, Suite 302
Los Angeles, CA 90013
rarebirdbooks.com

Copyright © 2017 by James Glickman

FIRST TRADE PAPERBACK ORIGINAL EDITION

All rights reserved, including the right to reproduce this book or portions thereof in any form whatsoever, including but not limited to print, audio, and electronic. For more information, address:

A Vireo Book | Rare Bird Books Subsidiary Rights Department,
453 South Spring Street, Suite 302,
Los Angeles, CA 90013.

Set in Minion Pro
Printed in the United States

10 9 8 7 6 5 4 3 2 1

Publisher's Cataloging-in-Publication data
Names: Glickman, James, author.
Title: Crossing point / James Glickman.
Description: First Trade Paperback Original Edition | A Genuine Vireo Book | New York, NY; Los Angeles, CA: Rare Bird Books, 2017.
Identifiers: ISBN 9781945572425
Subjects: LCSH United States—History—Revolution, 1775–1783. | Rhode Island—History—Revolution, 1775–1783—Fiction. | African Americans—Fiction. | Canadian Invasion, 1775–1776—Fiction. | Québec (Québec)—History—Siege, 1775–1776—Fiction. | Ward, Samuel, 1725–1776—Fiction. | Historical fiction. | BISAC FICTION / Historical
Classification: LCC PS3557.L53 C76 2017 | DDC 813.6—dc23

DETROIT PUBLIC LIBRARY
3 5674 05637118 1

Praise for **Crossing Point**

"*Crossing Point* is engaging as a work of history, where realistic detail grounds and girds the story; but it's a work of imaginative grace and vision as well. James Glickman is a gifted writer, and he makes the American War [of] Independence credible, physically and emotionally real. I don't think many of us know this war as well as we think, especially the story of black participation. Glickman has provided a genuine service here, imagining our history for us, summoning the warp and woof of daily life in a pressured time. I recommend this book for anyone who wants to come closer to the wellsprings of the American story, our conflicted and fiery origins.

—Jay Parini, author of *The Last Station* and *The Passages of H.M.*

"I was quite won over by the skill with which [Glickman] humanizes the abstractions of military history—the relations of officers and men, rebels and loyalists, blacks and whites, slaves and masters, and makes the incredible horrors of war credible."

—C. Vann Woodward, author of *The Strange Career of Jim Crow* and editor of *The Oxford History of the United States*

DUFFIELD BRANCH LIBRARY
2507 WEST GRAND BOULEVARD
DETROIT, MICHIGAN 48208
(313) 481-1712

NOV 0 7 2017

DU

CROSSING POINT

...I would remind you that in this noble land, memory is all: touchstone, threat, and guiding star. Where we shall go is where we have been; where we have been is where we shall go—but with a difference.

—*Juneteenth*, Ralph Ellison

Most of the characters and all of the major events in this novel are based on the known historical record.

Prologue

The smoldering embers of the morning's fire scent the fall air of the meeting room. Thin gray light filters through the thick leaded panes of the eastern windows. At the front wall, the thirteen hearing officers range along the far side of a long oak dining table turned broadside, their faces alert. Escorted by the sergeant-at-arms to a small scarred desk at the center of the room and told to sit, Guy Watson settles himself, his hands gripping each other in his lap and the muscles in his neck and back knotted with tension. At a slanted writing desk to the left of the hearing officers, a secretary dips his quill in the inkwell and carefully wipes the excess off on the well's edge. He moves the pen to the paper, pauses, and, hunching over it, begins to write. Guy, listening to the pen scratch in the silence, can feel the eyes of the officers level on him like gun muzzles. The man at the writing desk stops, rests the quill in its holder, and nods at the officers. The court-martial president, General Varnum, requests everyone to rise. The chair legs scrape the floor as everyone complies.

General Varnum asks the twelve other officers to raise their right hands. "You swear," he says, "that you will well and truly try, and impartially determine, the cause of the prisoner now before you, without partiality, favor, affection, or hope of reward, so help you God."

"So help me God," the officers reply.

General Varnum then tells the secretary to raise his right hand. "You, Caleb Whipple, do swear that you will, according to your best abilities, accurately and impartially record the proceedings of the court, and the evidence to be given in the case in hearing, so help you God."

"I so swear," replies the secretary.

"The general court-martial is now in session."

They seat themselves. Guy, uncertain of what to do and not having been spoken to, remains standing. Varnum passes the secretary a paper to read aloud.

He peers at the page for a moment, his lips moving silently, as he reviews its contents. Then he clears his throat and reads in a thin, reedy voice, "'By direction of Brigadier General James Varnum, a general court-martial is hereby appointed to meet at East Greenwich, Rhode Island, on the fourteenth day of September, 1778, for the trial of Lieutenant John Hazzard Junior, and such other prisoners as may be brought before it, accused of violating article fifty-two, "misbehaving before the enemy, shamefully abandoning the post he was commanded to defend and casting away his arms and ammunition." Also for the trial of Guy Watson for violating article fifty-seven, "holding correspondence with, or giving intelligence to, the enemy, either directly or indirectly." Conviction of said crimes shall result in death or such other punishment as shall be ordered by a sentence of a general court-martial.'"

The secretary turns to Guy Watson and says, "How do you plead?"

Guy's grip on his own hands tightens. He stands straight and unmoving. He has been told about this part and knows he is supposed to say something. Here in the pale morning light of this room with the officers looking at him and the word "death" still hanging in the air, he cannot for the life of him remember what it is he is supposed to say.

Part I

Chapter One

1775

THREE MEN DRESSED IN black rode their horses on a rutted dirt road that threaded through the spring stubble of a wide pasture. Beyond them, a low steady surf tumbled against the shore. At first only dark dots against the sunbright blue horizon this April morning, they slowly grew larger. The grim-faced riders took shape—stiff, upright, alert—and they followed along the low gray stone walls heading toward the main house.

Ice entered the hearts of the slaves. They believed these men with the flat-topped black hats shading their lean faces had come to consider them for purchase. For weeks the rumor had winged among them that as soon as the spring planting was done, Master John Hazzard would have to cut back, raise cash. Sell. He did it last year. Now they feared he was going to do it again.

Everyone in the yard near the house grew still. They could hear the steady clop of the horses' hooves. A rooster skittered toward the barn.

No question the Hazzards were being squeezed. The port of Boston had been sealed up by the British for nearly twelve months to punish the Massachusetts radicals, and the results of strangled trade now pressed eighty miles, throughout Rhode Island and all the way down to the Hazzard farm. The prices for their wheels of cheddar cheese and egg-laying red hens had plummeted, and the markets for their fat sheep and fleet riding horses, Narragansett pacers, completely vanished.

*

MASTER JOHN HAZZARD, ESQUIRE, set his hands upon his silk-covered couch and peered out through the panes of his parlor window at the three men. He narrowed his eyes. The expansive Master Hazzard enjoyed talk, strong beverages, and games of chance, and often he wore a brilliant vermilion vest under his waistcoat even for the Sunday services at the Kingston Episcopal Church. He loved an argument. His admiring, intelligent wife liked to say he was the only man she had ever met who had more answers than there were questions.

Ah, he thought, *the Greenes are back. All three of them this time! Jacob, that tough old bird. His younger brother, the asthmatic, barrel-chested radical, Nathanael. And their lanky, cadaverous cousin, Christopher. Your basic slave-owning, arms-carrying, hypocritical Quakers here to poke into my affairs.* He lifted his long split-tailed jacket from its peg and dusted the sleeves.

Because of the seven other Hazzard (and Hazard) families in the county, each having several Johns, nicknaming became a custom to tell them apart. Master John's eighteen-year-old son was known as Young John, a name by which he would be called even if he lived to be a gray-haired great-grandfather. Master John himself made his way deliberately down the brick steps from his white house while donning his jacket over today's canary-yellow vest. Master John's neighbors knew him as Gambling John.

He enjoyed that his spacious two-story house made a fine backdrop for his appearance. It braced him like a powerful friend standing squarely behind him. He tugged at each of his white shirt cuffs, settled his scented hands on his lapels, and with a broad smile and a hearty voice, said, "Brother Greene, this is a surprise! You are most welcome, and your companions as well."

Jacob Greene, who was called "Brother" only by other Quaker Friends or family, smiled wanly at this presumptuous greeting.

"Can I offer you some refreshment after your ride?" the master continued. "The ardors of your travel must have left you gentlemen with a terrible thirst."

"A few words with you," Nathanael said, his voice low enough to make the master take a step closer to hear him, "in the shade and shelter of your house will be all we require." Master John knew that Nat Greene was two or three years past thirty, but he was standing close enough to notice for the first time that his dark hair was already threaded with gray—doubtless from worrying over other people's affairs.

"Of course. By all means." He extended a hand toward his red front door, instructed his old body servant Quamino to take their horses, called out to his wife that they had guests, and, with a brisk step, cheerfully led the three men past the broken gate post. He thought of them as the buzzard, the bull, and the corpse. They had looked uneasily at Quamino, an aged black man with an alarming sense of dignity.

Guy Watson leaned over the splintered post and, with lengths of string, continued his measurements. The white men did not look at him, but once they passed, Watson looked at June Harris near the milk house, her dark hands ringleted with suds from the soapy washtub. He caught her eyes, bright and shiny with sun and fear, and shook his head. No. Not slave traders. She let out a long, relieved breath, and quietly began to pass the word. As always, he found it hard to look away from her.

*

INSIDE, AFTER MASTER HAZZARD introduced his wife, Elizabeth, and son, Young John, John invited the men to sit in his front parlor. While only the strictest Quakers kept their heads covered at all times, Jacob Greene kept his covered now. They sat stiffly on their wooden chairs. "Mrs. Hazzard," the master said to his wife. "Can you offer our guests some refreshment?" She smiled, walked a step closer to the men and in a soft polite voice offered water, ale, or coffee, that new bitter drink she confessed she had not gotten used to. All three men declined. She dipped her head and excused herself. The master knew that she would be listening from the next room and would not be shy in offering her opinion later. It was an opinion he looked forward to, since Elizabeth had a gift for noticing things that he overlooked. Her eavesdropping was as reassuring as having his house to back him up.

"And to what, sirs, do I owe the pleasure of this unlooked-for visit?"

He expected the buzzard Jacob to do the squawking, but it was the bull Nathanael Greene who replied. "We come as members of the Committee of Inspection."

Of the three Greenes, it was only Nat, with his steady gaze, who unsettled him. "I'm the member of half a dozen committees myself, and though I'm flattered you are interested in my poor services, I'm afraid I lack the time to…" He paused, looked at the others, and waited to be interrupted. Instead, the lean-faced Jacob regarded him silently, his deep-set eyes hard to read. "…To ride about the countryside and ensure compliance on the resolves of the Continental Congress."

"We are here, Mister Hazzard, to discuss your own observance of those resolves. And of Rhode Island's."

"My *observance*?" he said as if surprised, rising from his seat. "I thought we had settled that on your last visit."

Nathanael took out a sheet of paper and read the list of offenses against austerity and British importation that had been reported by his neighbors: meetings in secret, tea-drinking, lamb-killing, powder-wasting.

John rocked back on his heels and then forward onto the balls of his feet. He was glad to be standing. All of these Greenes were taller than he by a good half a foot. Fortunately, he never had to impose himself physically on others. He always had greater energy and cunning than most of the lummoxes he dealt with. He had found that it was actually the short men like himself he had to be on his mettle for. The big ones, like these Greenes, usually carried around a misplaced confidence in their own abilities. "Well, we clearly have some misunderstandings here. Mrs. Hazzard and my son both had a grippe last month, and Doctor Babcock himself suggested they would recover more seasonably if they could bring themselves to consume some tea. I know it went against their own convictions, but our tiny supply is from before the restrictions on import and I urged it on them for their health's sake." He waited to see if they challenged this. They did not. "As to lamb-killing, we have only consumed animals that have succumbed by age or accident, and we shear every thread of their wool for homespun. I don't know what powder-wasting is known by, but I would be a poor steward of my own affairs to waste anything, and surely not something so dear as gunpowder." He noted their skeptical faces. "The slaves have their own firearms for game and against predators, and I warrant it's possible they have not always been as slow to shoot as I might wish. But, gentlemen, they have their own limited supplies, and they know if they expend 'em they will get no more."

"The meetings?"

"Church meetings, social gatherings, a celebration of Young John's birthday! Nothing secret, no cabals! Two nights past we had a meeting to decide what to do about this year's slave election." He lowered his voice to a confidential tone and glanced about as if nervous. "As I suspect you know, some of us with large properties are concerned that one faction or another may try to stir our bondsmen to rebellion. In our neighborhood, taken all in all, as you well know there are more black souls than white. If you have reports of whispered gatherings, you may depend that we are only whispering to not tempt the ears of our servants."

"Then you will have no objections if we examine your smoke house, root cellar, and larder," Nathanael said.

John Hazzard's face darkened. The confidence exuded by the powerful-looking Nat Greene annoyed him. "Mister Greene, this mistrust is unwarranted and unneighborly. Do you wish to tell me my answers have not given you satisfaction?"

Jacob fixed his gaze on John Hazzard. Close-set eyes, a hooked beak of a nose, Jacob was a bird of prey if he ever saw one. "We would wish to tell you that we will not examine your house or outbuildings if you forbid it."

They considered each other in silence. Gambling John drew himself up, stared stonily at Jacob Greene for a long moment, then sighed, an honest man in a rigged game throwing in his cards. "If you insist on a search, I will not prevent it. But I must tell you, I will not soon forget the affront."

Christopher Greene turned up his palms. "Duty, sir. Nothing personal." By God, the cadaver moved! It even spoke!

"And we appreciate your obliging us, Mister Hazzard," Nathanael said mildly.

The three men remained in a group and requested John Hazzard to accompany them so he might be satisfied they had not mishandled his property.

"Even under the circumstances, I would not dishonor you with such a suspicion," the master said. "Johnny," he called to his son, who appeared almost immediately. "Show these men to the root cellar and smoke house."

Since the daily tea was below a loose board in the kitchen, the lamb already dried, jerked, and stored among the wheels of cheese in the milk house, and the extra gunpowder tucked away in the barn in a sack marked *CORNMEAL*, he had little anxiety about their search. The only thing that bothered him was that he had failed to put away last week's *Rivington's Gazette*, a loyalist paper. But he believed Jacob could not read with much skill, and Nathanael failed to look into his study when he came in.

Still, these inspections were getting to be a bother, and they were getting more pointed each time.

The theater of it is entertaining, though, Hazzard thought.

*

HE HAD THE *RIVINGTON'S Gazette* safely in the drawer when the dour threesome returned.

"Are you quite done, gentlemen?" John asked. "Any other nook or cranny you need to peer into?" As Nat looked at him, he suddenly thought of the large supply of tea in the attic, and he decided not to press his luck. "And may I offer you something to drink before you go?"

Nathanael shook his large head. "We have only to raise the request Samuel Ward left with you about leasing your bondsman. I understand it has stood unanswered for some weeks now."

"And what, pray, has this to do with the Committee's business?" The old bastard Ward, the gnarled up, pettifogging former governor and chief judge had been at him for months about the matter. Ward. Was there anyone worse?

"As you know, sir, Mister Ward's presence is required in Philadelphia for the next meeting of the Continental Congress. His family would be made easier and his important business conducted with undivided attention if he knew the needs of his farm were being met. You gave him to understand that once the winter repairs were done and the spring planting completed, you would be free to lease one of your servants. One who was skilled in carpentry."

"I might have done. And if I was to lease to Mister Ward such a one, would I then be spared these offensive visits from the Committee of Inspection?"

As Nathanael paused, the old buzzard Jacob Greene offered in a deliberate voice, "The Committee looks favorably on those who support the Continental Congress."

"Is that a 'yes,' Mister Greene?"

"When Mister Ward reports himself satisfied with the man's work..." He nodded.

Master Hazzard walked them to the door and toward the path to their horses. "And what about price?" He suppressed a grin, knowing that the question made them look like lackeys.

Nat snorted—*just* like a bull!—and his voice took on an edge. "That is for you and Mister Ward to determine. We are not brokers."

"Are ye not? Well, Samuel Ward is a fortunate man to have such good friends..." He grinned.

Nat Greene looked at him in silence for so long that John shifted his weight from one foot to another.

Old Jacob finally broke the silence. "God bye you, Mister Hazzard."

"Farewell, gentlemen. Tell Governor Ward to send us a means of conveyance, and he shall have his man."

The three men in black mounted their horses.

"Not before Thursday," the master added. "He's got work to complete."

"The day after the morrow, then," Nathanael Greene confirmed.

John Hazzard tried not to snort himself. Old Jacob probably called it the fourth day. Some of these religious zealots were so pious, they refused to profane themselves even by using the names of the damned days of the week! Thor'sday, Mars'day, Sunday, Saturnday, as if a little pantheism and pronouncing the names of a few Roman gods was going to consign their pinched little souls to roast in hell. "Thursday!" he called again cheerfully, waving to the departing men.

As he turned to go in the house, he stopped in front of Guy Watson who was still repairing the front gate.

"Two days, Guy. You have two days to finish your tasks. Then you'll be going to Weekapaug for a bit." He began to go inside once again, and then stopped. He laid his finger to his nose for a moment and said, "If you keep your ears open, there may be some money in it for you. How would you like that?"

Guy looked up and shaded his eyes. The dank smell that most white men had of wet potatoes cascaded around him, mixed with the master's smell of lime and spice that came from a brown glass bottle. Master Hazzard looked serious, his pointed small clever face reflective, yet at the same time quite pleased with himself.

"Yessuh," Guy said.

With enough money, one day Guy hoped to buy himself and June. He did not know what enough was. He could not count above twenty. He could neither read nor write. But he did know that for years the master had hired him out only in the winter. For it to happen in the spring, and for him to offer a money reward, he believed the three men in black must have squeezed the master hard, very hard, and in a soft place.

✷

THIS WAS NOT A time when Guy would have chosen to leave, if he had the power to choose. Sometimes he and June Harris together were smooth as old cambric, sometimes bumpy as a rutted road. It had been more bumpy than smooth recently. There were bad changes going on—threatening ones like selling off more slaves, and certain ones, like Young John taking over as overseer.

Young John, just turned eighteen, was the only Hazzard child to survive past the age of three. He had been his parents' hope for the future his whole life, and he was being groomed to inherit their estate. They had already sold off Cuff, the cause of Lucy's pregnancy, and when young Caesar died last year of the smallpox, the Hazzards made no move to replace him. Guy had heard the master say replacing the overseer would not only save the Hazzards some expenses, but let them tighten up on discipline. The old overseer treated the slaves the same way he treated the livestock. He tried to keep them healthy and working, and while he spared no one who stepped out of line from being struck, compared to many, he was not harsh.

Young John, however, was just back from visiting relatives in the Carolinas, and he had gotten some new ideas there on how to tend slaves. From what Guy had heard of these ideas, he did not like them. He especially did not like leaving June alone to deal with them. Not that he wasn't convinced she could handle Young John—who had not only grown to be much taller than his father, but was now almost Guy's height. She could handle him, and another two or three like him.

*

AT DINNER, WHILE ALL the slaves were reaching into the common bowl for shreds of boiled, spiced squirrel and chunks of yellow squash, Guy told June what the master planned for him. He could tell she had heard him only because she stopped chewing for a moment. They were careful to let Lucy, June's pregnant younger sister, have some extra food.

After a time, June asked, "How long you be gone?"

"'For a bit,' he say."

"Like the other times? All season?"

"Too much need doin' here for that."

June nodded.

A grave, self-possessed old Quamino, who, as the master's body servant, sometimes ate inside, tonight was outside with them. He listened, quiet and still, his back straight as a tree trunk. He was so still that when he slowly shook his gray head, it was as arresting as if a rock had suddenly begun to move.

"What?" June asked.

His gaunt, dark, deeply lined face was, as always, serious. His hollow eyes and high cheekbones were shadowed in the flickering firelight. His reputation as a *ndoki*, or sorcerer, wise in the old ways of the African people, made listeners take heed when he spoke. From his work in the house, he often heard conversations no one else was able to.

"Could be a long time," he said.

There was something about his dignity and clean, always-buttoned-to-the-neck shirt that made whites nervous. Some mocked him. His manner also tended to annoy Jubah, the cook. She had a reputation throughout the county among the slaves as a *nganga*, a root person and conjurer, someone you might go to for troubles of the body or the heart. White people in the area used her as a midwife. Her round face, black and shiny in the light, wrinkled up as if she had just tasted some bad food. "Have 'nother one of your dreams?" she asked the white-haired old man.

"No dream," he said softly, looking into the fire. "Mastuh Hazzard makin' too many plans now. Man tryin' to keep hold of something he think slippin' away."

Jubah wiped a hunk of bread in the bowl's savory bottom. "Man's always makin' plans. You always makin' predictions. Some work out. Some not."

"It's a jumble time," Quamino said, staring into the fire. "Plans don't hold."

"Predictions don't neither," she said through her mouthful. Then she muttered, "Make enough of 'em, though, a few of 'ems goin' to come out."

Lucy giggled. The rest of them continued eating.

Guy said, "Mastuh say he give me money if I listen."

Jubah and Quamino both looked at him sharply.

"Listen? Where you goin' to?" she asked.

"Wards."

Both the cook and the servant grunted in surprise.

The Wards and the Hazzards? Night and day. Dust and water.

"Mastuh won't leave you there one minute longer than he has to," Jubah said.

"What if he leave him there to keep spyin'?" June said.

Quamino broke his rock-like stillness once more. He nodded.

"Be careful 'bout Young John," Guy said. "He not overseer yet, but he still startin' to smell his own pee."

As the women gathered the plates and bowls to rub them clean with beach sand, Quamino motioned Guy over to the fire. "Tomorrow night, we go to the crossing place. Find out what we can."

Quamino very rarely summoned spirits. He must sense something coming.

*

JUNE WANTED TO TALK to Guy. He was uneasy about being alone with her, for that was when they got along least well now. It was his fate that he had found himself, as if by a great tide, hopelessly drawn to a woman who, before she came to the Hazzards', was raised in America by a devout, churchgoing family. He found in Newport that women slaves newly arrived from Africa or the Sugar Islands often had a sunny disposition about the pleasures of the body. If it suited them and the time and the place, they would take a man like they might take a meal. But slaves raised in religious families—as most slave owners tried to be—usually thought bed pleasure was only for couples who were married. Even Lucy, who liked to be bad when she could get away with it, thought that way. She was not married to Cuff, but it was close enough. That didn't keep the Hazzards from selling him off. Sooner or later, that was what he and June would end up arguing about.

"We certain to marry," he'd say, stepping close to her and breathing in the smell of her skin.

"When?" she would reply.

"Soon's the mastuh let us."

And then, as always, she would sniff. The Hazzards did not want her pregnant. Another useless mouth to feed right when times were bad? A second slave so big with child she can't work as hard as usual? Then having to nurse the baby when she supposed to be working? No, sir. Nuh-uh. "So keep your hands to yourself," she would conclude.

"Why you let them say how we be?" he would say.

"You wan' get me sold, too?"

"No," he would say and step in closer to her, reaching to put his arm around her.

Then she would shake her head and push him away. He suggested that Quamino should marry them by having them jump the broom. June said that would not change what the master would do if she got bigged up. He went to Jubah to see if she had medicines, *belongo*, that might keep June from getting big.

Jubah, who was always working something over in her mouth, stopped chewing. She looked at Guy for a moment, meditatively. Then she nodded.

"What you have?" he asked urgently.

"Keep yo' breeches up. Work every time."

"Nothin' else?"

"Nothin' else that work every time."

*

Tonight, he thought. *Tonight might be different.* He was leaving, and if Quamino was right, maybe for a long time. When he found June at the edge of the woods, looking out through the trees at a bright sliver of moon, her breath making a fine plume of mist in the cool air and her shadow flickering in the dwindling firelight, he stepped up behind her. In the distance, they could hear Lucy singing in her beautiful, melodious voice about sleep and stars. Slowly, he touched her, then wrapping his arms over the upper slope of her breasts he squeezed her warm shoulders with his hands.

She leaned back against his chest, and his heart began to pound and his breath to quicken. He knew if he pressed himself against her bottom and she felt his arousal, she would move away. Instead of all softness and silence and warm skin, she would become grave and shake her head and press her hands flat against his chest. Then, with a steady light pressure, she would remove him to her arms' full length.

"Cold?" she asked him.

He murmured no into the back of her head. Her arms smelled of soap and her warm scalp like old copper.

To his surprise, as if reclining into a hammock, she settled herself all along him. Through their clothes, he could feel himself pressed into her.

"Guy," she said.

"Mmm," he said back, squeezing her shoulders.

"Guy. Get the mastuh to let us marriage."

As a pleasurable shudder coursed through him, he found it hard to attend her words.

"Mm-hm," he said.

She gently lifted his arms from her, and Guy thought she was going to turn to face him. Instead, she slipped away back to the fire, leaving him standing there throbbing in the darkness, alone under the fingernail moon.

The next night, after the old overseer was asleep and all the windows in the master's house were dark, Quamino nudged Guy to tell him it was time to make their way through the woods to the crossing place. As usual for a night journey, they dressed with their clothes inside out to protect themselves from hostile spirits, ghosts abroad who might otherwise recognize them. Quamino was carrying a small bag of tools and potions. Guy had with him the amulet his mother made him in the week before she died.

"Want you to try it tonight," Quamino said in a low voice. "Come a time you need to, and no Quamino there."

Guy shook his head. He did not think he had the gift.

He had known ever since he could remember the picture of the world the old *ndoki* had talked of, one he must have gotten at the place he was raised, old Asa Robinson's farm.

The world—and he had known this even before he had the words to describe it—was a great circle quartered by two great axes. One of them was the line of water and life, the other of the realms of God and of the Dead. And where they met in the middle was the intersection of all the spirits of the universe, the great crossing point. From that center, if you were able to put yourself in it in the proper spirit, you might hope to summon the spirit-forces, the *simbi*, and cast a spell to seek power or achieve prophecy.

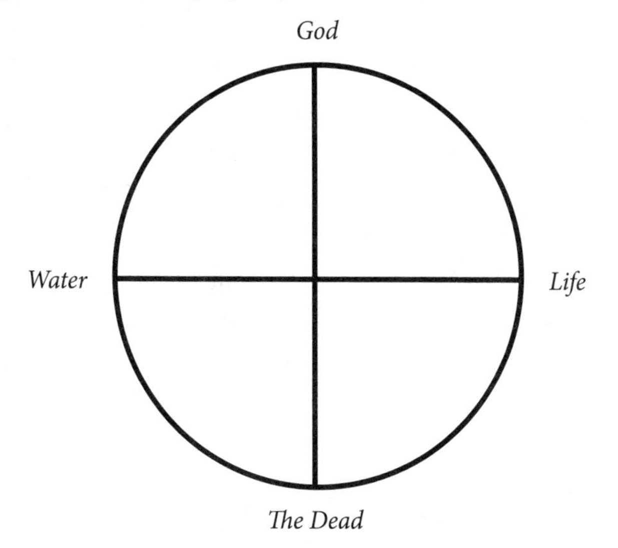

But to summon the spirits, you had first to be clear of heart, clear with all the ancestors, in harmony with the waters and with the spirits of the dead. Once the spirits entered you, they might not offer the gift of power or of sight, but instead try to destroy you. You were at the mercy of the greatest God, *nzambi mpungu*.

Guy did not feel prepared inside himself to step into the ritual circle. But he watched carefully as Quamino readied himself to do so.

From a pouch he carried inside his shirt, the old man took out a candle, two small bags of sacred herbs, a tiny leather pouch of dust taken from his daughter's grave, and a stick no wider than his hand, worn smooth with handling. He struck sparks from a flint into some straw, blew them to life and, lifting a flaming piece of straw, lit the candle. He took a tiny pinch of the grave earth and sprinkled it in his palm over a dusting of the herbs. He rolled them together in his hands, slowly sifted them into a seashell, and then poured them into the candle flame, carefully inhaling the smoke of their combustion. Facing first the night skies and then the spring-smelling earth, he chanted some words ("*bisimbi*," "*mpati!*") that Guy did not understand. He chewed on some of the herbs. Shuffling his sinewy old legs and feet, he began to dance, and his chant intensified. He rounded the prayer circle three times, stopped, grew silent, and stepped solemnly to the crossing point.

The old man stared through the trees at the water and held the prayer stick aloft to the skies. Water, life, the dead, and God all brought to a single point. The old man shut his eyes, dropped to his knees, and then grew very still. His white hair looked golden in the candlelight. Quamino straightened his bony back and grunted in surprise. His face contorted and grew shiny with sweat even in the cool evening air. He pressed his palms against his eyes.

Long minutes later, Quamino left the circle and sat down, exhausted.

"What?" Guy asked.

Quamino took a deep breath and shook his head.

"Confusion. White men shooting. Snow, lots of snow."

"June? Me? You? Jubah?"

Quamino was quiet for a while. He started to hoist himself to his feet and, for the first time in all the years he had known him, Guy had to help him get up. "Death. So much it hard to make out a face. All I know is, somebody right here, a slave, goin' die before the big deaths. I saw 'em upside down with the ancestors."

"Who?" Guy asked. Quamino said he couldn't tell, but was too sad and shaken to talk further. They made their way back to the Hazzard place in silence.

Chapter Two

When young Ward came to fetch him early the next morning, Guy tried to say goodbye to June. Young John Hazzard, who could not get Sammy Ward off the property fast enough, would not give him a second to make a farewell. Guy looked across the yard and stared at June's face, half-illumined by the morning sun, watched her fine shape bending over the sage. He was seized with longing. She stood from the herb garden and waved, her anxious face growing sad. He could feel in his chest that leaving her was different this time.

Master John came to the steps and said to Guy, "Remember well what I told you."

Guy was not about to forget. As long as he was with the Wards, Guy needed to keep his eyes and ears wide open—the master would be sending a messenger to visit him to ask him questions. "If you value everyone's well being, including June's," the master concluded, "you will answer that person in as much detail as possible."

*

Guy rode the eight miles of woods and pastures from the Hazzard house to Weekapaug with Sammy Ward, a tall, blond, blue-eyed eighteen-year-old who was so brilliant he finished his years at the Brown brothers' Rhode Island College at the age of fifteen. Everyone called him "Sammy" to distinguish him from his father, old Samuel Ward. His smooth pink face made him appear not much older than his years, but his great height, depth of chest, and breadth of shoulder were a full-grown man's. Though he dressed more like a farmer than the son of a famous gentleman, he spoke rarely but with the quiet assurance of someone who was used to being listened to. This was hard for Guy to get used to, since he was the opposite of Young John Hazzard, who spoke loudly and sharply, like someone who feared that if he did not raise his voice he would be ignored.

While there was not much the Hazzards and the Wards saw eye to eye about, there was one thing they did agree on: Rhode Island politics. Master John said it was a rough and dirty game, full of fraud, deceit, back-biting, trickery, lying, slander, influence-peddling, and graft. And it was why British officials loved to sneer that Rhode Island, with its peculiar habit of electing a governor, was "a downright democracy." But the master also admitted it was a game Samuel Ward and his family had played for more than forty years with skill. Samuel had been elected governor of Rhode Island three times and his father had been governor before him. And for the last thirty years, Samuel's brother had been elected to the Rhode Island's second-highest post—though many thought it was the most powerful—as Secretary of the Colony.

✳

Over the years, Guy had heard a lot about the Wards, but he had never seen them, even though they did live less than ten miles away. Because he worked each year in Newport, he had seen the present governor a few times. He was a large, plump man named Wanton who favored long ringleted wigs, jeweled fingers, ruffled shirts, and gauzy lace cuffs. That was what Guy assumed all governors looked like. So he was surprised on his arrival at former Governor Ward's place to find the many Ward children on the place to be plainly dressed and plainly spoken. He was even more surprised to see the famous Samuel Ward himself wearing no wig nor powder in his long, graying-blond hair, which fell loose about his head.

When Sammy reported to his father that the Hazzards' servant was with them now, the famous and powerful elder Ward paused in his correspondence, placed his pen in the inkstand, and, after nodding at his son in silent greeting, stopped to give Guy a full inspection. Having been through this many times, Guy believed he could almost read the old man's mind. He was pleased and a bit alarmed at Guy's size and strength, and also concerned about how much food he would eat. Until he was able to reassure them he was not a troublemaker, they would watch him like a dog they fear might be rabid. He waited for the silent inspection to end. Out the casement window behind Samuel Ward, just past the tall, pale-green beach grass, gleamed one of the many small inlets of Narragansett Bay. From where he stood, Guy could hear the whispering sound of fair weather surf.

"You're to be with us for two weeks," the old man said. "Do you know how long that is?"

Guy nodded, proud that he could count that high. "Yessuh."

"Good. We have many tasks that require your attention. For tools or materials you require, you are to ask young Master Ward. For your needs, you will ask Violet or Cujoe." He turned his blue-eyed gaze on his son. "Have you introduced this man to our other servants?"

"We've just returned, Father. I thought it best to see you first."

The old man nodded his head once, briefly. Guy could suddenly feel the tension even before the son asked, "Any news?"

"No news. Keep a sharp lookout."

"By sea?"

"By sea is the most likely." The old man's tone changed as he looked back at Guy. "Do you have any questions?"

Guy glanced over at Sammy, assuming the son was being addressed. It suddenly became clear to him that the former governor was asking *him* if he had any questions.

"Nossuh. No questions."

The old man nodded again. And that was all. They had been dismissed. He took the quill from its holder to resume his writing.

Sammy asked Cujoe, the elder Ward's body servant, to show Guy the farm and outline his tasks. His hair gone gray and his face black and weathered, Cujoe looked as old as the man he helped dress every morning. His voice was raspy, as if his vocal cords had weathered as much as the rest of him, but he spoke more like whites than the slaves at the Hazzards' place.

Smaller, with fewer crops and fewer slaves than the Hazzards, the Ward place was devoted mostly to being a dairy farm. The house was almost as large as the Hazzards' but it was less grand and had rooms added on here and there as if they were stuck on by a child playing with blocks—and there were also at least six Ward children living there. Cujoe said there once were eleven of them, but some had died and the oldest boy lived on his own, and after Mrs. Ward died five years ago, the older daughters began to marry and moved away. Guy listened to all this, but his mind was mostly on the family's tension about someone arriving by sea.

Guy soon saw there were many more repairs than he could hope to complete in two weeks. Cheese presses, fallen sheep pens, cracked plow handles, the barn walls, two carriages, and a hencoop. First, though, some of the tools he would be using himself required repair, everything from the beetle mallet to the adze. If he got all that done, Cujoe said, the house itself needed some work.

Guy had learned that the best way to get to the end of a day without trouble was to speak little. But you had to speak enough so that they didn't decide your lantern wick was turned too low. He settled himself down near the front of the house where he could see, but more important, he knew, where he could be seen.

"Start here?" he asked.

"Good," Cujoe said. "Something to drink?"

Guy was thirsty, but it was bearable, and he knew the sooner you established you were a hard worker, the sooner they would leave you alone. And the sooner that happened, the more work you could get done. The early April sun had some warmth in it, but not enough to be hot, and it was a good two weeks too soon for the tiny black flies whose bloody bites itched for days.

He sharpened the blades of the cutting tools, and he tightened and smoothed the handles of the pounding tools so they were comfortable and secure. The Ward children all seemed busy enough themselves, some milking the cows and cutting wood, others tilling the fields, still others working the gardens, and they had a field hand out with a plow and an ox. The children looked up frequently from their work to peer out into the bay, Sammy stopping once in a while to lift a spyglass to one eye.

As they neared time for the midday meal, Cujoe pointed to a basin of water and told him he should wash up before he came in.

"Come in?" Guy asked, thinking he had misheard. He had never eaten in a white person's house before. There was just a small table in the corner of the kitchen. They told him to sit.

The meal was savory and plentiful. Cujoe and his wife, Violet, used some kind of eating tool. He and the other field hand used their fingers.

After a while, he asked the question that had been burning in him almost since he arrived. "Why the mastuh tell his son to look out sharp to sea?"

Cujoe and Violet looked at each other for a long time before answering.

Cujoe stopped eating and looked straight at him. "Master got reports that the British goin' to arrest him. You see any men coming, you tell Master Ward right away."

He finished eating quickly. Rather than wait for someone to tell him it was time to get back to work, Guy got up and returned to his tasks.

*

He settled into a work rhythm over the next few days, often getting lost in the details of his labor. Hours passed, and sometimes he would barely notice. The sun moved across the great dome of the sky, times for meals arrived, and Cujoe had to come get him. Guy's mother had taught him that trees were the outward, physical signs of a person's spirit on its way to another world, so he loved to work with wood. In truth, he had learned how to make wood do most anything—be as smooth as young skin, but have a spine of iron within.

The secret with white pine, he knew, was to get the wood from the tree's north side.

Last year at the Hazzard place, Young John made him clean out and fix his personal privy. He gave the order to clean it out just to show Guy he was no one special, and to show all the Hazzard slaves he was old enough and important enough to be giving orders now. As a result, Guy decided to use south side pine. It comforted him to think as he cleaned out the Hazzards' stinking shit and buried it that, come winter and a windy night, the walls would be creaking like an old ship's and be as porous as a torn shirt. A few months later, they were.

Give him beech, maple, oak, hickory, walnut, chestnut, and birch. Give him apple, fir, spruce, or ash, and he could make them do whatever they did best. He loved to fix things. His mama said that he had a gift. He could find the *kolo*, a Mande word she used to name the kernel, the seed, the live-ness that was at the center of all the things of this world. Sometimes even now, whether he put his hands to a leaking bucket or a seized buggy wheel, he would picture his mother while he went about the repairs, looking just as she did when she was alive, upside down among the ancestors in the earth, smiling at him from among the dead. He worked on, never forgetting that the sooner he was done, the sooner he could go back to the place that June made feel like home.

Chapter Three

RHODE ISLAND'S ELECTION DAY—WEDNESDAY, April 19, 1775—dawned fair and sunlit.

Samuel Ward had gotten warnings and heard intensifying rumors for days about hostile actions in Massachusetts; he tried to put them out of his mind. He spent the day packing for his journey tomorrow to the Congress in Philadelphia, giving counsel to his children about what to do during his absence, and taking Sammy to Westerly to cast their vote at town hall. There he walked along the worn dirt roads and shook the hands of the people who had supported him all his adult life. And while he was not so secretly hoping young Sammy might follow in his footsteps, his smart young son seemed far more interested in apprenticing to a doctor than to a politician.

Folks in town clustered around to bid him Godspeed. And though they knew Samuel's brother Henry would win the post of Secretary of the Colony for the fourteenth consecutive time, and that his brother-in-law Judge Greene would lose in his race for governor, he and his friends and neighbors still joked and winked about sunny, blue-skied "Ward Weather" carrying the day.

The news did not come until in the middle of the spring night. It was borne by his oldest son, Charles, who, though often drunk and inconstant—he had sold his own vote for a pretty price to the Hopkins forces the same year Samuel went on to lose by only twenty-seven ballots—this time had ridden faithfully straight through from Providence.

Samuel heard the door bang open and voices yelling downstairs in the cold dark, and for a heart-clutching moment he feared the rumors were true—the British had come for him. He had heard from friends in Boston that the British were plotting to kidnap Sam Adams and John Hancock, both of whom were frightened enough about the possibility to have fled their homes. More than one acquaintance reminded him of his own growing prominence among those who had been at the First Continental Congress. If the British could go after Hancock and Adams in Massachusetts, they would surely go after Ward in Rhode Island.

Sitting upright in the dark, his mouth dry, he listened for the voices of strangers. He had thought to take one precaution, and he reached for it, the pistol he had for several nights kept by his bed. His knees and hips stiff with arthritis, he made his way to the top of the stairs, pistol in hand, the palm of his other hand hard on the hammer.

His oldest daughter, Nancy, called up into the darkness in her throaty voice. "Daddy! Charles is come with news from Uncle Henry! Terrible, terrible news!"

By the time he found his spectacles and made his way barefoot down the stairs, the whole family, still in their nightclothes, was assembled and the lanterns lit.

Samuel, seeing Charles's grave and ashen face in the flickering light, broke the red wax seal with hands that already were beginning to tremble. He read the note aloud for all to hear.

Providence, April 19th
9 o'clock at Night

Dear Bro'r

We have rec'd Intelligence that our Brethren in Mass Bay are attacked by a Body of regular Troops & that many of our Friends are slain.

A gasp from his children and servants interrupted his reading. Charles nodded. The youngest girl began to cry. He looked at his children's stricken faces and, his heart pounding, tried to collect himself to read on with a steady voice.

> *The Provincials are alarmed and mustering as fast as possible. The Gen'l Assembly will meet together to make preparation for the common Defense as soon as it may be convened. Gov. Wanton's response remains uncertain. I must close as my Letter will be left. God preserve you and yours, dear brother. Charles will bring this to you. Your counsel and presence much in need here. Militia General Potter is ill. Yours in haste, Henry Ward.*

He folded the note and rested his hands upon it. He asked Charles if there was further information to add. Charles shook his head. Samuel asked them all to bow their heads in prayer. His children grew quiet at once.

"Let us remember our slain friends in the blessings of the Lord. May their souls be at rest and their spirits at peace. And may our friends and family be sheltered in the days ahead from the coming storm."

Everyone murmured amen, and the youngest girl continued quietly to weep on her older sister's shoulder. The three younger boys tried to look brave, but they stared at their father and grown brothers with glassy eyes. "Nancy," Samuel said to his twenty-five-year-old daughter, the eldest. He had hoped for her sake that she would have married by now, but her presence now was the one he was most grateful for. "You will tend to the farm in our absence. Sammy and Charles and I must head for Providence at first light."

Nancy rested her hand on Dicky, the youngest Ward boy. She had refused two proposals of marriage, one of them from Nat Greene, and tonight she might have been living like her sister

Debbie whose husband was Nat's younger brother. Instead, she sat in her father's house, her back straight.

Dawn on April 20 found them still awake and assembled at the table, piecing out their plans.

*

SAMUEL SAID THEY WOULD have to keep an extremely close eye on the servants, the field hand, Toby, especially. With all the disorder, it was a time when Tories would take every opportunity to encourage flight or even revolt. They were not, under any circumstance, to permit the servants any discourse with strangers, and none of them were to leave after dark.

Nancy and Polly, the two oldest, looked at each other with frightened eyes. They drank in every word of advice and warning.

"What do we do about the Hazzards' servant?" Nancy asked.

"We need him too badly to return him," he said simply. "But we cannot trust him enough to leave him here."

Finally, he turned to Sammy and Charles. "Our problem in Rhode Island will not be getting our men ready. Our problem is going to be Governor Wanton."

"The assembly and Uncle Henry will handle him," Charles said.

Samuel looked at him, barely masking his irritation over his oldest son's customary hollow confidence. "It is not that simple. No action of the militia and no commissioning of officers is legal without his signature. And that is why you and I and Sammy must go to Providence immediately. You will both be needed first as posts to get information in proper hands as swiftly as possible. And when that important business is done, you will be needed as soldiers."

"It is begun?" Sammy asked.

"If this act has been countenanced by the king, it is begun."

Sammy's eyebrows rose. "Do you think it possible that General Howe or Gage is acting on his own?"

"They are disciplined men. I believe they have received orders."

Guy heard the clomp of a single horse's hooves in the night, and he sat up and saw the lanterns glowing inside the main house. He could hear the excited murmur of voices, but when no one emerged for many minutes, he lapsed back into a fitful sleep. At dawn, he was given some cold bread and meat and told to get ready to travel north on horseback.

"British soldiers killed some people outside Boston," Cujoe said. "They think it's war now. They wan' you take care of the horses. Can you do that?"

Guy nodded, his heart thudding in his chest.

War, Guy thought. He had heard the word before. He knew it was about soldiers with guns, but it was distant, remote, as hard to imagine as a poorly told story. He wondered, too, if Quamino was wrong about his returning home.

It took them much of the day to ride from Westerly to Providence. Samuel's slow-moving carriage had to wend its way through roads crowded with frightened people hurrying in all directions. Packet boats plied the waters to and from Newport, the vulnerable city across the bay that everyone expected the king's fleet to assault first, each ferry bringing back crowds of terrified people to the mainland. Women and children with dazed expressions rode away from the shore on wagons piled high with goods, and men of all ages and sizes rode and marched toward South Kingston and Warwick and Providence. When people recognized Samuel Ward, as they often did, they asked if he had fresh news. He yelled, "No! But the Lord blesses us! Prepare your arms for defense!"

The Wards stopped at Samuel's sister's and her husband's house, Judge Greene's, in East Greenwich to give the horses food and water. They learned there that thousands of men from Connecticut and

New Hampshire had left their homes and were heading toward Boston to join the Massachusetts forces.

Judge Greene said it was far worse than Samuel had heard. The slaughter after the main exchange of fire at the towns of Lexington and Concord included old men killed at their firesides and helpless women bayoneted in their kitchens. Near Charlestown, a small boy sat gaping upon his fence as the soldiers passed his house. A passing redcoat casually shouldered his musket and shot the boy to death. Other soldiers broke into a church deacon's house in Lexington and by bayonet forced his wife, still confined after the recent birth of their child, to flee with the infant in her arms. Then they set the house on fire with their other five children still inside.

But as fast as they traveled, he and the others arrived in Providence too late. Governor Wanton had already done what Samuel had predicted. While the entire Rhode Island militia under the command of the Wards' young friend Jimmy Varnum was marching, armed, toward Boston, an express from the governor intercepted them. He ordered them to turn around and to "await his lawful commands."

When Samuel and his sons arrived at Stephen Hopkins's house, men clustered outside were still angrily muttering, "Treason!" Nat Greene had already refused to obey the governor's order and, along with two of his brothers and some other men, continued to Boston.

Sammy asked his father if he might ride on to join Nat.

Samuel shook his head. Sammy and his brother were needed for something more important than furnishing lead and powder. He ushered Sammy and Charles inside to join him, their Uncle Henry, the Greenes, the Hopkins, and the Browns, for it was they who would be deciding how to handle Governor Joseph Wanton. And the Ward boys would be the ones carrying the expresses to make the news known.

"Too bad the election was not today," Stephen Hopkins said, his face grim, as he invited Samuel to sit. "Judge Greene here would have won in a rout. And I would have been the first to give him my prox." Two of the Brown brothers, Joseph and John, stout Wanton backers, growled in agreement.

*

Guy tended to the horses behind Stephen Hopkins' house. His own legs and backside hurt from riding—he had never been on a horse so long in his life—and he imagined the horses themselves must be sore, too. As he wiped them down, he kept thinking about what he had witnessed in the final yards of his trip. He had seen soldiers before, British ones in Newport dressed in scarlet, carrying long guns with gleaming sharp knives at the end, and Rhode Island ones here and there in blue and buff nankeen. But he had never seen so many as he saw encamped upon the Providence green, some in uniform, most in ordinary clothes, but all carrying muskets and fowling pieces. There was something frightening about seeing so many armed men, so much power: what couldn't they do if they chose? And something awesome, too, like watching a wolf preparing to close its jaws on a terrified rabbit.

He saw that one of the carriage horse's harnesses needed mending. He wondered whether to draw this to old Ward's attention. One of the horses chuffed and tossed his head. He rubbed down its lathered side with his hand, trying to soothe him, and like an ache that would not leave, he missed June.

Guy slept with the horses behind the Hopkins house for the next few nights. He spent his days doing repairs at homes nearby. Finally, on the fourth day, he was told to go back to Westerly with Sammy. He had not seen much of the young master, for he had been carrying messages morning until night to places all over the colony. Sammy told him the ride back to Westerly was going to be interrupted with six or seven stops along the way to deliver expresses.

He wanted to ask when he was to be sent back to the Hazzards', but he could not bring himself to frame the words.

*

Of all the errands he had to complete, Sammy was looking forward most to one stop on his journey home. He had some news to deliver to his old friend Nathanael Greene. He thought if ever a man had earned the privilege to hear some good news, it was Nat.

Born with a bad leg and chronic asthma, Nat Greene had to struggle his whole life for things most people took for granted. His dour father didn't believe in education beyond the Bible, so, though he pleaded to, Nat never got to continue schooling after he learned to read. Nonetheless, he was up every day in the hour before dawn to continue his education, frequently consulting Sammy about the works of Caesar and Livy, Horace and Herodotus. Despite his handicaps, Nat was a handsome man, with wide muscular shoulders from his work at the family forge. Still, Sammy's oldest sister rejected Nat's proposal a few days after Nat's thirtieth birthday. This blow to his heart was followed within a week by another terrible loss. His entire Coventry forge burned to the ground. Then in the hours following the fire, he suffered from an asthma attack so severe it almost killed him.

His livelihood and that of the dozens of people who worked for him were gone. For four days and nights he was unable to lie down without choking. In the midst of the ruins, struggling to breathe, dizzy with fatigue, he wrote Sammy a wild and rambling letter, calling him "a Bosom friend and Brother in soul," and launched into expressions of bitter jealousy over the friendship Sammy had developed with one of his college instructors.

Sammy told his father about the letter. Within three days, Samuel gathered the whole family to go visit Nat in Coventry and arranged to submit a special bill to the General Assembly to start a colony-wide lottery aimed at helping defray the costs of rebuilding the burned forge.

Shortly after it was rebuilt, some Rhode Island men dressed like Indians rowed out at midnight to burn a British man-of-war that had run aground. Nat Greene was falsely accused of being the ringleader, though he approved of the act entirely. He soon became so convinced war was coming that it became an obsession. And instead of reading Horace, suddenly he was reading Thucydides on battles in the Peloponnese and Marshall Saxe on the art of warfare. At his new forge he stopped making anchors and began making cannons and shot, and with Jimmy Varnum, he started and funded the militia from Kent County out of his own pocket. His thanks? The militiamen of the Kentish Guards met in East Greenwich to elect its leadership. Wearing their bright red uniforms with blue facings and polished silver buttons Nat's hard-earned money had paid for, the men elected sergeants, two lieutenants, a captain, a major, and a commanding officer by secret ballot. Varnum was elected commander. And then the other names were read.

Nathanael Greene was elected to nothing.

Sammy had been there when it happened. Nat slipped off early after the votes were tallied, and Sammy heard some of the men saying in the wake of his departure that Nat's limp marred the marching order, that his pthisic, as they called his asthma, made him too slow to respond. One of them said, "Make old Nat an officer, and never mind *minutes*, they'd have to call us *Hourmen*." Sammy felt like punching him.

And so tonight he was glad to be bringing some news to Private Greene of the Kentish Guards that the tide of his affairs had changed. And, as always, he was looking forward to seeing Nat's wife, Sammy's pretty and vivacious cousin Caty. She was his favorite cousin, along with one other who reminded him of her. Judge Greene's daughter, Phebe, though young, was full of a spirit that was perpetually expressed through her quick intelligent eyes. Sammy sat up straight in the saddle and reminded himself to keep his thoughts on his errand.

*

AT DUSK, HE GUIDED his horse out from under the lacy spring canopies of oak and chestnut that tented the Coventry road, and he and the borrowed servant headed up the sloping brown path toward the level spot where Nat had sited his house—Spell Hall, as he liked to call it. The soil here was quite poor, and the saplings he and Nat had planted a few years ago still struggled half-heartedly to survive. It was a standing joke in the Ward family that cousin Caty had the same touch at gardening that she enjoyed in knitting—none at all—so the house had a perpetual raw newness about it that no vegetation softened. Nonetheless, it was a handsome place, white sided with fine milled lumber, and with eight rooms and a garret attic, very substantial for two people. Here on the hill, you could hear the narrow Pawtuxet River making musical sounds in the still of twilight as it streamed through the water race toward the mill. Sammy knew that the morning stillness would vanish as Nat's large ironworks stirred abruptly to life. Members of most of the families in Coventry were employed there, and once they arrived in the hour after dawn, the wooden race would be raised to engage the huge water wheel that then drove the bellows and powered the trip hammers in the bloomery. The clangor would ring throughout the town all day.

As they approached the house, he saw Caty—who had doubtless heard their approaching horses—peering out through a pane in the front sitting room. Bluish smoke rose out of the central chimney, and, behind Caty's trim figure, the room was a wash of gold light. The chill air near the house carried the smell of boiled beef, burning applewood, and spice pudding. Something melancholy in this quiet picture suddenly pierced Sammy. Most of his life, he had been aware that he was someone who Nat wished he could be. But tonight, at this moment, it was he who wished he were Nat. And yet, unaccountably, he felt all at once not like someone who was coming to bring good news but like a thief who was going to steal something away.

They dismounted and Guy led the horses to the barn to water them and wipe them down. Caty pulled open the door, stood on her toes to kiss his cheek, and, one hand resting on his chest, said, "Oh, Sammy! Nat plans to leave tomorrow and all our plans are blown to dust!"

Three years older than he, and despite all his book learning, she had always seemed to know the world better. He had never heard her sound helpless in his life. Looking at her wet-eyed and anxious face, he remembered she and Nat had been married less than a year.

"Some say," he offered, "that when the king hears of the strength of our resistance, he may offer a settlement." He kept to himself his father's belief that not only would there be war, but that it might last long enough for Sammy's younger brothers to have to fight. The last one with the French and the Indians lasted seven long years.

Caty tilted her head skeptically and sighed. "That is not Nat's view."

"Where is he?"

She glanced at the parlor, and said in a hushed voice, "Sleeping. He was up all night securing the house."

The door to the parlor swung open and Nat, red-eyed and in his stocking feet, came out to peer at his visitor. "Master Ward! I thought it was your voice..." He rubbed his eyes and smothered a yawn. "What gelatinous, narrow-spirited thing has our governor and the assembly done these past few days?"

"Made a disgraceful new appointment."

Nat's eyes narrowed in alarm. Sammy, trying hard to maintain a severe frown, handed him the sealed letter. Nat tore it open, read it through—his face flushed.

"What is it?" Caty asks.

"They've appointed me to Sammy's father's old post." He began to read aloud, "As 'representative to the New England colonies for mutual safety.'"

Nat knew this was a high honor. Sammy waited until he looked up to tell him the greater news. Despite Wanton's resistance, once they formed an army, Nat was being discussed as someone who might well be chosen to head it.

His astonishment was as open as a flung door. "Me?"

"It is not a settled matter," Sammy said. "Three candidates are under review. Jimmy Varnum." Nat nodded. "Daniel Hitchcock." Nat nodded again. "And you."

"Me," he repeated, searching Sammy's face for the possibility of a joke.

"There are those who feel Jimmy is too young at twenty-seven. Others think that he is too deistical."

"Many of us could suffer that charge."

"And Dan Hitchcock has lived in the colony for only five years."

"Nat may lead the entire Rhode Island army?" Caty asked.

"My father and Uncle Greene and Uncle Henry all support it. From trade in the past, the Browns and Mr. Hopkins have formed a high opinion of him. And there are many who like the idea of a Quaker being strong for American liberty."

"But my disabilities..."

Sammy ticked them off. "Youth. Lack of rank. Lack of war experience."

Nat nodded, calculating his chances. "I think Jimmy Varnum is the most likely."

Caty's eyes brimmed. "But if Nat is chosen..."

"These are but speculations and flying reports, Caty," Nat said.

"I have known Sammy too long to know he would misjudge." She turned to him. "Tell me if this is serious."

"It is far from decided, Caty." She held his gaze patiently, waiting for him to complete his thought. The words came slowly. "When Jimmy Varnum returned home, everyone noticed that it was Nat who pressed on to Boston. It is serious."

*

GUY WAS TOLD TO sleep in the barn that night. As Sammy spoke to him, they heard some clanking and a low moan from the house's attic garret.

Before he could ask what the noise was, Sammy volunteered that one of Nat Greene's servants tried to run away during the recent confusion. "He's been put in irons for the nights."

The young white man said good night and returned to the warm house full of golden light. Guy made his way into the darkened barn, a place warmed by cows and horses, with their steady breathing sounding like a wash of tides upon the shore. He found a clean mound of hay up in the loft and settled in for sleep. Still, whether in his mind or from just outside the walls, he kept hearing a low moan and the clanking of irons.

Chapter Four

PHEBE COULD NO LONGER recognize the world she had known her whole life. Her family of six had already ballooned to fourteen when the refugees from Boston arrived. It was not safe for Jane Mecom, the sister of the famous patriot Benjamin Franklin, to remain in Massachusetts, and she and her entire family fled to the Greenes' house within days with scarcely anything but a few clothes. All their furniture, property, and valuables in Boston were promptly looted and their house taken over. The Mecoms were working hard to find a more permanent place to live, but that was proving impossible. From the day they arrived, Phebe had gone from someone who worked hard to perfect her skills in music and needlepoint to someone who washed and cleaned and cooked and cared for half a dozen children. And, difficult as it was, that was not the only change. In truth, it was hard not to feel that all her bright girlhood hopes were shattered.

How foolish she felt. Less than a year ago Caty Littlefield, her cousin who had lived with them for almost ten years, had married Nat Greene right in their house, and Phebe thought her life was at last about to flower. Her beautiful, vivacious mother was someone she hoped she could grow up to be like, but the sun of her warmth and attention—and the world's—was soon shed upon and often blocked by Caty, arriving to share her room and her house just after the death of Caty's mother on Block Island. Caty, too, was strong-willed, charming, and spirited; strangers often asked if she were the daughter and Phebe the cousin. Still, when Caty moved to her new home with Nat, then the monthly red herald of her own womanhood arrived, and her body began to change in ways visible for everyone to note, she thought her time had finally come.

She knew this not just in her flesh and her heart, but in the cues the world began to offer. When she entered a room, even back at Caty's wedding, she was no longer invisible. She could feel the eyes of friends and relatives linger on her face and shoulders and clothes in the way they had so long done with Caty, with her mother, and with all of Sammy Ward's lovely older sisters. At last, it was her turn. And she knew it best of all at the husking bee last fall.

When the Wards, Greenes, and Rays gathered for their family celebrations in Warwick, Newport, or Westerly, there was music, dancing, quilting, games to play, and songs to sing—her Quaker father and Sabbatarian Baptist uncles made exceptions to their austerity when it came to what they allowed in the bosom of their family. They would not participate themselves, of course, but they knew their wives had been raised to enjoy a wider range of expression. Proper, always—that went without saying—but often involving so much laughter that tears would stream from the women's eyes. And the husking bee in the hours before the last evening meal was best of all. There, everyone participated, man and boy, woman and girl, stripping the corn and preparing it for drying. It was work and exuberant play all at once, full of competition and jostling, a kind of sport where flirting and the exchange of confidences and feats of strength were all rolled into one.

It was always her favorite few hours of the year no matter what age she was, and it had never been better than last year. Sammy was there. To her, there was no one handsomer, smarter, or kinder in the world. Though he was three years older, she was finally gaining on him, the top of her head, she judged, reaching all the way to his chin. He seemed much older, though, as if every year for him counted as two or three. He had mastered all the courses and was given a degree at the Brown brothers' college in Providence when he was barely fifteen years old. He had grown stronger, too, with all his strenuous farm work at the Wards'. When his father was away at the Continental Congress, it was Sammy who ran their affairs and balanced their ledgers. When family problems developed, he was included in the discussion of how to solve them. Even his older sisters treated him with a touch of awe. Always warm and friendly to anyone who spoke to him, he acted all the time, too, as if he were no one very special.

But this last time at the husking bee, Sammy acted as if *she* were special. When he looked at her, she could tell he was seeing something new in her, though she worried, intelligent as he was, he might see straight into her heart. She could feel her face grow hot and she had to lower her eyes every time they talked. She could usually speak articulately enough to anyone, even to her grandmother, the stern old widow of the longtime former governor of the colony, or to her own father, the judge, who had just lost on his own first run for that office. Yet around Sammy, suddenly she stammered and stuttered and could not get her mind to enjoy the balance she otherwise had as nearly a fixture of her nature. When they crowded into the Westerly barn to start the husking, remarks rather than full conversation became the currency of exchange, and soon she had Sammy laughing with some of the imitations of family members she found so effortless to do. His favorite? When she mimicked her mother, laying a hand lightly on his forearm, tilting her chin up, and in a lilting and floridly expressive voice saying, "Oh, *Sammy*, how *lovely* it *is* to *see* you!" The trick was to gaze intently into the person's face and emphasize every other word as if it, and it alone, was the most important thing in the entire world.

Of course, her own belief in the words redoubled their force. When she exclaimed how lovely it was to see *him*, she was wearing a mask that fit snugly over her own feelings. Caty was there, too, with Nat, but Sammy gave her no more attention this time than he did to her. Though she knew it was a terrible vanity in her to do so, she could not help exulting in this newfound sense of her reach.

In the back of it all, like a faint rumble of distant summer thunder, was talk of the military and of conflict with the king, but she had heard talk like that almost as far back as she could remember. She and her family went down to see Sammy and Nat train with the Kentish guards in February, but she had no chance to speak with him then. She could simply wave and admire what an impressive figure he made in uniform.

And then came the attacks at Lexington and Concord, and the world was blown to dust.

Since their house overlooked the ocean within easy reach of a surprise landing or shelling by a British warship, and her father was known, along with the Wards, as one of the most prominent supporters of resistance to the Crown, together with having Benjamin Franklin's family with them, they had good reason to be afraid. Phebe's usually imperturbable father sent her little brother, Ray, outside with a spyglass as soon as they heard the news to survey the full horizon of Narragansett Bay. He arranged for neighbors to do the same and created a schedule of watchers to cover all the daylight hours. But a night landing was something they could not anticipate, so he set about making plans for all of them to move inland to Coventry. Goods had to be packed and carriages and wagons loaded, messengers sent to request housing.

But her first thoughts were of Sam Ward. When he and her Uncle Samuel arrived on their way to Providence after the terrible news arrived, Sam's thoughts seemed far away. She felt as if she were watching him through a glass on the other side of which he could scarcely see or hear her, though inside she was calling out with all her force. All the young men of East Greenwich, all the ones she knew, had immediately prepared themselves to leave to join the army in Boston, and while some were angry or fearful or excited, within a day, they were gone, all of them, leaving behind only old men, women, children, and a few assorted servants.

The world had been one way until that warm mid-April day, and the next, it was another—dark and fearful. The future which had once seemed to spread out before her, various and new, was now full of pain and uncertainty. People had died before, young ones, including her baby brother and three of Sam's sisters, but that seemed like the hand of fate or the will of God. No one had died from the terribly planned and organized violence of men at war. And now every young man she knew might meet that end.

Once a system of watchers was in place all up and down the coast, and tenders were placed offshore to intone hourly in the night, "The coast is clear," the Greenes and the Mecoms moved back to the big house in East Greenwich. But life did not return to anything resembling what it once was. Everywhere, women had begun to work farms, and servants who had been in the city or in the house were hired out to help. Her father, when he got back from his meeting at the Colony House on the crisis, began to work the farm himself in ways he hadn't since she was small. A few boys filtered back to town and took up arms in the local militia, a group whose presence was needed in case of attack. While her father believed Rhode Island's safety was best assured by keeping the British bottled up in Boston, he also conceded that the redcoats' best strategy would be to cut off New England from the Southern states. Finally, with a grim look, he said it was best to prepare for a long war. He looked sadly at ten-year-old Ray when he said this, and Phebe felt her throat tighten.

So there were spinning bees now to make coats and blankets, but they were serious and heavyhearted affairs, and worry was like a thick haze in the room.

Then they got news that the First Rhode Island Regiment was going to march right through East Greenwich and very probably camp for the night near the town green. One of their newest officers, her father said, was Sammy Ward. He said that they should prepare to receive him and have a fine meal ready to offer. He did not say, "Because we do not know when we shall ever see him again," but she knew her father's face and his tone, and she knew those were his unvoiced thoughts.

She and her mother prepared against that day, and she was scarcely able to tamp down her mounting excitement. She freshened her best dress, or at least the one she thought she looked best in, helped plan the menu, and when word arrived the regiment would be there the very next day, she could barely close her eyes that night for thinking about what she might say. She looked out the dark window of her room, one she now shared with three other children, and gazed at the stars against the velvet sky and saw his face, his broad forehead, his fine high cheekbones. When she saw him smile, slowly, as if at her, she finally drifted into sleep.

Court-Martial Proceedings

"You are charged," the court president says, looking up from the papers in front of him, "with giving intelligence to the enemy. Do you understand the nature of this charge?"

Guy listens carefully to these words. He grips the arms of the oak witness chair to steady himself. He understands that he is accused of passing information to the British. What he does not understand is why these thirteen officers are letting him be accused. He only did what his master told him to do, but it is his master who is leveling the charge. The court waits. He cannot make the words that occur to him match his thoughts. As he gropes for words, he feels as if he is trying to sort pebbles all of the same size in the dark.

General Varnum says in a louder and slower voice, as if he is talking to a child, "Do you understand the offense you are charged with?"

Guy Watson nods. "I don' und'stand why you let him," he says softly, tilting his head toward Master John, "do dis."

"Do what?"

"Put on a trial."

"This court is obligated to hear Mister Hazzard's evidence and examine his witnesses. But we will arrive at our own judgment as to your guilt or innocence. As I believe it has been explained to you, in the view of this court, you are considered innocent until or unless it is proved otherwise."

Yes, *Guy thinks,* they did explain that. *They did not explain, though, why he is going to be held in jail and under guard all during the trial. Something about the Hazzards convincing the court that Guy Watson might, if given the chance, run away.*

General Varnum says, "Respond, in your own words, to the charge of giving intelligence to the enemy."

"Didn't do it," Guy says, and having rehearsed this part, speaks in a steady, clear voice. "I never meet a British soldier or officer. Never been behin' enemy lines. I don' know how to write, so I never sent a message, not to no one. I never was aksed to deliver a message to no one. I done what my mastuh tell me, and when he send me out, I do what he, a new mastuh, tell me." He is unused to speaking so much, so he takes a breath and swallows. It is hard for him to talk under any circumstances, and with all these important white men looking at him, his mouth is as dry as corn husks. "Don' know a thing 'bout giving 'telligence to a enemy."

General Varnum nods, his lips pressed together. He asks the other court officers if they have any questions. The men shake their heads. Guy does not know if this is a good sign or a bad one.

Master John rises from the back of the room and steps forward, looking as much at home as if he is striding across his own parlor. Guy dreads what is to come.

"You just testified," Master John begins, "that you have never delivered a message. Is that correct?"

"Yessuh," Guy says.

"Every winter, it was my practice to hire out your work, was it not?" Guy nods. "And when I sent you off, usually to Newport, did I not send letters and messages for you to carry?" Guy pauses, and tries to frame an answer. "Remember, Watson, you are under oath."

"You give me leather pouch and tell me to give it to my winter mastuh."

"And in the pouch were letters. Yes or no?"

General Varnum breaks in. "Where is this questioning going, Mister Hazzard?"

"I am trying to establish for the court that this witness is not always... reliable...in his testimony. Perhaps it is because his memory is faulty, or perhaps it is because he does not have a precise command of the English tongue. Or perhaps it is because he is a habitual liar—that is for the court to decide. I simply wish to establish that his testimony as just given to this court is not factual. And the officers of the court may then draw what inferences they may."

"The witness may answer," General Varnum says to Guy.

Guy looks at Master John uneasily. "I don' know what you put in the pouch, suh."

Master John shoots him an irritated look and rolls his eyes at the court officers. "You are saying you don't recall my calling you into my study before your departure and my putting sheets of paper, some of them sealed with red wax, in a correspondence pouch?"

"I 'member you givin' me de pouch all closed up."

"And you don't remember your winter master opening up the pouch when you delivered it?"

"No, suh. He use to put me right to work."

"Your answer is no, then?" Guy nods. "Do you know what the word 'correspondence' means?" Guy thinks he does, but he is afraid to say yes in case he is wrong. As he hesitates, Master John says, "Let me put the question another way. When I gave you my correspondence pouch every winter, what did you imagine was in it?"

"Didn't think it was my concern, suh." He can see that he is being successful in parrying the master's attempt to show that he has, in fact, carried messages and letters before, but he worries that he may seem too clever. Clever enough to deceive people if he wished.

"You testified a few moments ago, under an oath to tell the truth, that you have never met a British officer or soldier and that you have never been behind enemy lines. Is that correct?"

"Yessuh."

"Do you remember last summer when Colonel Barton and his servant appeared at Mrs. Hazzard's and my farm?"

"Yessuh."

"And what did they appear for?"

"Dey want me to help 'em."

"And I permitted you to go, did I not?"

"Yessuh."

"And you rowed with others to Middletown, behind enemy lines, to capture a British officer, did you not?"

"I did what dey tell me."

"But the truth is, you have been behind enemy lines. You have encountered British officers. Isn't that correct?" Guy doesn't know what to say. He glances nervously at the court president. Master John leans forward, towering over him. "Answer the question."

"Guess it is," he mumbles finally.

Master John nods and says softly, "You guess it is." He turns to the table of court officers and raises his voice. "The truth is, gentlemen, that Guy Watson," he points at Guy with an accusing finger, "has delivered letters and messages, he has been behind enemy lines, he has met British soldiers and British officers. And I will show, and present witnesses who will testify to the fact, that he has shared intelligence with the enemy, crucial information, that has cost American men their lives and their freedom. And if there is any justice in the heavens above, it should cost him his!"

He turns on his heel and walks to the back of the room. Master John's words ringing in his ears, Guy looks at the court officers. None of them look in his direction.

Chapter Five

For weeks Sammy, in the last light of day, took out his commission and read it. Written on creamy, thick paper, it was a grand document, and clever, too.

By the Honorable the General Assembly of the English Colony of Rhode Island and Providence Plantations in New England in America. To Samuel Ward, Junior, Greetings. You are hereby in His Majesty's Name George the Third by the Grace of God King of Great Britain, etc., authorized, empowered and commissioned to have, take, and exercise the Office of Captain in the Army of Observation.

It was signed by his Uncle Henry, secretary of the colony, on the eighth day of May 1775, "in the fifteenth year of his Majesty's reign." His father had thought up the key concept: confound Governor Wanton by fighting the king's men in the name of the king.

He knew Nat Greene had an identical document, but his concluded, "Appointment of Brigadier General of the Rhode Island Army."

Though Sam liked thinking about his new appointment, he also worried about it. At eighteen, he was heading a unit of sixty men, most of them older, some of them over twice his age. He knew that he was unusually tall, something that lent him authority—unearned and undeserved, of course. And he was from a renowned family. His muscle strength was visible even to casual observers. But one look in the glass told him the inescapable: he had the lineless face of a very young man. His lieutenant, Elisha Lewis, was five years older than he. Mostly, he had no idea if he had the fierceness that was required to make orders be followed.

Sam had no misgivings about the cause for which they were going to fight. He was not even worried about his lack of military experience. But how was someone like him, who would rather be a doctor than a political leader, fare in a war? Saving lives appealed to him more than taking them.

*

HIS BREAKFAST EATEN, HE pulled on his high, brown leather boots over his white breeches, settled his buff-colored coat, strapped on his newly whitened webbing, slung his dispatch case across one shoulder and cartridge pouch over the other, tied his hair back in a queue, set his triangular hat, and mounted his horse. He and all of his sixty men left Westerly in high spirits. But they had little time to enjoy the friendly reception of the people they passed. They had been asked to hurry forward "with all speed" because of reports that a dozen large, newly arrived British ships had begun to disgorge thousands of fresh soldiers in Boston.

Just as they were nearing East Greenwich where he hoped to visit his aunt and charming cousin Phebe, nearly all sixty of his men—at least those who ate their morning portion of salted fish—fell ill with the flux, Sammy among them. Some of them who had the energy decided to stuff some rags in the backs of their pants and, despite orders, head home. On the doctor's orders, they set up a makeshift infirmary in a field outside of town where they dug vaults for the men to leave their erupting diarrhea. Sam and Lieutenant Lewis were themselves too sick to enforce the rules against gambling, drinking, and leaving the area—an area where, Sam admitted, the stench was nauseating. He was far too ill to visit anyone. He sent someone to give his regrets to the Greenes, along with the advice that, for the sake of their own health, they should not come to the camp to visit him.

✷

FIFTY-THREE OF HIS ORIGINAL sixty men straggled into Providence five days later, their original pace slowed in half. To Sam's surprise, Colonel Varnum met him not with orders to head to Boston but to attend divine worship at the Baptist Meeting House.

"Services, sir? I thought we were required urgently in Boston."

Varnum, a handsome, fine-featured man with watchful, dark eyes, sighed. He looked weary. "'Tis the request of some patriotic merchants here."

"The entire company, Colonel?"

Varnum smiled without humor, his lips pressed tight. "Where do you think our friend Brigadier General Greene is?"

"At the lines in Boston."

"A reasonable assumption. But mistaken." He explained that their new general had left raw recruits, a confused officer corps, and a threatening enemy for one reason: supply. So when John Brown or any other local patriotic merchant made a request, it was honored. Varnum held up Nat's letter whose looping careful handwriting was as familiar to Sammy as his voice. "He writes that he was forced to leave the lines at Boston, come within seven miles of his home without having time to visit Caty, and gone without two nights' sleep, all in order to ensure supply. He returned to the lines in Boston barely in time to stop a soldiers' revolt over poor food. But he will back here in Rhode Island tomorrow. Why? Supply. The local Massachusetts merchants charge outrageous sums for the filthiest food, and most of our men lack the money to buy it. We must provision our men from here, or they are stripped by profiteers."

"Our carriages and wagons are full."

Colonel Varnum looked at them. "You have enough there, I judge, for ten days. Two weeks at the outside. Let me tell you this, Sammy, if no one else has: look to your men's stomachs and to their pay. If you do, they will follow your orders. If you do not, nothing else matters."

"We have learned something about illness already." Sam knew about the difficulty of enforcing discipline. Rhode Islanders were an independent lot, not ones who relished taking orders from anyone.

"So encamp your men on the green, Captain. Services will begin in two hours."

Just before he turned to comply, Sam asked the colonel whether he would be joining them the next morning on their march to Boston.

"No, Captain Ward, I will not. My youngest daughter has what the doctor calls a putrid malignant sore throat and is in quite guarded condition." Sam expressed his sympathy and wished a swift recovery. Varnum added, "I will join you as soon as circumstances permit."

Something in the cool and measured way the colonel said these words reminded Sam that Jimmy Varnum was passed over for the choice of general. He got the sense that while Colonel Varnum was concerned about Boston, his pride still stung, he would fulfill his duty, but only at a time that was convenient.

*

FROM THE MORNING THEY marched out of Westerly, it took them sixteen full days to reach the lines outside Boston. After they left Providence they pushed themselves to stay on the move for eighteen hours a day, well into nighttime marches, something few of them had ever done.

They approached the lines through a cool, fog-damp night, weary and excited and nervous, several hours after full dark. Sam and the two other captains of the regiment had studied the maps. There were tens of thousands of men in the lines around the city, soldiers from Connecticut, New Hampshire, and Massachusetts—and even the Stockbridge Indians and Mohawk warriors had furnished men. Their task was to find the

Rhode Island brigade. Everyone knew maps could be wrong. They also knew that a stumble into the wrong area could be fatal.

A fetid, rank smell announced their nearness to the army, as if it were some great beast breathing and excreting in the quiet dark. Minutes later they were able to make out through the thinning fog a great arc of campfires in the distance. He looked at the flickering points of yellow light, and Sam began to take in the vast size of the encampments. Nothing he had seen in his life was remotely like it. It was like looking deep into the nighttime reaches of a starlit sky, each campfire part of a great constellation. The entire company stopped and stared in silence.

As they continued north up the road and began to pass tented encampments, they came across a man leaning against a stile at the side of the road. He had his hands folded over the top of the barrel of his propped musket. He was dozing, his head dropped on his chest.

Sam's company stopped in front of him. Behind, the entire regiment came to a dead halt. A Rhode Island ensign walked over and offered the man a gentle nudge.

The man gave a quiet snort, tilted his head back, and smacked his lips sleepily. He looked around incuriously at the assembled men and said, "Huhm… Who are ye?"

"Rhode Island Brigade," said Sam. "Third Regiment, Companies Three, Four, and Five. We are looking for headquarters."

The man took off his sweat-stained hat and scratched the top of his head. He yawned broadly. "Over toward Jamaica Plains." He pointed down a road heading west and put his hat back on.

"Who are you, sir?" Sam asked.

"Massachusetts militia. I forget the numbers. M'on sentry tonight."

The three captains looked at each other in the dim light. A sentry sleeping amid reports of an attack that was said to be directed against precisely this sector? Sam, though not especially close, was close enough to the man to smell the fumes of rum.

The captains waved their companies forward down the western road. Before the last wagon left the area, the sentry, his head on his chest, was snoring.

*

They were finally directed to the Rhode Island headquarters that had been set up in the mansion on the captured grounds of the former royal governor. Sam and his fellow captains passed a guard who stood at attention at the red front door of the bright yellow house. They were ushered by a servant into a crystal chandeliered central hall where they found Major Christopher Greene, Nat's cousin. Tall, rangy, and older than Nat, with his lean wind-burned face and serious, dark eyes glowing in the dim light, he had the same air of authority as his kinsman. Sam had not seen him since Nat and Caty's wedding a year ago, when, in his ill-fitting best clothes, he seemed out of place. Here, though, even alone in the mansion's largest room late at night, he looked entirely at home. Christopher Greene had been read out from under the care of and expelled by the East Greenwich Society of Friends for "having taken up in the military way." Though quiet, he inspired confidence among the Kentish Guards long before he was brevetted major. Sitting in a chair at one end of a dining table long enough to seat thirty people, he looked up and greeted the three officers without rising.

"You are welcome, gentlemen, to the Boston lines."

"Is the general back yet?" Sam asked.

He shook his head. "No. Colonel Church's regiment is unable to control their men. Colonel Varnum is delayed. An attack is due any time." He added dryly, "Matters could be better." He stood and motioned them to the head of the table to look at the map. "But we have enough shot and enough cartridge." He placed a lantern closer to the center of the unfolded map.

On the map, Boston looked like a fat tadpole swimming north. It was surrounded by water except for a small run of land at its tail where it was connected to Dorchester and Roxbury. Major Greene pointed to this spit of land. The lines of the Rhode Island brigade were placed in Roxbury, right astride the tadpole's tail. "Here we are. This, gentlemen, is the point where a surprise attack will be easiest to mount. To go anywhere else," he drew a finger in a circle around the rest of the tadpole, "requires ships." He paused to look up at them to make certain they were listening. "Our friends in the town tell us landing crafts are being prepared now. We wanted you here as soon as possible because we expect a landing here behind the lines at the undefended Dorchester Point," he put a finger down on the coast of the area near where they had met the sleeping sentry, "and a land attack here on the lines at Roxbury." He moved his finger once again directly to the spot where the Rhode Island lines were established. "Then Howe will attempt to roll up the flank of the New England army all the way to headquarters at Cambridge." He swept a hand in a semicircle.

"Is this a flying report?" Sam asked.

"As firm as can be gotten without having Howe tell us himself." Major Greene straightened up from the table. "It is an hour past midnight. Five o'clock is parade and drill. Six o'clock prayers. Seven o'clock breakfast. You will want to see your men are properly established for what remains of the night."

"Yessir," the captains said together.

*

Sam awakened mosquito-bitten and dry-mouthed to the rattle and toot of a fife and drum. He could see a slice of dark gray sky out the front of his tent. Within minutes, the air swelled with the sounds of men talking, cows lowing to be milked, dogs barking, horses neighing, and cooks clanging breakfast kettles and banging gruel pots.

They had encamped squarely in the governor's gardens, and they found in the morning light swirls of yellows and reds and pinks in full June bloom, cut in precise rectangles and crisp squares, full of unfamiliar, exotic flowering plants imported and cultivated by a platoon of English gardeners. On the east side of the garden was a hothouse that was now serving as a powder magazine. On the west side, scores of wagons and carts were drawn up with mounds of supplies all disgorged into heaps.

An old family friend and neighbor, Augustus Mumford, Colonel Varnum's adjutant, appeared with a quick grin, but he was soon all business. Gus read the general orders to the captains and to their lieutenants, ensigns, and sergeants. He explained the supply arrangements and apologized for the disorder. Sam was not quite clear about which "disorder" he had in mind until he followed Mumford's glance to where some men were peeing and crapping in various corners of the garden.

"For reasons of health and order," the adjutant read in a loud voice, "the command wishes that the men always repair to the necessaries and that you appoint colormen to dig and fill the vaults at least every two days."

Sam heard one of his sergeants say, "Hah?" to another, who replied, "We gotta use a hole for the shite."

Mumford ended his list of announcements by pointing to a well-worn road heading north. "The Rhode Island lines are two miles that way. You will be encamping there on a permanent basis. Or," he added, "until orders come to the contrary."

As they made their way in the brightening morning light toward the lines, Sam was surprised by what he saw around them. His Rhode Islanders had tents made of sailcloth, and the officers had marquees that opened over the entrance; most of the men also had a few pieces of uniform, and some a complete outfitting. The Massachusetts men—furnished by the same province that exuded military ardor—were dressed from captain to private like the civilian farmers, mechanics, and shopkeepers they were. Their tents were ramshackle rigs of boards, turf, stones, cloth, bushes, and birch bark. And their behavior was worse. Several men were obviously drunk, others sick and unattended. All were dirty and unshaven, idle, slack, and bored.

The Massachusetts soldiers didn't look encouraging, but the defensive works they manned were impressive. Designed by the old British-trained veteran Colonel Richard Gridley and Nat Greene's friend, young Colonel Henry Knox, the fortifications took the terrain as it came and used it brilliantly. Sam was relieved to find that the Rhode Island lines at the crucial tail of the tadpole of the Boston peninsula were well secured. A large pond protected one flank, and a trench with foot-thick walls dug into rocky ground ran from the shore all the way up to a full redoubt on the other. Sam and the rest of the officers clambered up to explore it. At the top of a slope, it had earthen breastworks on each side with huge stick-packed bundles called fascines in the middle. It had an outcropping for artillery on one side and arrow-shaped projections on the other to permit soldiers to directly fire in nearly any direction at once. It even had sally ports dug in the front to permit the soldiers to exit for a swift counterattack.

A quarter of a mile straight off the flank of the Rhode Island lines were two hills, each with a dozen eighteen- and twenty-four-pound cannons bristling from their brows. Between them passed the Boston Neck Road, the only clear passage out of Boston itself. It was obvious that if the British came by land, they would have to come this way. You also did not have to be a military expert to see that it was a path that would make them pay a steep price.

While Sam knew that the Rhode Islanders' compared to those from Massachusetts were a model of order, that order did not extend to their firearms. The variety of guns and muskets the men carried made uniform training impossible. This was a problem. Armies, he knew, had to work like the gears in a water mill—everything meshing. If they did not, they would grind to a halt and be destroyed.

Some of his men had blunderbusses, others fowling pieces or muskets. Three in Sam's company had long, heavy rifles. And even among those who had muskets, there was a bewildering variation of flint, firing pan, and barrel caliber. Each man had his own powder requirements, and no standard charge could be prepared. The riflemen had to melt and mold their own lead shot. So as the men began pouring powder into their paper cartridges, they had to be reminded that a lopsided charge meant a lopsided shot. A few of the men had Brown Bess muskets that took a standard one-ounce ball, lead lumps the size of the end of Sam's finger. The rest were left to their own skills.

By midafternoon, the trenches, redoubts, and fortifications were manned almost shoulder-to-shoulder.

Though the weather was clear, the officers recommended that their men daub each of their cartridges with tallow for waterproofing. When Gus Mumford rode up to the lines, he did not make any of the friendly conversation he usually did. Instead he asked him to walk with him behind a supply wagon and, after looking sharply around, spoke in a low, urgent voice, his eyes darting with nervousness.

"We have received firm intelligence that Gage and Howe plan to attack here within two days. Colonel Hitchcock has sent expresses to Varnum and Nat Greene telling them to get here immediately. Major Greene will continue in command until then." Sam nodded, but the tremor in Gus's voice brought his own nerves to a high edge. Mumford looked around once again and stood close enough to Sam for the brow of his hat nearly to touch his own and smell the coffee on his breath. "Tomorrow night," he whispered, "under the greatest possible secrecy, Putnam of Connecticut and Prescott of Massachusetts will steal a march. They will be entrenching their men to the north around Charlestown."

"Charlestown," Sam repeated.

"That will put all their men-of-war in the harbor and most of their soldiers in Boston within cannon range. The noose will be around their neck. They will have to come out and fight, or be hanged." Gus looked anxiously about him. "We believe there are spies among us, so this news must not be shared with *anyone*. If news of the plans got out…" He shook his head.

"We must plan today for a fight tomorrow."

"More likely the day after. The redcoats think we'll just turn and run. They are in for a bloody surprise."

*

Everyone gave Guy orders. Everyone.

As soon as he was separated from Sam Ward, no matter what he was doing, someone came along and told him to do something else. Fix this, dig that, chop, clean, stoke the fire, cover the shit. Wash this, hold that, get some wood, haul some water. Sergeant, private, age sixteen or age forty, everybody worked him.

He found his best defense was to be busy with a project he had been ordered to perform by someone high in rank—but who remained in sight while he performed it. If there was no officer available, Guy found it was best to drop what he was doing and get about whatever it was anyone told him to do. When four different Rhode Islanders gave him jobs he could not complete, they nearly got into a fistfight with each other.

No one was afraid of Captain Ward. The soldiers seemed comfortable about him, but they did not worry about taking his servant off a project. He knew, though, that they were glad to be serving under him. At night around the fire, he heard one of them say, "No way they goin' to risk the son of the delegate to the Continental Congress on some damn foolish errand. And that's all right by me."

Another added, "And I bet they don't fail to send food our way, neither."

Ever since he left Westerly, Guy had been waiting for a contact from Master Hazzard's man. He thought while all the soldiers were sick in East Greenwich, someone would come asking for information. He thought while they waited in Providence, someone would come. Because no one did in either place, he was sure someone would contact him soon at the Boston lines. What he did not know was what he could possibly offer that would be useful.

He had seen something that he longed to tell June and Jubah and Quamino. When he worked winters in Newport, he had seen several free blacks, so he knew that such a thing was possible. Here, though, he had seen while marching to the Rhode Island lines, not one or two, but a dozen or more black soldiers in the Massachusetts army, men carrying muskets and cartridge pouches! One of them had his wife along with him, just like some of the whites. At home, they would never believe it.

There were women in the camps, too, mostly tending fires or visiting their husbands for a few days, but some seemed to live and work for the army. And there were camp followers, washerwomen and cooks by day, who, by night, sold their bodies to men. There were tinkers selling wares, peddlers selling food, sutlers selling beer and spirits, and dark-clothed clergymen who came and preached sermons about virtue. One wanted to take their money, the other to tend their souls.

He tried, as ever, to stay clear of trouble.

*

SAM WALKED BEHIND HIS rows of men at the lines and assigned them into two ranks, the first to step forward and fire while the other prepared their guns, the second to fire while the first reloaded. He relayed Major Greene's instructions. "If the attack comes," he said, "Aim first for their officers. Shoot no higher than their cross belts. Wait until you see the nose on their face and the sweat on their lip. Do *not* fire until ordered!"

He repeated the instructions, passed among them, checked their cartridges and weapons, repeated the instructions still again, and waited. Huge British men-of-war floated lazily about in the harbor. Men who sweated with nervousness in the morning began to sweat with the heat of the sun. As time passed, some dozed, others sang tunes. Some men gambled, played cards, wrote letters, or read their Bibles. A rumor raced through the lines: someone had heard drums flamming in Boston. Someone else had seen the *Glasgow* open its gun ports. Yells ran up and down the lines. Fear reached a cold hand into their bowels and squeezed. Officers' spyglass lenses glittered in the sun. Soldiers peered over the edge of the trenches and checked their powder. An hour later, another rumor. And so the day inched along. Boredom and waiting and vigilance punctuated by violent jolts of fear.

As the thick yellow light of the long June afternoon began to fade, Major Greene came to the lines and instructed the regiment to prepare themselves for the night. They would not be returning to their tents but were to sleep where they were, in their coats upon the rocky ground. They were also to maintain a four-hour rotating guard, one who was to adhere strictly to the parole and countersign to be demanded of anyone—and that meant anyone—who attempted to approach the area. At full dark, the skies a rich blue-black, they were permitted only one campfire per company and to maintain complete silence. So quiet was it that men up and down the lines at Roxbury could hear the British sailors' watch aboard the *Glasgow* intoning, "All's well."

Augustus Mumford came to inspect the lines and whispered to Sam that at this moment Putnam and Prescott were entrenching on Bunker Hill on the Charlestown peninsula. By the time the sun rose, they expected to have the fortifications completed, with Colonel Gridley there himself to make sure it was done properly. "If he does half as well up there as he's done down here," Gus Mumford said, "they'll be in a nutcracker."

Chapter Six

On Saturday, the day he had been raised to believe was the Seventh Day and had always tried to keep as the Sabbath, Sam was awakened from a ragged sleep at first light by the deep cough of cannons firing on the far side of the bay. Seconds later, alarms, bugles, bells, drums, and fifes sounded all over Boston. He knew with a tightening in his chest that he would not be attending church this morning.

The colonial troops digging in during the night on the Charlestown peninsula had been discovered. The deep thump of firing British gunships in the harbor began to sound. The British battery on Boston's Cobb Hill joined in. In the graying dawn, American soldiers all up and down the lines prepared themselves for an assault.

Sam, his hands unsteady enough that he had to set them on his knees to still them, peered at his rolled-out map to analyze what was happening. In the large C-shape of land around Boston harbor, the Rhode Island brigade was at the bottom of the C. If he drew a line straight to Charlestown and the newly fortified hills beyond it at the top of the C, the line passed right through the heart of Boston. He raised his spyglass and could see the city streets beginning to fill with masses of red-coated soldiers and civilians, all of them heading north away from his view. The hills and the church spires of the city blocked his view of the Charlestown peninsula, though just to the sides he could see foresails being hoisted as the great warships tried to swing round. From the side of one of the ships, three of its cannon muzzles flashed fire and pushed out puffs of smoke. A few seconds later, a dull distant *whump* reached his ears.

Major Greene and Colonel Hitchcock arrived at the Roxbury lines, their unshaven faces tense, to ready the Rhode Island companies to hold their positions. Everyone thought the British would try to break out of the city—directly upon them.

The shelling of Charlestown grew intense. The sun burned off the morning fog and the sky moved from purple at the horizon to a brilliantly clear blue. Minutes dragged by. They could see red-coated British soldiers continuing to gather in the streets, many of them mustering at the waterfront. Finally, the tiny figures in uniform began, one company at a time, to board boat tenders. In groups of three and four at a time, the tenders carried them out to the warships and to rows of barges. Then the big boats began steadily to row toward the Charlestown peninsula.

It became clear to the Rhode Islanders that whatever was going to happen, their lines in Roxbury would not be the target.

"It would be a proper time for us to attack," Sam said to his lieutenant. "They're not paying us any attention at all."

Sergeant Bond muttered, "Not me. I like these trenches." Sam looked at him. "I hope they attack us, though," Bond added when he saw the captain regarding him.

"If we attack, we would have surprise on our side," Lieutenant Lewis said.

"That may be," said Bond. "But I wouldn't want to go marching out in the open and get shot in the legs. Ever seen a crippled farmer, lieutenant?"

"No…"

"That's right. If I get shot, might as well be in the head."

Sam wondered how many others in the army felt the same way. Most of them were farmers. Would they be brave fighters in a trench but be shy to attack?

Major Greene passed behind them, reviewing the lines. The whitening sun rose higher as the British boats, laden with soldiers, made their way north.

Sam intercepted him. "Any word, sir?"

"Not yet."

Sam showed him his map. "Look at this, Major." He pointed to Charlestown, connected to the C of land outside Boston by only the narrowest neck of land. "If the redcoats land troops here at the Jews' burying ground, our soldiers on the hill will be completely cut off."

Greene nodded, interested but undisturbed. "We will know soon."

Sam hated sitting there, and he thought they would have to hear about what was happening because they would never be able to see it: their view of the entrenched hill was blocked. They could, however, already see great billows of smoke rising high above the area of Charlestown itself. Though their eyes ached with watching, everything in their own area was quiet.

When Augustus Mumford finally returned, Sam stepped in close to hear his report that General Thomas has requested a hundred men from the Rhode Island brigade to head toward Charlestown. With no colonels at the lines to get the request, Major Greene, the highest-ranking officer present, took charge. A call for volunteers for a detachment went out, and Sam stepped forward before the words had finished leaving Christopher Greene's mouth. A few minutes later, he exchanged his dispatch case for a cartridge pouch, and he was ready.

For three miles, over Jamaica Plains and across the Muddy River, the one-hundred-man Rhode Islander detachment competed with messengers, curious onlookers, supply wagons, and moving artillery trains. They didn't stop until they were halfway to Cambridge and the peninsula first came into view.

Charlestown was ablaze. Even from their distance and in full noon daylight they could see two church steeples forming the base for huge orange pyramids of fire. Behind the town, what had been smooth green slopes a day ago were now trenched with brown earthen cuts—cuts dotted with men. Through his glass, Sam could see the Americans still digging. Even with the naked eye, the hot sunlit scene was clear to view. The lower peninsula was amassed with brightly clad British infantry and a second flotilla of barges filled with redcoats was completing its crossing of the bay. The British soldiers waiting on land for reinforcement were sorting themselves into sharp, straight lines. To Sam, their scarlet coats seemed like terrible extensions of the fire that was reducing the town to ash.

The Americans continued digging.

Sam and the other officers on horseback waited for the men at the back of their detachment to catch up. They gaped at the awesome sight before them. The British warship the *Somerset* lobbed shells into the middle of the town even though most of it had finished burning and was beginning to subside into embers. The second landing of British troops was completed as they watched. Lieutenant Lewis said unhappily, "They mean to give us a pageant today." He took a sharp intake of breath. "Great Lord," he said, voice quavering. "It's going to start!" He raised a hand and pointed.

An eerie silence bloomed. Spectators on shore stopped talking. Sam's group stood rock still. The British batteries in Boston stopped firing. Suddenly there was the sound of bands playing martial music on fife and drum. The ships resumed their cannonading, focusing their fire on Charlestown Neck to try to cut off American reinforcements who were making their way to the lines.

At last the British soldiers started forward, marching in a methodical, orderly, brilliantly colored wave. As they crossed fences and climbed outcroppings, the companies stopped and reformed themselves once again into knife-edged lines. Sam's heart pounded in his ears louder even than the cannons' *whump*. At that distance, the soldiers looked to him as unreal as dolls as they moved toward the

American lines. But he knew, and felt the knowledge as an ache in his chest, that these toys were about to deal out agony and death.

Some of the men yelled for quiet, and then they could hear the ticking sound of distant musket fire. Just out of their sight, on the far side of the peninsula at the left flank of the entrenched hill, the fighting had begun. The redcoats they could see marched ever closer to the entrenchments, steady as an oncoming wave. Sam heard the Rhode Islanders around him praying for victory. The British line still advanced implacably. Finally, the red rows were directly on top of the Americans. Sam wondered for a terrible moment if the dreaded British were simply going to pass through and crush the colonials without having to fire a shot. "Fire!" Sam heard himself yell, and the strained praying men around him took up the call. "For God's sake, fire!"

They saw a line of gray-white puffs come silently from the American redoubt, the fences, and the breastworks. Red figures toppled like bottles. A moment later they heard the muffled crack of muskets. A second row of puffs issued from the entrenchments and more red figures fell. The lines appeared to merge for an instant, waver, and then the red ranks broke apart, first in one place and then another, and then they began to fall back in clumps and bright splinters. Some groups retreated slowly, and others ran, fleeing down the slopes they had just marched up. Scarlet splashes dotted the ground where wounded and dying British soldiers lay. A great cheer rose around Sam and, his own face suddenly wet with unnoticed tears, he found himself screaming with everyone else.

Amid the din, Major Greene waved them forward. They pressed toward Cambridge at top speed. They had nearly reached the Charles River when some civilian spectators overlooking the bay began to yell and point at the peninsula. Word reached them that the British had reformed their lines and were preparing for a second assault. This time, though, they could see nothing of Charlestown or the peninsula. They continued their quick-time march toward headquarters in Cambridge, praying again in a blind sorrowful rage for the Americans to hold on.

The Rhode Islanders were supposed to get further instructions at headquarters, but the little college town was in bedlam. Streets were clogged with horses, wagons, carriages, undirected soldiers, scurrying women, carts, cannon platforms, and dirt-streaked, crying children. Major Greene surveyed the scene and ordered the men to continue.

"What are we doing?" Sam called.

"We are going to help," the major replied. "If help is needed."

Sam looked back and estimated that almost half their original hundred men had either gotten lost or turned back.

The closer they got to Charlestown Neck, the more crowded the way became. They were told everywhere by thrilled, excited witnesses that the British second attack had been repulsed more convincingly than even the first. Some were saying that the Americans had been reinforced and were impregnable now.

Amid the air of uncontained celebration, the Rhode Island officers noticed that few men were crossing Charlestown Neck, no one seemed in command in the area, and those who had recently crossed were entrenching on a hill well short of where the fighting had taken place. Sam judged there to be easily a thousand men on that unchallenged hill—but they were not reinforcing anyone. They were setting up new positions that appeared to have no relevance to the field.

Gunboats and armed transports continued to send grapeshot and cannonballs whistling over the causeway and across Charlestown Neck. Every few minutes a group of ten or a dozen men returned from the peninsula helping some soldier who had a cut on his head or a wound in his arm.

Sam and many of the others wanted to cross over, but Major Greene held them back. Something, he said, was wrong. "Exposing ourselves and our detachment to that compassless crowd over there is foolish. They look to be on the wrong hill." He pointed to a powder-blackened and exhausted artillery company that was retreating over the Neck. "Why are they leaving?"

"With respect, sir," said Elijah Lewis, "why not cross over?"

"It is dangerous, lieutenant, to take an action without a clear purpose. Look at this map." He and the other officers dismounted and gathered around the major. "Our men were sent last night to throw up works on Bunker Hill. We are looking at Bunker Hill now."

They raised their heads and looked at the unscarred hill a mile distant, swarming with unstained troops. "But that is not where we saw the fight," said Lewis.

"Correct. What we saw, according to this map, was Breed's Hill." Greene stopped one of the retreating powder-darkened artillerymen. "Why have you left your post, private?"

"We're out of ammunition," he said, still panting.

"Where are your cannons?"

"We left 'em." Greene frowned. "For the relief troops," the man added.

"Were you relieved?"

The man shrugged and said no.

Shaking his head, the major asked, "Where are your cannons, exactly?"

"On Bunker Hill."

Greene pointed to the near hill. "There?"

"No," the weary artilleryman said. "Farther on." He coughed and straggled off to join his retreating company of ensigns and matrosses.

Major Greene turned to Sam and told him to arrange the company into two files. "We're crossing over," he said. "To the *far* hill."

Before they could be formed for marching, however, they heard the British fife and drums once again. They looked at each other in disbelief. There was a long pause and then they heard the crackle of muskets.

Incredibly, the British had begun a third attack.

Within minutes they saw the first wave of Americans falling back from their positions. More and more of the wounded appeared. Some of the spectators began to panic. Major Greene ordered the Rhode Island detachment to return march, and he himself began to ride about the area and roar at gawking civilians and sutlers and soldiers to clear out. Sam immediately saw the major's concern: a full retreat across that tiny strip of land would be a disaster. If it was not cleared ahead of time, they would be stopped up like a corked bottle, perfect targets to be swept by canister and grapeshot from the gunboats.

Once people on the Cambridge side saw bloodied men withdrawing from the peninsula, they fled at a run. Within minutes, there was over a square mile with nothing in it but an overturned cart with one wheel turning slowly in the air.

A steady retreat from the entrenchments began, those from the farthest hills arriving first. Some of these men had gone twenty-four hours without sleep or food. Most were too tired to run and a few looked almost too exhausted to walk. Major Greene ordered the Rhode Island detachment to hold its position in case they needed to protect the rear from pursuing British soldiers. An hour passed and the New England soldiers trudged by, looking more as if they were heading home from a grueling day's labor than fleeing a battlefield. Not a single redcoat came in sight.

The retreating men all told the same story. They would have held off the third assault, too, but they ran out of ammunition. When the redcoats heard some of the men in the lines calling aloud for powder and ball, they knew precisely where to press their advantage.

The grenadiers and light infantry and Welch fusiliers came in among them at the end with their terrible bayonets fixed. In fury over the slaughter their companies endured in the first assaults, they took revenge. Accepting no surrender, they were pitiless in running through the slow and the wounded. Some men tried to surrender, pleading for mercy, and were run through as they begged.

Sam felt his flesh crawl. There was something unspeakable about death by bayonet. And the executioners themselves! They did their work personally, plunging the blade in at close range and twisting, watching the man's face as they did it. It was an act that seemed to him as barbaric as the scalpings the papers said British General Gage was bribing Indians on the western frontiers to perform. A lead ball at fifty yards seemed almost civilized.

*

AS THE AFTERNOON PASSED, the ocean tide dropped, reversing the currents away from Charlestown Neck. The Rhode Islanders knew they were fortunate. Pushed away, the British gunboats were unable to remain close enough to fire effectively upon the shore. While there were several hours of light left on this day, one of the longest days of the year, everyone knew by late afternoon that the battle had ended. In the silence that succeeded the ships' withdrawal, the men on shore began to hear groans and cries of the wounded and the dying.

Sam tried not to listen but found it is as impossible as not to breathe. One man called for his wife. Another for his mother. Many called on God. Some called for water. Many groaned and others whimpered. One man screamed in agony, horribly, over and over and over until Sam wondered how he could keep it up.

He was still screaming when Major Greene ordered their return to Roxbury.

*

GUY WAS GROOMING THE officers' horses when Captain Ward asked him to tend to two more. He followed young Ward to an area just outside the headquarters' dazzling flower gardens. All the officers inside had come out to greet the new guest, someone named Dr. Church. For two days now, ever since the battle ended, everyone from the highest to the lowest rank had been discussing the fight on the Charlestown peninsula. It still was being debated who won and who lost. At the end of the engagement, the British occupied the embattled ground, which some men said meant they won. Others insisted the British suffered such high losses of officers and men that it was a spectacular loss, and that a few more such costly "victories" would mean a total American triumph. As Guy waited to take the two horses, he heard a lieutenant say that Church was the head of all the army's hospitals and that if anyone knew what losses the Americans had, he would be the one.

Guy did not know who lost, but everything in the mood of the soldiers he had seen told him the Americans won. Most seemed jubilant and, as more and more information about the battle reached them, their nerves settled. Dr. Church, a portly man in expensive clothes, his long hair powdered white and tied back in a queue, had an air of intelligence and high confidence about him, and though he seemed tired and said he had been working long hours these past days, his mood was upbeat. He seemed to know several of the Rhode Islanders personally, Captain Ward in particular.

Guy held Dr. Church's horse as he dismounted. Once on the ground, Church thanked the officers for this warm greeting and clapped a hand on Sam Ward's shoulder, telling him he had just returned from the Congress at Philadelphia a few days ago and that Sam's father sent him his special regards and a personal letter. Church turned to the man on the other horse, his assistant, and told him to find the missive for Captain Ward. He and the captain talked about their families for a while, and the doctor mentioned pursuing the captain's old wish to become a doctor himself. The captain said that it was a peacetime pursuit. Then, to Guy's surprise, Church looked directly at him and asked Sam if this was his servant.

"For the time being," Sam replied. Church nodded, and then told his assistant to give Guy his horse as well.

The assistant, a tall thin man with prominent cheekbones, intense grey eyes, and a dark red birthmark on his temple about the size of thumbprint, dismounted. He removed his hat and began to leaf through some papers in a thick leather bag attached to his saddle. As Dr. Church headed inside with the Rhode Island officers, the assistant told Guy he would have to walk with him to where he groomed the horses and remove the saddlebag there, the better to look through it.

Guy led him to the nearby barn and set the thirsty horses up before the water trough. He asked the man how long he would be staying.

He rubbed his lean cheek. "A good hour," he replied, and began to uncinch his own saddle.

After removing Dr. Church's saddle, Guy took an old blanket and began to wipe down the well-lathered horse. Either Dr. Church had been riding farther than his assistant, or the doctor's considerable bulk made his horse work harder; the assistant's horse, he noticed, seemed as fresh as if it had just left the barn. As Guy began rubbing down the horse, the assistant asked him how long he had worked for Captain Ward.

Whites never held personal conversation with him, so Guy was surprised to hear this question. "Since spring," he said guardedly.

The narrow-faced man nodded, putting on some silver-rimmed spectacles before peering in his mailbag. His birthmark glowed dully. His glasses on, he looked both ways, glanced at Guy and then said, as if casually, but in a low voice, "Mister John Hazzard is a particular friend of mine." He paused for a moment, letting this information sink in. "And he has asked me to see if you have anything you would particularly like to report to him."

Guy felt his muscles tense from his neck to his knees. He looked nervously around. "You see him?"

"I saw him last week. Which is when he asked me to check with you to see if you had anything useful to tell him."

"Useful…" Guy repeated, stalling in order to think.

"Information that would help him understand the situation here."

Guy had already given the matter long thought. He knew if he wished to be seen as valuable to the master, he had to give valuable information. He also knew, though, that if the information was very useful, the master might arrange to let Captain Ward keep him there. And that would keep him away from June still longer. But if he got sent home now, he would be going back to a life he could not change—being around June, yes, but not being with her.

He took a deep breath and told the thin-faced man what he could.

The man nodded, the sun glinting off his glasses. While most of what Guy told him he would already know on his own—that the Rhode Islanders seemed ready to fight—and he knew nothing except what he had seen, he was able to tell him about the near mutiny in one of the regiments over a lack of food and money.

When he was done, the man asked him a few questions about Nat Greene. And then he asked Guy if he could read.

Guy shook his head, "Nossuh."

"Pity," he muttered. "Are you able to be present when Captain Ward gets his orders?"

Guy shook his head again. Sometimes yes, mostly no.

"Can you serve at table?"

Guy thought back to a party in Newport where he once carried and offered trays of food. "Yessuh."

"All right. You listen to me, now. I am going to arrange for you to be at headquarters, not at the lines." He waited for Guy to nod. "And part of your time, you will serve at the officers' table." He raised a finger and pointed it at Guy's head. "Your job is to listen to *everything* that is said. I will check in with you every several days or so for a report." Guy nodded. "Now, what did I just say?"

Dutifully, Guy repeated what the man told him.

"Good." The thin man pulled himself up to his full height and fixed his gaze on Guy directly. Again he pointed his finger at him. "On your life, not a word of this to anyone. Do you understand?"

"Yessuh."

"Your well-being depends on it. And June Harris's, too."

His heart squeezed in his chest. Before Guy could say anything, the man turned on his heel and was gone.

*

When Guy was told an hour later to bring the freshly watered horses back, he found Dr. Church with a broad smile on his face making his farewell to the Rhode Island officers. The doctor stopped and chatted with Captain Ward for a time, and Guy heard him advise the younger man to keep a proper distance between himself and the men under his command. "Too close, my boy, and you undermine your own authority. Be sure to spend your nights here, not at the lines. Better rest and improved conditions will keep your strength and health up, and that will make you a better officer. I speak here as a doctor."

"Yessir, Doctor Church, thank you. It is an easy order to follow when it increases your own comfort."

Church laughed and clapped Sam on the shoulder. "Yes, but we have higher aims in view than mere comfort."

Sam nodded. Then his face grew serious. "If you are in Philadelphia again soon, perhaps you can urge father to vaccinate himself against the smallpox."

"He hasn't done so already?" Sam shook his head. "I shall write him as soon as I have a moment free. Smallpox is thick as hail in large cities." Guy held the reins as Church mounted his horse. "Farewell, gentlemen," he said to the Rhode Island officers. "Good courage!" He gestured to his thin-faced assistant who then mounted his own horse.

The assistant bade goodbye to the officers, and, as he wheeled his horse about, looked directly at Guy before he rode off.

The next evening, Guy was told he would be required from now on to help serve the evening meal. Dr. Church had found that the past server was not attentive enough to cleanliness and recommended a change. The fat and sweating cook, wiping his hands on his filthy, food-encrusted apron front, told Guy he had to be very careful about cleanliness.

Chapter 7

RUTTING SEASON BEGAN JUST after Guy left, and June saw that Master John was in an expansive mood. He was happy that Lucy miscarried and recovered so swiftly that she barely lost a day's labor. He also told everyone that war was going to be excellent for business. "The market for beef, milk, and cheese is going to be lively," he explained to Young John. He gave orders for every cow whose undertail got a bit swollen to be sent to the bulls. His cheerfulness seemed to make him popular. In the days and weeks after the fighting at Lexington and Concord, many of the master's panicked friends and neighbors came to him for advice.

Some wanted to move to Nova Scotia until the storm passed, others threw their lot in with one side or the other, but most in southern Rhode Island did not want to choose sides until they could tell who would prevail. He told his loyalist Tory friends that the rebels didn't stand a chance. He told his few rebel-supporting neighbors something similar but in a more measured way. June heard an early version of what became a standard speech for him one afternoon in the creamery.

"This little bruising is precisely what we have needed, Johnny. The home government will see now the necessity of sending over some additional soldiers, and in a few months, t'will be over. Have you read the latest *Rivington's*? No? It reminds us that there are eight *million* British citizens, and only two and a half million colonials. And when you reduce the colonists' available soldiers by excluding loyalist friends, the devout Quakers, the uncertain, and the one-quarter who are black, what do they have? A handful of rag-tag, ill-equipped farmers, some lawyers, and a silversmith or two. And think of it, son, *they* propose to take on the greatest navy and the best trained fighting forces in the world. Hah! All we need is for the colonials to get Parliament to settle this damned taxation problem, and then, Johnny, we shall have our cakes *and* our ale. And in the meantime, please don't forget this—there are profits to be made."

"How?" Young John asked, brightening at this last news.

"There will be soldiers coming and soldiers gathered. And as long as men have breathed and fought, they have needed three things: food, clothing, and supplies. And we shall furnish them to whosoever needs them."

"But how can we get our goods to the British in Boston?"

He waved a hand in dismissal. "Boston will come to us."

"The Committee of Inspection will…"

"We provision both sides, son. No one will want to bite the hand that feeds them."

But for all the coming-and-going of nervous neighbors and the atmosphere of tension, life did not change very much for June and the other slaves. Jubah worked hard every evening at teaching June more about herbs and medicines, and Quamino was more silent than usual. But otherwise life went on almost if no war had begun.

Rutting season disrupted the cheese- and butter-making work in the creamery since the dairy slaves were needed to help herd cows into the narrow wooden driftways behind the barn. Once the cow was in the driftway, Quamino would herd an already aroused bull in after her and then they would let nature take its course.

June tried not to think about Guy living in some far-off place between two hostile armies, but so much of his handiwork was everywhere at the farm it was hard to go more than a few minutes without something calling him to mind. He had built the driftways himself. Lucy, who seemed to have recovered from losing her baby in body, was very downcast. Jubah gave her some herbs, saying it would take time, but she would feel better. Quamino's face grew inward, and he said he wondered if this was the death he had foreseen at the crossing point.

Everyone on the farm had seen matings between sheep, horses, pigs, cows, dogs, cats, and dung chickens, but this season Young John started to take a special interest in it, particularly with the bulls. So June was not surprised to find he was often there to watch Quamino at work. There were two ways Quamino aroused a bull. One way was to let the bull begin mounting a cow they knew to be in heat and then drive the bull into the driftway with another cow. This was effective, but risky. No one wanted to interrupt a mating bull. The other way, and one Quamino used more and more often as he got older, was to take a stick with its end wrapped in rags, something they called The Tickler, and stroke the bull's penis until the bull was ready to rear up, mount, and service the waiting cow.

It was Mistress Hazzard's standing order that this was men's work. Everyone but Quamino was sent back to work once the bull and cow were safely in the driftway. One morning something unusual happened, but it was not until dinner that Quamino had the time to explain what it was. The bull was a three-year-old, young and inexperienced at mating, but he had begun his task with vigor. Young John edged closer, bending his knees in order to watch the action. During one of the bull's most emphatic thrusts, the cow shied, lunged forward into the fence, and one of the slats broke with a sharp *crack*. The startled bull lost his balance. Staggering backward, the bull became disengaged from the cow, lost his balance, and his penis swung around like a tree branch in a gust of wind. Quamino looked over to find two paths of bull sperm dripping down the chest of Young John's shirt. Though he tried not to, Quamino found himself smiling at the look on the boy's face and had to turn away before the boy saw him.

Quamino went to get a rag for the boy to wipe himself, but by the time he returned, Young John had vanished.

Everyone laughed at the story until tears rolled down their cheeks.

It was soon less amusing. Just before their Sunday dinner, their biggest meal of the week, June started down the steps to the root cellar to get some vegetables for Jubah when she heard someone grunting. Immediately wary, she stopped and peered quietly down into the cool darkness. A second passed while her eyes adjust to the lack of light, and then she saw Young John, his pants around his ankles, thrusting into Lucy who was bent over a cutting table, her dress pulled up around her chest. June stared in disbelief. Barely able to stifle a gasp, she backed slowly up the stairs into the daylight.

She told Jubah what she saw. Jubah's initial look of surprise faded. She shook her head slowly and sighed. "What we gone do?" June asked.

"Goin' do nothing," Jubah said. "I talk to Lucy, but that girl not doin' much listening these days."

June listened to the conversation Jubah had with her that night. Jubah asked Lucy to sit and then chewed on a little piece of sweet wood, working it around her teeth. She regarded Lucy in silence for a while. Finally, Lucy said, "What?"

"June saw you this afternoon in the root cellar. With Young John."

Lucy took a big breath and looked at June. "What you see?"

"What you think she see?" Jubah said before June could respond.

Lucy took another deep breath and then straightened. "He give me some pie and a new mobcap."

"Did he, now?" Jubah said. "How long this been goin' on?"

"Maybe a week."

"How many times?"

Lucy looked uncomfortable. "'Bout every day."

"'Bout every day?" Jubah said quietly. "Every day, now?" Lucy nodded. "He give you somet'ing every time?"

"Every time," she nodded. "Some ribbon, stockings, sweet taffy. Something."

"So this seem pretty good. The mastuh's son sniffin' after you, giving you gifts an' treats an' things?"

"What I'm s'pose to do? Mastuh's son tell me what to do, I'm goin' say no and get whip or beat or worse? And he jus' lie to his parents if I try an' tell 'em."

"What you goin' do if he gives you another baby? Jus' because your first one not live don't mean next one won't. You gonna say Quamino done it? Think he goin' marry you? No? You not that stupid? So what you goin' do if his momma or daddy finds out he wiggling his thing in you?"

"How they goin' find out?"

"Thousand ways. June ain't the only one goes down the root cellar. Mistress Hazzard might start wonderin' where you suddenly get these nice things an' why your breath smell like apple pie. Young John might be start braggin' to one of his friends."

"Then maybe he finally get the trouble he deserve."

Jubah shook her head. "It don' go like that, Lucy. Next thing you know, you goin' South, lady, down where they don' give you nice things when they buck you."

Lucy blinked. A little while later she asked, "You got anything keep me from getting bigged up?"

Jubah sighed.

*

THE NEWS OF THE battle of Bunker Hill hit Master John like a log speeding downriver. One minute he was full of confidence, the next he was in a blue haze of astonishment and dismay. By the time an emergency meeting began at his house that night, though, he sounded positive once again.

Tom Hazard, who Master John liked to call "the old bore, One-Z" behind his back, made regular trips to Newport to exchange information with the British man-of-war officers porting there. It was he who also brought the intelligence that the new commanding general from Virginia chosen to take over the colonial army in Boston would be arriving any moment.

"The problem is not just Bunker Hill," Tom Hazard said. "More and more soldiers are arriving in Boston from the southern colonies every day. Give them a Virginia commander and this is no longer between Boston's Massachusetts radicals and the home government. Or even between the New England colonies and the Crown. Now it'll be all the American colonies involved in a full-scale war."

As usual at these meetings, Master John let those who were feeling frightened do the talking for a while. When the anxiety grew highest, he stepped in. "What General Washington knows of the military," he said of the new commander from Virginia, "he learned in defeat and disaster under British General Braddock in the Seven Years' War. He looks the part, I'm told, but 'tis all looks. And his great and much bragged-of personal fortune he inherited and acquired through marriage. No, defeat and disaster is what he knows, and what he will know again. It is what he does best."

He let this sink in before he went on.

"And let me remind you about one thing concerning Bunker Hill. The British army occupied the rebel positions at day's end. They drove them completely from the field. Yes, many were lost and wounded, but the news of the terrible casualties will speed back to England and remind His Majesty, and remind him pointedly, that a great force and many new men will be required to bring events to a happy conclusion. The painful cost of this victory will thicken the king's resolve and speed the end of this rebellion."

The assembled neighbors nodded their heads. Their panic slowly subsided like air from a bladder.

"Besides," the master added. "It is clear that Americans know how to fight from behind fences and fortifications. Wait, my friends, until they face the grenadiers and a few companies of dragoons are out in the open. We shall see a very different story then. As will General Washington."

His visitors left in much better spirits than when they had arrived. But after they were gone, Master John had a large glass of port to steady his own nerves, dropped it, and cut his hand on some broken glass. The next morning the cut was red and inflamed. The day after that, his arm all the way up to his elbow was swollen. The day following, he was too sick to get out of bed, and Young John was sent urgently to fetch the doctor. Jubah offered her skills, but Mistress Hazzard said she was sure Dr. Babcock could attend to the problem.

Dr. Babcock, who examined him carefully, seemed very concerned. He wrapped the master's hand in black wool soaked in rum, prescribed Anderson's Pills, two taken twice a day, and told the master to stay in bed. The master replied hoarsely that he couldn't do anything else. The doctor nodded and said to change the wool often.

When the doctor came to check on his patient the next day, he found him worse, much worse. Master John was running a high fever and the swelling had run up to his armpit. The doctor applied an egg cataplasm, bled him twenty ounces from his good arm into a posset cup, and left some styptic powder for the master to consume in hot water. Babcock, who was an ardent patriot, even suggested black tea and offered some of his in case the Hazzards had observed the ban on it so closely as to have none themselves. "'Tis no offense taken as medicine, I warrant."

When the master failed to improve on the next day, Mistress Hazzard finally called Jubah in. Jubah looked at his hand and arm, studied the master's blotchy face, and did not like what she saw. "Wish you call me sooner," she muttered.

"Beg pardon?" the mistress said.

"Nothing, madam," Jubah said.

Jubah and June made a concoction of feverfew, pennyroyal, sage, and chamomile and asked him to drink as much of it as he could bear. Jubah then showed June how to make a basswood, honey, and camphor poultice for Master John's swollen hand.

"Got me here in time to fix his hand," she told June, "none the rest of this happen. Now we got to cure the whole body."

The master slept better that night but his hand was worse. Mistress Hazzard, now quite frightened, told Jubah her spells were no good. She knew better, though, than to ask what was in the medicines Jubah used—as Jubah told June, the two biggest rules of working with the sick were to use the right thing at the right time, and never to tell anybody what was in your cures, simples, and medicines. Ever.

"Haven't tried a spell," she said to the mistress. "Someone want that, they should aks Quamino. It a good sign his hand is hurting. Hand gets worse, he get better."

The mistress put a hand to her chest and said, "But he says it feels like someone is sticking it with a red hot iron!"

"That's about right," Jubah said. "We headin' down the right path."

The next day the master became delirious and began babbling about boats and battles and red skies. Jubah told June that a lot of folks believed in cat's blood as important in cures but she didn't. Instead she bathed the master's bad hand in a tansy, hyssop, salt, and mugwort solution until the site of the original cut started to ooze a whitish goo, then a pale, cloudy liquid, and finally a pink watery fluid. While she supervised the bathing, she had June tie sliced onion to the bottoms of the master's feet and cover them tightly with a warm, damp cloth. Finally, she put a moldy wheat bread poultice, which she had been preparing ever since the night the master first cut his hand, directly over the cut. She bandaged it tightly. Every few hours, she changed the bandage and applied more poultice.

She spent the night awake in his room tending to him. In the morning, June came in to see if she needed anything.

The master was lying on his back, mouth open, breathing shallowly. His face was very pale in the morning light.

"Smell his breath," Jubah said. "Go ahead."

June leaned over and sniffed. "Smell like onion."

"Exactly. And look at his hand."

"Swelling go down."

"Almost regular size," Jubah said, nodding in satisfaction. "Master John goin' be better. But don't tell the mistress that. Let her find out for herself. Not that it make any difference. She goin' thank God and Doctor Babcock, not me. Not until the next time somebody get bad sick, that is. Then see who she call for help."

By evening, Master John was sitting up in bed and eating with the first appetite he had felt in three days.

*

WHEN THE MASTER WAS back on his feet and taking one of his first walks around the farm, he came across Young John leaving the barn, checking to see if his trousers were buttoned properly. Since the barn was far from the outhouse, Master John found such behavior odd, but he did not think anything of it until, as he was talking with his son, he saw Lucy emerge a few minutes later brushing the front of her dress.

"Feeling better, sir?" Young John asked.

"Much, thank you." He saw color mount in his son's face as they watched Lucy round the barn and head toward the buttery. "I know in Carolina your cousins said they treat the slaves differently than we do here." The boy looked nervous but nodded. "Do not think in so small a world as ours that such conduct can go unremarked."

"What do you mean?"

"I mean you should not engage in something that would embarrass your mother or be a subject of public shame on Lecture Day."

"Sir?"

Master John lay a finger alongside his nose. "Do not think you can fool your old father." He nodded toward the barn. "Lucy."

"I was making sure she finished raking out the stalls."

"I'm sure you were. But let me repeat myself. We are in a very dangerous time now, and we need no scandals. Do you understand me?" He stared at the boy hard.

Young John opened his mouth to pretend ignorance when a faint breeze carried the smell of sex into his nostrils. He swallowed hard. "I understand," he said.

Chapter Eight

GUY SAW AFTER THE battle at Bunker Hill that the men's daily fear of attack had given way to crushing boredom. The British began to shell them after the battle was over, and after an initial wave of terror during which they cowered in the trenches, they saw that the cannons could not reach their lines. So the soldiers began to count the shots—eighty a day. They practiced watching the flight of the ball during daylight; at night they timed the intervals between firing and impact. When the novelty of this wore off, during lulls in the shelling, the men went out and gathered balls that were not too banged up to be reused. Then they offered them to the supply officers, at a price—a little extra food, some thread for their fraying clothes, and a few pennies.

A Massachusetts man was out gathering cannonballs when an almost-spent ball rolled off his leg and shattered it instantly into kindling up to his hip. His screaming and the splintered tangle of bloodied bone fragments reminded them that their game had risks.

The most prized trophies were bombs—or "boombes" as the men called them. Shells with fuses, launched with a soft belch from thick-walled mortars, the bombs retained the power to frighten the soldiers when nothing else did. They landed quietly, almost gently, and then they exploded into a thousand whistling pieces that passed through bodies like needles through cloth. Several men had been wounded by fragments, and though no one had died, the sight of all that sliced-up flesh was hard to forget. But an unexploded bomb was so valuable for its store of gunpowder—worth money and a week's leave—that men took all kinds of chances to recover one.

Guy understood why the soldiers wanted a leave. Most men had lice. Few had a change of clothes. The officers insisted on no gambling, no swearing, no drinking, and no visits to the lewd women gathered at the camp's perimeter. All of these rules were quickly broken, quietly at first. But when the long-promised uniforms failed to arrive, the beef was sour and the bread so moldy they could not make out what it was, the rule-breaking became open. Amid the boredom and heat, they played cards, threw shells, rolled lead dice, and drank rum. Tempers flared. After three days of eating a paste of fat and hairy hide that was called pork, the Providence regiment got three barrels labeled *Beef*. They were horsemeat. A riot broke out. General Nathanael Greene was forced to ride from headquarters to promise a remedy in person.

The men were not happy about becoming part of a Continental Army. Instead of being supplied by their own colony, whom they could barely trust as it was, they would become the dependents of some distant, new and less-accountable body called a Congress. Worse still, they might soon have to take orders from one of the hundreds of stupid, loutish, lazy Massachusetts officers where the colony had created so many of them, they lacked plain soldiers to order around.

Captain Ward began to spend less time at the lines than he did at the quartermaster's trying to get food and supplies. In Guy's view, the captain was having a hard time figuring out when to insist on having his orders followed. Sometimes he offered the threat of whipping or having to ride the wooden horse for a few painful hours. Other times, given the poor conditions, he just let the men quietly misbehave.

Because Guy helped serve and clean up after the evening meals at headquarters, he got to eat one meal a day that was better than any of the men at the Roxbury fortifications ate all week long. This made him grateful to Dr. Church's assistant, and he tried to reward him with information whenever he saw him. The assistant was most interested in military plans, but no plans were possible until the new general from Virginia arrived.

As bad as the men's mood was, most of them were looking forward to seeing this new general, hoping he would change their conditions and provide them with some proper food and clothes and a fresh supply of powder. They said he was one of the wealthiest men in America, so how could he not help? "They think things goin' get better," Guy told Church's assistant, "so they put up with it now."

Guy was working at the lines in the early afternoon when the fabled new general came to review the brigade. They were nervous about this stranger from a place none of them had ever been. The man himself was supposed to be wealthier than any ten Providence manufacturers and the Newport merchant princes all rolled together. Guy had heard someone say that he, by himself, owned more slaves than there were men in their entire regiment.

The soldiers were shaved, their muskets cleaned, hands washed, itches treated with vinegar, and their filthy uniforms put in as good condition as possible. They presented themselves in parade order at full attention. Finally, a group of officers approached on horseback, some of them with faces and in uniforms Guy had never seen. It did not take any effort, though, to guess who the new general was. Not only did he ride toward the front of the group of riders on a majestic horse, he was himself at least a head taller than any man in the group, and that was while he was sitting down. (Dr. Church called him "the generalissimo," though others had taken to calling him the Commanding General.) With him was a remarkably ugly man who continued with an unending British-accented commentary on all he saw. Disheveled as many of the men lined up before him, he was the second in command, a General Charles Lee, whose defection from the British was said to be a serious loss to them. Guy assumed his talent must be in his ability to think since his appearance was nearly as poor as the Virginia general's was grand.

As General Washington rode his majestic white sorrel slowly before the Rhode Islanders, Guy was able to take a long look at him. He passed right in front of Guy, his heavy-browed blue-gray eyes looking steadily ahead toward the regiments he was about to review. Dressed in a blue uniform with tan breeches and high black leather boots, he was muscular and thick-shouldered, his back straight as a tree trunk. He had extremely long arms and legs and unusually large hands, and with them he controlled his powerful horse as easily as if it were a pony. His brown hair had lost most of its morning's powder and was tied back in a queue. Guy did not know whose idea it was, but as General Washington and General Lee passed before them, one of the Rhode Islanders pulled off his tri-cornered hat and began a "hip-hip-hooray!" All the others immediately took up the cheer, and when Washington nodded and smiled, the cheers became louder still.

✷

TWO DAYS LATER, CAPTAIN Ward's regiment was alone detached from all the rest of the brigade and ordered to Cambridge. Dr. Church's assistant could barely disguise his excitement at this development. He said if he was able to get Guy to serve in the Cambridge headquarters, Guy would have a chance to hear the plans for the entire new Continental Army. But the assistant's hopes were dashed one day later. Captain Ward's regiment, after a day of fasting and prayer and a required reading of Congress's "Declaration on Taking up Arms," was assigned to Prospect Hill. It was a hill one short mile from Bunker and Breed's Hill and in plain sight of the thousands of encamped red-coated British soldiers.

Ward's men looked fit enough that they had been given one of the most important assignments on the entire front. They were placed directly among the Massachusetts regiments who had fought so bravely in the recent battle and were in a position that would be critical if any new attack from the British were to come.

It did not take long for Guy to see that the Rhode Islanders would have preferred not to have had this honor. They had been placed among new amputees who were still too sick to journey home, near graves whose ground was still raw, and within range of huge ships of war and a bristling array of British artillery emplacements. There was, by now, the almost customary boom and thud of mortar and cannon, but this time the balls and bombs landed much closer. And he was at the lines long enough to hear the anger among the Rhode Island privates the day they discovered they were to be paid as Continental soldiers the same as they were before, but not under the colony's lunar four-week month—which paid them thirteen times a year—but under a calendar month which would pay them only twelve times a year. The men needed to mend their shoes, re-foot their stockings, buy soap and writing paper from the sutlers who charged outrageous prices. And many of them needed to send money home to wives and children or parents who had already lost their labor and wages. And they still had not been given their long-promised new uniforms.

Guy did not follow all the numbers, but he was able to report to Dr. Church's assistant that while the men liked the new general, they were not happy about being cut off from their brigade, nor taking a pay cut, nor serving at a dangerous post. He was also at the lines long enough to hear one of the men who had heard "The Declaration" say, "It says we are 'with one mind resolved to die like freemen, rather than to live like slaves.' Aye, well friends, can't speak for you, but I know I didn't know what real slavery was until I got here." There were grumbles of assent from the others, though one of the younger men glanced at Guy uneasily.

A few hours later, right after Dr. Church's assistant found he was unable to get Guy assigned to headquarters, word was passed from

Master Hazzard that he was required in Kingston and Captain Ward was to send him there as soon as possible.

Guy wondered how long Dr. Church's assistant had been holding onto this "word" from the master.

*

Sam Ward saw that he had a problem. He was too young and too mild to make his men afraid. He was almost as tall as the commanding general from Virginia, and he was strong enough to impose himself on most of the men if he had to. But he was not fierce enough to scare them. Dr. Church said Governor Ward was likely to be made Chairman of the Committee of the Whole in the next session of Congress, and he was already chairman of the committee whose secret task was to make arrangements with foreign powers for the provision of powder and arms. Church concluded, "It is no exaggeration to say that his success could determine the course of this whole conflict!"

But when his lofty connections provided his men with little better supplies than anyone else's, and his efforts to create a well-trained regiment succeeded so well—*too* well, some of the men said—that put them closer to the cannon's mouth, he was no longer so well-regarded. Sam studied the problem but found no answers except to try to find better food, more powder, and a change of clothes for his soldiers. But at these he was having no success. Christopher Greene—newly made lieutenant colonel in the Continental army—told him that one thing was true. "The Rhode Island regiments at Prospect Hill have earned a reputation with General Washington as the best prepared in the army. And if your men grumble, put their minds on the task. Remind them that we know that the redcoats are in very poor shape. Their supplies are scarcer than ours, smallpox has broken out, and if they do not crack our siege soon, they will be desperate. They will have to attack, and it will likely be on these very positions. Remind them of that, and they'll have less room in their heads for grousing."

The weather turned wet, and they waited, day after day, in the mud and the rain, for an attack that did not come.

*

Guy was not back on the Hazzard place five minutes—dropped off by one of the Gardiner boys who had come home for a leave—before the master pulled him aside under the shade of the large white oak at the side of the main house. His clothes still wet from last night's rainstorm, Guy preferred to stand in the sun. He kept edging that way until the master told him to stand still. And though he tried keep his head down, Guy could not keep from looking around for June. He noticed, though, that the master looked unwell, thinner than when he last saw him, and with darkened half circles in the papery skin under his eyes. He sounded hearty enough, however.

"'Tis about time you were here," he said to Guy in a voice loud enough for the departing Gardiner boy to hear. "We have a list of tasks for you longer than a horse's leg. Johnny will be going over them with you." He noticed Guy looking around. "Thirsty after your ride?"

"Nossuh." He saw no one out on the grounds. "Ever'one all right?"

"Fine-fine-fine." He watched the disappearing figures of the Gardiners. "You're back just in time for 'Lection Day."

"'Lection Day?" Guy thought that celebration had come and gone.

"For slave governor. It was delayed this year because of all the… excitement around Boston."

'Lection Day was the second biggest holiday of the year for slaves whose masters, like Master John, were Episcopalian. Since none of the other Christian groups celebrated Christmas, 'Lection Day was the biggest celebration of them all for everyone else. Hundreds of slaves gathered in one place for dancing, wrestling, fishing, racing, fiddle music and drums, games of quoits and paw-paw, everyone eating 'Lection cake and drinking 'Lection beer. And unlike the other big gatherings on Lecture Day, there were no sermons, no whippings, no threats of awful suffering in the next world. Still, Guy could not understand why the master told this news with Captain Christopher Gardiner long out of hearing range. He had never cared before about Guy except for making sure he did his work.

"Don't know if you'll be going back to join Captain Ward again, so we've made some plans for you here. You're going to run for governor."

"Suh?"

"Governor. I would like you to be in a position to get information locally. And perhaps help take action on a few matters." He laid a finger alongside his nose, saying in a low voice, "I also have a small wager on the outcome."

Guy thought that Gambling John might look peaked, but he was acting like his old self. Guy knew that the slave governor had to set punishments for slaves who misbehaved, and he would like not to do that. But he had no choice. Unless, he supposed, he got other slaves to vote against him—but he knew this would make the master angry. He sighed. He had been hoping to simply come back and see June. If it was a life that had not changed as much as he wished, it was still one where no cannon fire enlivened his days nor crashed through his nights.

An idea surfaced in him like a fish rising in a pond, and this time he came right out with it. "Mastuh, I wan marry with June."

Master John nodded, made no answer, and asked him about the army at Boston, as if Guy had just commented about the weather or the squash yield. Guy did not know how to respond. He paused, thought, then said, knowing he was risking serious punishment for stepping above himself, "Can I marry with her?"

Master John took a long breath. "She with child?"

"Nossuh."

"Good. This is a hard time to make plans, Guy. Talk to me after the election. But now tell me about Boston."

At least the answer wasn't a flat-out "no."

The more Guy told him about how bad everything was, the brighter the master's eyes grew. Young John emerged from the house and, without a nod or greeting or any indication that Guy had ever been gone, told Guy he was to start by making new handles for the scythes and fixing the door latch to the root cellar. When his father went back inside, Young John said, "Start with the cellar latch."

As Young John led him around to the root cellar to show him what he wanted done, Guy saw June, a bucket in one hand, leading in one of the cows for milking. She was wearing a pale blue smock he had not seen before, and she carried herself well, upright and vigilant. To see her made his pulse quicken. When she saw him, her hand flew to her mouth in surprise. With one of her rare radiant smiles, she rose on her toes and waved at him, her hand above her head as if he were at a great distance. He nodded and gave her his fullest regard, but he did not lift his hand to wave. He did not know why he felt this way, but he did not want Young John to be a witness to June's reaction to his return. He stole a glance at him from the side. The boy's thoughts at the moment seemed safely elsewhere.

Young John said he wanted a latch on the *inside* of the root cellar door—to keep it from swinging open when someone was putting food down for storage. A strip of leather and a piece of wood, and Guy was done with this simple task in a few minutes, though he thought the request was an odd one. He was told when he finished all the urgent repairs, he was supposed to build a box that fit so snugly under the master's bed and matched the grain and color of the frame so well, from the outside it would look like a supporting plank. "Think of it as a drawer without a handle," Young John said.

"How you get it open?" Guy asked.

"You just make it. I will worry about the rest." He wondered what it was for.

That night, June was called into the big house to help with the preparations for tomorrow's 'Lection Day activities. The busy mistress had her sewing and preparing food by lantern light almost until midnight. Guy, weary and sore from three straight days of riding and soothed by a night not punctured every few minutes by cannon and mortar fire fell asleep before she came out.

Chapter Nine

By ten the next morning, they arrived at the largest of all the plantation farms in the southern Rhode Island: Stantons' Field. They found its gates and fences draped with red and white bunting and a crowd of several hundred slaves and almost that many white spectators. Usually, the slaves were dressed up in some of their owners' best cast-off finery, and some of the men arrived atop polished carriages and on good horses wearing powdered wigs, tri-cornered hats, vests, and three-quarter coats, their feet squeezed into bright-buckled leather shoes. The women wore smocks and dresses and skirts with flounces, usually with some personally created bright scarf or feathered hat to set off their shell and polished-rock jewelry necklaces. This year, though, everything was much more subdued. The nervousness among some of the white owners was great enough that they had even banned the use of drums outright, fearing it might offer a secret code to communicate with the enemy or stimulate the slaves to a "hazardous level of excitement."

Still, old Polydor Gardiner played the fiddle and tables of food and drink were set out, and though there was much less beer and much more water sweetened with apple cider than usual, the children had races and some of the men and women began to dance. The whites gathered on one side of the field to point and laugh and enjoy the festivities, though they, too, were subdued.

Jubah dropped into the celebration like a fish dropped into water. She hugged old friends and relatives she hadn't seen since last year and, before Guy even had got out of the wagon, was singing and dancing and clapping her hands as if she were still a girl. June and Lucy went off with friends to watch a wrestling match. Quamino, though, hated these gatherings. He stood next to Guy, pulling up the waist of his breeches, saying what he said every year: "Dress us up like pet monkeys, hold a fake 'Lection, drink enough beer, and some start thinkin' how *lucky* they is."

Guy wished the election was more fake than it was. Every year they chose not only a governor but a high sheriff, a man who took a whip or a cobbing board and applied it to the backs of slaves convicted by magistrates of pilferage or meeting a loved one after dark or disobeying an order or breaking a dish. The judges were black, and so was the high sheriff. Quamino said it was all a way to get them to do white folks' bad work for them, but Jubah said the black judges went easier on them than white ones would. Guy didn't know. And he did not want to know.

For years the families with the most slaves, like the Robinsons and Gardiners and Stantons, determined who the governor was going to be, but in the last few years, there got to be so many slaves in the area, it was hard for even these mighty families to determine the outcome.

The man who had been governor for the last few years, a huge gentle old man with a badly disfigured face, Cato Fayerweather, ought to be chosen again, Guy thought. Almost burned to death when he was a boy by a giant fireplace summer beam collapsing on him while he was tending logs beneath, all these years later his face was scarred enough to alarm children and some adults. Once they got to know him, though, most thought the fire must have scorched out all his bad feelings. Calm, soft-spoken, and good-humored, he was someone everybody liked.

He was one long way from Mingo Rodman, the high sheriff. Not tall, but powerful, with a round chest, wide neck and arms roped thick with muscle, he kept getting elected because people were afraid not to vote for him. They said he didn't go light when he used the whip or the cobbing board, either. On smaller places like the Hazzards', the master or the overseer administered the punishment, but the big places sent their misbehaving slaves to see Mingo Rodman. Some said he enjoyed it.

They clapped hands and rang bells, announcing the start of the election. The Chief Marshall, Pomp Tilman, took his staff and carefully drew a long line in the dirt. Chief Marshall every year because he could count far past even one hundred—and do it quickly, too—he called out for the men who were "of age" to vote. Many of the slaves, like Guy, didn't really know their own age, and Guy had been voting for seven or eight years, since he was, he guessed, fifteen. No one ever complained unless the voter still looked like a child.

Guy looked around for Cato Fayerweather, but his owner, the minister, announced that Cato was too sick to run for governor today, and that this year the candidates would be "Mingo Rodman and Guy Watson!" He murmured a few words to Pomp Tilman, who nodded.

Quamino looked at him and said, "You runnin' for gov'nor?"

Guy sighed. "Mastuh John tell me I got to."

Usually there were long candidates' speeches, something Cato did every year with such seriousness and dignity the whites stopped laughing for a while. This year, Pomp Tilman simply called for Mingo and Guy to take their places at the head of the line he had drawn in the dirt—Guy thought it was probably that the whites were too nervous to let speechifying take place. He thought that if somebody said the word "freedom," the masters would shut the whole celebration down.

He could see Master John over at the side taking bets on the outcome. The Gardiners, the Stantons, and the Robinsons were all on the side of the rebels, and Guy figured they would want Mingo to be governor. They would feel confident he would keep the slaves frightened and under control—and they certainly wouldn't want to trust any slave owned by Gambling John Hazzard.

The male slaves started to line up on the side of the candidate they preferred. This was when the speeches usually took place, after which the voters milled around, talked and bargained, changed sides, laughed, and then Pomp Tilman called solemnly for the final vote to be taken. This year, though, Pomp Tilman just said "Mingo Rodman" and "Guy Watson," holding a hand behind each man's head as he intoned the name. Then he said, "Cast your votes!"

Though Guy did not have Pomp's counting skills, he could see that the contest was close. To Guy's surprise, Quamino and a few old friends of his came out of the crowd to vote. Quamino and his friends had never voted before, always saying, just as he did this year, that it's all foolishness, and he was too old for foolishness. Guy noticed that many of the slaves were too frightened of Mingo Rodman to look at him. The lines shifted around, and some of the men taunted and cajoled and wheedled others to change sides, but it was all muted compared to previous years.

After a time, Pomp Tilman called, "Quiet!"

Men had moved back and forth so much the line had disappeared. Pomp redrew the division in the dirt with his long staff, slowly passing down the middle of the silent voters. When he finished, he sized the groups carefully and began his counting. The whites, Guy could see, watched as intently as the slaves. Master John held a coal to the bowl of his clay pipe, puffing calmly, so Guy knew before Pomp even finished the counting what the outcome was. In the end, Pomp Tilman announced that Guy Watson was the next gov'nor, having won by just two votes.

After that, Mingo was easily reelected high sheriff.

Afterwards, Guy asked Quamino why he came out and voted for him. He shrugged. "See and hear more as gov'nor. You got a better chance find some daylight. 'Sides. Vote for Mingo Rodman? Nuh-uh."

Cato Fayerweather always gave a speech afterwards and, putting on the governor's special cape, walked among the crowd and thanked his supporters. This year there was no procession, and everyone was invited straight away to come eat the 'Lection cake, have something to drink, and head home.

*

"CONGRATULATIONS, GOV'NOR," SAID THE master to Guy as he got back in the wagon. He pressed a Portuguese half-Jo in Guy's hand. Guy stared at the gold coin in surprise. This was far more money than he had ever been given before, and he had not done anything to get it except stand where he was told. Guy showed it to June, and everyone soon was making a big fuss about it. Even Quamino looked impressed. Guy held the coin in his hand and wondered what it was the master was going to ask him to do now. He tried to talk to him, but the master was headed with his friends directly to Arnold's tavern. He told Young John and the mistress he wouldn't be back until late.

*

THAT NIGHT, AFTER THE evening meal was over and the dishes were scraped clean and the fire was banked for the night, Guy went to June's cabin. Jubah was working with her on sorting and drying some herbal medicines. Jubah, who usually treated Guy with dry kindness, did not look pleased to see him. She sharply called for June to pay attention to what they were doing. June nodded and told Guy she would talk to him later. Lucy, half-asleep in the corner, gave a long sigh.

Guy walked back to his shack, grateful to be home. The air was soft and the pinewood they burned in the fire kept the mosquitoes back. He thought about lying down but was too restless to stay still. He propped the oiled paper window wide open at the front of his cabin to get a breeze inside and resumed carving on the head of a walking stick he was making for Quamino. The sound of crickets swelled and subsided and the purple sky deepened to a darker shade. He stared at the trees and watched the occasional blinking of a firefly and enjoyed the sweetness of silence. He heard footsteps. June came to say goodnight. She smelled of herbs.

"You back," she said. He nodded. "Things happen while you gone," she said.

"What?"

She told him more about the master's illness and how she and Jubah cured him, a story she'd told him in bits and pieces on the wagon ride this afternoon. In a sudden guarded whisper, she told him about Lucy and Young John. He was troubled by the fact that June saw them down in the root cellar—but now he understood why the boy told him his first task was to put a latch on the door down there. He told June about it.

"Lucy say she keeping away from Young John now."

"He not plannin' to keep away from her," Guy said. "She got any more presents?"

"She do, she hiding them. She bein' quiet a lot."

"They see you seein' them?"

"No," June said. "But I told Jubah and she told Lucy."

"She must've told the boy."

"Why you say that?"

"Why else he want a *inside* latch on the door?"

June was quiet for a while as she considered this. "See what you mean."

Around the evening fire, he had already talked a lot about Boston and the army and the guns. He was tired of talking. "I aks the mastuh if we can marriage."

"You did?" Her eyes widened. "What he say?"

"Say talk to him after the 'lection. Then he go off." He took her hand and gave a gentle tug. "Come inside."

She shook her head. "Jubah be lookin' for me."

"Everybody tellin' us what to do." He tugged again.

"Can't tell *you* now, Gov'nor," she said.

Suddenly, the moment she called him "gov'nor," he was angry. He did not know why. He was not angry at her so much as at everything. She saw it in his face and dropped her hand from his. "What?" she asked.

"Ever'thing change," he gestured in a big circle. "But nothing change."

She stood in silence for a while, nodded, then walked into his cabin.

He closed the door and lowered the oiled paper window. They lay down together on his pallet. When he put his arms around her, he found she was shaking.

He began to remove her summer shift, but she shook her head, took a thin muslin sheet he used on summer nights when the air cooled, blew out the betty lamp next to the pallet, and covered herself. She was embarrassed to have him see her naked. Under the sheet she removed her dress. When she was done, he took off his shirt and breeches and slipped underneath the sheet. Her teeth chattered.

"Cold?" he asked. She shook her head.

"Afraid," she said.

"Don't be," he said softly.

She nodded, then whispered, "Don't put your seed in me."

"Yes," he said and nuzzled her neck. He kissed her shoulders and her breasts, and then he kissed her everywhere. Her shaking stopped and a tiny shuddering began. Finally, after a time, he rolled her onto her stomach and kissed her neck and back. Then he spread her legs with his. He was as gentle as he could be, though once he was inside her, he could tell she felt more discomfort than pleasure. He was careful to withdraw at the end. His panting subsided. He wiped her back with the sheet.

"Stay here," he said. "Sleep here." She shook her head, rose, and with her back turned, put her clothes on.

"Jubah be mad."

"Jubah be mad anyway."

"I goin' go."

"June." She turned. "It better next time."

Offended, she looked at him sharply and said, "How you know?"

*

June found it was not very much better the next time. The time after that, though, Guy changed from what he called "African" to what he called "Christian," front to front. He had her wrap her legs across his back, and holding her bottom in his hands, she put her arms around his neck. She found she could move herself using her arms and legs almost as she wished. And soon, she wished and wished and wished, and she squeezed him to her harder and harder and more and more until it felt as if there was a hot sun glowing inside her and she had to bite her lips not to moan out loud with pleasure. And then, to her surprise, she felt herself congest heart-stoppingly from head to foot, and then she felt herself gather and release in great radiant circles.

The next day in the house, Jubah twice had to remind her to stand and walk in a more ladylike manner. June was embarrassed. Something in the tilt of her pelvis or the way she walked had changed. A week after that, Jubah said on hearing that she was coming to bed late almost every night, "Don't forget to save some. For when you gets old." She shook her head. "You keep this up, you *be* old."

Guy asked Master John again if he and June could marry. The master replied, "We'll see. This is not yet a good moment."

But for Guy suddenly everything seemed different now, though he knew the only thing that had really changed was how he was with June. But that was more than enough. However he looked at it, and he thought of June when he woke up in the morning and while he worked all day, he knew he had never felt this deep of happiness before. Not close. At odd moments, he felt a small surprising edge of sadness, though, knowing however long it lasted, he would never feel quite this way again. The knowledge made him savor every moment.

*

Severe-looking Jacob Greene, the man who had been there to arrange to first send him to the Wards', and two new members of The Committee of Inspection, arrived early that morning. Guy had finished building the secret drawer for the master and mistress's bedroom. He knew there were papers in it, nothing else. Old Greene refused the master's offer for food and drink, and he even refused an offer to go inside to discuss whatever was on his mind.

"We have been told, Mister Hazzard, that you have offered money to several men to induce them not to join the army at Boston." Greene opened a sheet of paper and read three names. "These men claim to have actually received money of you in return for not serving under arms."

Without so much as a twitch, the master said, "'Tis quite true. Many of us here in this county are extremely worried about a British landing in Narragansett. If all our ablest fighting men are off in Boston, who will be here to defend us?"

"That, sir, is not a question you are empowered to decide."

"And I did not, Mister Greene, pay these men not to go. I urged them to remain here where their need is urgent. All three men are mechanics and day laborers. Without them here, and with the slave trade come to an end by order of the Congress, we have too few to help harvest and transport our goods to market. You can have the shopkeepers and the lawyers, sirs, but laborers? We *need* laborers. I will go anywhere you wish to answer these charges."

"We are not here to make charges, Mister Hazzard. We are here to make inquiries."

"Inquire all you wish."

"You accept the Rhode Island scrip and the new Continental currency."

"I have and I will. If you doubt me, ask the quartermaster who bought fourteen wheels of cheese from me just last week."

"You agree not to eat mutton and to shear your sheep seasonably for homespun?"

"My wife was at the Gardiners all day three afternoons ago for a weaving bee. Their sons are captains in the lines at Boston, you know. I believe she said she made enough material for four army blankets."

"Have you any arms or powder to spare?"

"Would that I did. I did send some lumber for the construction of the new powder mill in town."

"So we have been told." Greene's lean face tightened. "You are aware of the new non-exportation laws set by Congress." He read from a paper in his hand. "'Nothing whatever is to be sold or bartered to the British or to any British factor or agent.'"

"I am aware of them and will comply with them. We all have to make sacrifices in these times, do we not?"

Greene looked at him steadily for a few moments before asking his last question.

"If you are so concerned about the safety of the area, why is your son not mustering with the Kingston Reds?"

This question appeared to have caught the master off balance. "It is our busiest season before fall. We have not had the services of all our servants, and our best mechanic was in Boston helping Captain Ward and the army." The members of the Committee of Inspection looked at Master Hazzard expressionlessly. "And, frankly, sirs, no one has asked him to join the militia. Are you doing so now?"

"We are. We will look to see him at first light on Kingston green on the sixth day of this week."

"Saturday?"

"Yes, Mister Hazzard. Saturday. He will be joining the three men you paid to stay here." The master tilted his head in acknowledgment. "One last thing."

"Sir?"

"Any future difficulties, and you will be required to answer them not to us here but in court in Providence. Am I clear, sir?"

"As day. Does that mean this is your last visit to our grounds?"

Jacob Greene gave him a long, silent look, his hawk's eyes unblinking. "Let us hope so," he said at last.

*

GUY HEARD THE MASTER tell Young John later that this would be an excellent opportunity for him to get further intelligence on defense preparations, and best of all that his participation in the musters will keep him from conscription into the Continental army.

"Conscription?" Young John asked.

"Forcing you to go," the master explained. "If the war lasts past the winter, it could come to that."

"Will it come to that?"

"Hard to say. But I could kick myself for not thinking of having you join the Kingston militia already! This damned committee would have left us alone. Well, 'tis not too late, not too late."

Guy mused on all that was said and then settled back into the long list of tasks he had to complete. Just before the evening meal, however, a rider arrived and Guy saw a familiar thin-faced man he would rather have not seen. It was Dr. Church's bespectacled assistant, his birthmark clear even in the declining light. After handing his horse to Quamino, he strode without so much as a word or a sidelong glance inside to see the master.

Chapter Ten

Gus Mumford, Sam, and Lieutenant Lewis leaned close to the camp fire, not for warmth on this hot and humid summer night, but to keep back the swarm of mosquitoes that rose in clouds to feed on the tens of thousands of men and animals ringing the city. The three officers, talking quietly to avoid being overheard by their regiment encamped a few yards away, rubbed dirt on their skin to soothe the bites.

They were used to the cannon fire. They were not used to the supply problems. They were not used to the camp itch that had spread everywhere. They were not used to the cases of dysentery or the meager, dirty, insect-infested, heat-spoiled food. They were not used to the drunkenness and indiscipline of the other regiments.

"Think we'll attack?" Elisha Lewis asked ironically. He had asked this question every night for weeks. When Washington arrived, the answer was yes. When rumors about imminent British reinforcements spread, the answer was yes. When the men from the rifle regiments from western Pennsylvania arrived last week with their amazing seven-foot-long guns and an ability to pick off British sentries at astounding distances, the answer was yes.

"Yes," said Gus Mumford. "When the rest of the riflers arrive."

"General Lee wants to attack now," Lewis said, knowing the answer. "General Washington. General Greene."

"Yes. Yes. Yes."

"So it's unanimous."

Sam Ward cleared his throat and spoke for the first time. He had gotten used to watching, observing, analyzing, but saying little. "Not everyone."

"What do you mean?" Gus asked.

"Our generals are as different from one another as three people can be," he said. "But they have one thing in common. None of them were here for Bunker Hill. You and I saw it, Elisha. And we saw what happened to the redcoats when they made their attacks on entrenched positions. Cut down like weeds. Ask any of our Massachusetts neighbors who were actually in the engagement how *they* feel about attacking on entrenched lines. Defend, yes. Attack?" Sam shook his head.

Gus Mumford sighed. Sam knew that he would report any views that held water back to the command. He also knew that sooner rather than later Gus and Lieutenant Lewis would be talking about their wives. Gus had married within the last year to a very attractive young woman Sam had seen at socials and bees, and he was going to be a father in less than two months. Elisha Lewis thought his wife might be pregnant, too. And while he felt excluded by their conversation—and was envious of them, too—Sam discovered that among officers or privates, rich or poor, once the most recent military rumors were dispensed with, there were but two great topics: food and sex. Mumford and Lewis talked about it discreetly, exchanging knowing looks when one or the other said he missed the pleasures of domestic life. About food, however, they were obscenely explicit. Sam thought if he heard about one more of Mary's cinnamony apple brown betties or of Debbie's hot blueberry grunts, he was going hit someone.

A number of Sam's soldiers spent their meager salaries paying haggard-looking female camp followers for sex. General Washington spent most of his daily General Orders calling for discipline, especially regarding drink, profanity, and warnings against improper conduct with improper women. This last task was made a bit easier by the rumor that the British had sent out whores infected with smallpox and other diseases to sicken the American soldiery. General Greene followed up by calling all the Rhode Island regiments together to witness the whipping with thirty-nine stripes of Rhode Islanders caught stealing, fighting, or refusing to follow officers' orders. The sound of the screams and the sight of the torn and bloodied backs had improved discipline noticeably. One man from Chris Gardiner's company who was caught at the whores' tents got to ride the wooden horse for four hours, his hands tied behind him. The humiliation was worse than the pain, and the pain was extreme.

Discipline improved, that is, until the Pennsylvania riflemen arrived.

When Colonel William Thompson's men first appeared in camp with their rifles and long white hunting shirts, buckskin leggings, and stitched moccasins, sporting tomahawks and scalping knives on their belts, they were greeted with enthusiasm. The riflemen were not in camp six hours when they began putting on demonstrations of skill with their rifles, picking off red-coated sentries who never knew what hit them. By nightfall, these Pennsylvania woodsmen, having heard that some Wampanoag and Ponagansett Indians had sneaked behind British sentries and captured arms and powder, decided to go them one better. They sneaked behind the lines, killed seven, took two prisoners, and lost a corporal of their own in the maneuver.

The next night, the frightened British set off such a firing of cannons and small arms, the whole wing of the army was alerted for an attack. Why were the British so frightened? The riflemen on this night had set off in a large raiding group, not content to sneak across Charlestown Neck as they had the previous night. This time they went deep past enemy lines and all the way to Charlestown Common. From two in the morning until five, they fired on British regulars who were attempting to entrench new cannons. When the British attempted to gather their dead and wounded from the night's skirmish, the riflemen shot them, too. Sergeant Bond reported seeing fourteen redcoats fall that morning alone. The New England soldiers were exhilarated to have these sinewy, tall, granite-faced men among them. Their daring and marksmanship was the talk of the whole army. British pickets became so fearful of venturing out, Sam's regiment was able to gather and feed the regiment's cattle and horses right in the front pastures of Prospect Hill with no worries. This was the good news. But good news tended in Sam's army experience to have a price tag.

A few more days passed and the riflemen began to recognize the awe with which they were beheld. Persuaded of their superiority over this motley gathering of New Englanders, they decided they did not have to behave like them. Orders about fatigue duty, using the latrine, presenting for parade, drinking liquor—these were for others to worry about. They ignored orders they did not like, got drunk, took whatever they pleased from whomever they wanted. They did no duty and got in fights. One night they wounded a Mohawk Indian and killed another "by mistake."

The Virginian and Maryland riflemen who arrived soon afterwards had different accents from the Pennsylvanians, but their conduct turned out to be similar.

Some of the officers reined in their men, or tried to. A few did not. Captain Matthew Smith and his Pennsylvania men maintained so little order that even the neighboring Pennsylvania regiments did not like him.

Gus Mumford was sitting at the evening campfire and talking about a fat roast capon he once ate when Private Tom Shepherd ran up, panting for breath.

"They've stormed the guardhouse!" he said.

"What? Who has?" Sam asked.

"A whole troop of the riflers came stomping past me and they were yelling about letting their friend out. They had their rifles with 'em, too."

Sam and Gus Mumford decided to go see what was afoot.

By the time they arrived at the guardhouse a few minutes later, thirty mostly drunken Pennsylvania riflemen had surrounded the little house where prisoners were kept. They were yelling to their friend, arrested for stealing food, that no one was going to keep him locked up. He yelled back to get him the hell out of there.

There were two musket-carrying guardsmen from Massachusetts facing thirty armed riflers. Gus Mumford took one look at the screaming fire-lit scene and said he was heading for headquarters to get help. Sam knew Captain Smith and his officers would be useless, or might even take the part of the crowd, so he sent Tom Shepherd back to look for Pennsylvania Colonel Thompson. "Tell him he must control his men. Tell him his men are in open mutiny." Private Shepherd disappeared at a run.

The two Massachusetts men were standing their ground, but Sam could see that any minute the Pennsylvanians were going to storm past them. One drunken Pennsylvanian was bumping up against the bigger of the two guards and telling him to make a move. "C'mon," he said. "Give him up." His friends cheered him on.

Three more Pennsylvania men started to struggle with the shorter guardsman who, outmanned, called to his friend for help. From inside the guardhouse, the prisoner screamed encouragement to his friends to get him out. As the tension thickened, the taller guardsman hit one of the Pennsylvania men in the head with his musket butt and threatened to shoot if they did not let the guard go. Two other riflers immediately stepped in front of him and began to wrestle him for his weapon. Sam realized with a sinking feeling that he had not brought enough men with him to be able to intervene. He was scanning the audience of Massachusetts men for some officers, hoping to organize a rescue of the guards, when he heard the thrumming sound of hooves grow loud and half a dozen galloping horses arrived on the scene.

Sam recognized the riders right away. Generals Greene and Lee and the unmistakable figure of General Washington himself appeared.

Gus Mumford, hat pulled down tight on his head, was in the middle of the group of their aides.

The yelling and fighting and disorder immediately increased. Generals or no generals, two riflers broke the door to the guardhouse open.

Without a moment's hesitation, Greene, Lee, and Washington rode directly into the mob of drunken armed men and told them they were to put their weapons down and stand at full attention. A few men followed orders, a few others began quietly to creep off, most simply ignored the generals. One of them called, "If you gave us decent food, we wouldn't have to steal it!" Others roared their agreement.

Washington and Lee pulled their swords. Nat Greene, still on horseback, began to take the rifles away himself, grabbing them by the barrels. Given that everyone knew many of these Pennsylvanians felt about their rifles the way a husband felt about his new bride, this was a brave act. Lee, disheveled and ugly as ever, was yelling in a scarcely controlled rage for this "worthless mob of miscreants" to come to attention or be run through. With the flat of his sword, he whacked two men across the head who do not heed his words. One of them sprawled headlong in the dirt.

General Washington walked his horse directly into the middle of the melee, found the largest, loudest, drunkest, angriest man in the crowd, and put the point of his sword against his chest. "Put down your arms!" he boomed. "You, sir, are under arrest!"

The angry man looked at the sword point, followed it up to the towering figure of the general on his enormous horse, and his face grew blank, then slack. The crowd grew quiet. The riot was over. Washington's aides disarmed all the rioters and six more arrests were made.

Gus Mumford explained to Sam that he was trying to reach Nat Greene about the riot when, completely by chance, he ran into the three generals coming back from dinner. He gave them the news, and without pausing even to discuss among themselves what to do, they swung their horses round and rode to the guardhouse.

The next day, the story of the three generals—the tough Quaker, the eccentric Englishman, and the large Virginia gentleman—spread throughout the army. Their reputation soared. Captain Smith's men no longer openly took what they wanted from surrounding companies anymore. Instead, they began to steal when they thought no one was looking.

*

SAM HAD BEEN CAREFUL not to take advantage of his friendship with Nat Greene, but he decided the time had come for them to talk. He knew that within a few weeks, the weather would begin to cool. The men would need blankets, coats, and wood for warmth and shelters, not just for cooking. Their terms of enlistment would be drawing to a close. If conditions did not improve, Sam was convinced that the entire siege would fall apart. His sector would for certain.

He sent a note requesting a meeting and was asked to come that afternoon. He had heard that Caty had just been up to visit her general-husband, so he thought he might find him in refreshed spirits. He saw immediately that he had guessed wrong. Haggard, preoccupied, his face puffy, his asthmatic breathing audible, his limp only barely disguised, Nat looked exhausted.

Sam worried that some personal concern had struck. "Caty is well, general?"

Greene nodded and gestured for Sam to step into his study. Sam walked past two aides copying dispatches. Nat told them he and Captain Ward were not to be disturbed. Once the door was closed, Nat offered Sam a seat, dropped into a chair, and at the same moment dropped the formality he maintained when others were present. "Caty sends you her love, Sammy, and brings Phebe's warm regards. She wanted to see you, but was here only for a day. We believe, if God wills it, that the new year will bring us a new child."

Sam congratulated him, and he wanted to talk about family and friends, but he knew that topic would have to wait for some other time. Instead, he went right into the heart of his concerns, outlining the soldiers' mood and plight, including the last week's endless series of baseless alarms about British attacks. "If a real attack comes, Nat, they will be so numbed, they will scarcely stir."

When Sam finished his description of the demoralized men, the general steepled his fingers and touched them to his nose in silence for a while. Sam could hear a faint asthmatic wheeze as he breathed. "Do you recall the inventory we had the regiments take of their powder magazines?"

"Three weeks ago. Yes, of course."

Nat nodded. "When we completed the returns, we had a surprise." He lowered his voice and leaned forward, putting his elbows on the desk. "This information cannot leave this room. To no one, no matter how much you trust him. Yes?"

Sam said yes.

He spoke in a hoarse whisper. "This news in the wrong hands could destroy us all," he snapped his fingers, "in a flash." He looked at Sam and waited for this to sink in.

"Not a word, general. To anyone."

He nodded. "Our inventory turned up a total of ninety barrels of powder. Ninety for the entire army. I personally had the duty of bringing the news to General Washington. He received this intelligence with such horror, Sam, that he sat for thirty minutes without uttering a single word. Ninety barrels of powder will provide our men with perhaps two rounds each—if we do not fire a single cannon or mortar. We sent urgent messages to every colony in New England, but we could not risk telling even them how dire our need is. If one message was intercepted or relayed to the enemy, you can guess how quickly an attack upon us would come."

Sam felt his scalp prickle as he took in the perilousness of their situation. "Good God, Nat. Have we gotten more powder yet?"

"Some," he said, "but scarcely enough to permit more than perhaps one more round per man. The supply remains dangerously poor. We hope to turn our attention fully to matters such as fresh food, warm clothing, and improving discipline, but it has been all our study to organize the newly arriving men and stock our magazines."

"How is General Washington?"

Nat leaned back in his chair and resumed a more normal voice. "I must tell you Sammy, I admire no man alive more than him. He has dealt with unimaginable difficulties from the day he arrived, and my regard for him grows every day. However," he smiled wanly, "his esteem of New Englanders has plummeted."

"Why is that?"

"It was too high to start with. He has found our common people have the same virtues and vices as others, and it is a disappointment to him. Many of us here have exalted the famous distant Virginians, and it turns out they have done the same with us. When His Excellency discovered we are not another race of creature entirely, he was let down. We have uncovered a score of Massachusetts officers drawing pay for men who do not exist. Others have taken leave without permission for weeks at a time in order to renew their acquaintance with the pleasures of domestic life. And the general is contemptuous of our merchants whom he calls 'stock-jobbing Yankees full of sharp practices and a filthy mercenary spirit.' It galls him to see these men, safe behind the lines, fill their pockets at the expense of their country. The point is hard to argue."

Sam, who had tried to buy extra food for himself, knew this well. "That is exactly why it is essential the army provide the men with adequate food. They steal from one another as it is. Discipline will be impossible without it."

Nat nodded. "As we have all seen with your Pennsylvania neighbors. I have explained to our general that the genius of our region's people is commercial, and it has made them avaricious. But he worries that we will starve the cause and protract the dispute. He is uncomfortable that so many of our officers are close to those we are supposed to command. In Virginia, he is used to the gentry being distant from the populace, and he finds New Englanders are too much levelers. I know he will find in time our men's bravery and spirit, but right now he is forced to contend with inadequacies on all sides. We need to remind our soldiers of the cause for which they fight."

"So there is little likelihood of our attacking."

"General Washington has thought about little else since he arrived. It is his chief wish. But," Nat shrugged, "circumstances do not yet permit it."

"When will food improve?"

"I cannot say. Though I can promise you a good meal tomorrow night." Nat rose from his chair. "General Washington has invited half a dozen Rhode Island officers for dinner, and you and I are among them. They do eat correctly on Brattle Street. And now, Sammy, I am afraid you must excuse me…"

As he rode back to the lines, Sam thought about the dinner he was to have with General Washington himself. He wondered how he might tell the general that his family actually owned a book Washington once edited on the rules of etiquette—a book as old as Sam and one he found a few years back made for brutally tedious reading.

On his way, he decided to pass by the encampment of some of the general's newly arrived fellow colonists. The First Virginia Rifle Company was this week even more talked of than the Pennsylvania riflers. They marched, incredibly, six hundred miles in twenty-one days, and they did not lose a single man on the trip. As Sam neared their encampment, he saw a knot of men in linen hunting shirts, a few of whom were wearing dark round hats bearing the legend *Liberty or Death.* As best as Sam could determine, they were gathered to watch two of their own men in a brawl. No one was yelling or cheering. They regarded the struggle silently.

One tall Virginian was leaning against a tree, his back to the fight, whittling a stick with his clasp knife.

"Pardon me," Sam said. "What is the problem here?"

The man glanced up for a moment. "No problem, sir," he said in an unruffled voice with a soft Southern accent. "It'll be over in a minute. The captain is showing something to one of the men."

"Captain Morgan?" Sam asked, having heard more talk about him than any other soldier below the rank of general.

"Yessir. Captain Daniel Morgan." He looked back over his shoulder. "Ah. See? Over already." Sam watched an enormous man emerge from the crowd rubbing the thick knuckles of his right fist. The private who had had something "showed" to him lay flattened on the ground.

Sam rode on to his men thinking that, despite General Washington's views, some Virginians were levelers, too.

Chapter Eleven

Sam walked into the handsome Cambridge mansion headquarters with Lieutenant Colonel Christopher Greene and Colonel James Varnum. Sam could tell that they—freshly shaved, hair powdered, carefully dressed as he was himself—were nervous. He knew he was. A half dozen other officers, including Nat and General Lee, were already inside. Jimmy Varnum shook hands with Nat Greene and nodded formally at General Lee, saying, "Your Honor."

"'Your Honor!'" Lee snorted. "I don't know who in the world devised so *ridiculous* a bauble to call me. 'Tis worse, I believe, than even 'His Excellency for commander in chief.' Please, Colonel Varnum, call me 'general.' Else upon my soul I shall spew..."

Everyone laughed at this, though Sam had known Nat Greene long enough to know his expression was one much more of tolerant amusement than enjoyment. A liveried black servant served them salty hot delicacies and they were directed to a table to choose a beverage. Through an act of will, Sam forced himself not to eat too many of the delicacies, though he could see the other Rhode Islanders eye them with the same longing. There was some talk of the Pennsylvania men. General Lee burst in, "They are paid more and worth less than any latrine-digger in the army. Dirty, mutinous riff-raff Smith's men are. Flogging is too good for them."

Colonel Hitchcock observed that at least Captain Hendricks' Pennsylvania regiment seemed to know what they were about.

Lee grunted agreement but pointed out that Ross's regiment was worse than Smith's, if such a thing were possible.

"Have they been invited to dine here, too?" Colonel Varnum asked with a grin.

"Aye," replied General Lee. "We set them up at the trough in the barn."

Every few minutes the men looked around for the commander. Almost a half hour passed, and were it not for the steady supply of trays carried by servants replenished with food and drink, Sam thought some of them might have grown restless. And when finally General Washington made his appearance, apologizing for his lateness, and still checking his white shirt cuffs to see if they were properly cleared of his elegant jacket sleeves, Sam was struck by a kind of warmth and easiness in him he had not expected. Instead of the silence and grave reserve he anticipated, and in place of stiffness and formality, was an easy dignity. Nat Greene introduced him one at a time to the assembled Rhode Island officers, and those he had met before he acknowledged with a few personal words, and those he had not he greeted personably and with something like friendliness. He listened to what each man said to him and responded to him without ceremony, standing an inch or two closer to each than was customary. Though Sam was himself over six feet tall, which meant he towered over most of his men in the line, the general was still the tallest man in the room. Sam judged by his muscular neck and the way he filled his clothes that he was also the strongest.

When he came to Sam, Nat introduced him, and Washington made a point of saying he knew and admired his father, was in frequent correspondence with him at the Congress in Philadelphia, and offered that his leadership and wisdom were widely and increasingly appreciated. Sam said that their family's acquaintance of His Excellency—a term he used knowing he was out of General Lee's earshot—extended back almost twenty years to his book on etiquette. Washington laughed aloud at this and said politeness had spared him so much embarrassment in his life—he was glad he made a study of it in his youth. "Though some will tell you I have failed to study the subject hard enough." Before he turned to be introduced to the next officer, he commented to Sam that he heard Sam had done an excellent job under trying circumstances at training his regiment. Sam's face grew warm at this compliment and found, his rehearsed remarks expended, that he did not know what to say except, "Thank you, General."

At dinner—roast beef! fresh vegetables! roast potatoes! warm bread and fresh butter!—the conversation focused on the question Nat Greene said was raised every night, and sometimes every day as well: when were they attacking the British lines? Sam was surprised to hear Washington give a speech almost identical to the one Sam had just given the day before to Nat.

"Cold weather will begin in two months," Washington said, putting down his wineglass. He looked at the men one at a time as he spoke. "Our powder is being wasted daily in effectless exchanges. The wood some men steal will be needed for reinforcements to the forts, to cook fires, and to erect winter quarters. Blankets and coats will be required when, now, we can scarcely even get enough food. Dr. Franklin's suggestion that some of you may have heard—that we should plan to use spears—tells you what he believes the future could hold. Does it not seem best for a speedy conclusion to be brought to this dispute? What are your thoughts, gentlemen?"

Colonel Varnum and a few of the others counseled patience. "With respect, sir, winter cold and insufficient supplies are a problem for the redcoats, too," said Varnum. "Cut off as they are, their experience at Bunker Hill has taught them another assault on our well-dug lines would be a desperate act. Our New England forests offer vast amounts of wood. If the snow comes early, we can sled whole trees in from the north. And we are told daily from home that the colonies will be furnishing more and better supplies—as it is, our wives and sisters and parents and children spend all their hours spinning, weaving, canning fruits, and smoking meats."

The discussion went on, with the generals more ardent for an American attack, the line officers for forcing the British to attack.

General Washington listened closely to the discussion, saying little himself after he launched the subject. When most had spoken their piece and one or two began to repeat themselves, he finally cleared his throat.

"An officer from Connecticut who helped retake the ruined fort of Ticonderoga a few months ago has come to me with a plan. A brilliant and daring plan. The man is highly intelligent, vigorous, and shrewd. And he is prepared to lead an expedition."

"What is the man's name, General?" Colonel Greene asked.

"Colonel Benedict Arnold. Do you know him?"

None did, but Sam volunteered that a Benedict Arnold was one of the first and best-known governors of Rhode Island over a century before. Old Benedict Arnold was buried just a few blocks up from the Ward family store in Newport. "It's likely this is his descendant."

Washington nodded. "And a man of mettle, too." He paused and waited until he had the table's full attention. "Canada," he said at last, "is the British back door to an invasion of the colonies. If we lock it before they discover it as an opportunity, America can look to offer the British a retreat by sea, a siege they cannot win, or the prospect of attacking a great natural fortress." His whole life long, Sam had been used to being around men who compelled attention by their position or by some personally imposing air of authority. General Washington had the ability to do both, but Sam was immediately aware of a level of interest in this subject that passed far beyond personality. Everyone stopped eating to listen to Washington speak.

"Congress has already authorized sending Generals Schuyler and Montgomery with New York soldiers to invest Montreal. By all accounts, it is weakly defended and will capitulate at the first demonstration of a presence in arms. What Colonel Arnold has called to our attention is Quebec."

Washington's large hands squeezed each other as he spoke. Not a man in the room stirred. "Colonel Arnold," he continued, "has proposed leading a detachment directly through Maine, up the Kennebec and Chaudiere Rivers to a point just above Quebec, there to join forces with General Schuyler. He hopes in the interval to befriend as many Canadian and Seven Nations Indians as possible—who we hear are warmly disposed toward our cause. And then to take Quebec itself. In a single stroke, this will threaten the British with the loss of all their colonies in North America."

Sam glanced at Nat Greene, who was nodding almost imperceptibly at Washington's words. He could tell from his face that this plan was not the news to him that it was to the rest of the officers. Colonel Greene asked how many men would be required for such a campaign.

General Washington leaned forward in his chair. "Colonel Arnold proposes to take a thousand men. Hardy men. The fatigues of a journey through the wilderness will be very great. I have been persuaded enough of the wisdom of this undertaking, though, that I have authorized it. It is not exaggeration to say that the safety and welfare of the entire continent could be determined by the success of this enterprise."

Despite himself, Sam felt a thrill at these words. Out of the muck and confusion and boredom of a siege came the prospect of clarity. Quebec! The words of a drill and marching song his regiment had used a hundred times bubbled into his head:

Come, each death-daring dog who dares venture his neck,
Come, follow the hero that goes to Quebec!
And ye that love fighting shall soon have enough:
Wolfe commands us, my boys—we shall give them hot stuff!

"How, Your Excellency, will the men be chosen?" Sam asked.

"We will take volunteers from Massachusetts, Connecticut, and Rhode Island, as well as riflemen from Virginia and Pennsylvania. We can also in this enterprise for the first time employ a *truly* Continental Army." He looked slowly around the assembled table. "As important as our homes are to each of us, we must begin to banish the idea of local attachments among our soldiers. A Virginian must feel the cause of Massachusetts as keenly as anyone from Boston. And so must a New England man for the rights of colonies to the south. It is the cause, not the place, which must inspire loyalty and the last measure of devotion."

*

SAM WAS STILL MUSING over these words as he and the others prepared to leave an hour later. He thought "banishing the idea of local attachments" would be hard going. Nat drew him aside at the door as the others made their farewells.

"His Excellency thinks the riflemen suffer from idleness and that a journey to Quebec will concentrate their energies. Colonel Arnold has already refused to take Captain Ross's regiment. Captain Smith and his men, however, will be eligible to volunteer. Do you still wish to go?"

Sam looked at Nat in surprise. "Is my face such an open book?"

"To your friends." Nat regarded him in silence for a moment. "And I want to warn you as your friend that this journey will be long, difficult, cold, and full of the worst dangers. Your father, your sisters, and your cousins will all wish you to remain in Boston. This expedition will break all but the strongest men. Two hundred miles alone, Sammy, through a trackless wilderness among unfriendly Indians. Hundreds of miles beyond that with long portages, uncertain communication, difficult supply, an upcountry march that could last into the teeth of a Canadian winter. The hardships will be extraordinary."

Sam nodded. "You would go if you could, wouldn't you?"

"If I were not needed here?" Nat's eyebrows lifted. "Excellent question. But let me ask you to give the matter careful thought. Let me also ask you a favor. Don't volunteer tomorrow at first light. Give it a week to weigh all the considerations."

Sam smiled. "Is that an order, General?"

"A personal request."

Before the week was out, Sam's entire family, including his father in Philadelphia, had written to urge him to remain. They were careful to code their warnings against his "venture north" for fear of their letters falling into the wrong hands. But his father's letter concluded without ambiguity, quoting Horace, someone his father knew well was his favorite writer: *They say it is a great thing to die for your country. But they might also say truthfully that is a great thing to live for your country.*

At the end of August and the time to decide drew near, Sam's regiment was called out to improve the fortifications on Plowed Hill, the last and weakest link of all the lines around Boston. Gus Mumford had been asked to supervise the digging, a task that continued all night under cover of darkness. He talked half the night to Sam about his favorite subjects, the joys of married life, the arrival of his first child, and, as always, the great meals he had eaten.

Steady British shelling from ships and from cannons on Bunker Hill continued all night. As usual, the cannonading had little effect, but as the sun rose to reveal the improved works and the American soldiers hard at work, the British Bunker Hill batteries coordinated themselves for a furious round of firing.

Sam and his men were weary after working all night with no sleep, but he knew they were to be relieved by other men at first light. He went to the brow of Plowed Hill to remind Gus to prepare to withdraw. He could see Gus's familiar silhouette against the sunrise a few yards off. He was supervising some men who were hammering in wooden supports to the inside of the freshly dug ditches and talking about what they all could have for breakfast in the next hour.

Sam heard an irregular whisking sound grow louder and louder. He never saw the cannonball itself, but the next moment Augustus Mumford's head and neck were gone. His body remained upright for a moment before it dropped under a welter of blood chasing the air for its lost skull. Sam looked around in horror. Gus's head was everywhere and nowhere. An eyeball sat all by itself in a small cradle of skull a few feet in front of him.

Rhode Island had suffered its first combat casualty.

Sam volunteered for the march on Quebec that afternoon. It was no longer a difficult decision. A man can die in Boston digging a ditch.

Chapter Twelve

"You are going to rejoin Captain Ward outside Boston," Master John said. "From there, I understand you will be accompanying him on a little journey to the north."

Guy had feared news like this might be coming ever since he saw Dr. Church's assistant arrive at the Hazzards', but now that he heard it said aloud, he could scarcely believe it. The blood rushed into his head. "Back to Boston? When?"

Master John stiffened. *Where did this servant's servility go?* "When I say so."

Guy looked down. "Pardon me, Mastuh. I thought since you wan' me be gov'nor, I goin' stay here."

He snorted impatiently. "None of us know how events will unfold. You will be governor for a full year, and I expect you'll be with Sammy Ward a far shorter time than that."

"How long I be gone, Mastuh Hazzard?"

"Depends on how long your journey takes."

"Can June come with me?"

"Come *with* you?" the master repeated in astonishment. "With the harvest coming up? The cows freshening and food to be put by? Are you daft?" He muttered, "Give you people an ell and you try to take a mile…"

"She could be paid fo' by the army. They have lots of womens doing washing and cooking up."

The master's lips tightened into a line, his eyes narrowed. "The answer is no."

He just had more conversation in a single minute than he had ever had with the master all put together, but he needed to press for one last request. "Can we marriage 'fore I leave?"

"You are that keen on it." Guy nodded. "If only so I won't have to hear you bring the subject up again. But," he leveled a finger up at Guy's nose. "But you had better provide Dr. Church's assistant with all the information he wants. Agreed?" Guy nodded. "Very well. I shall talk to Reverend Fayerweather about posting the banns. Understand this: making June your wife does not make her any less my servant. Or you, for that matter. Do you have that well in your head?" Guy nodded solemnly.

He understood this much too well.

*

June's dismay over his leaving lessened after Guy explained that, at last, they had permission to marry. Within minutes, she ran excitedly to tell Jubah and Lucy the news. Jubah started to discuss what food they might have and Lucy said she would help sew a special dress.

Quamino nodded and gazed impassively into the middle distance after Guy explained what the fuss was all about. He did not congratulate him nor touch his arm nor say what a good thing it was to marry.

Guy said, "June think my goin' is like my workin' in Newport every winter."

"It not like that," Quamino said.

"June think marriagin' goin' keep us together."

"Didn't keep her momma and poppa together. Mine neither."

"She think it keep babies with their family."

"Till they be worth somethin'. How old was you when the Robinsons sold you?"

"Maybe eight."

Quamino nodded.

The two men stood together in silence for a while. They regarded the three women smiling and discussing the wedding.

"'Fore I go, can we try the crossing place?"

Quamino turned his weathered face toward Guy and looked him straight in the eye. "I was thinking that just now. Need to know what we can know."

*

"WE COULD DO WITH a celebration," the master said over dinner.

His wife's observant face clouded for a moment. She sighed. "It would be a sight better after the harvest than in the middle of it."

"After the harvest, there will be only half a couple."

"Perhaps we should wait, then."

"We need Guy to cooperate from afar and June not to be sullen at home. No?"

The mistress mused for a few seconds before answering. "Yes."

"A wedding will serve that purpose well."

She looked at her husband directly and steadily. He could tell by the slight narrowing of her blue eyes that she was going to negotiate with him. "Can you spare June for inside work?"

"A small celebration," he said.

"Still…"

They regarded each other in silence. Their overall interests were the same, but how they got there was not. "After she is done in the dairy," he conceded.

"Good," Mistress Hazzard said with a relieved smile, standing to pour her husband some more tea.

"You know," Master John said, watching her pour. "I am exceedingly grateful I do not have to bargain with you for selling our goods."

*

AND SO JUNE WAS called into the big house in the days before the wedding.

Without really thinking about it, she always pictured the mistress leading an easy life behind the closed red main door. But after a day of helping her wash and dust and clean and scrub, and another day of spinning and mending and weaving, and then crushing apples for cider and preparing dough to bake bread, and then cleaning some more, she discovered the mistress's life was not easy after all. And she also found they wasted as little inside the house as they did outside. The Lecture Day sermons on thrift as a way to be custodians of God's handiwork were ones the Hazzards took to heart.

The slaves had eaten intestines, brains, feet, and internal organs of the slaughtered animals long enough to know food was never wasted, but her days of work in the house showed her what became of the rest of the carcass. Guy and Quamino were ordered to slaughter one of the cows that had grown too old to milk. The blood they drained into wooden buckets was used for puddings and broths. The tanned hide was to be used for leggings, shoes, gloves, fire buckets, belts, and coats. The fat was rendered for soap and candles and used for waterproofing. Even the bones were made into knitting needles and toothpicks, the remnants shared with the dogs and put in the kitchen midden to be used for compost next year. June had just taken the flat wooden shovel and removed a loaf of bread from the bake oven when she heard Young John talking with his father in the room off the kitchen. Though it was almost noon, he was still wearing his new militia uniform from this morning's drill, something Jubah said he did to remind his parents that they should be generous to him for doing what they asked. Their voices were low at first, but then they became louder.

"With the slave trade supposed to be illegal," Young John said, "now is the best time. She'll fetch a fair price."

"Wait a few months, and the price will only go up."

"Wait too long, Father, and who knows what will happen. Some in the militia are saying all this liberty talk could infect the legislature."

"To do what?"

Young John lowered his voice. June could not make out what he said.

"Hah! If they decided to do that tomorrow," his father said, "it would take twenty years to realize. And they would themselves suffer in the bargain."

She will fetch a fair price? June said to herself, her heart pounding. Who? Not Jubah. Couldn't be. Not likely herself. It must be Lucy, she thought. But why? She told Jubah about it as soon as she could.

"They talking about selling again?" she said. "They always talking about buying or selling somethin'. Horses, cows, chickens, us. It what they do when they get bored. Don't mean nothin'."

"But it was Young John pushing for it."

"Young John," she said, surprised. She stopped for a moment. "Don't like that."

Jubah went straight to Lucy. She said Young John was trying to get back at her for not letting him have her any more. Jubah looked at her in silence, drawing her teeth slowly across her lower lip. June knew that look right away: it was what she did when she thought someone was not telling her the truth.

"Young John goin' arrange sell you off 'cause you stopped liftin' your shift. He wan' you so-o *bad* he goin' sell you where he can never touch you again." Lucy nodded. Jubah nodded back. "Don' make a lick of sense."

Lucy nodded again, looked up at Jubah, and then shook her head no. "And…"

"That's right," Jubah said. "And."

"And he think I'm bigged up."

"Ah. Is you?"

"No. But he don't believe me."

"Show him your stomach."

"Jubah!"

"You showed him a lot more n' that."

"He say some women don't get big."

"So you showed him your stomach already." She nodded, embarrassed. "So show him some bloody rags."

"Bloody rags?"

"From when your time come round with the next moon." Lucy looked down and said nothing. "You stop bleedin' down there, Lucy?"

"I think so."

"Lord," Jubah said. "Lord, Lord."

"Sometimes I just stop. Weeks. Months."

"Happen before?"

"Sometimes," she said, hopefully.

"How you feelin'? Tired-like? Tummy all right?"

"Feel all right." Jubah drew her teeth across her lip again. "A little sick-ish 'fore breakfast."

Jubah said, "Uh-huh."

"And a little tired sometimes."

Jubah didn't say anything. She didn't have to.

"What we goin' do?" June asked.

"I don't know," Jubah said. "I truly don't. Right now keep our mouths closed."

*

DESPITE HER FATIGUE AND everyone else's short temper, June found her spirits lifting as the wedding approached. Guy seemed worried, and so did Quamino and all the Hazzards. Jubah and Lucy were worried with good reason. But when Reverend Fayerweather and some of the neighbors came along with their servants, the sun was shining, the air was soft and full of birdsong, and she had a ringlet of bright, fragrant flowers to wear in her hair, it was hard for her not to believe her life was better. She worried about Lucy, too, though she didn't want to. Sometimes she thought Lucy had helped bring trouble on herself. Other times she thought maybe Lucy was cornered and it was not even a decision at all. But she put these thoughts by as she readied—so nervous, so excited, so happy—to pledge herself to Guy, who looked strong, straight, and substantial, dressed in clean clothes and carrying himself as calmly as if he did this every day! Pledge herself in the sight of God and all these witnesses from this time forth, now and forever, amen. And when Reverend Fayerweather said at the end, "What God hath joined together, let no man put asunder," she felt a thrill that threaded all through her body. Just before she kissed Guy, she looked at the Hazzards and saw that they said "amen," too.

And then there was food and singing and dancing, as if there were no war and this was 'Lection Day and Christmas all rolled up into one.

Just as the heat of the sun of this beautiful August day began to fade, a young soldier rode up at a gallop to tell Young John he must report to the Westerly green for immediate muster.

"What is it?" the master asked.

"Listen," he said.

The company all grew quiet. Over the panting of the man's horse, every few seconds they heard a distant thumping, as if someone far in the forest was sinking an ax into a hollow log. Guy, who had heard the sound before, said it was cannon fire.

The man announced, “Captain Wallace from Newport is shelling Stonington.”

“Stonington?” Master John repeated. The Connecticut seaport town was a few miles to their south. “Whatever for?”

“Wallace is insisting that sheep and pigs be left on shore for him to take on board. The townspeople refused. We think Westerly will be next.”

“You ride on, lad,” the master told the soldier. “Spread the alarm. Johnny will be ready to muster before you reach the next farm!” He turned to his son. “Run and get your musket, son. Quamino, prepare his horse!”

The soldier road off and Young John dashed inside, pulling off his jacket as he ran. The mistress urged the guests to take home some food and thanked them for coming. Carriages and wagons and horses were readied, and in five minutes the party was over and the frightened guests were gone. Young John, in his militia uniform, was ready to go. They could still hear the distant thump of the cannon.

The master dusted off his son’s lapel. “This is annoying.”

“Annoying!” his son repeated, astounded.

“Believe me, none of Captain Wallace’s cannonballs will land in Westerly. The Wards and Gardiners aside, he knows he has many friends in this area. But here is the true problem. If he starts forcing provisions out of towns on the coast, he will have no wish to pay for anything. And one of our best markets will vanish.”

“Am I still to go?”

“Yes, of course, Johnny. This is a splendid moment to show your readiness to defend the colony. With this one muster, I suspect you will spare us a visit from the damned Committee of Inspection for weeks, perhaps months. Just remind them when you’re there that the Rhode Island militia must remain in Rhode Island—and certainly don’t let them pull you across the line into Connecticut.”

"Yes, Father. But what will we do if Captain Wallace no longer buys from us?"

Master John's eyes narrowed in calculation. "Well, son, if he forces livestock out of towns for free, the price of our goods will rise. People in Stonington still have to eat. The price of salt is going up faster than people can pay for it, so they won't be able to slaughter their stock and salt the meat down for storage." He fished a gold half-Jo from his waistcoat and flipped it in the air. Catching it, he slapped it down on the back of his hand. "Heads or reverse?" he asked.

"Heads," Young John said.

The master lifted his hand, revealing the coin. "Heads it is." He showed his son the coin and then put it back in his pocket. "What you must always ensure is that whatever side the coin falls on, the coin itself remains yours." He patted his jacket pocket. "Come back safe, son, and this particular coin will be yours for your trouble."

*

Once more, Guy and Quamino wore their clothes inside out for a trip into the forest, hoping to deceive any spirits abroad who were seeking to do them harm. Guy brought his bundle of sacred objects, his *nkisi*, painstakingly gathered under Quamino's instruction. He had the white quartz stones which gleamed and sparkled in the faintest light, a prayer stick, herbs, a candle, and the coin his mother had given him when he was a child, one with a hole in the middle and a string running through it to wear around his ankle. It was to keep his circle complete and make him safe from harm through his childhood.

Tonight he was going to step into the middle of the circle himself, stand on the crossing point, and see if he could peer into the dark to discover what the future held. He hoped his heart and his spirit were strong enough to withstand any malignant spirits. Being with June had cleared his mind, bringing him to some harmony he felt deeper than he thought possible, driving away the fear that had crouched in the dark corners of his heart.

They made their way to the place in the forest with a clear line of sight of the waters of Narragansett Bay. Quamino redrew the crossing point with his prayer stick. He instructed Guy in the words of the chant and showed him the leg drive and foot placement of the sacred dance. There was enough of a breeze from the ocean to make candle burning unsteady, but Quamino set it close against the shelter of an elm tree and invited Guy to begin. First the chant, then the dance, a burning of the herbs and sacred dust whose smoke he breathed in. Finally, he stood on the crossing point and raised the prayer stick to the heavens while gazing at the point where the water met the sky.

"Empty yourself, rinse clean of anything but the sounds of the chant. Kneel. Close your eyes. Listen hard. And see what you see."

"What if it nothin'?"

"Nothin' is something."

Guy danced, chanted, breathed the sacred smoke, and knelt. His mind was blank, layers of dark over dark. He thought about June wearing flowers in her hair, and he knew he had spoiled his chance. He rose and shook his head.

Quamino did the ceremony. Guy saw from how the old man's body stiffened at the end that he had seen or heard something. When he was done, he rose from the circle in silence. He refused to talk about it.

"You try," he said.

Guy tried again. This time Quamino drummed with a thick piece of branch on a hollow log, adding his chant to Guy's and pounding a rhythm into Guy's dance. He speeded the rhythm and Guy speeded his dance. The sacred smoke in his lungs, his prayer stick held high out to the length of his arm, the stars small pinpricks in the black sky, Guy saw and heard something even before he knelt and closed his eyes. The picture intensified, grew more vivid. Then vanished.

A few moments later, Guy rose, the evening world of the forest seeping slowly back into his thoughts, and he nodded to Quamino.

They listened for a while to the soft sound of the waves lapping against the shore.

They put out the candle and carefully gathered their *nkisi* back into pouches.

"I saw men skinny as dogs," Quamino said. "I heard booming of guns. And blood, bright red, in the snow."

Guy opened his mouth. Quamino looked at him. He found he had trouble even getting the words out. "I…I…"

"I know. You saw the same thing."

*

Two nights later, Lucy announced over dinner that she had decided to run away.

June and Jubah both cried, "No!" Guy and Quamino shook their heads.

Lucy said, "June sleepin' every night in Guy's cabin now, I all alone. None o' you can stop me."

"Lucy, you listen me now, girl," Jubah said. "Where you think goin' go?"

"Far away as I can get."

"How far you think you can get, no money, knowin' nobody? Bring you back here, get whipped, put in irons ever' night. That what you want?"

"They goin' sell me South. You say yourself they pay the most for slaves."

"Maybe they not goin' sell you. Maybe they sell you over to the Gardiners."

"What if I'm bigged up?"

"What if you not?"

Lucy shook her head, lowered it into her hands, and sobbed.

"They catch you runnin' away," June added, "and they sell you off for sure."

Quamino added, "If you big, the Hazzards be mighty worried 'bout a light-lookin' baby. Reverend Fayerweather not glad. You might make a bargain, Lucy."

"Bargain?" Lucy said. "What you mean?"

"Tell them they keep you, you swear a white stranger attack you in the woods."

Lucy paused on that. "They won' make no bargain with me," she muttered.

"Maybe," said Jubah. "Maybe not. But you run away, you be caught sure. Young John not doin' the decidin' round here. Just bide your time. Maybe a big army come through here need help and you can sneak off with them. Maybe you not bigged up. Maybe you are and you miscarry. But runnin' away now? Lucy, don' even think about it."

June sat next to her and comforted her.

✷

Before he left to return to Boston, Guy tried to leave everything fixed tight. Though fall had not yet begun, he secured his and June's cabin for winter. He showed her where he kept his money. He took one small copper coin to use if he was dying for lack of food or clothes, and he took the one gold coin if he had to bribe someone to save his life. The rest he left in a small box in a hiding place in the cabin. June looked at his collection of various coins, more than twenty of them, and was surprised.

"How you get all this?"

He shrugged. "Save 'em."

She knew he must have kept them for years. "Save 'em for what?"

He was embarrassed to say this, for it was a dream so great even this pile of coins was pathetically small in the face of it. He looked at her. She was his wife now. So he said, "Save it to buy…you."

"To buy me out?" He nodded. "You have enough?"

"Not close. I saw Africans bein' sold in Newport last winter. They a lot cheaper n' ones born in Rhode Islan'." He pointed to the heap of coins. "I need ten piles like these just fo' one a them."

June looked at the coins and found she could not speak for the tightness in her throat. His strong body and serious, watchful face were two reasons she loved him, and as strong as they were for her, this was something more that she had sensed about him all along but not really understood until now. Trapped as they all were, he was still willing not only to dream, but to work, save, and sacrifice. She knew he got tips and gifts and small payments from the master. Other slaves she knew on other farms did, too. He could have spent that money in Newport. He could have spent it or gambled it playing paw-paw shells like other slaves on holiday gatherings. But he had something they did not: a capacity to hope. It amazed her. She pressed her cheek against his arm and said he should buy himself out.

"I seen 'em in Boston, June. I seen 'em."

"What?"

"Seen black mens, and womens too, who nobody owned. Not rich like the baker woman or sick or old like free ones in Newport. Just… people." He had told her this before, but now she understood him in a way she did not before.

"Who knows?" she said. "Like Quamino say, it's a jumble-up time." She smiled at him and he nodded.

Suddenly the thought of his leaving was as if someone were going to tear her arm from its socket. She hugged him fiercely, tears spilled from her eyes, and she begged him not to go. She had thought the marriage would make it easier. Instead, it made it worse, far worse.

*

On the morning he was to leave, he and June exchanged amulets. She gave him a talisman wrapped in a tiny piece of her wedding clothes. He gave her the coin with a hole in it his mother gave him to keep the circle of his life unbroken. He crouched to tie it round her ankle. They were both weary and sad, but they knew they had not wasted their last night together.

The supply wagon he was to accompany was waiting. It was packed so full, they could find no room for him to ride. He knew he would be marching most of the way to Boston. He said goodbye to Jubah and Lucy, telling them to look after June. Finally, he asked Quamino in a low voice the question he had wanted to ask for days. Will it be his blood in the snow? Quamino sighed. He did not know.

Guy nodded. He was going to miss this old man. He did not know how to say this, so instead he said, "Bless you."

Quamino looked surprised. "You got your *nkisi*?"

"Yes."

"Well, you got part of me with you, then." He gave Guy a wan smile. "You be off, now."

Chapter Thirteen

After Gus Mumford's wrenching memorial service and in the middle of his preparations for his march north, Sam was suddenly seized from nowhere by an absolute, pitiless, blinding lust. It afflicted him for days. One evening after dark, the men posted for the night, he made his way to one of the many stews near the encampment. He had no difficulty finding the place. He had never had sex before. He stepped into the perimeter light of a low campfire and a fat red-faced woman who had been sitting in the shadows came forward. She quickly sized him up, sucking on her teeth and looking at him from head to toe.

"Lieutenant, are ye?" she said.

"Captain."

"A' been cheaper if you was a lieutenant. Connecticut?"

"Rhode Island."

"A day's pay and we'll oblige you." She gave the sum of his pay correctly to the penny. "Ye want to be lieutenant, one pass. Captain, ye get two."

He did not bargain. His captain's wages stuck safely in a leather pouch around her waist, she took him into a low tent, lay down on a muddy blanket and pulled up her skirts. Uncertain of where to put himself, she sighed impatiently, muttered something unintelligible, reached down, and poked him in. She smelled dankly of rum and bad breath and pipe smoke and other men's sex. Once inside her, he came almost immediately with a groan, but stayed where he was, plunging slowly into her inert form, and then, not so slowly, bucking away until he began to drip sweat. Minutes later, panting, he came again.

As he was buttoning his pants to leave, she was already outside sizing up another customer.

Sam returned to camp expecting to feel assailed by guilt and the fear of a wrathful God who would lay him waste with disease and grief. As he lay on his straw-stuffed bed, to his surprise, he felt only a sense of relief, a faint crawl of mortality on his skin, and the dry, sweet sensation at the back of his throat that preceded sleep.

✷

MOST OF THE MEN from his regiment volunteered to go north, Elijah Dole and Sergeant Amos Boynton, and even practical old Tom Shepherd, who said he was "bored to tears" with this siege life. His friend and lieutenant, Elijah Lewis, shaken by Gus Mumford's grisly death and not wishing to put any more distance between himself and his wife and home, decided to stay behind. It was not easy for Sam to say goodbye to him, nor to Nat Greene. Sam was not glad to hear that Captain Smith and his riot-prone riflers would be coming. Regardless, he knew it was time for him to go.

Nat tried hard to talk him out of it—he even offered him a position on his staff—but once it was clear Sam's mind was made up, Nat arranged for him to meet Colonel Arnold.

It was a good list of volunteers, Sam thought. Tall, quiet, authoritative Pennsylvania Captain Hendricks and the powerful and legendarily determined Captain Daniel Morgan of Virginia were leading riflers. Experienced men from Rhode Island, Connecticut, New Hampshire, Massachusetts, and Maine—among them Nat's cousin, Colonel Christopher Greene—made up the rest.

At Cambridge headquarters, as he was looking down the list of names, a man of medium height and dark complexion in a Connecticut officer's uniform approached. "Captain Ward?" he said, extending a hand and regarding him closely with watchful bright blue eyes.

"Yes, sir," Sam said, straightening from the table.

"Colonel Arnold." His handshake was brief but fierce, conveying a sense of satisfaction at this encounter and a full alertness to the moment.

"Honored to meet you, sir." Sam looked at him intently. So this was the man upon whom his own life and the enterprise's success would depend. He had heard about Arnold's ambition and creativity and drive, but not about what he looked like. Not conventionally handsome nor tall nor powerful of build, he still carried himself nimbly and as confidently as a prince.

"You're a polite lad," he said, his voice deeper and louder than Sam would have guessed from a man his size, an amused look on his lively face. With a rolled map he held in his left hand, he swatted Sam on the shoulder. "Not *too* polite, I hope."

"His Excellency says politeness is a valuable skill."

"Oh, it is. A talent, truly. But we descendants of Rhode Island governors know that is not how to get work done."

Sam grinned. "Benedict Arnold was…"

"Great-great grandfather. No, no. Politeness won't get us to Quebec. We're going to need the strength of those wide shoulders of yours." He unfolded the map and, at the same moment and without ceremony, he released the coiled spring of his restless personality. As if Sam were Washington himself, Arnold explained the whole complex campaign, growing more ardent and animated the more he explained it.

Colonel Arnold repeatedly drove his finger into the map as he hammered his points home. In a strong voice, he outlined his plans and preparations. From time to time, he fastened his piercing gaze on Sam. Sam, listening carefully, recognized two things: Arnold understood the need for meticulous planning, and he knew how to lead. A practiced listener to inspirational speakers, Sam still found himself swept up by the torrential force of Arnold's conviction.

A young aide excused himself and interrupted Arnold to hand him some expresses. Arnold stepped back from the table and broke the seal on all of the messages before reading any of them. As he read rapidly through them, the aide introduced himself.

"Aaron Burr," he said. Short, so handsome as to border on the beautiful, thick eyelashes as long as a girl's, slim, and possessed of an absolute aura of self-confidence, Burr managed to look up at Sam while, with a trick of the head, somehow conveying that he was the same height.

"Of New Jersey," Sam said, having heard from Nat Greene a few things about this aide. Burr nodded, appearing quite unsurprised that others had talked of him. "Sam Ward," Sam said, extending a hand. As Nat had put it to him, "He's a lad of about your years who graduated from the college at Princeton at the same child's age you did. His father was president of the place. He knows the Abenaki Indians well enough to be already biblically familiar with a pretty one. He's fine of build, though. You have to hope he'll have the strength to make this tour."

Burr glanced back at Arnold. He stepped closer to Sam and said in a confiding tone, "After consulting who knows what oracle, General Washington has urged the colonel to disorder the traditional chains of command. He wants Southerners commanding New Englanders and New Englanders commanding Southerners! He believes this will banish the idea of 'local attachments' and make the army 'truly continental.' Hah!" The young aide did such a skillful imitation of General Washington's soft Virginia accent, Sam could not keep from smiling, though he was surprised to hear criticism of the commander in chief, and certainly not offered so matter-of-factly to someone Burr had just met.

"That all the soldiers have volunteered to go to Quebec says it is more the cause that animates them, not attachment to place."

Burr gave Sam a sharp look. "But these men fight—if they do fight—and follow orders—if they *do* follow orders—because of local attachments! It is only human nature to want to look well before your neighbor and to help him if you can. And there are a hundred reasons a man might sign for this journey, not all of them having to do with 'the cause.'" He eyed Sam closely for a sign of assent. None came. "No, General Washington is making a political decision on this matter, not a sound military one."

Sam was annoyed. No uniform, nineteen years old, unattached to any unit, and he was sitting in Olympian judgment of General Washington's military competence. "There are eighty-four men in my new company, half of them from Massachusetts and New Hampshire. What difference would it make if they were from Pennsylvania or Virginia? Speaking for myself, I know I would rather be commanded by a Virginian than by most of these miserable officers from Massachusetts. And when we attack Quebec together and our lives depend on one another, I hope every man there will consider me a local attachment."

"You speak of officers. I speak of the average soldier. You argue well enough, though, Captain Ward. But we'll see soon if a good argument is the same as the truth."

"No argument is good except insofar as it describes the truth," Sam said.

Burr grinned disarmingly. "Ah! Now there we disagree!"

*

SEVERAL OTHER OFFICERS ARRIVED at headquarters who had also signed on for the march north: Captains Thayer and Topham of Rhode Island, Captains Goodrich and Hanchet of Connecticut. They introduced themselves to Colonel Arnold and, leading them to his map, he began to explain to them with undiminished ardor what he had already explained to Sam. "If we are respectful of Indian and Catholic alike, we will appear in the north as bringers of freedom, not as invading conquerors. Our success will secure victory for America months or even years sooner. And extraordinary undying honor will fall to every single man on this expedition."

When several more officers arrived, Arnold gave the same explanation all over again, almost word for word in his deep, loud voice, but as energetic and expansive and fresh as if it were not the third time he had done so in thirty minutes.

In the days before the men prepared to leave, Sam had two visitors—his aunt Catharine Greene and her nearly sixteen-year-old daughter, Phebe. It was passing odd to see well-dressed and proper women at the lines—just a clean face, much less pretty female ones, was as rare as a double rainbow. Sam found it hard not to stare at them to drink them in, like watching brilliant sunflowers blossom above a crust of snow. Aunt Catharine, his mother's younger sister, was charming enough that her friend Benjamin Franklin had once strenuously tested her virtue on a long coach ride to New York. Beautiful, animated, smart, and resourceful, she had little problem deflecting his attentions and maintaining his friendship. But it was soon clear she had come to the lines to test her considerable powers of persuasion on behalf of the entire Ward family directly on Sam. After giving him treasured gifts of fresh food, clean clothing, and bringing him up to date on all the family news, she looked him straight in the eye.

"Sammy," she said, resting a hand on his forearm. "You *mustn't* go north. You *simply* mustn't."

"Aunt Catharine, I should deeply regret declining any request you make."

"Good, then."

"But this is a project whose completion is our surest safety."

She frowned briefly, then cleared her brow, locking her eyes with his. "I know you are young and have an appetite for adventure and the ambitious pursuit of honor, and that is to your credit. But the hard truth now is that your entire family depends on your well-being. With your father in Philadelphia at the Congress and your brother Charles gone God knows where, let us be clear—*you* are now the head of the Ward family. To volunteer to put yourself at what everyone agrees is very great risk, no matter what the cause and when it is not in any way required, is to play dice with the future of your brothers and your sisters. It is not your own destiny here that is put at hazard, but the fate of your family. So please, Sammy, you must rise above a thirst for personal glory and do the responsible thing and remain here at the Boston lines." She gripped his arm tightly as she said, "I not only speak for myself here, but for the memory of your dear mother, who I am sure would counsel as I do."

Her voice reminded him so much of his mother's that his throat tightened, and it was a while before he could bring himself to speak. "It is for my loved ones that I plan to go, Aunt Catharine. If this venture is successful, our country and our colony will arrive all the sooner at a happy conclusion. If we do not, this conflict could drag on for years, long enough for your youngest sons and my youngest brothers to have to take up arms. There will be more grieving widows and more grieving orphans and more families like Gus Mumford's." Phebe looked at him with such warmth and intensity, it took him a second to recover his thoughts. "General Washington would not authorize this journey if it were not one to slice through the Gordian knot of a long struggle and save the lives of thousands of sons, brothers, and fathers. I have committed to go, the plans are set, and my men depend on me. Wish me fair weather and safe passage, Aunt Catharine. I cannot remain here."

His aunt's mouth turned down and her eyes brimmed. "You are a brave young man, and a foolish one. It would break our hearts to lose you." When he took a deep breath and said nothing to this, she turned to her daughter. "Phebe, you reason with him. Perhaps he will listen to you." His aunt rose to go, leaving him alone with his cousin, who had clearly arrived at womanhood since he'd seen her the year before. Nearly as tall as her mother, with a trim waist and a round bodice, she had the clear, intelligent, watchful and wide-set eyes of their cousin Caty, Nat Greene's wife.

"Captain Ward," she said, her voice soft. "Have you received my letters?" Sam nodded and thanked her warmly, apologizing for not having had the time yet to reply. In fact, his mental picture of her was as dated as an ancient sketch and scarcely matched the lovely young woman in front of him. He wondered if he would have found the time had he had a fresher picture in mind. "I imagine you know I would never ask you to do something that your own heart and judgment do not prompt. My mother is mistaken to think otherwise." She lowered her eyes shyly.

"Your mother, Phebe, never thinks tactically and is rarely mistaken. She is always strategic."

She looked at him once again. "I am afraid I do not follow you."

"She knows you do not need to make an argument at all." She tilted her head in puzzlement. "I hope you will not take this amiss. But you are yourself an argument to stay even if you do not say a single word."

She blushed. "You mean she is exploiting my concern for you as a final plea?"

"We know your mother is effective in all she sets her mind to."

Phebe nodded and laughed softly. "That is certainly true."

"And I think she believes, shrewdly enough, that it is my concern about *you* that will make the case." There was a brief silence, during which they regarded each other, unblinking. Phebe's pupils dilated to cover almost her entire iris. He spoke softly. "She is also quite correct to think that, to me, you make the case most eloquently." He paused and thought that this was the moment that he might, in normal times, propose spending social evenings with Phebe.

Cousins married cousins in his family all up and down the Ward family tree, as they did throughout New England. In normal times, indeed, they could explore their degree of attraction over weeks and months and see what their hearts prompted and how their families felt. These were not normal times.

"Where you are going, I believe my letters cannot reach," she said.

"They may. Couriers are sent. Permit me to say that my thoughts will be with you even if my letters cannot reach you. But I will write you."

"So will I," she said. "Please be careful, for all our sakes."

"I will." She smiled at him in a sad way that he, afterwards, found haunted him, materializing night after night in the minutes before sleep.

*

A LONG WEEK WAS to pass before they left, and more days were lost when, at the Newburyport shore, the frugal New England men insisted on being paid a month's wages in advance. While they were marching into a wilderness with no place to spend the money, they also knew they were soon going to be beyond the reach of any payroll delivery. And then, as Aaron Burr predicted, the Southern men balked at being led by Colonel Christopher Greene—no offense to him, they said, but they would prefer Captain Morgan. Finally, after more precious days slipped by as they waited for the payroll, on Tuesday, September 19 at nine in the morning, they were cheered with loud huzzahs and wished Godspeed by a crowd of locals who did not have a clue where these men were headed. They at last set sail for Fort Western, one thousand strong, complete with assorted guides, pioneers, teamsters, quartermasters, oxen, two pet dogs, aides, a chaplain, two doctors, and two soldiers' wives.

*

When Guy Watson arrived at Fort Western four days later in the company of a messenger bearing orders from Cambridge, Sam and most of the other men were just straggling in. Their schooners proved too heavy to sail upriver, some boats ran aground, and the rest had to be towed on foot for fifteen miles. No one was pleased with how the great march north had begun.

As Guy stepped off the shallow-drawing transport, a young man was waiting at the dock standing between two armed guards, his hands manacled behind him, his head hung low on his chest.

"What's this?" the messenger with Guy asked a guard.

"This?" said the guard. "This is Jimmy McCormick of Maine. Quiet boy, Jimmy, until last night when he got good and drunk. Shot and killed Sergeant Bishop, a Pennsylvania rifler. Sentenced to death by court-martial this morning, he was. And you and me and the corporal here will be taking him back to Cambridge for them to carry out the sentence."

McCormick lifted his head, and Guy saw his eyes were red and swollen and his face was stained with weeping. He looked to be no older than eighteen. When his stricken eyes met Guy's, he felt a prickling run up the back of his neck.

✷

Guy was directed to find Captain Ward in a large field just outside the fort. He was easy to spot, tall, and his blonde head uncovered as he made his way amid a field full of upside-down bateaux. The captain's damp Rhode Island uniform was steaming in the morning sun. He glanced at Guy and said, exactly as if Guy had never left, "Give me a hand with this."

Following the Ward boy's lead, Guy helped him right a bateau so he could examine its inside. Guy was aware that the two of them were strong men, just as he was aware that the captain's face reddened and the veins stood out in cords on his neck as he strained to roll the beige beast over. Guy had a hard time merely keeping a purchase on the boat's dew-wet sides, and he grunted with the effort of lifting. A third man, Sergeant Amos Boynton, rushed over to help them.

The boat turned over at last, the Ward boy said, breathing hard, "Must weigh three or four hundred pounds."

The sergeant nodded, surveying the rest of the field. "God knows we got a lot of 'em, too."

"Two hundred, to be exact," Captain Ward said. "Each is made to carry six or seven men plus supplies." He leaned down into the bateau to examine the inside.

Guy studied it with him. Like the dories he had ridden on for ferry crossings to Newport, this flat-sided vessel flared out from its narrow bottom and had a pointed, overhanging bow and a flattened stern. Squat and high-sided, it would almost be as hard to overturn in water as it was on land. He sniffed it, stroked it, dug a fingernail into its wood. It was pine, which meant it was soft, and green, which meant it was wet and heavy, and it would warp soon. You scarcely needed to know wood to know this.

Some other members of the Ward regiment gathered.

"New boats," muttered Captain Ward. He looked around at the vast field of other bateaux. They were all fresh made. "Like an unbroken horse." He sighed. "Well, for most of this trip these are our steeds." He looked at Guy and, judging from the light that appeared in his eye, remembered something about him. "You're a carpenter," he said to him. He swept a hand across the field. "You and Privates Tolman and Dole and Sergeant Boynton. Pick out ten or twelve of the most likely of these crafts as you can find, and mark a 'W' on their hulls."

"Double-yew?" Guy repeated in a low voice, embarrassed.

The captain handed a hunk of charcoal to Boynton. "Sergeant, you make the marks. Lieutenants Shaw and Clark and I will be back in thirty minutes to review your choices. Choose them as carefully as you would choose yourself a wife."

Once the captain was out of sight, Guy heard Private Ebeneezer Tolman mutter to Elijah Dole, "What's he know about choosing a wife? And what's this about ordering us to work with his nigger? Don't care a fig who his father is." Pinching three fingers and a thumb together, he raised them in a sharp upward gesture. "I volunteered for this duty as a free man, not some rich boy's slave."

Tolman, from Massachusetts, did not know that Dole and Sergeant Boynton were Westerly neighbors of the Wards. They looked at him and shrugged and went off wandering through the bateaux, trying to find ones that looked likely. Guy, not wishing any trouble, walked off in a direction away from Tolman. Tolman followed him, still muttering that he sure as hell did not leave his farm in Weymouth just to end up working with a bunch of nigs. Guy was careful not to look at him and moved steadily away, changing directions several times, hoping to put some distance between them. Tolman kept trailing after him and continuing his angry monologue. Boynton and Dole tried joking him out of it, Dole saying he's found one, and he thinks he has fallen in *lo-ove*! Could Sergeant Boynton mark it, please, oh, please? Boynton told him to get down on one knee and propose first.

Tolman called that he'd found one and Boynton came over to him. "This one?" he asked. Tolman nodded. Boynton marked a *W* on its hull. Tolman snorted and moved on. Guy, taking his time, finally found one that appeared to be made from northside pine—the grain was tighter—and, more important, most of the boards in the hull were, too. Too many of the bateaux he'd seen had mixed north and south, straight and waved, so they'd be sure to check and warp at different rates. New boat, new wood, you wanted them at least to warp in the same way at the same time. He called for Sergeant Boynton. As Boynton stepped toward him, Tolman exploded.

Pointing at Guy, he yelled, "You are actually going to let him choose one?" Some soldiers from other regiments began to turn to look.

"Now, Eb," the sergeant said. "You heard the captain."

"Damned right I did. You're letting a nig choose wives for the whole regiment."

"At least all the pine is white."

"You think this is a joke?"

Boynton, who was a head shorter than Tolman, stepped close to him, and though he spoke softly, Guy could hear him. "No, private, I don't. But we've heard enough o' your whining. Unless you want to be put on report, 'tis time for you to keep yer mouth shut." Tolman's eyes blazed with anger, but his lips tightened into a thin line. "Now go about the business of picking out the best craft here."

By the time the Rhode Island officers returned, they had picked out and marked off seventeen bateaux. Captain Ward and his two lieutenants examined the choices slowly and carefully, at length arriving at their final selection. All four of Guy's selections were chosen, only one of Ebeneezer Tolman's. Amos Boynton and Elijah Dole had not paid much attention as to who had picked what. Guy was aware, though, that Eb Tolman knew very well what the score was. He avoided looking at him until the process was over and Captain Ward ordered the final twelve to be portaged to the regiment's campsite. When he glanced at Tolman, he found the Massachusetts man staring at him, his green eyes sparkling with unvarnished hatred.

*

Dr. Church's assistant found Guy hauling wood for a wash fire. Some of Ward's regiment had made the mistake of sleeping in the fort's barracks last night, a privilege they paid for by renting their beds from some Virginians who had arrived first, and they had been eaten alive with fleas. They covered themselves in borrowed blankets while they boiled their clothes. The top of the water looked like a soup someone had lavishly peppered with the corpses.

He called Guy aside, his spectacles glinting in the firelight. "We are going to be divided into four groups, 'divisions' they are called. You will be in Major Meigs' group, the third of the four. I will be traveling right behind you with Colonel Enos."

"You come, too?" Guy asked in surprise.

He nodded shortly. "I will be in touch." He said in a cold, impassive tone that Guy could later not stop worrying about, "Congratulations on your marriage."

Chapter Fourteen

Colonel Arnold was concerned enough about the snags and problems of these first days that he called for a banquet before their departure from Fort Western. "Journeys well begun," he told the officers, "are more likely to end in success. Let us have a feast and make every effort to put our men in a proper spirit." That night there were no bonfires and no speeches, but fresh killed meats, rich cheese, warm yeast bread, fresh-baked fruit pies, and an extra portion of rum cheered the soldiers.

Sam himself heard about the final command structure at the banquet. Colonel Greene explained to him that Captain Morgan and the Virginia and Pennsylvania riflers would be in the vanguard. Experienced in woodcraft, they had the demanding job of blazing the trail for the portages, felling trees, setting campsites, sending back couriers with information on the terrain and the waters. Following them would be Colonel Greene's division with four New England regiments, Major Meigs with Sam's and three other regiments, followed by Colonel Enos and his Connecticut men. "Since as each division passes the travel will become easier and the path better blazed, each division will carry more in supplies than the one ahead of it. The ax-handlers and pioneers will go first, carrying less but with the hardest work, and the teamsters and quartermasters will travel at the last."

With all the delays, Sam had by now met all the officers, and his only discomfort was that he was by far the youngest. Captains Thayer and Morgan and Hanchet and Goodrich were in their mid-thirties.

Colonel Greene was nearly forty. Only Captain Henry Dearborn of New Hampshire was anywhere near Sam's age, and at twenty-four he had already fought at Bunker Hill and before he joined the army began training back in Portsmouth as a doctor. Since Dearborn's company would be just in front of his, Sam hoped to have the chance to talk to him about medicine. Everyone knew who Dearborn was because wherever he went, he was followed by his large and friendly black dog, his companion since he was a boy.

Sam admitted his anxiety to Aaron Burr, who knew as well as Sam the burdens of precocity. Burr said, "Major Meigs has had his eye on all the regiments he knew would fall under his command, so let me ease your concern about one thing. He placed you fourth of his four regiments. As everyone knows, the last of a group always determines the pace of the whole. If the major had any concerns about you, he would have placed you in front to keep an eye on you, or put you second or third to be led from the front and pushed from the rear. Colonel Arnold also holds you well. If we complete our journey, they're saying this will be one of the most arduous marches since the time of the ancient Greeks. As the days pass, I expect you and I will be praising almighty God that we are not older than we are."

"What I want is to be underway," Sam said. "Each day that passes puts us farther into a cold northern season."

"Tomorrow," Burr said. "At first light."

*

IN FACT, THOUGH, SAM and his men did not leave Fort Western for days, not until the afternoon of September 27. Two divisions had to leave before them, and loading the bateaux took longer than any of them anticipated. Before they could put the bateaux in the Kennebec, they had barrels of beef, pork, fish, flour, and dried peas, firkins of butter, cones of sugar, bags of salt and yeast, rifles, muskets, cartridges, powder, shot, tents, blankets, clothing, cooking utensils, shovels, axes—provisions, on and on and on. And this was supposed to be just enough to get them to Quebec.

They made ten miles a day for the first few days, passing Fort Halifax and at last coming to the Ticonic Falls, their first carrying place. There, all of the cargo and supplies that went into the dozen bateaux now had to come out. With handspikes slipped under each bateau, four men had to raise the soggy, four-hundred-pound boats up a steep, weed-tangled, rock-strewn bank. They reloaded the boats with as much of the supplies as they thought they could carry, and then, straining under the weight of the enormous load, they made their way to the other side of the falls. They had to be relieved every few hundred yards. At day's end, there was not one of them who didn't have blistered hands and aching arms, legs, and back, not one who wasn't wet from wading the Kennebec, and not one who didn't have fingers cramped into claws.

They made it only four miles. The afternoon light thickened toward dark early, the Maine fall weather growing chill and sharp for the first time. And if their carefully chosen bateaux leaked less than others on the river, they still leaked enough to wet their tents and extra clothes. As darkness fell, the men crowded around the cookfires and slowly turned themselves to dry off one portion at a time.

*

ON THE LAST DAY of September, as the sun faded, cold settled over them with a blanket of ice. Two of Sam's eighty-four men deserted. Several more were sick.

The first barrel of beef they opened, summer killed, was rotted from top to bottom. It was pitched in the river before Sam had time to say a word.

For a time, though, they began to do better. They got more familiar with their tasks and their muscles strengthened. At Skowhegan Falls, Sam put his lieutenants in command of arranging encampments, and then went to visit Henry Dearborn. He found the young captain sitting close to a fire draped in a blanket, trying to dry out. His face was slack with fatigue but his intelligent eyes remained undulled. He nudged his large black dog to make room for Sam by the gently licking orange flames.

"Pardon me if I do not get up, Captain Ward. I cannot get my legs to follow orders. I went up behind one of those damned bateaux myself today. It's unstrung me."

Sam settled himself between the dog and the captain. "My lieutenant tells me they have run into some of Captain Goodrich's men up ahead. They report the travel from here to Norridgewalk is the easiest yet."

Sam petted the dog, who edged closer to the fire and let out a long sigh. "We could use it. Had a desertion last night. You?"

"Two."

Dearborn poked the fire. "I expect another one tonight. It's written all over him."

"How?" Sam asked.

"He's stopped complaining, which is welcome. Stopped talking with the others. And while I have half a dozen sick, he is not one of them. When he sneaks off, we'll not lift a finger to stop him."

"I have four sick ones, too." He thought about Dearborn's training as a doctor. "How do you decide who to send back?"

"I've got two who're very bad. One's got bloody flux, can't keep food or water down and fainted today at the river bank. He'd have drowned if someone hadn't pulled him out. The other one is about as yellow as this fire. Colonel Arnold requested we travel fast. Anybody too sick to walk can't be kept."

Sam described his sick men to Dearborn. He recommended one be sent back to Fort Western, the others carried forward for a day or two to see how their conditions progressed. As they talked, Sam could hear men coughing all around. "Half my men have full chests. Another third, including me, have running bowels."

"Well, I'll say this," Dearborn said. "I doubt we shall ever have an easier command than this one."

"What? *Easier*?"

"The men are too tired to make trouble."

Sam nodded. He sensed all was not right with his command, but he could not put a finger on it. And he was embarrassed to raise his concern with someone else. "I have begun to hear a few rumblings from men who can add. Colonel Arnold's calculations depend on us to make ten miles a day. We have been doing barely half that."

Dearborn nodded, his face serious.

*

WHILE TRAVELING THE NEXT day did improve, including five miles on the river as smooth as a pond, by day's end they still had barely surpassed their best distance yet, eleven miles. According to Major Meigs' map, they were in Norridgewalk, the end of the first leg of their trip. Less than one-third of the way to Quebec, the place offered only the remains of an old Abenaki village, a ruined fort, and the gravesite of a French priest. It also offered the last settlers they would see until they reached Canada. The voyage into the true wilderness had only started.

*

GUY TOOK A BREAK from unloading the bateaux—Colonel Arnold had hired caulkers to make repairs before they started again—and, wiping the back of his hand across his forehead, took a slow look around for the first time since he left Fort Western. He knew that this day he had the luxury of not having to hurry. The three divisions, all encamped at Norridgewalk, were waiting for the fourth under Colonel Enos to arrive.

It was the full blaze of fall here, and the sunlit trees along the light-sparkling river glowed red, orange, and gold. The sky looked a more brilliant blue than he had ever seen and the pine-smelling air was impossibly clear. The high raking light of the Maine fall sun brought every leaf and blade of grass into sharp focus. The trees were taller and denser, filtering the light into patches of deep cool green among the stands of firs and dotting the forest floor with scarlet and bright yellow. The hills, pine green in the distance, rolled with thick carpets of bright color. There was a scattering of birdsong and the sound of trickling water. Guy, standing by the bateaux amid the blue shadows, with the men of the regiment dozing nearby, thought he had never seen anything so beautiful in his life. He wondered if his constant feeling of foreboding was wrong. He thought of June. He missed her so much his chest hurt.

Lieutenant Shaw walked in front of him, silently inventorying the unloaded food. Guy knew nothing about numbers, but he knew, for good or for ill, they would be traveling far more lightly when they left this place. All the beef in all the divisions was rotten, inedible for anybody but Captain Dearborn's dog. The dried codfish, soaked inside even the tightest of the leaky bateaux, had lost their salt and turned to mush. It, too, was thrown away. The casks of dried peas and dried biscuit had taken on water, spoiled, and blown the staves of their barrels apart. Captain Ward told Guy that he must help recooper the barrels. At the bottom of each bateau, Guy found a thick stew of spoiled food.

All they had left was pork and flour, but not much of them.

With another two desertions in the night and another half dozen sick men who would have to be sent back, they would need fewer bateaux and have fewer men to feed. So there was that.

Guy stayed clear of Ebeneezer Tolman. Twice Tolman asked him to do chores for him, and Guy promptly fell to the tasks. This was not a hard calculation. Tolman had friends and carried a musket.

Though the air was dead still, brightly colored maple leaves released themselves from their boughs and in slow spirals eddied their way to the ground.

*

They waited a full day for Colonel Enos's men. Nothing. Captain Morgan decided to lead his division out. Colonel Greene's division followed. On October 6, just as Sam's company finished their portage above Norridgewalk Falls, he heard the first of Enos's division arriving at the camp below. Since they, too, would have to repair their boats and repack food, they would be two days behind him.

*

Better rested and traveling lighter than any time since they began the journey, Sam and his men made good time even through fast, shallow, rock-strewn waters. The men caught fish and ate their first fresh moose meat. The trees, majestic and untouched since the dawn of time, towered in thick stands all about them. They camped on an island early this first night, having caught up with Dearborn's men, and bedded down on blue-green joint grass that was as soft as a straw-stuffed bed. They made driftwood fires, roasted their freshly caught fish, looked at the velvet black of the sky, and dreamed of the success that was to come when they took Quebec.

Sam wrote to his father and his sisters, hearty upbeat notes that said all was well and indicated nothing about where he was or where he was headed. And then, pulling off by himself to the far side of the fire to be alone with his thoughts, he started to write to Phebe. The act of writing to her made her appear in his imagination with piercing vividness, her face as palpable before him as the smoke rising from his campfire. His pen hovered above the thick cream-colored vellum, and he could not think of what to say. Finally, he said the best version of the truth he could offer. *I carry with me over my chest a small volume of Horace, that grand poet who was a fine soldier. And while he reminds us how death cannot be shunned, he insists joy should not be, either. "Now I hold you in my chain, And clasp you close, all in a nightly dream." And so do I. "And when you are left, I am of myself bereft." And so am I. At all moments, Phebe, I carry thoughts of you.*

In the middle of the night, it began to rain, softly at first.

The rain continued the next day. Even at midday, the forest was thick with a dark green light. They no longer saw so much as an abandoned shack. It felt as if they were the only human beings who had ever set foot in a vast wilderness. The rain surged and slackened, surged and slackened. They pushed on.

Up ahead they rounded a bend, and as if they were growing out of the icy river itself, bloomed snowcapped mountains. Lieutenant Shaw pointed to the tallest of them, Sugar Loaf Mountain, and said that it marked the start of the Great Carrying Place. Once they crossed it, they would not have to pole and paddle upriver any longer. The water changed direction, and they could at last go with the current. Sam sent a courier to Major Meigs promising to make it to the mountain by nightfall.

As he watched the mountain all that day, Sam felt as if he were having one of those dreams where he ran toward some vital goal but never got closer. He offered his men an extra gill of rum if they picked up the pace. As they marched, the sky finally cleared, followed by the sharpest cold yet.

By dusk, they had made their best day, fourteen miles.

At the Great Carrying Place's first of three portages, Colonel Arnold himself passed Sam's company. He left orders for Sam and Captain Dearborn to pull ten men from their units to help McCobb build a block house for the sick and as a supply depot. No sooner was it thrown together—and named Fort Meigs—than it was full of very sick men, including two men from Sam's company. He left them with a young surgeon's mate who said he was on his own there until Dr. Ervin came back.

"Where is Ervin?" Sam asked.

"Building a hospital at the next portage."

The next morning a driving northeast wind delayed crossings on all three ponds. With it were occasional thick pieces of snow. While they waited to cross, Sam sent his men in two hour shifts to improve the portage in back of them to make it easier for Enos's division coming up behind.

That night, the wind howled with such force it was hard to sleep. They awoke to the news that it had blown a tree down on one of McCobb's men, crushing his ribcage. Colonel Enos reported there was no chance the man would survive. Everyone grew quiet.

They crossed the pond in bateaux, prepared for their second portage, and Sam, at Dearborn's request, went to check on three men Dearborn had to leave behind at Dr. Ervin's hospital.

The sickest man there, barely conscious, covered in his own filth and swarming with insects, was Dr. Ervin.

Chapter Fifteen

Major Meigs brought new orders that effective tomorrow, Sunday, everyone was going to be placed on short rations. Colonel Arnold expected that they would be able to supplement their rations with fresh fish, moose meat, and anything else they could harvest from the surrounding rich forests.

After three more punishing portages, Major Meigs promised them a reward for their labors, and once the last boat was across, they found it. The last two oxen of the division had been killed and quartered. Sam's company was given permission to camp and feed. As they roasted their portion, a full company from Colonel Greene's division, ninety strong, marched rearward to help Enos catch up. Sam and his men also hoped the reward would include messages from home, but none awaited them.

The next day, he and his rejuvenated men made an extraordinary twenty-one miles on the Dead River. To celebrate, that night they broke out their last supplies of rum and whiskey. His men safely encamped, the alcohol rising pleasantly to his brain, Sam decided to head up to Colonel Greene's tent a quarter mile upriver. He had not spoken to him since they had left Fort Western, and he knew he might not be this close again anytime soon. If anyone would, perhaps he would have word of news from home.

He found the colonel quickly enough. He was sitting alone outside his tent, his lean face drawn-looking in the firelight. Sam greeted him.

Colonel Greene slowly raised his head, nodded, and invited him to have a seat. Sam was startled at the dark hollows under his eyes. He offered him some coffee. Sam declined. Gloom was suddenly as vividly present as another guest at the fire.

"Are you unwell, sir?"

Greene shook his head. "Remember Colonel Arnold's optimistic view of the rest of our march?" Sam nodded, feeling a clammy embrace by Greene's dark mood. "It was based on Lieutenant Steele's scouting. Steele left some of his party behind to jerk some moose. They showed up a few days ago," he said quietly. "They were half-starved."

"Starved," Sam repeated.

"These are riflers, tough forest men. They could find not so much as a ground squirrel. Not a rabbit. Not a fish. The only living thing they saw for days was a yellow-eyed wolf. I saw two of the men myself. Young Private Henry and tough old Sergeant Boyd staggering out of the woods, faces filthy, jaws thick with beard. They wept, the both of them, at finding us."

Sam gave a long, low sigh.

The colonel threw another stick on the fire. "And we now have two impossible demands. We are told to make speed for the Chaudiere and help clear the passage across the Height of Land. But we cannot possibly go forward without provisions from Colonel Enos." He poked the fire. A few sparks lifted from it, fading quickly.

Sam looked up at the starless sky and felt a sudden wash of cold that penetrated his coat. Most of the men he passed in Greene's division had no tents and were sleeping in brush huts or out on the open ground. "Smells like rain," Sam said.

Greene nodded. After a minute, the colonel added, "Boyd and Henry say Steele told them that it will be one hundred and fifty miles before we will see another human being."

*

Sam's company left in the rain on October 19, hoping to make long daily distances on the quiet of the Dead River.

It rained for three days without break. The waters of the river began to stir to life, slowing the men to an exhausted crawl. By the time they made camp on Saturday, the wind began to pick up, stripping the trees of their last leaves. As they took shelter for the night, word reached them that Colonel Greene's entire division still had not gotten food from Enos and they remained stuck a full thirty miles behind.

*

Guy, like everyone else, was dizzy with weariness, but sleep was hard to come by. The wind kept rising, howling him up out of a doze. Finally, in the dead middle of the night, he found himself sitting bolt upright listening in terror to the sound of trees being uprooted and crashing down near him in the forest. The first thought that entered his mind: the only man killed so far in the march was crushed by a falling tree.

He peered through his thin covering of pine branches. Lieutenant Shaw and Sergeant Boynton were screaming and gesturing at them to move closer to the river and away from the densest stands of trees. Guy moved, pulling his blanket and branches with him. He bedded again on the cold, wet ground, and, despite the roar of the wind, sank into sleep like lead in water.

Suddenly he heard the screams of men from Dearborn's and Goodrich's companies upriver. He felt in the earth under the entire length of his body a strange rumbling and heard a roar deeper than anything he had ever heard in his life.

This time Captain Ward and Lieutenant Clark were yelling for them to move *away* from the river. The roar and alarmed cries grew louder.

"Flood!" came a scream out of the tumult and darkness. "Flood!"

Some men were too tired to move quickly, others did not hear the orders over the wind, and still others were desperately trying to save supplies when the roaring, muddy cataract of water swept down on them. Guy, who had gone into the forest itself, was still pulled off his feet and smashed into a tree. He came up in the shockingly cold water sputtering, grabbing at bushes, ropes, roots, anything, trying desperately to snag onto a point of stillness above the foaming flood. His hands, slick with mud and water, slipped. Finally, he wedged himself between two trees with a tent pole. He saw three heads bobbing on the waters of where the riverbank used to be. They vanished downstream and out of sight.

A cold dawn showed them the water had risen eight feet. The spot where Guy first lay his branches down for sleep, pocked with drizzle, was under three feet of water. Men, drenched and dragged downstream, scattered off in search of lost bateaux, began to straggle back. Amazingly—miraculously, the captain said—no one was missing. It was probably the only good news. Clothes, tents, food, guns, and cash had all been swept away. Many of the bateaux were gone or smashed beyond repair.

The clouds thinned. Arriving with the gray outlines of daylight, through the bare trees a cold, biting wind knifed in from the northwest. Shivering and wet to the skin, the men found not a single campfire they could use to dry themselves.

Everything Guy found was broken, torn, or spoiled. The weather steadily grew colder. Captain Ward, eyeing the sky distrustfully, decided to lead a detachment ahead and into the woods to find burnable materials for their evening campsite.

Guy wished he had been chosen to go into the woods. Instead, he was left with Ebeneezer Tolman and thirty other men to march on shore. As soon as the captain disappeared, he heard Ebeneezer Tolman's voice.

"I think the nig has cursed us."

Guy's stomach tightened. For a long time there was no response. He thought perhaps no one heard or cared. Then someone said, "Cursed us?"

"What d'ye think he carries in that pouch around his waist?" Tolman asked. "Spells and magic. Never takes it off, not even to shit."

"What about Ware's lucky coin? Bartram's rabbit foot? That square of your sister's needlepoint? More curse material? Let it rest, Tolman."

"I've seen him out there in the trees, making marks on the ground and mumblin' words. I've seen him."

Another voice said, "Think he's Catholic then, Eb?"

Several men laughed, then coughed.

"Day he arrived at Fort Western, they sent that Maine boy back for hanging."

No one said anything this time.

The next morning, two of the men looked over at Guy for an extra second. He averted his eyes. Before, he had been able to move among them as unremarked as a horse or dog.

✷

On Monday, October 23, the skies cleared and the river dropped. They pushed on, making enough progress to catch up with Morgan's division.

Sam was preparing for sleep when the messenger came.

He, Major Meigs, and all the captains of the division had been summoned forward to Shadagee Falls. They were going to meet with Colonel Arnold for a Council of War. Sam was instantly wide awake.

✷

As he made his way through the trail of campfires toward Shadagee Falls, Sam saw that all the other soldiers were in tough shape, too. In the dim yellow light of several fires near the command tent, Aaron Burr and some other men were standing at the river's edge, looking grimly into the water. Burr's prettily handsome face had grown gaunt and his once-pink skin was mottled grayish brown. It occurred to Sam he must look the same way. "What happened here?" he asked.

Burr glanced at him, his mouth drawn tightly down. "Seven fully laden bateaux went over." He pointed into the dark waters. "Food, money, clothes, guns. Gone."

Sam looked into the river. He had been planning to ask Colonel Arnold to help make up for his own lost supplies. His company had started with sixteen bateaux. They were now down to four. Ahead was a chain of ponds for which bateaux were the only means of travel. When he looked up from the swirling current, Major Meigs told him the Council was about to begin.

After Reverend Spring said a short prayer, Colonel Arnold told Burr to make certain there were no enlisted men near enough to the tent to eavesdrop. "We must have free and open communication, gentlemen," he said "Any disagreement must remain between ourselves." As he waited for Burr to return, he looked at each officer, his hands behind his back. His eyes were serious and he showed none of his usual physical restlessness. Burr stepped back in the tent and nodded.

"The first question we must consider is whether, under the present circumstances, we should turn back."

There was a moment's silence. Sam thought it was one of surprise to have a question that was on everyone's mind posed so bluntly. There was a brief murmuring followed by a chorus of "no!"

Colonel Arnold looked relieved. His mouth drew into a fierce line. He began pacing, slowly at first, his hands still locked behind his back. "Excellent. We need to send back all the sick and feeble to Norridgewalk, pull Enos forward, cut loose any who are faint of heart. And we need to get food."

Another chorus of assent.

In the meantime, he asked, how could they make it to the French settlements on such short supplies?

"Fast as we can," Captain Morgan said, facing the other officers. "Remind your men that Mrs. Grier and Mrs. Warner are doing fine in our division, and I am told they are working as hard as anyone else."

Major Meigs said, "To speak of my men, Colonel. They don't need encouragement so much as their bellies filled. And Lieutenant Steele may have seen plentiful game on his canoe trip, but no army who cuts trees, drags bateaux, and marches through woods is going to see an animal of any stripe. Too much noise."

Sam, Hanchet, Goodrich, and Dearborn nodded.

Arnold said, "How about this, gentlemen. Let us pick fifty hearty men to march under Captain Hanchet at full speed for the Chaudiere River. There they can get provisions from the inhabitants and send the supplies back in a flying relief column." He turned to Hanchet. "Captain?"

Though Sam wished he had himself been chosen, it was hard to quarrel with the choice of the tough and determined Hanchet. Hanchet said, "Yessir. We'll make it."

"And we must get all spare supplies sent up from Colonel Enos."

Sam said, "We are told that Colonel Greene is having great difficulty getting his division properly supplied by Colonel Enos. May I suggest, Colonel, that you put your request to Enos in a direct, written order?"

Arnold frowned, nodded, and turned to his adjutant and told him to see that Captain Ward's suggestion was carried out. He concluded with a fine speech about their assault on Quebec, but Sam was too tired and hollow-stomached to thrill to it. As the colonel said good night to each officer in turn as they left the tent, Sam thought Arnold did a good job under the circumstances. Yes, they were supposed to already have reached settlements by now, but who could have foreseen floods, storms, and so many lost bateaux?

*

THEY MADE POOR PROGRESS for several days. In the morning, out of nowhere, a skinny, somber, bespectacled man from Enos's medical personnel came by, asking how his men were. Sam thought he might be Dr. Church's old assistant, but with thousands of faces having passed before him in the last few months, he could not be sure. The man talked to Sam's servant in low tones for a minute and then moved on.

They woke up the next morning to three inches of snow on the ground.

Just as Sam was about to get the men underway, Colonel Greene appeared in camp. He was by himself, not even an aide in sight.

"Colonel?" Sam asked.

"Where is Colonel Arnold?" Greene asked, his face unreadable.

"Ahead with Captain Hanchet. He would be a day or two's journey from here." Greene's brows pinched together. "Why?"

The colonel spoke quietly. "My division has sent back fifty sick men. Fifty. But Colonel Enos reports he is too short on provisions to supply the rest of us. After I last saw you, we waited on Colonel Enos *for six days*. He gave us two barrels of flour. Doctor Senter tells me that last night some of our men were eating melted candles for the tallow." He peered up the river at the dark, looming bulk of the mountains. Snow blew about, obscuring their tops. "How far to the Height of Land?"

"About twenty miles."

Greene lowered his head, composed himself with a visible effort, and then straightened. "Twenty miles. For my division, about twenty-five. And to the French settlements?"

"Another hundred," replied Sam.

"And Colonel Arnold cannot be contacted."

"Not immediately."

"That is a problem." The colonel paused and looked at Sam in the way someone does who is about to give very bad news. "Colonel Enos has called for a Council of War this noon."

Sam's stomach dropped. "He got Colonel Arnold's written order?" Colonel Greene nodded. "There is no need for a Council. There is only the need to go forward."

"Colonel Enos has been skillful in making himself unavailable to us. He and his men have hung back for weeks. Why now, on this snowy day, are he and all his officers suddenly pushing forward?" He took a breath and rubbed his temple, the same gesture his cousin Nat used when he was worried.

"Should we send an express to Arnold?"

"Too late for that. But can you return with me, Sam? Leave one of your lieutenants in charge. We are just short of the falls at the last encampment."

"I can, but what service can I be?"

"Captain Hubbard is sick. My guess is that this Council will be asked to vote on some questions. I would like my men fairly represented on whatever matter is raised. Your vote will ensure that happens."

Sam agreed. With fewer men to command, only three bateaux left to haul, and two able lieutenants, he did not doubt his company could part with him. He dispatched a messenger to Major Meigs to inform him of his plans and instructed Lieutenants Shaw and Clark to advance as quickly as they could despite the snow and strong currents.

As he and Colonel Greene made their way back through Hubbard's, Thayer's, and Topham's companies, he saw they were even worse off than the men of his own division. Skin and bone, their clothes in tatters, with no tents and almost no food, these men were marching north, Council or no Council.

He also saw at the rear of the line the eighty sick men who were making their way back to receive medical care. It was hard for Sam not to picture what an effect this parade of illness-ravaged bodies might have had on Enos's skittish men.

"Who will be in the chair of this Council?" Sam asked.

"Colonel Enos. He has called for the meeting." Sam was just about to object when the colonel added, "It also means he cannot vote."

Sam looked again at Colonel Greene. As his own father used to do with the General Assembly, the colonel, he could tell, had been counting noses.

By the time they made it to Colonel Greene's command tent, Colonel Enos and his officers were already there.

*

This Council was thick with the unsaid. Where Colonel Arnold laid out the main concerns directly and bluntly, Colonel Enos, looking tired and old, sidled up to them. He gave a long speech about the difficulties of the march and the morale of the men. He listed all the problems they had encountered and the unforeseen delays. Finally, he held up Colonel Arnold's orders and settled some reading glasses on his nose. "I am told here," he said, reading, "'to proceed with as many of the best men of your division you can furnish with fifteen days' provisions.' The problem, gentleman, is that we do not have enough food to furnish *any* men with fifteen days' provisions without instantly starving all the rest."

Colonel Greene's officers looked at Colonel Enos's officers. Dirty, yes. Tired, yes. However, none of them looked as drawn and pared of flesh as Topham's, Thayer's, Bigelow's, Ward's, and Greene's officers.

There was an uncomfortable silence. It was Major Timothy Bigelow who said, his voice flat, "Your division has had the most supplies and food of the entire army. Coming last, you have had the best directions and clearest paths. Morgan's, Greene's and Meigs' divisions have all preceded you. You have encamped in places where the fires still burned and the huts had been built. We have sent back relief columns for you. Colonel Arnold's orders are clear. I am at a loss to understand why any of us was here in this Council when we should be marching north."

Captain Williams of Enos's division said, "My company did a full inventory this morning. We have five days' provisions left. Colonel Arnold says we need fifteen days. The trip has already taken longer than he expected. What if he is wrong again?"

"You don't suppose," Simeon Thayer said, "that your men have undercounted their supplies or hidden away some private portions?"

"You don't suppose," Enos's Captain McCobb said, "that with one hundred and fifty additional sick men to feed, most of them sent back by their companies unprovisioned, we don't have burdens your divisions do not?" Sam knew McCobb had fought all day at Bunker Hill. He was a brave man, and giving these excuses was obviously difficult for him.

Sam felt a sudden uneasy grip of responsibility. It was his suggestion that Colonel Arnold put his orders in writing for Colonel Enos—Enos having already ignored oral requests a dozen times. But Enos was using his supposed inability to comply with one aspect of the written orders—fifteen days' supply—to question the whole enterprise.

"If we don't have enough food," Sam said, "we can find some. Today's snow is perfect for tracking." He saw this observation was listlessly received, and so he decided to cut directly to the question Enos had dragged them all here to consider. "Colonel Enos, if I understand you, you are considering turning back. Is that correct?" A tense silence fell in the crowded tent, and Sam could hear several of the men breathing.

"All of us wish to go forward," said Colonel Enos. "The question here is whether, under the circumstances, that is possible."

Enos's Captain Scott added, "I want more than anything to go on. The truth is, my men will not follow me."

Sam reflected for a moment and was willing to think both these things might be true. He knew, though, that did not change what must be done. “It is our duty,” he said, “our lawful obligation as soldiers, to comply with Colonel Arnold’s orders.”

Colonel Greene spoke for the first time. “Captain Ward is right. Following every provision of Colonel Arnold’s orders is not a matter for debate. We are ordered to go forward. We are to send back the weak and the ill with a humane minimum of provisions and divide the rest equally among us. For the rest, we will have to trust Providence to see us to safety.” A murmur of assent rumbled through the tent. As it subsided, an ashen-faced Captain Hubbard made his appearance unsteadily in the tent.

Major Bigelow called for a vote. Everyone knew it would be six to five to continue. Suddenly Enos’s Lieutenant Buckmaster was called inside to join his fellow lieutenants Hyde and Peters. The vote was now six to six, and Colonel Greene’s prediction of the chair having to vote came to pass.

Colonel Enos removed his glasses, sighed, and pinched the bridge of his nose. Sam’s stomach sank. He glanced at Christopher Greene, wondering why he wanted Enos to have to vote. And then he got it. If Enos voted to return to Cambridge in opposition to a direct written order from his superior, he would be on record as supporting a mutiny. A court-martial would be a sure thing.

“I vote,” said Colonel Enos, “that we continue our march north. That is my personal wish and private choice.” There were groans of dismay from his officers. They slumped in their chairs. Greene’s officers glanced at each other and nodded their heads in tight-lipped approval. “It is my order, however,” Enos continued, “that my division make its own choice, independent of me, whether to go forward or return.”

So there it was. Enos was protecting himself against a military court’s judgment. Everyone knew by the looks of guilty gratitude on his officers’ faces what their “choice” would be. And Sam had lived too long among courts and politicians not to know how the rest would play out.

Enos's men parleyed and voted unanimously to turn back. They also pleaded for Enos to return with them and help them face whatever fate would confront them. If they made it back, Sam knew they would all face a court-martial. He also knew that with the remainder of the army heading north, the only witnesses available to testify would be those who had returned, putting the best possible face on Enos's decision.

Sam wondered if Enos had this all worked out in advance. He supposed not. Some of his captains like McCobb probably did wish to go on. Sam knew he would never forgive these men—but it was more for what happened after the meeting.

Enos sighed and said it was his duty to remain behind with his men.

They agreed to share their supplies with the men who were going on, promising four hundred pounds of pork and eight hundred pounds of flour. But the next day, when Captain Thayer came downriver, Enos's men reneged. They would not share anything after all.

Enos's men had decided overnight that they had farther going back to civilization than the others did going forward.

Sam found as he made his way north that he was in no hurry to catch up to his company. He was bearing the news that, against orders, an entire division had turned back, taking with them all their supplies and ammunition and, if you counted the sick, almost half the men. From over a thousand effective men who left Cambridge, at a single stroke they now were scarcely over five hundred.

Along with that news was the fact that all of them could starve, and that it could happen soon.

Chapter Sixteen

Sam made his way back in the face of a biting north wind, uphill, laboring across swamps and bogs and so many ponds he lost count. Towering before him were the huge and jagged crenellations of the Height of Land. He passed two "blow-downs," several-acre plots where every tree in the thick forest had been blown flat by some extraordinary wind.

He wondered if any of them would reach Quebec alive. As he plodded, he listened for a voice in his head, anyone's: God's, his father's, his mother's, Nat Greene's, or even Phebe's telling him what he might do, what he might say. Nothing. He heard nothing but the endless whoosh of the cold wind through the desolate forest.

He found his men at the last pond, all of them so ragged there was no way to tell an officer from a private. They were glad to see him, something they conveyed with looks of guarded relief and short nods, salutes having been abandoned weeks ago. He heard a few of them saying to friends, "He's back." And then they went about their business. In Sam's absence, they had received orders from Colonel Arnold to take only one bateaux for the sick and for transporting large essentials and to leave the rest behind. Lieutenant Shaw said it was odd to have dragged the damned things all this way only to leave them right when the traveling was going to become all downstream. Lieutenant Clark added that Colonel Arnold reported that land passage would be preferable. Clark shrugged, "And he ought to know."

"He ought," Sylvanus Shaw said. "But Captain Morgan has ordered his men to take 'em anyway. He wants them all to float their way downriver."

A number of men began to gather around their returned captain. Sam took a slow look around and, pulling in a breath, decided now was the time. No matter how he worded this announcement, it would be a great blow.

"Colonel Greene's division will be joining us soon," he said flatly. "The three companies of Colonel Enos's division have grown discouraged. They turned back." He held his face expressionless, determined not to show them his own loss of hope.

There was a stunned silence that stretched so long, Sam wondered if he made himself understood. Finally, the mild and soft-spoken Sylvanus Shaw said, "Those filthy bastards." In a few seconds, the weary men filled the air with profanity.

Having feared the silence of despair, Sam was so relieved at their outburst his eyes stung with tears.

*

BEFORE NOON THE NEXT day, the men climbed their way to the Height of Land. They descended into a spacious green meadow as open and as welcoming as the Westerly green. Already there, sprawled and dozing in the fall sun, was Captain Morgan's division. Colonel Greene's division, making excellent time—and no doubt driven by fear of starvation—joined them by midafternoon. It was the first time what was left of the army had been together at a single spot since they left Fort Western. Morgan and his men, still exhausted from hauling all their bateaux around blow-downs and up the mountainous passes, decided to encamp on the greensward until morning.

Sam, Goodrich, and Dearborn decided to put their companies in the lead at last.

Who was where and at what hour became important to Sam later when he tried to reconstruct the next three days. They were days that nearly destroyed their entire army.

Two hours after the last of them marched as fast as possible into the woods along the river, an express arrived from Colonel Arnold. It concluded with a warning that Arnold underlined with a thick stroke of pen. By no means, he wrote, should they keep to the river. It was a river *which will carry you into a swamp out of which it will be impossible for you to get.* They were instead instructed to follow the guide and bearer of the letter, Issac Hull, to Lake Megantic. Not having heard the news about Enos's division desertion, Arnold also sent a separate and unknowingly pointless letter to Colonel Enos with instructions on how to attend to the sick, concluding, *I hope to see you soon in Quebec.*

Colonel Greene dispatched a messenger to recall Sam, Dearborn, Smith, and Goodrich.

Not only did the messenger fail to reach them, he was never seen again.

*

BY NIGHTFALL, SAM FOUND himself the head of three captainless companies. Captains Dearborn and Goodrich went off by canoe in search of Goodrich's food-bearing bateau. Smith's company had disappeared in their bateaux downriver. The rest of them were stuck on a small knoll in the middle of a swamp with enough firewood for one fire. The men of three companies crowded round it, their breath coming out in white plumes, hoping to dry themselves before their clothes froze to their skin.

The next morning, in a cold dawn, Sam ordered his company to stretch their supplies to try to feed all three companies. He could see that his own men were outraged at having to share their terrifyingly small supply of food with other companies, some of whom were hiding their own food in order to use others'. He surveyed the camp in a glance in the gray morning light. There would be fights if they remained in place any longer. He ordered everyone out. Stuffing their knapsacks, the men headed in the direction the lake was supposed to be.

Just as they filed out, appearing from some tiny stream they could barely see through the thick forest were Dearborn and Goodrich in their birch canoe. They announced the welcome news that they somehow had found the right lake. They also had bad news. All three companies would have to be ferried across two rivers in their single, small, flimsy Abenaki canoe to get there.

After five hours, only a fragment of the three companies made it across the first river. If they made it across that river, there would be a second. After that would be thirteen miles of lake. Some men, following the example of Captain Ward's African servant, started digging for roots to eat. He pointed out what was safe. They could find no fish and no game.

*

EBENEEZER TOLMAN LOOKED AT the men who were imitating Guy Watson and said, "It's the nig, I tell you. Has he been sick? Look at 'im. Has he lost an ounce of weight in all this time? He's hale as a fuckin' horse. I tell you, he's hiding food. He's cursed us. He's put a spell on Enos's men and he got us lost in these woods, and if he keeps on with us, we're all going to be dead. Send him back. Send him forward. Send him away or," his hand tightened on his musket and he looked at Guy with murderously narrowed eyes, "who knows what'll happen to him."

Guy looked for Captain Ward. He was far ahead talking with Captain Dearborn. There was neither a lieutenant nor a sergeant anywhere near. Men were looking at him, and suddenly his face grew hot with anger. He straightened from the lovage and snakeroot he was digging. "You t'ink I can make spells and curses, an' you still alive?"

The other men were silent for a second and then burst out laughing. Eb Tolman's face swelled and he came running forward in a furious rush, swinging his gun butt like a club. Guy stepped back and leaned away from the blow, but the weapon still caught him across the forehead. He felt the thunk on his skull, saw a flash of red and gray light, and tasted something like tar. A warm trickle of blood ran down his temple.

Two men grabbed Tolman's arms before he could swing again. When he calmed down, they slowly let him loose. He pointed a finger at Guy as if it were a pistol. "Watch your mouth, nig," Tolman said.

*

At that moment, Colonel Greene, Major Meigs, and Captain Hendrick's riflers were in worse shape than Sam's. Their guide, Isaac Hull, had taken a wrong turn. While Morgan's men were making their way across Lake Megantic, Meigs and Greene were one mile away. At the wrong lake.

Order disappeared. Companies dissolved into fragments. Those who could walk fastest did. Others fell farther and farther behind in the vast cold forest.

*

Morgan and his men, exhausted from hauling bateaux, crossed Lake Megantic and were careening down the Chaudiere River. Going full speed through a foaming, tumultuous passage, one after another, Morgan's boats were shattered. Gasping men floundered through the rips and rocks and tons of oncoming water toward shore. A man named George Innis was snagged on a tree branch six inches under the surface. They found him downstream with his eyes and mouth both stuck wide open as if in astonishment, glass-smooth water washing over him. Behind Morgan's boats, Smith's and Goodrich's bateaux were also completely destroyed one after another.

The name of the place was Talons du Diable. Just downstream were the wrecks of Arnold's bateaux and the remains of one of his canoes. These rapids, and the falls after them, were exactly why he sent word ordering the men not to haul their bateaux for water travel. The falls, a quarter of a mile further down from the rapids, would have killed not just George Innis. It would have killed all of them.

*

It took Sam, Dearborn, and the others three full days to find the lake that was only six miles from the sunny green meadow where they all loitered a brief while.

They awoke on the morning of October 31—where some thought the earth would exhale spirits of the dead at nightfall—to the coldest temperatures yet. Lieutenant Clark brought Sam the news he has been dreading: five men in his company could not continue the march. They were too sick.

"Can they march at all?" Sam asked.

"None of them more than an hour, sir."

Sam's hands and feet burned with cold. He pulled his long coat tighter around him and banged his arms against himself.

He looked at his feet and clenched his jaws. Everyone knew Colonel Arnold's order. Those who could not keep up were to be left behind.

"Assemble the company," Sam said.

"Here?"

"No. Near the five men. And Lieutenant, wait until the sun is up a little higher. I want everyone to be able to see this."

He had a request no one was going to want to fulfill. Last night they had gotten Arnold's last message. No help would be coming for at least three more days.

Sam's men slowly assembled. Many of them were shivering and rubbing their hands, hoping to generate some warmth. Sam stood in front of them. Half the men had no shoes and wrapped their feet in rags. Along the way, some had wrapped their feet in old hides, but all of them were roasted, boiled, and eaten in the last forty-eight hours. They had eaten shaving soap, candles, shot pouches, lip salve, and tent waterproofing. Behind Sam, sitting weakly or lying flat out on the ground, were the five sick men: Jacob True, Elijah Dole, William Dorr, Jabez Brooks, and Bishop Standley.

Sam said their names slowly, one at a time. "These men cannot go forward with us today. If we go as slow as our slowest, all of us may die. If we go as fast as possible—faster than possible—we can reach the relief column that much sooner." He looked at the emaciated, bearded, grimy faces of his ragged company. "Then we can send back food and medical assistance sooner." He cleared his throat and raised his voice so the men farthest away could hear him. He extended a hand behind him. "Jacob True. Elijah Dole. William Dorr. Jabez Brooks. Bishop Standley. They have been with us through forests and flood, mud and snow, up streams and down waterfalls. They were lost when we were lost, found when we were found." He paused, breathing in the still air of the freezing dawn. "Some of you have food left. Not much, I know. But by the grace of God, we will be supplied before long. These five men will not."

He asked Tom Shepherd for his old slouch hat and banged it clean against his thigh. From his own tiny and carefully preserved supply, he put in a handful of oats. He passed the hat on to his lieutenants. They added some flour and passed it on. Men raked out the bottom of their pouches with their fingernails and carefully pulled out their pockets, sighing—some groaning—as they scraped together the last of their food. When the hat came back, it was almost full.

The company marched out a few minutes later. Sam left last, setting the hat down next to Jacob True, Elijah Dole, William Dorr, Jabez Brooks, and Bishop Standley. "We will be back," he promised. "Or we will send those who can travel fast." The men, hollow-eyed, sick, and weak, two of them with faces mottled a terrible yellow with jaundice, thanked him and apologized for holding them up and taking their food. They wished him the best. To show them how determined he was that they were not to be left for lost, Sam left them a ribboned stack of the letters he had written to his family, the most personal items a person could entrust. And when he invoked the Lord's blessing on them, Elijah Dole, who had been fighting all morning to maintain his composure, burst into racking sobs.

Sad, embarrassed, helpless, and angry, Sam headed out to rejoin his marching company, damning Colonel Enos with every step.

*

He and his remaining men made it fifteen miles along the deeply cut channel of the Chaudiere, a distance that would have been hard for them on their first day. Sam's and Dearborn's companies were far ahead of what remained of Arnold's army. Morgan's division, having lost their bateaux and supplies at the Great Falls, were stripped and shattered. Goodrich and his company no longer functioned as a military unit at all and pressed forward as a mob.

*

On November 1, they awakened to a thin blanket of new snow. Hunger, for most of them, no longer had the sharpness of a knife in the belly. It passed into a dull ache. Their brains lost clarity and their legs weakened. Lieutenant Shaw slipped on a patch of snow and went straight down the embankment and into the river. He would have drowned had Guy Watson not pulled him out.

Sam, plodding forward, was aware of a kind of billowing faintness of mind. He tried to keep his company together, but as the day proceeded, they began to string further and further out from one another. They passed several stragglers from Dearborn's and Smith's companies, including the beautiful twenty-three-year-old Mrs. Warner. She was tending to her exhausted, skeletally thin husband. Sam stopped for a moment next to them. Sergeant James Warner's eyes were closed and under a thin blanket his narrow chest was rising and falling in tiny rapid movements. The last time Sam saw him for any length of time was back at Fort Western, when the then-handsome twenty-five-year-old was as vigorous as a Highland pony. Now, the sockets around his sunken eyes seemed enormous.

He recognized in Mrs. Warner's expressionless, dry-eyed, hollow-cheeked face what he had seen in every man on the march in the last few days: a drained sense of detachment by people who had reached the furthest limits of human endurance.

"Is there anything I can do?" Sam asked.

She shook her head. "He cannot go another step."

Sam nodded. "We will send you relief the moment we reach inhabitants." It took him a long time to get these words out. His speech had slowed and tongue thickened. He hoped for Mrs. Warner that Colonel Greene's division might be able to offer some assistance—though he believed her husband was very likely beyond help.

They marched forward. Some of the men swayed and lurched as if drunk. Shadows lengthened, raking sharply in the thin northern light. In the late afternoon, they passed twenty of Goodrich's men who had three kettles cooking over two fires.

Sam saw a heap of black fur. He knew without asking. They had eaten Dearborn's black labrador. They had ground the dog's bones into a slurry and were making a soup of it, preparing to eat it, too. Tough old Tom Shepherd, who loved dogs better than people, stopped and stared. His face suddenly wrenched up in pain, he gave a dry sob, and, stumbling a bit, he turned to march on. One of Goodrich's men lamely called out, "It's a bear," but everyone knew better.

*

The November night was cloud-covered and less cold than on recent nights. In the morning, after a thin exhausted sleep, Sam gathered what was left of his scattered company and went forward. Anything beyond a slow, leaden walk left him winded and faint. Just before noon, the sun having grown warm and bright, two men collapsed within five minutes of each other. Only one of them was able to go on. The remaining men dropped their equipment as they shuffled forward. Occasionally, he or his lieutenants, their weary voices hoarse, would try to cheer the men up with what a great tale this would all make to tell their grandchildren. But soon they lacked the spirit to talk. As the day passed, he could tell he was tapping into his own last reserves. The trees and landscape began to leave gray-green traceries behind as they swam past. An ache ballooned inside his skull. He forced himself to drink some cold water and chew on a root Guy Watson had given him. He had not been hungry or thirsty in three days.

Up ahead along the winding river, he saw movement. He figured they must have caught up with Dearborn. Lieutenant Shaw stopped and took out his field glass. Sam did not like stopping, afraid he would not be able to start again, but something in the tenseness of his lieutenant's body indicated he should. When Sam stopped next to him, the entire line of men gathered slowly behind them.

"What?" Sam asked.

Sylvanus Shaw's voice cracked with emotion. "Two horses. Some horned cattle. Half a dozen men. A relief party."

Some men wept, others hugged each other. Eb Tolman took out some food he had kept hidden and wolfed it down. Sam, who had seen George Innis's body streaming water as it was dragged onto shore and Mrs. Warner's dying husband's fluttering breath, and had prayed for the five weak and suffering men they had to leave behind, suddenly could not stop thinking about Dearborn's dog. While his men were feeling surges of joy, Sam was all at once ambushed by a crushing sense of grief about, of all things, the poor pink-tongued black animal that Henry Dearborn had brought with him to stave off loneliness.

Chapter Seventeen

June had never been to Newport before. She had never been on a boat, even on a little packet like the one that at the moment ferried her and Master John to Little Rest across Narragansett Bay. The winter winds gusting across the water were sharp, piercing her coat and neck kerchief. She stared nervously at the greenish gray water sliding by just a few feet away from her and blew white-plumed breath into her cupped hand. Master Hazzard had insisted he needed the money from her winter leasing. Mistress Elizabeth wanted to send Lucy, but the Hazzards no longer trusted her. And they knew that June would never consider risking herself with Guy Watson away. "This master," Master Hazzard warned, "expects real work to be done." Simon Pease had wanted Guy back again, or, failing him, some other man. But men were in short supply.

The sun on the water broke into a thousand bright points, and each of them felt like a stab of anxiety. She missed Guy. She was frightened just by the idea of a big city, and she was told Newport was one of the largest in the country.

As the boat began to draw closer to the wharves, they could see, looming off the island's point, eight armed British ships with their gunports open. Their red and white flags luffed in the breeze. Huge and silent, their decks dotted with men, the enormous black vessels looked like floating forts.

As their packet pulled in and its sails were dropped, June saw a great knot of people clustered on shore, all of them staring anxiously right at them. She wondered if they were waiting for mail or some special passenger. She saw no one among the few other passengers aboard who was striking, so she glanced behind them to see if some other vessel was due to arrive soon. Nothing. Then she saw that all the people were carrying trunks, crates, and sacks, and kept looking at the men-of-war like field hands looked for lightning under a lowering thundercloud.

She and the Hazzards were barely able to clear the deck before the Newporters began to pour aboard. Though they were dead silent, June could smell the fear.

As the three of them made their way to the new winter master's house on Mary Lane, June tried to avoid stepping in the garbage and bumping the hens that foraged on the cobbled streets. All the while she gaped at the remarkable place around her, her home for who knew how long.

Newport's houses, all huddled close together, were dyed in bright red, blue, green, and yellow. Most houses had pigs, cows, and chickens in their tiny yards. They passed two huge houses made entirely from red brick and three enormous wooden churches. And then they passed the brick Market Place at the foot of a large, open green Master John called the Newport Parade.

Master John said to the mistress, his voice full of astonishment, "Where is everyone? This place is always loud with the crying of wares!" Though he was not loud, his voice echoed off the street. "Look. Even the wharves are still. No brigantines, no schooners, not even a snow getting fitted…" He swept a hand around at the silent scene. "Look at this," he repeated, now in a hoarse, amazed whisper, shaking his head. "Simon said it was bad."

Mistress Hazzard looked down the street in the other direction and peered at the row of stately sea captains' houses along the water. "Look!" she said.

"What?"

"You said there would be a dozen homes with pineapples atop the front post to announce the captains' return."

The master paused and looked at the empty posts. "Either they are not making it to the Sugar Islands for the trading of slaves, or they are not making it back." He continued to look down the row. "Winter is the season they put 'em out—no rot and no wasps nesting in them."

Long ago, Quamino had explained to June how the trade worked: the islands sold the molasses that the Rhode Islanders made into rum. They used the rum to buy slaves in Africa, and then they sold them in the Sugar Islands for money and molasses, and then the three-sided trade started all over again.

She looked for the place Guy had told them about, the house made entirely of glass where they grew amazing flowers, some of them looking like a woman's sex. And she looked for the stores that sold tubes you could look through that brought far away things very close, even stars! She didn't see them, but she did see a store selling dresses that made a woman's waist smaller than a man's thigh, but her hooped hips look as big as the top of a hogshead. Just as Guy said, she saw black servants dressed as well as Master John himself! She saw no evidence of the free blacks he spoke of, but then she wondered how she would know even if she saw one.

*

Master John lifted the brass knocker made in the shape of a pineapple and used it to rap on the front door of a bright yellow house. The house was so big that it had four chimneys. A white face appeared briefly in one of the windows at the side of the door, and a moment later a trim, middle-aged white woman pulled open the door with a nervous smile. June could feel the heat from inside flow over them like some thick, delicious liquid. "Elizabeth," she said. "John. So glad you are here." She glanced at June. "If you go around back," she said to her, pointing down to the right, "you will find the servant's entrance. Basheba is waiting for you."

"Yes, mistress," June said, and she backed out into the cold, turning to make her way carefully down the icy stone walk.

Just as she lifted her hand to knock on the side entrance, the door opened. A tall, slim, deep-brown woman with large, intense, observant eyes stood before her. Her handsome unlined face was one that made her age hard for June to guess—older than herself but younger than Jubah. Her hands were careworn.

"I'm June," she said.

Basheba nodded. "You lettin' cold in," she said in a deep voice. June stepped quickly inside. There were two fires in the enormous brick fireplace, one with cook and wash kettles over it, and a smaller one under a bake oven. June could smell some fresh yeast bread.

"Hungry?" the tall woman asked.

June set down the flour sack in which she carried her clothes and some of Jubah's medicinal herbs. She stepped closer to the big fire to drink in some of its warmth. "A bit," she said. Basheba ladled her a steaming bowl of thick bean soup and gave her a spoon. Her coat still on, she took a small bite. The soup, sweet, salty, and tasting of bacon, was wonderful. She heard someone on the steps behind her. A dark-haired, richly dressed white man came down. He looked at her for a brief moment with cold, keen eyes, and headed to the back door. He opened the door, looked both ways, and quietly walked out. Still feeling his glance on her, June's flesh crawled.

"Who was that?"

"Ship captain from Bristol. Name DeWolf. He one of the biggest slavers in all Rhode Island. The look he gave you? He priced you."

"Priced me?"

"How much you sell for."

"What he doin' here?"

"He and Mastuh Pease are partnering on something."

"Slaving?"

"Not this time. Don' know what they workin' on."

June believed that Master John was in on it, too, whatever it was. She looked at Basheba. "Master Pease hard?"

"There are worse," she said.

June ate her soup in silence.

She could hear the rumble of Master John's voice in the room above them and, once in a while, the lighter voices of Mistress Hazzard and Mistress Pease.

"What tasks I goin' do?"

"You probly be working at his 'stillery makin' molasses into rum. Hard work, but warm. Or you might be workin' at his cocoa manufactory grinding beans. What he really need is somebody to work at fixing up his ship in the port. A carpenter like that man on your place."

"Guy Watson. You know him?"

"Been here last two winters."

As she set the bread on the side table to cool, June looked Basheba up and down. Guy never mentioned her. "He stay in the house?"

Basheba shook her head. "He stay down at the wharf. Was up here building bins for the root cellar a few times, hangin' pot hooks in the kitchen."

"He get along all right?"

Basheba glanced at her. "With who?"

"Everyone."

"Didn't get whipped that I ever heard." June, frustrated, could see that this woman didn't talk much. Basheba looked at her again. "He came sniffin' round me once, if that's what you wan' know. As I see it is. You wan' know something from me, you got to learn to *ask.*"

"Came round you once?"

Basheba looked at her in silence. All at once June could see in her challenging eyes as clearly as if she had said the words: *That's what*

I just said, didn't I? June, not used to asking anything directly, forced herself to try.

"And what did you do 'bout it?" she asked, shocking herself with her boldness.

The tall woman smiled faintly. "Told him I don' fool round with boys."

"He fool round with someone else?"

"Wasn't my task to know what he did. Have to aks him."

"He's my husband," June said, feeling herself blush.

Basheba looked at her, her face blank as the oven door. "Now, why am I not surprised?"

*

As Basheba served the Peases and the Hazzards the midday meal upstairs, June lay a fire for the wash kettle outside, hauling wood that had thawed in the kitchen back outside and replaced it with wood from the outside pile so it would be warm enough to burn. She carried a good dozen pails of water from the backyard well to fill the kettle, put in a handful of some gluey brown soap, and waited for the water to get hot. A stray dog came by and watched her expectantly for a while. Once it smelled the soap, it trotted away.

June went inside to get the bedsheets; Basheba told her she was wanted upstairs.

"What for?"

The tall servant shrugged. "Take your coat off before you go up."

June did as she was told. She stepped hesitantly into the sunny parlor where the four were drinking tea. She could smell the tea all the way from the entrance, and they made no attempt to hide the teapot the way the Hazzards did. They ignored her for a minute, finishing their conversation. Finally, Mistress Hazzard turned to her and said that after they completed a few errands at the market, they would be leaving for home. "You do what Master and Mistress Pease tell you," she said.

"You will be required to work on Sundays here," Master John said, looking stern.

"After church," her mistress added.

"If we get a good report of you when you come home next month, there will be a reward," Master John said. "There could be some actions by soldiers during your stay. If there are, you needn't worry. You will be entirely safe here."

"*Only* here," Master Pease said, looking at her with his shrewd gray eyes.

June dipped her head. "Yes, sir."

"Farewell, June," Mistress Elizabeth said.

She nodded again and to her astonishment found her throat was suddenly closed with emotion and her chin was trembling with sadness. She was about to be left by the only people she knew in a strange place amongst strange people. Out the window she could see the huge warships floating in the harbor.

"Back to work," Mistress Pease said.

*

"Might as well know this," Basheba said after the evening meal was served and darkness had gathered outside the windows. June was about to bring the clean but frozen sheets back to dry in the kitchen overnight. "You know the town you pass on your way here from the mainland?"

"One they call Jamestown?"

"Somethin' bad goin' happen there sometime soon, done by some friends of the Peases. Some slaves goin' be helpin' the British make it happen. So don' you go wanderin anywhere. Word gets out, bein' a negro in Newport goin' be a problem."

"Thank you for tellin' me. What goin' happen?"

She shrugged. "Find out soon enough."

June didn't know if she knew and wasn't telling, but either way she was grateful that Basheba had trusted her.

*

Basheba awakened her from her attic bed before dawn to help her stoke the fires and prepare breakfast. "Daylight so short now," she said in her low voice, "we be workin' before sunup every day. After sundown, too."

June raked the ashes in the big kitchen fire to bring up some embers and asked where she would be working today.

Basheba peered out the back window into the darkness. "You goin' have to do some men work."

"Where?"

"Out on the mastuh's big boat in the harbor. Wear thick clothes. Eat a big breakfast. Do what you told."

"Out next to those big men-of-war?"

She nodded. "They leave you alone. But there goin' be two men workin' there. Don' go below deck alone even if you freezin'. Like as not, one of them be down after you like a duck on a bug." June felt her eyes open wide. "Thick clothes isn't just goin' keep you warm. Goin' cover that nice shape you carry round."

"What if they tell me to work below deck?"

"You tell 'em Mastuh Pease's said 'bove deck only."

*

At dawn, a heavy man with black hair and pale skin named Thomas Briggs came to the kitchen door to fetch her. Waiting outside with him was Jonathan Easton, a slim fine-featured young man with long bushy sideburns.

Briggs growled to Basheba, "The sloop or the brig today?"

"The brig," she answered. "The *Betsey.*"

He peered into the kitchen behind June. "Where's the man?"

"No man," Basheba said. "Just her. Mastuh Pease says above-deck work only."

He frowned and shook his head. "Let's go," he said to June.

She followed the two men down to the wharf to the huge twin-masted square-rigged *Betsey*. On top of a brick-paved area at the stern of the ship, she was told to build a fire under a black kettle filled with dense black goo. The two men were repairing the upper deck. After laying new strips of deck, they were tarring it with the black goo as they went. By the time she got the fire going well and the tar softened, it was full light. The heavy buckets of hot tar she brought stiffened so rapidly in the cold, she repeatedly had to run back to the pitch kettle with the buckets for reheating.

The two men did not talk much at first except in grunts and clipped phrases. As the pale yellow sun brightened the blue-black sky, they began to discuss the ship. Briggs wondered why they were working on it at all. "British won't let her out of here without a big payment. No profit, and there's an end."

Easton replied, "*This* ship's owned by Dr. Hunter, the Wantons, and Pease. She'll pass in and out as slick as you please. It's men like your brother who'll have to pay."

Thomas Briggs looked up and said sharply, "Captain Briggs hasn't made a trip to the Guinea coast for over a year."

"This brig will be ready to go soon enough."

"The *Betsey*? Not to the Guinea coast. She's to be set up for local trade." He pointed with a tar swab to a low wall on the top deck near the bow of the ship. "Pass us the tar," he said to June.

"Tar gone thick again," Briggs grumbled, handing the bucket back to June. "Get it hot this time."

June turned toward the front of the brigantine where the tar fires smoked. She saw, beyond the ship's bow point, a small privateer slicing at full sail right between the British warships. There was a flash from the British sloop, the smaller of the two men-of-war, and an instant later she half-heard and half-felt a loud thump. Easton and Briggs were on their feet. A few people working on the wharf stopped to look out into the bay. The swift privateer came on.

Within a minute, clumps of spectators had gathered. Within five minutes, the docks were nearly full. The larger of the two British warships gave chase to the little American ship.

The privateer was heading straight for the wharves. The cumbersome man-of-war wallowed behind. To the cheers of the spectators, the privateer pulled safely into an open slip, and the crowd cheered merrily. Some of them jeered and taunted the fat twenty-gun British pursuer for having lost its prey.

The warship drew up broadside, its gun ports open. A few of the townspeople continued to gesture obscenely at the sailors.

Briggs and Easton stood near June at the bow of the boat. Easton shaded his eyes and said to Briggs matter-of-factly, "Time for the weekly threat, eh?"

June could barely stand still for fear. Briggs said, "Without us they'd starve. If they didn't freeze first. Feel as safe here as home in bed."

Easton's voice grew tense. "They've got a live torch down in the gun pits."

"Where?" Briggs asked, and then interrupted himself. "Great God! Look! They're putting fire to the touch hole!" He turned and screamed to the crowd at the top of his lungs, "*Take shelter! They're going to fire!*"

The crowd scattered amid shrieks. In all the tumult, a little clergyman stood stock still on the wharf and glared fiercely out to sea.

"Dr. Stiles!" Briggs yelled, his voice trembling with fear. "Remove yourself!" There was a bright flash from the warship. With the loud boom, June and the two men instinctively dropped to their knees and ducked their heads behind the ship's railing.

Reverend Stiles stood unmoving as the ball made its short journey and instantly destroyed the chandlery store behind him. He raised a fist and yelled, “Deicides!” Finally, he turned to make his way off the wharf. Two nine-pound balls landed almost on top of each other, one crashing into a house and the other ripping a gaping hole in the dock on the spot where, seconds before, the little clergyman stood. June heard a single loud voice from the British warship. “Die, ye rebel scum!” She turned and ran to take shelter below deck, seeing that Easton has already done so. She heard Basheba’s warning in her head and stood paralyzed, not knowing what to do.

The British ship slid slowly past the town and back out to sea. Acrid smoke hung in the air. The throng of excited onlookers returned. Briggs was gone. Easton emerged from below decks and promptly left, too.

June stood alone on the deck, her heart thudding in her chest, and wished as much as she had ever wished that she was back at the Hazzards.’

Chapter Eighteen

It was Basheba who came to the wharf and recalled June from the ship. She walked her past the rope walks, the candle factories, and the wooden synagogue to Master Pease's distillery on Jew Street. "Nobody hurt, I hear," she said to June, her breath issuing in white plumes. "Lucky for you. You get some warm, quiet work now. When no one lookin', help yourself to some molasses. Don' drink the rum."

Basheba seemed so unworried! June could not stop trembling. She thought she would never forget the sound of the tremendous crash the cannonballs made as they ripped through houses and stores made of the stoutest wood. At the distillery, she had so much trouble concentrating, the man in charge they called the "factor," thought she was too stupid to do anything but wash floors. And she thought she was. Over and over, she kept seeing the cannonballs crashing onto shore.

At dusk, the factor head pointed the direction to Mary Street only a few blocks away and discovered she was not too stupid to find her way back to the Peases. The Peases, after making certain Basheba and June took up a pile of mending to do by lamplight, left Basheba strict instructions for them to go to church on the morrow.

The Peases, like the Hazzards, were Episcopalians. But, since here in Newport they did not let many slaves attend their services, the Peases permitted Basheba, who was raised Baptist, to go to whatever church she pleased. As long as she went to church, and it was not Samuel Hopkins'.

"Hopkins? Who is he?"

"Tall, fat man with a serious face. Preaches big against slavery. He like to say, 'Am I not a man and a brother?' Gets people all worked up."

"Whites like him?"

"Not much. He talk all the time about perfect love, but he act cold, face the expression of a loaf of bread. And he is confusin'. To go to Heaven, he say you gotta be ready to be damned for the greater glory of God. Can't sort that out."

"Sound like you do go there..."

She lowered her voice. "Once or twice."

"Where we go tomorrow?"

"Baptist Meetin' House. Problem with it is, cold as ice. But they don' make you sit up in nigger heaven."

"What about that man almost got kill today on the wharf?" June asked.

"Little man?" June nods. "Heard about that. Reverend Ezra Stiles. He invite slaves into his home sometimes, reads from the Bible. He send a couple of slaves to a college to be ministers."

"*Ministers*? You tellin' the truth?"

"Knew 'em both. John Quamino and Bristol Yamma."

June shook her head in amazement.

She felt as if she had hardly closed her eyes when she heard alarms and church bells splitting the air. She sat up, terrified, thinking she was dreaming about the destruction at the wharf. She again could hear the dull thump of cannon fire. It sounded distant, but she still immediately imagined a ball crashing right into their attic. She opened the shutter and peered out into the first gray of dawn. People were milling in the streets, some only half-dressed despite the cold. Basheba called her over to her side of the attic. Standing in their nightclothes, they peered out her window. From their high vantage, they could see clearly a flickering glow at the western horizon. It began to grow larger, brighter.

"Sun comin' up backward today," Basheba said dryly.

"What is it?" June asked. "What?"

"Jamestown burnin'."

June stared. Outlined by the growing fire, she could see men-of-war lobbing shells into the flames. Newporters in the streets stared in open-mouthed awe.

The Peases, Basheba discovered, were gone.

"Where are they?" June asked.

"Probly went up to Middletown or Portsmouth. Did this last month when the British shot up Bristol. Left the night before. Bunch of militia arrive the next day to arrest Tories like the Peases. Week later it get quiet and the Peases come back like nothin' ever happen."

"What we goin' do?"

"Tell you what we *not* goin' do. No church today. Peases ask, we just tell 'em we was too scared to leave the house."

Basheba, muttering to herself, made them a master's breakfast: fresh eggs, hot oat and cornmeal porridge with plenty of molasses, some smoked ham, and mugs of steaming coffee. Outside, June saw people still staring at the conflagration to the west. Even sitting in the kitchen, they could hear propertied Newporters gathering in worried knots in the streets, some weeping with fear. When June went to fetch some wood, she smelled not wood smoke but the layered smell of burned wool, leather, and linen—a Jamestown house and all its contents spilled out onto the air.

Wagons and carriages with women and children aboard and packed with household goods began to roll down Farewell Street, heading for the countryside. Houses were shuttered closed. No smoke rose from their chimneys.

*

The Peases' nephew came back in the early afternoon. June was told to clean out the barns, milk the cows, feed the hens, and slop the pigs at half a dozen nearby abandoned homes. He arranged for the milk and any eggs to be carried to market. Basheba was told to attend to cleaning at these houses. While they set about their duties at the first home across the street, the nephew inventoried all the Peases' dishes and silverware to make certain that nothing was missing.

June's work was easy compared to home. And best of all, she was spared more work on the *Betsey*. Days passed, and still the Peases did not return. The British navy threatened Newport with the same fate as Jamestown if it did not furnish them with full provisions. Basheba said the town had decided to hold a town meeting.

While only white freemen of property could vote, anyone could attend. Basheba said they should go. June did not want to, but neither did she want to stay in the Peases' enormous home alone as the day grew dark. And so she found herself standing at the back of the crowded, lamplit hall of the brick Colony House—a vast building that was empty except when there were meetings. June had thought it was some wealthy person's private living place. She could certainly see why no one would want to live there. It would be like living inside an enormous chimney throat. Voices echoed hollowly about as if they were in a cave. Its damp cold oozed into every pore. They stood amid a throng of blacks, poor whites, women, and older children.

"We are here to consider one question tonight," called out the town clerk, a plump old man who had some trouble making himself heard. He was forced to repeat himself to the cries of "Louder! Louder!"

"We are here to consider one question! Do we supply Captain Wallace and his men or do we not?" He explained that if the town voted to do so, Captain Wallace would call a truce and let its market ships pass in and out unmolested.

Only one man rose to speak against supply. With a short cough he cleared his high-pitched voice. He was short and plump and his metal spectacles kept sliding down his small nose. The huge hall fell into a tense and unhappy silence.

"I am William Ellery," he said, looking as mild as milk. And then he proceeded to explain that food that went to Captain Wallace might fall into the hands of General Howe and his army garrisoning Boston. "That army is reported full of scurvy and smallpox and dysentery," he said, smiling at the hostile faces around him. "A lack of fresh provision will doom their cause. Their destruction is Newport's surest safety."

He sat and an uneasy silence greeted his words. Finally, the men voted to send a delegate to Providence to plead their case for supplying the British warships. By a unanimous vote they requested the little cannonball-spared clergyman, Ezra Stiles, to represent them.

The little clergyman rose and in a clear, loud voice said that he could not present the position of supplying Captain Wallace with any conviction, and he must respectfully request they find another advocate.

In the ensuing days, Providence authorized money and transportation to remove four hundred of Newport's poor. The day after, they were taken away to the mainland on packets, and a large group of Rhode Island militiamen descended on Newport to defend the island. The warships drew closer to the wharfs, and violence looked inevitable.

A tense week of cold and miserable weather later, on Christmas Day, the second most powerful man in the American army, General Lee, and eight hundred American soldiers arrived together with a pack of his huge wolfhounds. It was a Monday, and only the Episcopalians and the Moravians were in church, since to all the other Christians in Newport—unsupported by any biblical evidence about the birth of the savior—Christmas was just another day. Or it at least it was until General Lee arrived.

He sent his soldiers right into Tories' homes, summoning them to the courthouse. For some reason, and to Basheba's surprise, no one came to the Peases' house.

A large crowd gathered on Newport's Parade to hear General Lee call on the accused Tories to sign an oath of fidelity to the American cause. He then advised everyone in the entire town "to clear out within ten days." June could not help noticing that at least every third person in the watching crowd was black.

Basheba pointed out that the entire town council of Newport had come to welcome this General Lee, something June did not think much about until she noticed, once again, that Master Pease was there, powdered wig and all. He was a member of that town council. They had not seen him once since he left town.

June thought that a world away from soldiers, cannon fire, and house burnings, the slaves on the Hazzard place were all celebrating Christmas. Safe, quiet, warm.

That night the Peases finally came home. Lamps in hand, they inventoried their belongings. Master Pease was too angry to focus his attention. He followed his wife about the house, damning General Lee and his soldiers, friends, dogs, ancestors, and descendants. "They've arrested a dozen men for refusing to sign! They were going to arrest Reverend Bisset himself until the last moment!"

Basheba whispered that the master should be grateful he wasn't arrested himself and his house ransacked. The Peases said nothing when the inventory was complete and retired to their rooms, so June assumed they were satisfied. The Peases soon reappeared, though, dressed in fancy clothes, prepared to go out for dinner.

"If someone look for you, what do I say?" Basheba asked.

"You may say," the mistress said, "that we have gone to dine with General Lee this evening."

"And his Goddamned dogs," Master Pease muttered.

As they headed toward the door, Master Pease complained bitterly that nearly all the Jews had now decided to leave and had gone over to the rebel side in the bargain. "Pollock, Rivera, and Lopez, and all their families with 'em. And their money, too!" Just before he pulled the door open, he cleared his throat, settled his angry face into a bland cast, and donned a pleasant smile as if it were a hat. Then they stepped out onto Mary Street and into the cold night air.

Basheba stared at the door after it closed behind them. She shook her head. "Nobody slice a loaf the way they do," she said.

*

One evening later in the week when the Peases were out, a wiry little hard-muscled black man came to the back. He asked to see Basheba, and the two of them talked in whispers while Basheba told June to lay some wood for the wash kettle. When she finished, she stood in the cold hugging herself and staring at the bright stars in night sky. Finally, she heard the kitchen door open and close.

"Everything all right?" she asked Basheba. Basheba looked at her impatiently and June remembered: she needed to ask directly. "Who is he?"

"That's Jack Sisson. Servant to Captain Barton. While you workin' on the *Betsey* yesterday, Jack was out putting on a show on the Parade. He break things with his head, boards and bricks. Saw him once hammer in a wood peg. With his bare skull."

"What he want here?"

"Some of Master Pease's letters."

"*What?*"

"Little Jack Sisson? He a spy." Basheba gave one of her rare smiles. "Wouldn' give him no letters. But he give me some interestin' information."

"What?"

"Ever since Colonel Wanton used his slaves for guides about what houses on Jamestown for the British to burn, everyone nervous. Nobody trust nobody. Captain Barton use Jack Sisson to fix that."

"How?"

"Show you tonight. We goin' spy on the spies."

*

UNDER COVER OF THE dark, Basheba and June neared the farthest verge of Brenton Point. Basheba held a finger to her lips. The air grew damper and saltier, and soon June could hear the sound of the steady fall of waves upon the shore.

Basheba seemed to know just where to go. She headed forward, looked carefully around, and pointed toward a large rock for them to hide behind.

June looked out to sea where two men-of-war floated in the light of a half-moon. Suddenly a group of figures off to their left came forward, their stealthy step muffled. June saw they were carrying long thin sticks, and then it dawned on her. They were armed. Her hand flew up to her mouth to cover her shocked gasp. This no longer seemed like a game.

"Shhh," Basheba said.

A short bandy-legged man stepped from behind a dune and went boldly right to the edge of the water. Though she had only seen him once, June recognized Jack Sisson's distinctive silhouette.

"Ahoy, the *Rose!*" he called. He cupped his hands and yelled again, "Hay the *Rose!*" There was a silence. The *Rose*, as June knew, was the British command ship. Sisson called again, his voice carrying easily over the waters of the bay, "Poor Negro wan' get aboard! I run 'way from mastuh! "

Finally a British accented voice came from one of the warships, coming clearly through the winter air. "We hear ye!"

"I am Captain Collins' man! Got papers!"

"Collins," whispered Basheba. "Member Sons of Liberty."

"Wait where you are," a British voice called. "And no more yelling! Hush!"

A small rowboat was lowered from the man-of-war with three British mariners aboard. Two of them rowed and the third directed them. Jack Sisson waved an arm slowly back and forth over his head. Within minutes, they pulled their small craft ashore right at his feet. They stepped out and motioned for Jack to get in.

At that moment a dozen armed men rose from behind rocks and dunes, seized the three sailors, and dragged their boat onto the sand. Voices yelled in anger and alarm from the men-of-war. The American militia vanished with their three new prisoners.

A few minutes later, Basheba motioned for June to begin their return trip. Once they reached a path leading back into town, Basheba said, "That ought to do it."

"Do what?"

"Keep British from luring slaves away. Jack Sisson say some lord down in Virginia offerin' freedom to any slave who come join his army."

"*Any* slave?"

"Any man slave. That's because there are so many rebels down there. Up here British don' set free Tory slaves. No difference. From what I hear, bein' in the army as bad as slavery."

Her chest ached at the thought of Guy.

Chapter Nineteen

Guy Watson trudged through the thick snow and made his way up the blue-white path to the well-kept McLean house. The McLeans, a couple from Boston who moved to Canada over a year ago, had turned over an empty bedroom to Captain Ward for his sickbed. Dr. Senter instructed Guy to visit three times a day and inform him of any change, any change at all. Stamping his tent-cloth-wrapped feet on the doorstep, Guy knocked on the heavy oak door, checking the sun to see if it was midday. It had taken him some time to figure out that the December noontime sun in Canada traced a lower arc than in Rhode Island. He was worried. He understood that if Captain Ward took what the doctor called "a bad turn," Ward could die in a matter of minutes.

It had happened to others already. A Connecticut man died from overeating the first night after the long famine-racked march. Lieutenant McClellan of Hendricks' company fell ill of the same disease as Captain Ward and was dead within twenty-four hours. Josie Carr of Ward's company was dead. Captain Dearborn, they said, was in his final hours—same illness. Cough, vomiting, fever, delirium, and their skin the bright yellow of urine in snow. Others were sick. For Captain Ward, Dr. Senter had tried medicines, teas, and blisters, as well as bleeding from his arm into a posset cup.

He grew worse as they watched.

Mistress McLean opened the door to him now. Behind her, he saw the grave face of the aged woman who served uneaten meals to the captain.

He stepped into the dim room where Captain Ward lay under a heavy quilt. His large and sunken eyes, where they were not bloodshot red, were yellower than his blotchy skin. He gripped the top of the covers with both hands. His lips were cracked, dry, and blue. "Mrs. Warner?" he croaked. His face and neck were slick with sweat.

Mrs. Warner, as Captain Ward knew, survived the wilderness trek. Her husband did not. Four of the five men they had to leave behind in the woods made it back, too. But, as everyone knew by now, pretty Mrs. Warner died a week ago anyway. She was in her cottage outside Quebec carrying a basin full of melted tallow to be used by the army to coat cartridges when she was struck by a thirty-six-pound cannonball that came through her thatched roof. Captain Ward had that information, too, but sometimes he no longer knew what he was saying.

"Guy Watson, suh," he said.

He said something unintelligible about Phebe. The room smelled sourly of vomit.

Guy looked at the pathetic figure on the bed and felt as if a trapdoor in his chest had opened. His heart plummeted through it. He did not want Captain Ward to die. Eb Tolman had been stirring the men against him while the captain has been sick. If he died, who would protect him? And how would he ever get home?

He thought back to the remarkable minutes after the relief party came and they had their first bit of food in many days. Though it was plain beef and some flat bread together with dried apples, each bite drenched their senses with the almost overwhelming intensity of flavor. He, Captain Ward, and Lieutenant Shaw watched the soldiers arrive from the wilderness one at a time, just as they had. The men would emerge and blink their eyes in disbelief. Awareness of their rescue would be dawn over their faces like a rising sun. Some laughed, others wept, and a few looked as if they were in shock. Each time, the arrival of this dawn on every face was something to see. He and the captain could not stop watching each man recognize that he was saved. Once, after half an hour and thirty or forty men had straggled out of the forest, Captain Ward happened to glance at Guy. Some of Captain Topham's company had just begun to arrive, their exhausted filthy faces became pictures of joy and relief, and the captain gave him the tiniest ghost of a smile. Guy could tell that Sam had recognized they were experiencing the same thing. For a split second, he was not a slave and the captain was not a master.

After that, though, as if breaking from a spell, each returned to his old identity. If Guy was strange to the whites he marched with, stranger still were the friendly dark-eyed, olive-skinned Frenchmen in blanket coats and knitted caps who wore their hair snaking behind them in a long Chinese-length queue. In their homes, villages, and churches they had barbaric, shocking, crude, brightly-painted sculptures of a bleeding Jesus suffering on the cross. Their bizarre religious artifacts, to Protestant eyes, were tame compared to the Abenaki Indians with their painted faces and elaborate broaches and bracelets. Still, all of them were friendly, even happy to see them, some of them staring at Guy as hard as everyone else was staring at them. Awaiting them all was the majestic sight of Quebec across the mile-wide St. Lawrence River, its crenellated walls, gray stone buildings, and needle sharp spires topped by red flags rising high over the waters like a king's castle, beautiful and startlingly real, the place they had all marched months and over six hundred miles to reach.

Captain Ward translated the words of the French priest, Father Verreau, about their journey: "A miracle must have been wrought for you. This undertaking is far above the common race of men in this debauched age."

Guy did not know what "debauched" meant, but he could feel the priest's awe.

They scarcely rested after their rescue and pushed on past the village of Sartigan and St. Mary's and made their way to the great goal of taking the city. But their problems were not over. Colonel Arnold, Guy heard, was hoping he would encounter the same situation he had earlier at a fort called Ticonderoga. He marched up to it with a small force of men, demanded surrender—and got it. The problem here was that they needed to cross the St. Lawrence River to make that show of force. To do so required getting past a twenty-six-gun frigate, a sloop-of-war, and a flotilla of guard boats. The colonel wished to surprise the British in Quebec, test their defenses, and, if all else failed, set up a siege and wait for reinforcements from another American detachment of New Yorkers that was attempting to invest Montreal to the west.

Colonel Arnold had bought leather and hired shoemakers to shod his barefoot soldiers, paid carpenters to build scaling ladders, hooks, and spears, and was purchasing boats for the crossing.

Arnold had thought of everything—everything, that is, except recognizing that he lacked the confidence of some of his officers. As Captain Ward explained this to his lieutenants, one of the other captains, Hanchet of Connecticut, now openly hated Colonel Arnold's guts. After watching Arnold drive ahead of him at the end of his own company's extraordinary effort to reach the Canadian inhabitants, and then taking Hanchet's boats right out from under him, Hanchet came to believe Arnold wanted to claim credit for the army's rescue all for himself. He concluded that Arnold was a reckless power-mad monster who would risk everyone and everything for his own personal glory. His fellow Connecticut captains, Hubbard and Goodrich, grew inclined to see things as Hanchet did. They certainly no longer completely trusted Arnold. And when Morgan's riflemen wanted more time to recover and Major Bigelow wanted more cartridges, even Ward, Greene, Topham, Thayer, and Meigs were not enough to carry Colonel Arnold's vote to cross the river. In a straight-out rebuke of his authority, he lost.

One day later, though he had just been rebuffed, Arnold called a new Council of War. There he announced he had freshly received the news that the New Yorkers, under the widely admired General Montgomery, had seized the fort of St. John's and Montreal as well. Then Arnold requested a new vote in light of the changed circumstances. Quebec could no longer be supplied, he said, nor was there any avenue of retreat for those in Quebec. A British deserter from the city promised to show them the best landing sites, and Captain Hanchet could remain on the far shore with fifty men to ensure a safe retreat, if one proved necessary. Their great end was almost within their grasp. Victory for themselves, victory for America.

This time, only Goodrich voted no.

They would need three crossings to get the five hundred men across and they would have to do it at full dark under a cloudy sky in order not to be seen. They waited impatiently for the conditions to be right.

The night they finally crossed the St. Lawrence, Guy's boat passed so close to one of the British frigates that he could hear its riggings brush against the mast. Its bulwarks loomed above them and they could hear clearly as their own frightened breathing the sound of a guard boat's oars grinding in its thole pins a few yards off to their left.

Once they landed, Captain Ward had to tell Newporters like Sylvanus Shaw to be quiet. "Lieutenant! You'll get us discovered."

"Sorry, sir. That frigate we almost hit? The *Hunter* out of Newport."

Guy straightened. He knew the *Hunter* only too well. It belonged to Simon Pease and he had worked on it for the last two winters running. He had set new harps for the very railing they had passed under. After Captain Ward's order for quiet, some still cursed Pease under their breath. They had risked their lives and futures, and he profited from supplying the enemy!

Guy thought of the bespectacled assistant to Dr. Church and wondered if Pease sent more than supplies.

The landings began at midnight and ended sooner than they wished at four in the morning. They were forced to build a fire to save Lieutenant Steele's life. Making his fifth crossing, and at the end of the second landing, his canoe smashed into rocks and overturned, dumping him into the freezing cold waters. Without a fire, he would die. With it, their discovery was certain. Colonel Arnold ordered that it be built.

With only two-thirds of the army present, Arnold consulted with the officers present about what to do next. They decided quickly enough. Half-running the entire way, Arnold led them up the steep path from the cove where they landed to the Plains of Abraham, bringing their hooks and scaling ladders with them. For the rest of the hours of darkness that remained, they deployed their diminished army to cut off the roads from communication and supply.

Dawn found the city of Quebec totally unaware of their arrival. The surprise was complete.

"In the name of the United Colonies," Arnold asked for their surrender. Instead, against all the practices of war, the British forces fired on the aide who brought the message under a white flag.

They soon heard a rumor from an escaping Quebecois citizen that the soldiers there planned an attack on Arnold's army. They had to come out—the city was too short of wood to suffer a siege. At first, the Americans were braced and cheered by this news.

No attack came that day. Or the next. Or the next. Continual rifle and cannon fire came from the walls. Sergeant Dixon of Smith's riflers had his leg shattered by a cannonball lofted from the city. Sam began to have the sinking feeling they had traveled a killing six hundred miles to end up in an identical circumstance to the one they had left. A siege. Fear and boredom were punctuated by rumors and random gruesome violence. Dr. Senter amputated the injured man's leg to piteous cries that could be heard on the far side of the river. Dixon died later that day.

Major Meigs did a full review on the state of Arnold's armies. They lacked winter clothes and, at mid-November, a real northern winter was preparing to settle in. They lacked the cash to buy any more supplies from the inhabitants. They had, at best, four to five rounds per man and no cannon or field pieces. If the British did attack from out of the city, they would encounter a force split into fragments, ragged, under-supplied, and not yet recovered from the ravages of their terrible march. Without an ounce of fat left on most of them, they could not withstand the cold, and to many, even the heat of standing near a fire was painful.

And so when no surrender was forthcoming, Arnold made the decision: they must retreat to winter quarters and wait for the arrival of General Montgomery's force. The entire army assembled at a place called Point aux Trembles twenty miles away. They nearly had Quebec in their grasp—but they had to let go.

Within days of their arrival at Point aux Trembles, Captain Ward fell ill.

*

GUY COULD NOT CLEARLY tell the sun's height in the sky on this cloudy day. And so he was not entirely surprised to find Dr. Senter still there when he arrived. Guy stood at the room's entrance while the doctor, who was sitting on a chair by the side of the bed, continued to examine his patient. He thumbed back one of Captain Ward's eyes, felt his neck and throat area, and talked cheerfully to him of recent news. It was unclear to Guy whether the captain understood what was said. His eyelids, half-open, kept drooping closed. Behind them his eyes rolled up so only the yellowed whites were visible. Dr. Senter talked to him anyway.

"General Montgomery has arrived," he said. "His New Yorkers are almost in as bad a shape as we are and no more numerous.

But he's brought winter clothes and one dollar in hard cash for every soldier. Your friend Aaron Burr has joined the general's staff with the rank of captain." He leaned down and put an ear to the patient's chest. "The clothes they brought, though, are all redcoat uniforms. You'd laugh at the men dressed in the colors of the enemy. Some are wearing white blanket coats over them and the hats inside out so the white lining shows. I'll wear mine tomorrow."

What could have been a smile, or simply a grimace of discomfort, crossed the captain's face. He coughed weakly.

"The British governor, Guy Carelton, escaped from Montreal and landed in Quebec with a schooner full of men, but he arrived just in time for an outbreak of smallpox. Deserters tell us their state is poor—cold, ill, and with few supplies. Of course, we have our woes. Captain Hanchet has taken to refusing direct orders from Colonel Arnold. You are lucky, captain, to be here in one regard. There is a foot of fresh snow on the ground." Senter leaned forward and smelled Ward's sour breath. "Your company fares well enough, but not as well as when you were there."

The captain strained to speak and finally rasped a word Guy could not catch.

"Dearborn?" the doctor repeated. The corners of his mouth pulled down. "Alive this morning when I left him. Barely, I'm afraid."

Dr. Senter picked up the captain's bedpan and swirled it around, sniffing at it and examining its foul contents. Guy could see he did not like what he found.

"One last story. We have yesterday received news from Cambridge that shocked all of Massachusetts and Rhode Island. Two weeks after we left, our old friend Dr. Church, the army's surgeon general, was discovered to be…a traitor."

Guy's chest thumped in alarm. He stared hard at the captain but could not see any response to this news.

"Church tried to send a coded letter through a prostitute in Newport to Captain Wallace of the *Rose*. She was acting suspiciously and the message was seized. Reverend Stiles could not puzzle the cipher out so they forwarded it to your Uncle Henry. He had it sent to Nat Greene. He and General Washington personally interrogated the trollop until she finally gave up the name of the man who sent it. They arrested Dr. Church, who insisted on his innocence and refused decipher the letter. General Washington found some adepts and had it decoded. The letter reported all there was to know about our army, including a proposed attack on Canada!"

Captain Ward moaned.

"Dr. Church is being held under guard. There are many who want to hang him, but there is some confusion in the law. We can thank God and a Newport baker that Church was caught at all! It was the baker who grew suspicious of the jade and seized her letter. All is well now. And we have no reason to think news of our Canada plans ever reached the British."

He examined the captain another moment, urged him to try to eat and drink anything offered to him, and rose to leave. He called Guy outside the room. "Try to keep him comfortable." He added to the owners of the house before he left, "He is in God's hands now." From where Guy stood at the top of the stairs, he could see Senter's eyes brim as he said the words.

When he was alone with the captain and the house grew quiet, Guy went to the kitchen to ask for a cup of hot water. Then he took out his carefully protected leather pouch and began to use some of the herbs June gave him to make a decoction. The only sound he heard was Captain Ward's raspy breathing. It was hard to get him to swallow some of the infusion. At length, he succeeded and Ward soon slipped into an exhausted sleep. Tansy. Mugwort. Feverfew. Pennyroyal. He tried to save some for himself. When he found no change that afternoon, he gave him some more. When there was no change the next day, he gave the captain the rest.

A day later when he arrived in the morning, he found the captain sitting up and trying to eat a bite of fresh-cooked egg. Guy liked to think it was June and Jubah's herbs that did it, and perhaps they did, but he heard from a now red-uniformed Dr. Senter that Captain Dearborn had begun to recover, too.

*

SAM FOUND IT DIFFICULT to get used to seeing his men and fellow officers dressed in the enemy's colors. He also found he was exhausted after being up for only a few hours, regardless of how little he exerted himself. But he was determined to make it for what Christopher Greene said was the most crucial vote of their entire journey. The question before them was whether they should storm the city once they had an adequate supply of bayonets and cartridges from General Montgomery.

As the council of officers sat in deliberation, he found himself staring absently at Dearborn's emaciated face and wondering if he himself looked as bad as the cadaverous New Hampshire captain. He was astonished by Hanchet's, Goodrich's, and Hubbard's open hostility to Colonel Arnold. In the end, the meeting proved brief. The Connecticut captains were the only three to vote against an assault on Quebec. Captain Morgan's division—having plundered every Tory house within twenty miles, slept in feather beds under wool blankets, eaten their soldiers' food with filigreed silver, and washed it down with wine and spirits—were back in fighting trim.

They prepared for their assault, right down to the details of having the men wear a sprig of pine or hemlock on their hats to distinguish them from enemies in British uniforms. As they murmured their prayers and wrote their final letters home, the plan was canceled at the last hour before it was to begin. Colonel Arnold and General Montgomery, who had spies, had learned that Governor Carelton was making defensive preparations and might well know of their plans.

Sam was glad for the delay. He felt stronger with each day that passed.

As the mostly Episcopal New Yorkers and Virginians prepared to celebrate Christmas, Colonel Arnold called for a final council of war. He called for the strictest possible secrecy before he unfolded the details for assault. Spies were on both sides.

A day later, every man in camp knew the plan. Under Arnold's orders, Major Bigelow investigated how this dangerous hemorrhage of information occurred. It took no special effort to find that the drunken rifle captain Matthew Smith had told all the details of the officers' council to anyone who would listen. He was in the middle of telling them once again to a corporal and two privates when Bigelow approached him.

Threatened with a court-martial, Smith promised he would shut up and promptly drank himself into unconsciousness. Sam, still incredulous that his father's old friend Dr. Benjamin Church was a cold-blooded traitor, grew nervous. If a patriotic doctor and head of the army hospitals could be a fraud and a spy, anyone could. Anyone.

When misgivings spread throughout the army, New York's General Montgomery assembled all the men, stood upon a tree stump, and called for quiet. He was tall and sturdy with a roughly handsome, pockmarked face. He bared his balding head to the winter air. He pointed to a rapidly clearing sky and a large yellow moon and said there would be no attack tonight. They would all be too visible against the snow.

"It gives me," he said, his deep voice carrying easily even to men at the far reaches of the crowd, "the highest pleasure to see you men here. Your willingness to fight speaks loudly of your great courage. I pray you do not be disheartened by this delay. A more favorable time will come and these few moments that we draw back will only add luster to our undertaking." He raised his voice still louder and the crowd, which had stirred restlessly, suddenly grew quiet as churchgoers. "You know that I am exceedingly sorry to detain you tonight, but I would not expose you rashly to the merciless rage of our common enemy. I would be answerable to our country and our Creator for the loss of any brave men whose lives might be saved by waiting for a more favorable moment." He looked slowly around the army and paused. "When that time comes, and it will soon, know, all of you, that I am willing to sacrifice my life to add, by any means, to the honor of my brother soldiers and our country. And I could not do this in any better company on earth than yours."

He stepped quietly down from the stump, and there swelled a great roar of approval for the man and his words. Hanchet, Hubbard, and Goodrich all changed their minds on the spot and decided they would lead their companies forward on the assault. Men who had had private worries about the wisdom of the attack grew more confident. Men who, in their anxiety, would not meet others' eyes now looked at their friends and grinned.

But four more excruciating days of crystal clear weather came. The fears and uncertainties began to return. Captain Ward reminded his men that if they met with success, in a single stroke they could end the war with Britain. Still, waiting felt like an illness. Sam wrote letters to all his family, knowing that these might be the last words they might ever read from him. Her sad smile fresh in his imagination as if he had just seen her, he wrote to Phebe that she was much on his mind.

As they reached the last day of 1775, it began to snow, gently at first. At midnight, they gathered under a thick and steady snowfall. At four o'clock in the morning, when they got the order to march, they were in the middle of one of the worst blizzards any of them had ever seen.

General Montgomery and his men were to attack the eastern side of the town by way of Cape Diamond near the river. Colonel Arnold's army was to attack the Lower Town from the west. Finally there would be a feint made from the Plains of Abraham east of St. John's gate. Arnold's and Montgomery's armies would then join together in the middle of the lower town, gather local women, children, and priests from the houses, mix them in among the soldiers in order to discourage indiscriminate artillery blasts, and march on the upper town. With some luck, they hoped to bring in the new year at a warm hearth and in control of Quebec.

General Montgomery and Colonel Arnold personally would lead the assaults, Arnold's group was to be spearheaded by Morgan, Hendricks, and their rifle companies. Captain Ward's company was to lead the center division, followed by the weakest companies of Smith, Hubbard, Hanchet, and Goodrich, and at the rear the ably led companies of Thayer, Topham, and Dearborn. Smith's men were leaderless. He had drunk so much in the last few days he had developed a brain fever and was incapable of speech or movement. Lieutenant Steele, a strong and smart man but not as well-known to Smith's men as their captain, had taken Smith's command.

When they first began their march, Sam could see the whole column of companies stringing out before him. A half hour later, as the storm grew violent and the drifts of snow piled past their knees, Sam had to struggle simply to keep the last men of Hendricks' company in view. The snowstorm that so usefully covered their approach to the city began to blind them from each other. Every third man carried pikes and scaling ladders. The rest tried to keep their musket pans and rifle locks covered from the driving snow by holding them under their coats. As they neared a great black bulk of wall looming over them in the night, the wind drove at them sharply from the northeast along the river, slamming against the wall and rebounding back upon them. White flakes swarmed and floated and twisted in great whorls. It looked as if it were snowing from all directions at once.

They discovered that the entire army had gotten lost in the white out. They stopped, and after some painful minutes of confusion where scouts and messengers crossed and recrossed themselves, their voices lost in the howling wind, they had to redirect themselves along the river to the entrance of the Lower Town. As they circled back, they discovered that Dearborn's company, in the storm, failed to hear the signal to march. He and all his men were nowhere to be found.

It was Sam's plan before they entered the gates of the town to give encouragement and a brief speech to his men to brace them for what they must do. When the time came, he found himself panting with fear, unable to utter a sound. From the moment they received orders to march, a high keening sound began in his stomach and ran up his back to become a loud, shrill, painful whine in his skull. The sound steadily grew louder as they marched single file through the snow-blasted night. By the time he neared the entrance to the Lower Town, he was shaking so badly he could barely walk. He hated himself for his cowardice but was powerless to change his reaction.

He heard the clanging of a bell high above his head and then the sound of bells throughout the town pealing out the alarm. Half the American army was inside the gates. Through the snow, Sam could see small bright muzzle flashes spark in the night from the cliffs. He could hear a crackling of shots from behind as he and his men drove forward. The shrill sound in his skull suddenly stopped. His heart was racing, but suddenly he felt possessed by a sudden, almost eerie clarity of mind.

Then the whole cliffside came alive. Cannons coughed, and bombs and fireballs the size of carriages arched over their heads. Sam felt the suck of air of a cannonball passing. Muzzle flashes in front of him grew as numerous as sparks from a bonfire. Then he began to hear, from all sides of him, small chirruping and whirring sounds like startled pigeons. As he moved forward, he realized with a chill that these were musket balls and rifle bullets. He stopped, turned, found his voice, and, with a wolf rising in his heart, yelled, "Forward!" Some of his soldiers were trying to return fire at the muzzle flashes, but their damp powder and snow-clogged pans were making sparkless clicks as their wet-flinted hammers came down. "Keep moving!" he yelled. "They can't hit us this close to the wall!" He waved them on. A man from Hendricks' company staggered toward him, heading in the wrong direction. Sam grabbed him roughly by the shoulder and prepared to threaten him with arrest when the light of a passing fireball illumined his face. There was a sheet of glistening blood. Just below the sprig of hemlock he had attached to his cap was a furrow of splintered bone.

The man blinked through the blood. "Permission to withdraw."

"Go," Sam managed to say.

Two more wounded men emerged heading rearward. Sam asked them to help the blood-soaked man make his way back.

Then Captain Ward led his men forward at a half run. He could hear Colonel Arnold's unmistakable voice rasping out louder and louder, calling them forward and urging them to attack.

"Another few yards and you're at the barricades. Take 'em! The city will be ours!"

Sam discovered why the fierce, confident voice was growing louder. Standing in the snow, supported by Reverend Spring on one side and an aide on the other, Arnold hollered them on. His white breeches were soaked from the thigh down with blood. Sam could see in the half light of the town's torches that his boot overflowed with it. The word was passed with sickening speed, "They got Arnold."

Sam could hear Morgan up ahead screaming at his men to keep going. After a quick word with Arnold, Colonel Greene moved ahead to take command. Reverend Spring begged Arnold to retire. He refused. He continued telling the men to press ahead to victory.

They made their way up Sault-au-Matelot, a narrow street whose end was blocked by a stockade of logs. The men knew they needed to spread out in order not to present a bunched target, but houses lined the whole length of the street with few openings between. Sam could feel his stomach muscles knot as the army neared the first barricade and the men began to press in dangerously close to one another. Two ports suddenly flew open from a barrier and blinding white flashes bloomed before them; thunderous explosions whose concussions he could feel in his bowels echoed down the street. A blizzard of whistling black metal shards raked over them, grapeshot that cut men to ribbons. There was a shocked silence in the wake of the terrible noise and Sam waited to hear the screams of the wounded, wondering if he was himself among them.

The shots had passed harmlessly over their heads. Morgan and his Virginians raised a pulse-quickening yell and surged forward, pouring over the stockade and setting ladders on the barrier. The rest of the army followed close behind, including Captain Lamb's New York artillerymen who planned to set up mobile emplacements when their field pieces were brought forward. Captain Ward ignored the ladders and led his men right up and over an enormous drift of snow that fronted the barricade.

Greene and Morgan seized the battery, took the barrier, and, clicking away on muskets that would not fire, managed to take a good sixty terrified British prisoners in the wave of their assault. Grabbing the prisoners' rifles and powder, they finally had some working firearms, and Arnold's army with Colonel Greene at their head went in a great swarm up the curving street toward a second barrier, the one where they were to join forces with General Montgomery's army sweeping in from behind. The enemy began to surrender before them in great bunches. Sam disarmed a brown-haired boy with a round, beardless face who could not be older than fifteen. He whimpered and his teeth chattered, his nose and eyes ran with torrents of tears and snot.

Three hundred yards on, they reached the second barricade. It was better built and better manned than the first and strong enough to withstand anything but artillery. It looked at least twelve feet high. Behind and above it were loaded cannons. Two ranges of muskets with fixed bayonets waited behind the stockade. Sam could see that the upper floors of the houses behind them were also filled with more armed soldiers waiting for them to come within range.

Colonel Greene and Major Meigs halted the army to regroup and consider how best to continue. Sam joined them in time to hear Captain Lamb report that he could not know how long it would take his pieces to arrive nor how well his cannon and mortars would fire when they did.

Meigs checked his pocket watch. Montgomery and the Yorkers were due to meet them soon. They would have to press on without the artillery.

The Pennsylvania men insisted this time on being the ones to storm the barrier with Captain Hendricks, Lieutenants Steele, and Humphrey to lead them on.

As they prepared the scaling ladders and readied their pikes, Topham's, Thayer's, and Captain Ward's Rhode Island companies pressed in behind in order to follow the Pennsylvanians. Sam explained to his lieutenants and to Sergeant Boynton and Corporal Brown that once they made it to the wall, they would be under the cannons, and the shot would pass over their heads just as the last volleys did. They nodded and passed this word back among the tensely waiting men. Sam prayed there were no hidden gun ports waiting for them.

Dawn was beginning to turn the sky a faint gray.

They still needed to make it across the fatal distance to the barricade itself. If they did, they believed the city would be theirs. Sam looked at the gap and began to mentally time how long it would take him and his men to run across it.

Morgan's riflemen began to take deadly aim on the platform where the artillerists waited. As the cannoneers dropped where they stood, they blindly discharged their pieces and retreated.

No one remained to reload them. Captain Hendricks raised his arm high in the air and then lowered it.

A low growl started in Sam's chest and in the chests of his men, growing and rising and bubbling up into his throat into a long shrieking howl of fear and rage, joining with all the other screams until it became almost a single unearthly voice. Together they ran for the wall, with Sam leading the way. He neither looked back nor sideways but pounded ahead, breathing only to scream some more. The black wooden barricade, like something in a terrible dream, seemed barely to float closer no matter how swiftly he ran, but he ran and screamed, and though it seemed to take forever, the wall finally loomed before him. He slumped, unhurt, in front of it.

Then he looked back in time to see Dan Davidson of Thayer's company take a musket blast point-blank in the chest from a gun port in the barricade. The half-blind drummer boy from Steele's company grabbed his own throat and dropped without taking another step. The men were still arriving at the barricade when a deafening blast of grapeshot was loosed on them, and poor John Stephens of Sam's company, who had slipped in the snow in his run, was torn to pieces. Newporters Charles King and Caleb Hacker were hit at the same moment by musket balls and they sank face forward into the snow. The men who reached the barricade were panting with terror and exertion, and their screaming stopped while they caught their breath. In the sudden silence, they could all hear wounded men's screams splitting the air, calling for help, calling on mothers and sweethearts and wives and almighty God to pleasepleasepleaseplease help them.

Hendricks' men set their ladders and, despite steady fire from the houses behind the barricades, began their terrible climb.

They were met at the top by more grapeshot and plunging bayonets. A man dropped next to Sam with a dull thud, landing on his back, his chest geysering blood from a gaping bayonet wound. His face was a mask of pain, but he could get no air to make the slightest sound.

Ladders began to topple on either side of Sam, with Pennsylvanians still clinging to them. Sam could hear Captain Morgan swearing and ordering assault upon the houses at either side of the barricades. Sam turned to take aim at a redcoat at the top of the barricade, and saw Lieutenant Steele next to him had already raised his rifle on the same target. He watched him take aim and in the next instant saw three of Steele's fingers on his right hand vanish, taken off by a musket ball. Sam shouldered his gun and aimed. He fired, and a dense cloud of smoke crossed his view. When it cleared a second later, the figure was gone.

The scaling ladders had all been repulsed.

Sam ordered his men to head for the houses to dry and reload their guns. He led them toward the houses off to the west and stood exposed in the doorway of the largest house to wave them in. As his men ran in front of him, he told each of them, "Good work." Suddenly he heard behind him Tom Shepherd's familiar raspy voice cursing about something. Sam stepped inside and found him holding what looked like a bloody rope. He realized in a sickening moment that it was Tom Shepherd's intestine, and he was trying to force it back inside his torn vest. He looked at Sam in astonishment and tried to say something, but a large bubble of blood choked his words.

"My guts are coming out. Dear God, oh God, dear God…" His eyes rolled back in his head and he dropped to his knees. Sam screamed for a surgeon, putting his head outside the door to call for Dr. Senter's assistant, just in time to see Lieutenant Humphrey get shot at the point where his white pack straps crossed in the front. He went down like a thrown sack. His own men, Corporal Brown and Jabez Brooks, both dragged themselves in, one with a bloody shoulder, the other limping from a shot leg. They said Captain Hubbard had been wounded in a very bad way. Sam saw Captain Lamb of the artillery being helped into a house across the street. It looked like half his face had been shot away.

There was no surgeon anywhere. By the time he turned back inside, Tom Shepherd was unconscious. Sam could feel himself growing numb second by second, like someone who had burned himself so badly he could not feel the charred area. He ordered his men to reload and prepare for another assault.

From a back window, Captain Ward got a report from Arnold's chief aide, Christian Feibeger. He blurted out his news: most of their prisoners had escaped in the tumult and hundreds of British soldiers had gone round to the far side of the first barricade. They were cut off. They could neither go back nor go forward.

"Where is Montgomery?" Sam asked.

Feibeger shook his head in frustration. "Past due."

"If he attacks from the rear, we'll still take the barricade." Then Sam had a bad thought. "How could they free up additional men to circle around us?"

"Don't know," he said, Danish accent noticeable under the growing stress.

Sam believed something must have gone wrong with Montgomery's assault.

As Feibeger was about to take his leave, laments came from the house across the way. Sam called to the men in front of the house to find out what happened. The word came back that Captain Hendricks, one of the best shots and best officers in the army, had just been killed while taking aim on the captain of the stockade guards.

Sam slammed his fist into the wall in front of him.

The snowfall continued. They were hemmed in. They continued exchanging shots with the enemy. Feibeger brought word that Dearborn and his men arrived just as the army was being sealed off at the first barricade. Overwhelmed by superior numbers, he and all his men were taken prisoner. Major Bigelow estimated there were three hundred of them left to pursue the attack. The rest had been wounded, killed, or captured.

Still no General Montgomery. Tom Shepherd's labored breathing slowed and grew shallower. Then it finally stopped. Though the battle itself was not over, when Shepherd died, Sam felt some hope die with him.

Four hours later, at ten o'clock in the morning, their ammunition was spent and there was no sign of the second army. An exhausted Colonel Greene showed a white flag. He surrendered the army. Having gone to fight for liberty and country and, most would admit, personal glory, they now had a new condition to face. Their great march had ended in a rout. Instead of liberty, they would all face prison in the new year, 1776.

*

First Colonel Enos, then Doctor Church, and as he sat locked up in his new makeshift prison, Sam finally learned a third name to add to the list of men he wished would roast in the deepest circle of hell: Colonel Donald Campbell of New York.

They had almost succeeded in their great task. And would have, too, if it weren't for, Sam believed, Donald Campbell. General Montgomery had led the assault from Cape Diamond as planned. Like Arnold, he presented himself at the head of his army, leading his men up the steep paths and through the blizzard to the first guardhouse. There, frightened, sleepy, half-drunken guards saw figures approaching through the whiteness. They fled. Their sergeant steeled himself, came running back, and blindly touched off their single cannon before taking to his heels for the shelter of the town.

The salvo instantly killed General Montgomery and his aides Captain Cheeseman and Captain McPherson—his newest aide, Captain Aaron Burr, was not yet close enough to the general to have been directly at his side. The command of Montgomery's army fell to Colonel Donald Campbell.

Campbell ordered a retreat. He did not try to advance farther. He did not reconnoiter the area. He left his general and two captains lying dead in the snow like spoiled beef. In his haste to flee, he abandoned a dozen other wounded men bleeding and groaning on the ground. Had he gone forward, he would have found the guardhouse empty and with nothing obstructing him from meeting with Arnold's men. Instead, in a spectacular failure of nerve, he chose to save his own skin, in an instant dooming all the efforts of the men struggling and dying in the center of town. They, too, had lost their commander, but pressed on in spite of it.

As the new year started, Sam heard their names when he was awake and asleep. Enos, Campbell, Church. Selfishness, cowardice, betrayal.

PART II

Chapter Twenty

Master Hazzard found the opening months of the new year crackling with a fierce hostility in the colony. Perhaps it was having so many Rhode Islanders in prison in Canada. Perhaps it was the Crown's unwillingness to compose the disagreements by negotiation. Certainly, he thought, it had all been made worse by that damned pamphlet penned by that despicable, rabble-rousing, regicidal English snake Tom Paine. *Common Sense* had created nothing but common hysteria—a hundred thousand copies sold in three months among a population that could scarcely read, for suffering Jesus's sake. Now there was no middle ground—either you were either a loyalist and a Tory, or you were a patriot and a rebel—and there was a clear, widening line between the two, a line that got harder to straddle every day. He knew it was only Young John's active participation in the militia that had spared him arrest. But he also knew that it had not spared him from falling under suspicion.

Even ever-nimble Simon Pease had not escaped arrest. He was carted in shackles to the mainland right after the British sloops attacked Prudence, the big island off the coast of Providence. Fourteen British sailors dead in that little disaster. And then at the end of last year there was the carefully planned "confiscation" at Point Judith where Commander Wallace landed and took off a few dozen sheep and livestock. No one among his loyalist friends could be accused of supplying the enemy. They simply were grazing their stock when the unconscionable piracy occurred! (Secret payments were made, of course, half in advance, half on "delivery.") Still, they were all questioned by the grim, black-garbed Committee of Safety for two hours. With no alarms sounded and no shots fired, even he had to admit it *did* look a bit suspicious.

Pease managed to get himself released and June back safely to Kingston, but Master Hazzard did not get Guy back from the army in time for the spring planting. When at the end of May they finally did drag Guy in, slung over the back of a horse like a sack of meal, he was half dead, and still barely of use even weeks later. In the meantime, puttering about like some ghost half-risen from the dead, he had offered almost no intelligence of any use about anything. The only good news was that from the day he returned June stopped being sullen and began to do her work unbidden.

Between no work and no information, his leasing Guy out to the Ward boy had been his worst bet in this whole sorry enterprise. When Dr. Church's man turned back with Colonel Enos on the march north, they lost their eyes and ears. Given how things turned out in Quebec, of course, they did not really need a spy. He admitted the only truly bad result of the Canadian adventure has been the colony's wasting its limited funding attempting to buy the release of its captured soldiers. Congress even went so far as to send that randy old bastard Benjamin Franklin all the way up there to try to negotiate a deal.

But poor Doctor Church. Why he used his trollop to convey his letters to Wallace was a mystery—or a piece of stupidity—he supposed they would never unravel. How could an intelligent man do such a stupid thing? Church's only piece of luck, if you could call it that, in this whole botched affair was that the military laws turned out not to say what to do with him. Last year, Congress said that anyone communicating with the enemy could be court-martialed, but they limited the punishment to two months in jail or thirty-nine lashes. After Church's arrest, they authorized a penalty of death right away, but that was for the future, and the good doctor himself ducked the noose. (Some accused him of treason, but how can one be treasonous when there is no country to betray? This line of thought led some of the worst rebels farther down that road to flaming perdition, wanting independence.) At the moment, Church was moldering away in Connecticut's Norwich Gaol. No one was permitted to visit or communicate with him. No books. No paper. Gasping with asthma, he had to petition the Congress to let him out to breathe some "clear, elastic air." Well, let him gasp, the fool! He had cocked up a lot more than his idiotic doxy.

The best spy they had been able to come up with in Rhode Island was Metcalf Bowler, the Speaker of the House. He sent his coded messages to Commander Wallace through Simon Pease and one or two other trustworthy sources. Mostly, though, he whined for money, and so far had damned little military information to offer.

He certainly was no help on the biggest and most shocking development of them all: Washington's sudden stratagem to force the British out of Boston. In mid-March of 1776, Washington entrenched some newly arrived artillery up on Dorchester Heights, putting the whole city of Boston in easy range. That left Commanding General Howe in a totally untenable position—either to come out and fight as they had done so disastrously at Bunker Hill, or to be shelled where they slept. The army already suffered from scurvy and smallpox, so Howe decided to vacate the city. He got to do it in an unhurried way. Washington knew if he pressed too hard, Howe could burn the whole city to the ground. Did Metcalf Bowler provide any advance notice of Washington's tactic? He did not. Dr. Church would have let them know in a heartbeat.

As soon as the British took sail, everyone wondered where they would head. Newport? New York? Philadelphia? Women and children from every coastal town in Rhode Island moved inland. The militia in Providence and Newport got reinforced, and Young John was roused at dawn and sent to Tower Hill to establish cannon emplacements and watch the horizon for ships. Every few hours the word was passed from one coastal watch to the next: "The coast is clear!" And it was, though Howe and tens of thousands of his men were still out there, somewhere, planning their next move. All Master John knew was that they were not going back to England. The government in London had hired soldiers from Central Europe, Hessians and Hanoverians and others, and if they were mercenaries, they were also some of the fiercest and most disciplined fighters in the world. Once they arrived on these shores, young Sammy Ward and his friends would be counting themselves blessed to be safe in a Quebec prison.

Still, as far as he was concerned, the best news of the year came back at the end of March. Down in Philadelphia, the old dragon Samuel Ward got himself a killing case of smallpox. Not a pretty way to go. But they say he was right in the middle of working out a foreign alliance—probably with the papist-loving French and Spanish—and was arguing for the radical step of actually declaring independence that he had persuaded a few timorous souls, including old man Hopkins, to go along with him. Not that the man they were going to replace him with would have different views, but whoever he was, he would be less effective in advancing them than the old snake charmer. After Ward breathed his last, the Continental Congress voted to wear black armbands for a month, a cheaper tribute than the Rhode Island Assembly authorized—erecting a damned monument on his grave. But at least the old bastard was dead.

Since no good news was ever pure, with Ward gone, it doubtless would be a problem getting paid what he was owed for Guy's services. The oldest Ward boy was a drunk serving as a common private somewhere lost in the ranks in Massachusetts, Sammy was in prison, and the several Ward girls who would now be running Ward Hall would be in no hurry to settle their father's debts, assuming they could manage the accounts. And with each week that passed, money was becoming a sorer issue. Most of Rhode Island's money was going to support the army, and the number of people who remained at home who could afford to pay proper prices was dwindling. The less they paid, the less he got. Markets were beginning to fall in on themselves, except for what the colony itself bought with its increasingly worthless scrip.

It was not a reassuring picture.

Which brought him to the thorny matter of what to do about the servants. Metcalf Bowler told him Rhode Island might soon outlaw the slave trade and do as they had already done in Newport—forbid freeing the sick and the elderly without filing a bond to pay for their support. Jubah and Quamino would not be able to raise much of an offer—too old. Guy Watson was much too sick. That left Lucy and June. Of course, Lucy was pregnant as a loaded barge and wouldn't be worth much while tending a baby. God knew who the father was; Lucy was closed as a clam on the topic. And Guy would likely get sullen if they sold June. But if he was going to sell one of them, he had best be quick about it.

In the meantime, he had one excellent chance to profit. The entire Continental army, with its thousands of hardy men, would be marching from Boston right though Rhode Island on its way south, trying to guess General Howe's destination. In the meantime, they had set up lanterns in the dairy barn for night work, and Jubah and Quamino had been working on the cheese presses as soon as their day work in the main house was done. He would soon be able to sell products in vast quantities at prices no one had ever seen before. He had been making Guy work, too, at repairing Mrs. Hazzard's looms for weaving. She had been spinning from morning until night so they would have as many goods as possible. He planned, of course, to be as public as possible in making his sales, a patriotic local farmer supporting the army in its noble work in defending America!

Unless the army settled nearby, however—something he considered highly unlikely—once the army marched out of sight, he would be faced with the same intractable problems. Money problems.

*

EVERYONE WAS SHOCKED WHEN Lucy disappeared.

June blamed herself for not seeing it coming.

June had prayed that she would make it home from Newport safely. And she did. She prayed for Guy to make it home alive. And he had. She prayed that Lucy would not do something foolish during her pregnancy. But she did.

Lucy was convinced they were going to sell her baby. Never mind what Jubah or Quamino said, that they never sell babies—children, yes, but not babies—Lucy said when this one came out looking white, the Hazzards wouldn't be able to stand it. Guy was silent, not healthy in his body or his soul, a powerful man grown weak in his bones and withdrawn in spirit. With the big army about to march nearby, everybody worked themselves from dawn until far into the night to make things to sell.

When June asked Guy what was wrong, he shrugged or shook his head. Once he said just before going to sleep that he felt more lost now than he ever did in the woods on the way to Canada. Quamino talked to him, but he had no more effect on Guy than he did on Lucy. He wanted Guy to come with him to the crossing point, but they worked too long each day to find the time. Guy was too weak to make it there and back even if they could.

"What would make you feel better?" she asked every night.

One night, after a silence so long she thought he either had not heard or had fallen asleep, he finally said, "A way out."

"Out?" she repeated.

Another long silence. She could hear his shallow breathing. "Out of being 'fraid."

"What you 'fraid about?"

He didn't answer. Not until the morning, as if the conversation had gone on all night in his head.

She looked at him in the gray of first light, and his eyes were open. He was looking at her. "I'm 'fraid they goin' sell you off. Or me."

"Why?"

"Anything can happen now. Anything."

She lifted herself on her elbow. "But maybe that anything be somethin' good." He shook his head. "You see something at the crossing point?" she asked in sudden alarm. He shook his head again.

"Don' see a way to stop a bad thing."

"You are feelin' weak. You are feelin' poorly. You get your strength back, you see things different."

His face looked sadder than she had ever seen it, his lusterless eyes downcast.

It occurred to her that Lucy felt the same way as Guy, that bad things could happen and she couldn't stop them.

Yes, June should have seen it coming. She should have noticed Lucy asking Guy all kinds of questions about the army—Lucy, who liked to talk, but almost never to ask a question. She had herself an idea all right, and when the huge army drew close, a few miles off to the west, and the Hazzards finished selling everything that wasn't fastened down, she disappeared, her belly big before her. Guy had told her the army from Boston that was marching south had crowds of women who traveled with it, mostly white women but with blacks and Indians too, all of them poor, but most were able to make some money and get by if they worked at it.

They awakened in the morning and she was gone without a trace. Nervously, Quamino broke the word to the master and mistress.

The Hazzards, though they did not trust Lucy, were still shocked. Then they were angry. They summoned the slaves to the front yard. Master John said he could not believe they did not stop her, and he did not believe them when they swore they did not know she was going to run off.

"She will be back," he said. "Though it will cost me money to send messages to the army authorities, and it will cost me money to publish public notices, and it will cost me in reward to the man who captures her, there is no way around this. You, all of you, will suffer for it."

June found herself hoping against hope Lucy would get away with it. At dinner, Jubah sighed and Quamino shook his head.

"Slave girl who doesn't know nothing 'bout nothing?" he said. "Walkin' around with her front big as a sow's belly?"

Each day, June awakened expecting Quamino's prophecy to be grimly fulfilled. Each day, though, no word of Lucy came. The master's mood grew darker every day that passed. In May, he got word that the assembly had decided to remove all use of the king's name from its documents and official prayers. He yelled so loudly, June could hear him from the summer kitchen. "Is there another colony in America who has done this?" he thundered. "Howe should attack here just to punish them!"

News of Lucy's escape trickled out to slaves on other plantations. Green shoots of hope sprouted around it. Jubah said she heard that when slaves were beaten down and exhausted, when they felt no better than burden-pulling farm animals, they now had another choice left to consider—doing what some of them called in whispered tones "a Lucy." When children dreamt of a life beyond the fields, it was through Lucy's eyes they did it. Her legend grew.

But not to Guy Watson. His strength began to return but his dejection did not ebb.

*

Master John learned in early June that the local planters had decided to cancel this year's 'Lection Day—there was too much unrest and talk of freedom. And they were uneasy about General Howe's intentions. He had seemingly disappeared, vanished, but friend and foe alike knew he would make landfall somewhere, and they said they preferred to know what his intentions were before gathering their slaves together in one place. Everyone believed they needed to have a celebration, a non-election 'Lection Day, to keep up the spirits of their servants. Too many of them planned all year about what clothes they would wear and what games they would play, what stories they would tell and what songs they would sing, not to give them their holiday. So the planters postponed it until the second Saturday in July. If Howe had not appeared off the coast by then, they would just have to take the chance.

Gambling John, as Master Hazzard was often called by his neighbors, smelled something more than faintly rotten about all this planning. Almost everyone knew, from the worthless spy Metcalf Bowler down to Young John in the militia, that Howe was going to head for the city of New York. If Howe could get New York, the British would command all navigation on the entire length of the Hudson River, be able to open communication with Canada by inland waters, and divide the northern colonies from the southern ones all in a single act. And that was why General Washington and his entire Continental army had abandoned New England and deployed most of their forces at Long Island and Brooklyn. The Rhode Island General Assembly—not the most courageous group of men Master John had ever seen—had decided it was safe to convene in Newport!

When he read at the beginning of June that the Congress had voted seven to six in favor of pursuing independence from England, he thought he knew why the Gardners, the Robinsons, the Watsons, the Stantons, and all the other rebel-sympathizing planters wanted 'Lection Day postponed. Still, when the news reached them that an entire regiment under Benedict Arnold had again failed catastrophically, he almost began to look forward to seeing their faces. Arnold, trying to reinforce a fort near Montreal, was surprised and overwhelmed, the fort fell, and instead of releasing the hundreds of prisoners in Quebec, he succeeded only in swelling their numbers. Congress's grand plans of the conquest of Canada lay in ruins. *Let them have their gathering and be jolly about* that, he thought.

Still, when the second Saturday in July did roll around, he could just smell it. The rumors were thick as gnats even before he arrived at the Stantons' parade grounds. Amid the cake, drums, races, ale, games, and dancing, the bastards would be reading Congress's freshly passed Declaration of Independence. As soon as he stepped from the carriage, he could picture it before anyone said a word. Fat old Jeremiah one-z Hazard, the one with the loud voice and the fat wen on his fat forehead, was going to get up on a tree stump and read it aloud. And he and Young John would have to do a brilliant job of pretending that it was all just fine-and-Yankee-doodle-dandy with them.

He warned Young John to keep a smile on his face. At least until they unveiled their own little surprise after the noonday reading by fat old Jeremiah one-z Hazard. It wouldn't wipe the smug, self-congratulatory looks off their faces, but it would let a bit of air from the slaves' sails in the event they started getting any more high ideas.

No, General Howe and the arrival of thousands of reinforcements from Scotland and Hesse-Hanau would sober them all up soon enough. Just before they stepped out onto the bunting-draped greensward, he said in a whisper to his son, "We'll see how cheerful they look *next* 'Lection Day."

*

UNDER A HOT SUN, slave children played and raced, fiddle music sounded, and storytelling began. Every once in a while, Guy heard someone quietly whisper the name Lucy and exchange guarded, satisfied looks. They didn't have the faintest idea what sort of life she was leading, but Guy did, assuming she was still alive. She would march all day behind the soldiers until they reached an encampment, and while they rested, she would have to work doing whatever she could find to earn enough money to be able to eat. She would not have any sure place to sleep, in good weather or in bad, and if she got sick or when her time to have her baby came, no one would tend to her. If she starved, no one would care. She was on her own, a lone kitten in the forest.

At least no one had come up to him and called him "Gov'nor."

Idle and heart-heavy, he watched a small crowd, including June, gather round a stocky bandy-legged little man who proceeded to pound pegs into a board using his head as if it were a beetle mallet. After banging home one peg as big as a thumb, he bowed to the applause and grinned. To his surprise, June led him over to where he was standing.

"This Jack Sisson," she said. She told him Guy's name. He nodded. A spy for the rebels. She had told him about Jack Sisson's adventure in Newport harbor.

"I'm Cap'n Barton's man," he said, and pointed to a dark-haired uniformed man who was standing next to a fat man while they read a long scroll of paper together.

Guy nodded again. "What bring you all the way down here?"

"Cap'n Barton interested in your mastuh. And his son, too."

"Interested how?"

"People say he walk on both sides of the road at the same time."

Guy was considering if he should make any answer to this when the fat man started to call for quiet. He motioned for whites and blacks alike to gather round. He called for a white boy in uniform to start flamming on a drum he carried by a leather strap around his neck. When the drumming stopped, the crowd grew silent.

Jack Sisson grinned and whispered, "You livin' in a spankin' new country."

Guy looked around. The sky was the same color as it always was, and so was his skin. He gave Sisson a dry look. "Look same to me."

The fat man climbed up on top of a tree stump and held up the scroll that he and Captain Barton had been reading a few moments ago. "This is dated at Philadelphia, the fourth day of July instant. Misters Ellery and Hopkins have signed it, and while representatives from New York have abstained pending the instructions of their assembly, it will soon be unanimously supported."

There was a burst of cheering from the whites. The fat man read the document. It was full of long words complaining about their treatment by the king. It ended with declaring the country's independence from Great Britain. More cheering went up.

Reverend Fayerweather got up and made one of his familiar jokes about it always being "fair weather" when he was there. And then he said a prayer of thanks and of praise. He ended by calling on everyone to join him in asking God to bless "the state of Rhode Island" as well as to save "the free and independent states of the republic of America." He said, "Amen," and the cheers began anew. Guy could tell Master John did not like his own clergyman saying these words, not one bit.

The slaves prepared themselves to return to their celebration when Guy noticed a closed carriage. A man in black slipped out the door and went up to Master John and spoke quietly for a time. Then the master called the king's county sheriff over.

Guy said to June, "Something 'bout to happen."

They followed his gaze.

"That a minister?" June asked of the man in black.

Jack Sisson said, "He carryin' a gun."

The sheriff began ringing a large hand bell and asked for everyone to remain quiet.

Suddenly the mood of the crowd shifted. Mothers hushed their children. When the sheriff rang the bell, everyone knew they were in for something more belonging to the punishments and sermons of Lecture Day than the festivities of 'Lection Day.

The sheriff gave a brief speech about justice and punishment for lawbreakers and said they had a person there today who had been tried and convicted in district court, but slave sheriff Mingo Rodman was going to mete out the punishment of nine-and-thirty lashes.

And then Master Hazzard got up on the stump. "In these tumultuous times," he said, "we must be especially heedful of the sacred bonds that bind us. These inviolable bonds, like those between a parent and a child, master and servant, shepherd and his flock, and, yea, the Lord and all mankind, can never be severed without terrible and awful consequences." On all previous Lecture Days, this familiar list included the king and his subjects. Guy did not give the absence any thought now. He looked at June, who was already crying. They knew who was in the carriage.

"Punishment must be given," Master John said, "not only because God is just. It is given as an instruction, as a loving parent might to an errant child to keep that child on the straight path, away from harm and out of the reach of evil. It is with joy and a measure of sorrow that I tell you that back among us today and soon to be reunited with her loved ones is Lucy Harris."

He gestured toward the carriage and the man in black pulled Lucy out. She was in shackles. Her name flew about among the slaves. Children began to cry and women began to moan. June noticed right away that Lucy's stomach was flat.

She looked awful. She was dressed in rags and her bruised face was full of sores. They dragged her forward toward a tree, and the swelling sounds of mourning and distress from the crowd took the masters by surprise. They began to look nervously around. There was no whipping post set up today, and the man in black looped a rope from her wrists over a tree limb and pulled until her arms were stretched straight above her head. He tied the rope around the trunk of the tree and nodded to Master John.

Surveying the agonized crowd, he announced that they had decided in charity to abate some of the punishment and, instead of thirty-nine lashes, Lucy Harris would suffer only twenty for the grave offense of being a runaway. He nodded at the impassive Mingo Rodman and told him to fulfill his office.

Rodman ripped open the back of Lucy's shift, stepped back, and prepared the whip as the sheriff read the charge and court sentence in a monotone.

When the sheriff was done, Mingo Rodman stepped up behind Lucy. Today, he did not unfurl the whip nor did he give a few trial snaps. Instead he began to lash her. Usually the powerful muscles in his wide back and thick legs worked together in one coordinated flow. He hit her hard enough to tear her flesh, but for the first time ever, he was not hitting someone as hard as he could. Still, the men in the crowd hung their heads and the women clutched their frightened children. And the lashing went on. Lucy quickly lost consciousness and the blood began to splash from her back with each stroke. The lashing went on.

Court-Martial Proceedings

*N*o one told Guy *how this trial would work except to say that Young John will not be questioned until after Guy himself is tried. Young John sits at the back of the hearing room with his father, sometimes rubbing a brass button on his militia uniform, but otherwise composed. The master has his usual half-smile playing across his lips, as if this is all a story whose end he knows and savors. So far, they have brought in three witnesses who were next to Guy Watson at the time he saw Young John turn and run from the lines. All three say they saw no such behavior, and in fact saw nothing of Lieutenant Hazzard at all. In different words and different ways, they have all said the same thing: it was hard enough just doing what they had to do to notice what anyone else was doing. Master John was going to call three more witnesses to say the same thing, but General Varnum said the court has "heard enough about what the soldiers near Guy Watson did not see."*

The general turns to the court secretary and nods. The clerk says, "The court calls Enoch Flinter." The door at the back opens and in walks a tall, skinny, narrow-faced man. The sun through the side windows glints dully off his spectacles. Guy isn't certain who it is, since, as the witness is sworn in, his back is to him. Once he takes his seat at the central witness table, there is absolutely no mistaking him or his birthmark. Enoch Flinter is Dr. Church's old assistant.

Guy's stomach drops like a brick.

Master John rises, pulls his vest to a comfortable fit, and walks up to the witness. "Your place of birth and present rank, sir."

"Born in Higganum, Connecticut. I am a sergeant in Colonel Enos's Second Connecticut brigade."

Guy glances at hearing officer Colonel Greene's face. He knows the name "Enos" will hit him like a tongue on a sore tooth. Sure enough, his eyes suddenly rivet on Enoch Flinter.

"And before that, Sergeant Flinter?"

"Before that I was an aide to Doctor Benjamin Church at the Boston encampments."

Now all the hearing officers' eyes rivet on the witness.

"And where," Master John asks, "is Doctor Church now?"

"Last I heard, he was in Norwich prison."

"Convicted on what charge?"

"For passing secrets to the enemy."

"Treason?"

"Yes, sir."

"Were you still his aide when he was arrested?"

"No, sir. I was with Colonel Enos on the march to Quebec."

"Very good. Now. Sergeant Flinter, when you were at the Boston lines, did you have occasion to meet the defendant, Guy Watson?"

"I did. He was a servant to Captain Ward of the First Rhode Island."

"Do you see him in this room?"

"That's him," Flinter says, pointing directly at Guy.

"And what, if anything, were your dealings with him?"

"Doctor Church asked me to arrange for him to serve dinner at the officers' headquarters."

"Did you?"

"I did. They needed the help."

"Was Doctor Church normally interested in officers' servants?"

"This was the only time I ever saw him be so."

"And what was his purpose in placing Guy Watson at headquarters?"

"He told me to have him report any useful information he might overhear."

"What do you mean, 'useful information'?"

"Military plans."

"Did he?"

"I checked with him once or twice a week. And, yes, sometimes he did pass along information he had heard while serving the officers their meals."

As clearly as if it is a breeze moving through the room, Guy can feel the hearing officers' eyes swing toward him.

"And what did you do with that information?"

"I passed it along to Doctor Church."

"Thank you, Sergeant," Master John says with a smile. He turns to General Varnum. "I have no further questions at the moment."

For the first time in the trial, most of the hearing officers are not looking at the witness as he leaves. They are looking at Guy, almost as if they are seeing him for the first time.

Chapter Twenty-One

Sam awoke with a sour, rusty taste in his mouth. His gums were bleeding again. The giant spider-shaped brown blotch on the ceiling over his head had not changed. His bed was stacked on top of two others like bunks in a ship's hold so his face was inches away. He put his hands behind his head and stared. He tried to think of Phebe, but her face would not come clear. He could tell dawn was nearing. There were some things he had gotten used to with the thirty-six officers jammed into a small room—the smell of shit and piss and unwashed bodies, the loss of freedom to do anything except when the guards said they could. And there was one principle thing he had not gotten used to: the complete and fundamental uncertainty.

The simple uncertainty of everyday life was true everywhere, but it got magnified here. Within days of their imprisonment, a deadly smallpox epidemic broke out. Dearborn talked Sam into writing up a petition asking to be inoculated. Dearborn said that seven or eight times as many people died who got the disease the natural way, and in their closed quarters the disease would go through them like a fire through dry straw. A local physician came in, made a small incision between Sam's index finger and thumb, and carefully introduced some yellowish variloid matter from a smallpox pustule. An assistant tied Sam's hand with a clean strip of cloth and the doctor went on to the next man.

Sam was permitted to stay with the others just long enough to witness from his barred window the solemn funeral for General Montgomery. They had already seen sleds and carioles pass up their snow-covered street loaded with bodies, American soldiers tossed like cordwood to be taken to the Dead House. The Dead House was where their frozen, uncoffined corpses would be kept until the Canadian ground thawed enough for them to be put in the earth. It was a scene Sam found difficult to forget: the men still in their uniforms, heaped together and frozen in the position they assumed in their death throes. When he saw Tom Shepherd pass, still clutching his belly, his gray face a fixed and frozen mask of pain, he could not look any more.

The next day he and twenty other inoculated men were moved to remote quarters to await their fate. One of their waiters, a boy from Maine, a private who was chosen to serve the officers, reported not feeling well. The next day, his face ballooned to twice its normal size and he was covered with great red pox that seemed, almost as they watched, to grow into a single swelling. Soon delirious with fever, he called plaintively for his "mothah" in a northern country accent. They carried him to the hospital in his pus-stained sheets. A day later he was dead. By nightfall, they all had raging sore throats, fevers, aching joints, and skin that was sore to the lightest touch. Dearborn got so sick himself, he had to be taken to the Hotel de Dieu, and Sam knew he was frightened at least as much by the hospital as he was of the disease. In the end, though, he and the other nineteen survived. Captain Lamb, the New Yorker head of artillery, whom Sam had seen with what looked like half his face blown off, miraculously survived, blind in one eye and deformed. But Captain Hubbard, who had suffered only a minor ankle wound, died before Sam was returned to his cell. Hubbard was heaped with the rest in the Dead House to await the spring thaw.

The bigger uncertainties were the ones that weighed, though, and their weight increased day by day. Would they be here months more? Years? Could they miraculously be rescued? Exchanged? Put to trial in London like Vermont's Colonel Ethan Allen? Executed as rebels and traitors? Weeks passed. Finally in March, Benjamin Franklin arrived with messages and money from home. The men's hopes for a release soared. Who in the world was better than Ben Franklin at negotiation? He left ten days later. Nothing.

They heard a new rumor almost every day: General Lee, "their long-nosed cousin with the thick-necked black dog is coming to their aid." They heard of a report that General Washington had tried to storm Boston and lost four thousand men, that Arnold had died of his wound, that Montreal was retaken, that Congress was overthrown and money had lost all value. They knew nothing.

Only one development was no rumor. Men who were born in England, Scotland, or Ireland were told they had to sign an oath to serve His Majesty in a new "Emigrants" regiment or be sent to England and tried for treason. They could "enlist in the king's service" or be carted across a wide ocean. Over a dozen men abruptly traded their prison cell for a British uniform.

They got dysentery and soiled themselves in their beds at night. The cell was so crowded there was no room to pace. Just as the dysentery passed, scurvy hit. The slightest bump caused blue blotches to bloom under their skin. Sam lost a molar. His legs and sides and back developed massive bruises, and the joints began to ache. There were no fresh vegetables or antiscorbutics in all of Quebec at any price.

When the bitter cold relented in late April, the lice began. They boiled their blankets and coats, washed their shirts in lye, scrubbed themselves in vinegar and wood ash. Little of it helped. Outside they could hear the sounds of digging. They were going to empty the Dead House.

And then in the first week in May, they learned that an American fireship had floated into the harbor. Washington had not forgotten them! Arnold was coming to their rescue at last! As soon as they heard shots announcing the assault, they planned to overpower the guards and make their escape.

Nothing happened. Two days later they were permitted to go out into a yard in small groups to take in the air. The guards gleefully showed them why: two frigates and an armed schooner had arrived from England. Church bells tolled all over the city in wild celebration of the enemy's arrival of reinforcements. Still more British ships arrived the next day. With them came the word that an army of American troops outside of the city under someone named General Wooster had panicked and fled pell mell into the forest, leaving behind cannons, supplies, food, and powder. Even the sick were abandoned. The disintegrated army fled west to Montreal in total disorder, where they hoped to take refuge with the newly promoted General Arnold.

This ended their last hope for rescue.

The American officers could see the groups of tall Hanoverian and Hessian soldiers marching past the prison wearing mitre-like brass helmets and dark blue regimental coats. The presence of these famously disciplined and brutal foreign soldiers told them everything they needed to know about the king's intentions. No settlement, no accommodation, no end to the war.

Summer brought only more bad news about strings of losses in Montreal and near Lake Champlain. They felt doomed.

In mid-August, on a sweltering afternoon, out of the blue, they were asked to sign a document. It was their release on "parole." Major Meigs, who had grown ill in July with a huge swelling in his armpit, had already been released on parole, giving his word not to take up arms until he was properly exchanged. Their hopes at first surged, they discovered that Meigs's agreement was not at all what they were being asked to pledge. Their statement said they promised "never to take up arms against His Majesty." If they signed, they were told they would be sent home by sea.

Meigs did not have that clause in his release. There was a long moment of silence as they digested this condition. Sam was the first to get it, and the first to say, "No. Never."

There was a burst of swearing. Goodrich argued for lying, but most of them insisted that if they were permitted to go home, after all they had been through, they would want to be able to hold their heads up honorably. At last, all of them refused to sign.

Sam, staring once again at the brown stain on the ceiling, began to consider what it would be like to spend years in this prison. He decided it was better not to imagine at all.

That evening at dusk, an aide to General Carelton arrived, the same one who brought them the parole agreement. A few men sprang to their feet, but the aide shook his head and gestured for them to sit. He had no news to bring them, except, "Some news for Captain Ward." His face, illuminated by a candle he carried, was grave.

Sam climbed carefully down from his bunk, his heart pounding in his chest.

"I regret to tell you," the aide said softly, "that we have received information that your father has died. A terrible case of smallpox at the end of March in Philadelphia. Our report says that half the city went to his funeral." He paused and extended a letter with a broken seal. "General Carelton feels it is safe to give you his old letter now."

Sam was stunned. Rumors that had reached them from guards usually proved untrue. News from adjutants and aides, however, had been accurate. He held out doubt for a second, but the look of genuine regret on the man's face hit him like a blow. Compassion from an enemy.

No mother since he was a boy. Now no father. It was as if the roof of his home had been suddenly ripped off and left him exposed to wintry skies. He took the letter and went to a corner of the room. The men murmured their regrets and Colonel Greene asked them all to join him in prayer. Sam could barely attend to the words. He kept looking at the clear, deeply familiar handwriting on the letter. When the prayer was over, the officers talked quietly among themselves, trying to offer Sam the impossible commodity of privacy. Written two weeks before his death, his father's letter reported all the family was well and the whole country was proud of him for his and all the other men's heroic efforts. And after he reminded him to behave honorably in captivity, his father added the news that sister Nancy had married Ethan Clarke. Not a word about Phebe.

Sam thought of the last time he saw his father, the morning he had marched off for the Boston lines on a day, only last summer, that now seemed years ago. He could see his father's lined face, his old slouch hat, his intelligent and warm blue eyes, his look of pride and worry. His father had called for God's blessings to preserve him. He looked down at the letter and, as the writing blurred, he thought how brightly the image of his father burned in his memory, and how terrible it was that he would not be given the chance ever to add a new one of him.

The same aide came back to the cells hours later. This time his face was neutral and every man in the room was on alert. "General Carelton," he announced, "has struck the offending words from the agreement." The burst of cheering was so loud they almost drowned out the conclusion. "If you sign, gentlemen, tomorrow morning you will all be sent home on five transport ships."

Over the months Sam had become aware that most of the men in the army had in their mind a picture of what they were fighting to defend. It was not just for an idea of freedom, though they wanted to secure that, too—but fighting to preserve from harm and servitude their wife or their children or their farm or their parents.

The world felt like a larger and much colder place. He no longer knew what "home" meant to him anymore.

*

THE CAPTAIN OF THEIR frigate in which they were all crammed would not tell them a word about their destination. They knew they were to be landed in an American port under British control, but where?

Because they stayed far from harbors, they believed the war had gone well for them along the coast. But when they passed Martha's Vineyard and drew within sight of Block Island, they knew they were not going to Boston and could not understand why. Sam and all the men from New England grew glum to see their homes disappearing behind them. The men from Pennsylvania and Virginia grew at once hopeful and fearful—if they landed near their homes, it would be more convenient, but it also meant the British army had moved to their doorstep.

Finally, they anchored outside what they were told was New York harbor.

The first intelligence brought from shore told the same grim story: the redcoats, the Hessians, and the Scottish Black Watch had taken Long Island, the city of New York, and most of the island of Manhattan. Over a thousand American prisoners had been captured, including New Hampshire's General John Sullivan, the commander of Sam's old wing of the army, outside Boston.

After all the months of captivity, standing briefly atop the decks in shackles, they at last could see the land they had fought to preserve. From the slimy hold below deck, Sam could not see anything.

Then they were told that General Howe would not honor General Carelton's promise to release them on parole after all.

A shuddering groan of dismay swept through the hold. Sylvanus Shaw burst into sobs, and a wave of desolation engulfed them, far worse than the hopelessness of confinement in the north. It was as if Howe had revived them from unconsciousness in order to torture them. Sam feared that several of the men might actually go mad. One beat his head on the gunwales until he was bloody.

Sam was in a bottom bunk this time, and the hot, thick, and fetid air made his cell in Quebec seem like a paradise.

And so, excruciatingly, they were held prisoner, chained together, anchored in the harbor, a musket shot from home. Just when they thought no worse news could come, as they waited, American prisoners were brought aboard who told them Howe was crushing what was left of Washington's army. At Kip's Bay, after another complete rout, Washington's troops fled in panic around him. They said he came within a few yards of being captured himself.

Once a day, like slaves on the long middle passage, they were brought up on deck and permitted to breathe the air and shuffle their shackled feet for exercise. They watched the shore even while the cause for which they had fought appeared to be collapsing all around them.

On the night of September 21, they were locked in irons, this time on the top deck, to watch, aghast, as a great part of the city of New York went hellishly up in flames. It was unlike anything any of them had ever seen or hoped ever to see again. Their faces were as brightly lit by the blaze of the huge fire as if it were full noon. They were hundreds of yards away but could feel the heat on their faces. Buildings, churches, houses, warehouses, and trees along the streets went up in whirling cones of red and orange. Within an hour, smoke and soot completely blocked out the moon and stars.

The guards told them that the ruthless George Washington ordered the city fired to keep its mostly loyalist-owned wealth from falling into British hands. Several Americans were caught lighting up buildings and were shot, bayoneted, or tossed alive into the flames.

The next morning, Sam, Topham, and Thayer had determined in whispers that the time had come to attempt an escape. Convinced that Howe's rage at the destruction of his proposed garrisoning place had wrecked forever their chances for release, they decided they would rather die in the attempt than starve in the pestilential hold of a prison ship.

On the twenty-third, as they were considering their final plans of how best to rush the guards—one year to the day that they left Fort Western for their march to Quebec—they were told their agreement with General Carelton would be kept after all.

Seconds later, without another word, they were lined up to await the shallops that would take them ashore. As they stood there, half stunned by their good fortune, the guards told them to watch their step. The British had just hanged a confessed spy in Artillery Park, some Connecticut schoolmaster by the name of Nathan Hale, and it could damn well happen to them, too.

Chapter Twenty-Two

THEY WADED THE LAST few feet ashore at a deserted sandy point across from Staten Island. Some of the men dropped to their knees and hugged the beach grass, weeping in relief at being free and back on native ground. Sam heard Captain Morgan's unmistakable voice bellowing in happiness. Some of the men began a celebration that lasted till dawn and wakened sleeping civilians in Elizabethtown, while others decided to seek out friends and family who were stationed in the area. Others still, like Captains Topham and Thayer and the other Rhode Islanders, decided to head straight to their homes and hearths.

Sylvanus Shaw, who planned to make it back to Newport as soon as possible, reported to Sam that their company had returned with more men than any company in the army.

"How many?" Sam asked.

"Thirty-three."

He tried not to think of the ones who did not return, but their names and faces swam up before him. He wished Lieutenant Sylvanus Shaw Godspeed.

"Where are you heading, sir?"

"Colonel Greene and I are going to find General Greene before we make our return. He may have news he wishes reported back to the colony."

"Colony?" said Shaw. "Ah, you haven't heard. 'Tis the free and glorious *state* of Rhode Island, one of thirteen independent but united states! Passed July second, signed in Congress two days later. They say the second will be a great holiday in years to come."

With the smell and smoke of the burned city still hanging in the air and, if the reports were right, the Continental army on the verge of destruction, it struck Sam as odd to be talking of national celebrations. But, for most, the exhilaration of being released from captivity mastered all. Sylvanus Shaw, he knew, had two parents, a wife, and a child to go back to. He wished he could feel what he knew the other men were feeling, but he could not. He did not know if it were too much death or not having a home to go to. And their names tolled in his head like a slowly ringing church bell. Gus Mumford. Tom Shepherd. Bishop Standley. Josiah Carr. Captain Hendricks. Captain Hubbard. General Montgomery. Sergeant and Mrs. Warner. The boy from Maine dying of smallpox and calling for his "mothah." His own father.

"Captain?" Sam turned to look at him. "Don't know when I will see you again. It was a privilege serving with you." He extended a hand and Sam shook it.

*

WITH THEIR LAST REMAINING money, he and Christopher Greene bought a predawn breakfast of fresh eggs and cooked ham and cornmeal bread and rented a pair of horses to make their way to what was left of Washington's army.

They were directed by some locals to Fort Constitution, newly renamed Fort Lee. The two men, light-headed from lack of sleep, made their way past bits and pieces of the American army. As the sun rose, they saw through the smoky air that some of the soldiers were lost, many of them had clubbed their muskets and were heading home, and a few new companies were arriving, bewildered about where to go. The veterans looked hard-faced and tired, and the militia recruits were skittish and nervous-necked. Most of the men were tentless, coatless, their shoes and boots patched and wrapped in rags. Colonel Greene said they looked about how most of them did halfway to Quebec. It looked bad, but they had seen worse.

They did not see a familiar face until they arrived at Fort Lee's headquarters, a large elegant home with a commanding view of the hills to the northeast. Inside they saw plump pink-faced Billy Blodgett, whom Sam had first seen in college do a turn as a comic actor in Providence and not seen since they were at the lines in Boston. As he was then, he was Nat Greene's aide-de-camp.

In a reaction that soon became familiar to all the survivors of the Quebec march, Blodgett glanced at them, glanced again, and then stared, mouth agape.

"You're alive…" he said, his voice gone suddenly hoarse with emotion.

Sam looked at Christopher Greene and down at himself. They were filthy, dressed in tattered blanket coats. Their unwashed skins were grayish-yellow, and Sam knew all the returnees looked like skeletal animals in the aftermath of a famine.

"You will not believe the stories we have heard of you." He shook his head in slow astonishment, still staring at them as if he could not believe his eyes. "How are Topham and Thayer?"

Colonel Greene said they were well and headed for home. He handed Blodgett a list of the men who had returned. And those who had not. As he was reviewing the list, he murmured a few names but, when he was done, drew a deep breath, smiled at the two men, and said, "God but the general will be happy to see you both. It'll be just the medicine he needs."

"Is he ill?" Sam asked.

"He almost died of a fever in August and his command had to be handed over to General Sullivan. It was at the worst possible time. He was in bed, delirious, and then unconscious for twenty straight hours on the day we lost Long Island."

"We heard that General Sullivan was captured."

"Not Sullivan's fault," Blodgett said. "He didn't know the soldiers, the defenses, or the terrain. General Greene had walked and mapped every inch of the place himself. When Sullivan was attacked by stealth, it was a disaster. He fought the best he could. Still a prisoner, you know."

"Is General Greene recovered?" the colonel asked.

"Completely."

"The army looks beaten up."

He nodded. "We have had some alarming moments. But we have more legs than a centipede." He glanced off at a far door across the large central room. "Nat may never forgive me if I keep you from his company any longer."

As he led them across the room, a large bulbous-nosed man with a short upper lip and a blue-eyed piercing glance descended some stairs to their left. He was reading some dispatches, and he paused when he saw Blodgett. Billy greeted him good humoredly as "Common Sense."

"'Common sense,'" the colonel repeated blankly.

"You may be the only men in America who have not heard of this man. This, gentlemen, is Mr. Thomas Paine whose book has been read, or read to, almost every man, woman, and child on this shore. I tell you this without exaggeration—the power of his words has shaken the thrones of Europe."

The sloppily dressed man extended a thick hand to shake. With a pronounced English accent, he said he was "merely an aide to General Greene."

"These," Blodgett said, "are Rhode Island officers who went with General Arnold to Quebec. Permit me to present Lieutenant Colonel Christopher Greene and Captain Samuel Ward."

Paine stared at them with the same sudden intensity that Billy Blodgett had when he first saw them. "Just released from prison?" They nodded. "You are great patriots. I am honored to make your acquaintance." He shook their hands again, apparently forgetting he had already done so a few seconds before. "I believe you make up some of the most renowned men this young country has to offer. Welcome home, sirs!"

Blodgett, meanwhile, had knocked on a closed door and then entered. Sam could hear Nat's familiar voice saying, "*Who? Here now?*"

The door burst open and Nat came forward and embraced each of them, ignoring their filthy clothes and pestilent stench. He murmured, "You are a sight for sore eyes!"

He was pale and thin and his dark hair had gone quite gray at the temples. The three friends looked at each other for a moment in silence and then all began to talk at once. Nat waved them into his office, asking Blodgett not to let anyone disturb him.

First Nat expressed his sorrow over Sam's father's death, said he missed him every day, and that the country never had a better friend. His voice thickened a bit when he said, "Nor did I. He was my best correspondent and wisest advisor." He cleared his throat. "He did live to hear the news that the British had evacuated Boston and was heartened by it." Nat was silent for a moment. "But let me tell you that all the rest of both your families are well." He turned to his cousin Christopher. "Anna and your children have gone to her parents' house in Providence. They make quite a crowd. They all await your return with wild impatience." Looking at Sam, he said, "Your sister Catharine has made my brother a father and you and me into fresh new uncles. And sister Nancy has married Ethan Clarke."

In the old days, Sam might have joked about her once-painful refusal to marry Nat. Instead, he offered, "I was able to read that news in my father's last letter."

Nat's eyebrows lifted. "You were permitted to receive mail?"

"Given the circumstances, General Carelton treated us with humanity."

Nat snorted. "You'll pardon me, then, if I say that you both look terrible."

"They provided for us," Christopher said, "as well as they were able. It was not until May when the British ships arrived that they were able to give us fresh food."

"A month closed below decks accounts for some of what you see," Sam added. "And you, General? How fares cousin Caty?"

He grinned. "We have a little boy named George Washington Greene. And, if our happy providence continues, she tells me he will have a brother or sister this winter. But tell me about Quebec."

Sam and the colonel looked at each other. To them this was old news. They were impatient to hear what was happening in the present. Colonel Greene gave a compressed narrative of their march and lost battle, and before Nat could ask more than a question or two, Sam broke in to ask how they stood now.

Nat sighed. "General Washington has brilliantly managed a series of retreats, though these are actions the country and Congress will not much credit."

"We have heard," Sam said, "that New York is awash in Tories."

"More than in New England, certainly. But once they see the cruelty of the occupying army, they'll change their colors." He pointed to a map on the wall next his desk table. "You see, with this fort where we stand now and Fort Washington just across the Hudson both in our hands, they cannot supply themselves without great risk. They are as cut off here as they were in Boston. And the enormous fire in the city I admit serves us well. I urged General Washington to set fire to it to render it uninhabitable. He forbade it. But some townspeople must have felt as I did. They did it on their own."

"The army looks to be in difficult straits."

Nat shook his head firmly. "We lack three things. A good corps of officers, an end to this use of militia, and a Congress who will fund us enough to make the first two possible. A good army is a permanent, well-paid standing force."

"Well all of us were militia once," Christopher observed.

"Some militia are better than others. There are too many one-month wonders. At Kip's Bay, they fled like running water and left General Washington standing *all by himself* within a few yards of the enemy. Without him, I doubt this army could survive a week. The next day, I should tell you, your old regiment behaved well under fire." He began to explain Newport's fears when Billy Blodgett knocked on the door.

"An express from General Mercer, sir."

Nat nodded and got to his feet to read it. "Tell the messenger to remain in case I need to send a reply." He scanned the paper, frowning. "The British have landed a detachment at Paulhus Hook. That puts them just ten miles south." He called, not loudly or with any anxious haste, for his aides Blodgett, Paine, and Colonel Cornell, whom Sam had heard called "Colonel Snarl" because of his strictness. He quietly began to give orders. Sam was struck by the ease of Nat's sense of command, everything proceeding with the naturalness as if he were simply continuing a conversation. Blodgett was to issue general orders for preparation for attack; Paine was to alert General Washington at Harlem Heights; Cornell was told to anticipate the needs for a defensive position if the British forces decided to make a move north.

When he was done, he apologized to Christopher and Sam, explaining he would have to ride to Bergen to consult with General Mercer. Colonel Greene said he had one question to trouble him with before he left. "What happened," he asked, "to Colonel Enos of Connecticut and Colonel Campbell of the New York line?"

Nat frowned. "Each man was court-martialed immediately on his return. Enos for turning back without orders, Campbell for not pursuing the attack after General Montgomery was killed. I regret to say...both were acquitted."

The quiet colonel could not keep the anger from his voice. "How? Why?"

"Since every man who might have a perspective different from theirs was a prisoner or manning the siege lines, who was there to contradict them? There was no one to challenge their account."

The colonel shook his head and sighed, and Sam slammed his fist down on the chair. "But for them," Sam said, "it would have been different."

Nat nodded. "But now we must go ahead." He put on a dark blue cape and settled a three-cornered hat on his head. "Gentlemen, we will get you exchanged as soon as possible. Nothing forbids you from visiting me. Rest. Eat. Sleep. Give my love to all our friends in Rhode Island. Welcome home, both of you, to America."

Billy Blodgett got them horses to ride home on, a change of clothes, and some cash for expenses. Finally, he walked out onto the front stepping stone and, pointing through the soft fall air, gave them directions to the post road.

Chapter Twenty-Three

As Sam rode up the path to the Ward farm in early October, he saw in the blaze of midafternoon sun that the leaves were just beginning to redden on the topmost reaches of their old maples. He reined in his horse and took in a few deep breaths of the cool air. It was the peak of harvest time. He was puzzled not to see the large group of men they usually hired. Instead, Sam saw the house servants, Cujoe and Violet, dressed in work clothes bent over in the field. Working nearby were his sister Nancy and her new husband, Ethan Clarke, and a lanky boy who it took a second for him to recognize was his fourteen-year-old brother, John.

They had not yet spotted him, and he was grateful to have these moments to adjust. His younger sisters Mary, Debby, Betsy, and Catharine were not there. His little brothers Ray and Dickey were not there. If they were home, they would have been out in the field. He knew this not because fieldwork was their usual task, but because Nancy had never worked in the field in her life, yet there she was. He could not remember their house servants there, either. Toby, their field servant, someone he would have expected to find twisting off ears of corn or loading butternut squash onto a cart, was nowhere to be seen. The fences and outbuildings were in disrepair, the crops weedier than he had ever seen them. Ethan Clarke, their minister's son, was a smart man, but he did not know about farming. Weeds would take their toll not on this year's but on next year's crops. Sam sighed. Perhaps if they dug the weeds out before the frost, they could hope to avoid major loss. But mostly he knew in a single glance that the Ward farm was in trouble. He was glad to have the chance to take this bad news in all at once, not learn it in painful bits and pieces.

Nancy saw him first. He took off his hat and waved. She dropped her burlap bag and, lifting her skirts with one hand, came at a quick walk toward him. "Sammy?" she called. He waved again, and she broke into a run, "It's Sammy!"

By the time he dismounted, she had flung herself around his neck and was weeping in great convulsive sobs. He patted her back, and Ethan Clarke ran up next, grinning and grabbing his hand. John looked almost as shy as Violet and Cujoe, but they all could not stop smiling. Nancy, who was normally composed and self-collected, cried on so stormily, everyone grew concerned. Giving Sam a puzzled glance, Ethan asked her if she were all right, and she sobbed on for almost another minute before finally she pulled herself back far enough to look at Sam's face and managed to say, "I've missed you." Everyone, including Sam, laughed gently at this. Nancy looked bewildered for a moment and then, wiping her eyes, laughed as well. She hugged him and every once in a while, through her laughter, broke into a sob.

*

NANCY AND VIOLET LAY out a huge meal and Ethan led them in a prayer of thanks for his safe return. After everyone exclaimed how alarmingly thin he looked, they gathered around to watch him eat as if this were a task, like repairing a door hinge or fixing a bucket, that they all wanted to see done properly. He savored each bite, and though he warned them he could not eat much at a single sitting, they looked disappointed each time he paused in chewing and drinking. They told him what had become of his brothers and sisters, with all of them apprenticed and living off with aunts and uncles. Sam listened to their accounts, their familiar faces and voices and the old familiar kitchen smell of wood ash and molasses all comforting as an embrace. When no one mentioned Phebe, he wondered if she might have found courtship elsewhere. He wanted to ask about her, but he was not sure he could maintain himself in the face of more bad news.

They told him what a hero he and all the men who marched to Quebec were, and he quickly grew embarrassed. John started to ask him questions about the army and the fighting and the imprisonment until Nancy asked him to hush and let Sammy just be for a while. He winked at his younger brother and said they had lots of days ahead in which to talk, but he was grateful to his sister for sparing him.

He told them instead about his visit to Nat Greene and the surprise of learning almost a year's news in the matter of a few minutes. They nodded, and Nancy told him what they knew about their father's final days in Philadelphia; they were good ones until the terrible illness. They all paused in silence, still feeling his loss.

"Our affairs here are strained," Sam said.

The corners of Nancy's mouth turned down and Ethan Clarke nodded. Sam knew his brother in law might not be a farmer, but he had an excellent head for business. "Your daddy left an estate with a large amount of land," he said. "But I am afraid he left even larger debts."

"So I've gathered," Sam said.

Nancy asked Violet, Cujoe, and John to return to work. As if he were a Bible or a lucky charm or they could not quite believe he was there in the flesh, they each found a way to touch Sam—his wrist, his elbow, his shoulder—before they stepped outside. Once they closed the door behind them, Ethan continued. "Your father appointed Attorney General Marchant and Uncle Greene executors—Uncle Greene is now chief justice, I should add. In any case, with you in the army, they felt it best to leave the management of it in my hands."

"Wise choice," Sam said. In the uncomfortable silence that followed, Sam could tell Nancy and Ethan did not know how to pursue the subject. "Where do we stand?"

Ethan sighed before looking him in the eye. "Judge Greene and Mr. Marchant have advised us to render the estate insolvent."

"Insolvent?"

"Yes. To protect the land from being broken up."

"Have we begun the proceedings?"

His brother-in-law shook his head. "We have kept hoping for a turn in fortune, but the only turns have been bad ones."

"We were also waiting," Nancy added, "for you to come home."

Ethan said, "Everyone is suffering. Shipping has been brought to a complete halt, and Newport is being blackmailed into provisioning the British fleet. War costs are mounting, and both Rhode Island scrip and the new Continental currency are fast losing value."

"And this is why Mary and Debby and Ray are working."

"Yes," she said. "And why Betsy and Dickey are living elsewhere."

"If the value of the currency is eroding," Sam said, "then isn't it best to delay repaying our debts?"

"Nearly half our debt is due in gold, and it is becoming more expensive almost hour by hour. We do not in any case have the means to pay them off."

"That leaves no choice," Sam concluded. He looked about his family home, the place his father liked to call Ward Hall, in dismay.

Nancy, following his look, nodded.

Sam, who had thought he was prepared to deal with bad news of a material kind, found he was not so well prepared after all. It felt as if losing had become a way of life. He glanced up and could see that Nancy, though seven years older than he, had been holding out the hope that he, on his return, might work some magic and rescue them all. They looked at each other, and each could read the helplessness in the other's eyes.

Sam pushed himself up from the table. He excused himself and said he needed to lie down for a few minutes before he joined them outside. Though the air still had some warmth, he was shivering.

He lay down and covered himself with his coat. He looked at the old beige water spot on the ceiling and closed his eyes. When he awakened and gazed up at the window casement, it was dark outside.

*

Barns, pens, fences, forage, and reaping tools all needed repair. Wood needed to be cut and split. Sam was forced to ask neighbors to whom they did not owe money if he could borrow their tools. He rose before dawn throughout the month and worked well past dark to complete the harvest. Though he doubted any Wards would be there to harvest another crop, he also insisted they dig out the weeds. At night he wrote letters to try to collect on old debts and defer payments on ones they owed. He wrote the state treasurer to request payment of his captain's salary for the months he was held prisoner. He wrote old friends and school acquaintances to see if any opportunities for work or investment were available. He did repairs by lantern light. Falling every night into bed exhausted, every morning, first thing, he thought of his sister Hannah who died of a wasting disease when she was one year older than he was now. He thought of his mother, dead of a purulent fever, and his father, dead of smallpox. At night he remembered the old intense, cheerful, noisy family dinners, the solemn book and Bible readings, the children's games on the parlor floor. Now it was quiet in the large house and, as the weather cooled, they sealed off several rooms. He reviewed the ledgers, and he knew that no matter how hard he worked, theirs was a lost cause. He worked anyway, each day feeling sadder.

While he split wood and dug weeds, the dead of the army crowded his thoughts.

During the worst moments of his time in prison, usually at first light or just after dark, he did not feel as lost as he did now. In Quebec, at the back of his mind had been friends and family and home, all of them having an unalterable, welcoming reality. Back in Westerly at last and sleeping in his own bed, he now felt adrift and homesick. He knew that what he truly missed now existed only in his memory, and day by day it receded further from his grasp.

*

His younger brothers and sisters came at various times to visit, and Sam put on a determinedly cheerful face for them, something he found more tiring than any fieldwork. They brought city newsprints, little of it bearing good news. He asked about Judge Greene's family and his aunt Catharine, but no one had anything to report about them or about Phebe but that they were as well as could be under the difficult circumstances. With the British in control of New York, an invasion of New England was almost certainly the next step. They would threaten them on three sides.

"Are we safe in Westerly?" Nancy asked.

"Safe from a landing," Sam replied. "The town is too small to garrison a large number of soldiers. Providence, Newport, and Warwick are not."

"Do you think they will attack us before Connecticut or Massachusetts?"

Sam tried to think of a way to say what he thought without alarming Nancy. "They have tried Boston already and are not likely to want a return visit. Connecticut is so close to New York, I should think they would want something farther north." He saw her eyes widen. "The season is late to begin a major campaign, so nothing may happen until spring. It is in their interest to make us fear an invasion so much that we try to get General Washington to divide his forces and send back militia."

*

THE GENERAL ASSEMBLY DECIDED the safest place to meet was a few miles to the Wards' north in South Kingstown. Uncle Henry and Governor Cooke and the assembly, knowing of the Wards' plight, had offered Sam a substantial fee for his services. They wished him to consult on the state's behalf directly with Nathanael Greene. An attack on Washington's army at the end of October in White Plains had made it clear that Howe had not taken up winter quarters, and anxiety was growing. The state's leaders wanted Sam to discuss with Nat Greene how to help the main army while leaving at home enough militia to protect the state.

Sam could guess the answer to this question—no militia anywhere could defend against a British landing, and the fate of the states would be determined by the fate of Washington's army—but he was preparing himself for a return to New York to get the answer. It was not going to be an easy journey. His own strength had not fully returned, but he could not afford to refuse the money, and with the harvest done and Ethan there to attend to the financial tangle, he felt he had to go.

The afternoon before he was to leave, he was inventorying tasks for the weeks ahead when he saw a small carriage bouncing up the road to their house. He shaded his eyes against the slanting sun and watched Cujoe help two passengers dismount, both women, caped and gloved against the November cold. He knew the instant he saw them they were not his sisters, but he could not see their faces under their bonnets well enough to make out who they were. He beat the dust from his father's old slouch hat and kicked the caked dirt from his boots before he went to greet their visitors.

It was Phebe and her mother, Aunt Catharine, people he had not seen since the Boston lines several lifetimes ago. He kissed his aunt and smiled at his cousin and said, "It looks as if hello and goodbye will have to be accomplished in one breath. I am off tomorrow for New York."

"We heard," said his aunt. "And since we know you will be gone an uncertain time, we simply could not let you go without seeing you. Phebe has been after me ever since you came back to make our way here."

Phebe lowered her eyes and blushed. Sam and Ethan helped them off with their capes, and Sam saw that his young cousin was not only taller but had grown more womanly. Her face was the same, though more oval, and her eyes had grown larger and her soft cheeks more prominent. He tried not to stare. She was, he knew, approaching her seventeenth birthday.

As they entered the house, his aunt said, "Heavens above, Sam, it is good to see you. I know you didn't follow my advice about the wisdom of making your march north, but it appears that we were perhaps both right. Surely it was a worthy pursuit but one with so many perils! In any case, we thank the Lord that you are home safe. We have brought you some clothes, but your sisters say you are nothing but skin and bone so we hardly knew what size. Nancy writes that you have gained back a great deal of weight, so we had to come see for ourselves."

The women looked evaluatively at Sam. Nancy said, "You can see my sisters are right. But you should have seen him a month ago."

"Your sisters are closer to the mark," Aunt Catharine observed tartly.

"Everyone has to sacrifice in this struggle," Sam said.

"So you say. But some of the loyalists around here are not doing much sacrificing. Yet Judge Greene says you may have to sell off some land."

"More than some, I fear," Sam said. Ethan nodded, his face grim.

His aunt made a clicking sound with her tongue and shook her head in dismay. "Phebe, girl, come help me with these buttons."

As her mother busied herself with the clothes, Phebe began moving buttons at the waist of a pair of breeches to make them snug. "I wrote you four notes to Canada," she said. "Did you ever receive them?"

"I got two kind notes in Boston, none in Canada." Phebe frowned. "But I am glad to know you thought of me."

As her face again grew pink, Sam noticed her mother glancing back and forth between them in a quick, interested manner.

At dinner, Aunt Catharine asked young John how he was bearing up. He had been silent for some time.

"As well as I can," he said glumly.

She snorted. "You are healthy. What can be the problem?"

Sam stopped chewing. Having not seen Johnny in a while, Aunt Catharine had forgotten how much like herself her nephew was. He watched his younger brother and waited for what he knew from the look in John's eye would be a bracing reply.

"What can be the problem?" John repeated quietly. "What can possibly be the problem? I am too young for the army. The family is too poor to send me to school, the store in Newport is closed, and so I am forced to milk cows and do farm work along with the servants and take orders from Ethan and Nancy who know as little about farming as I do about being an apothecary. I am fourteen and we are on the edge of financial ruin and my parents have both passed away and my brothers and sisters are all flung to the four winds. And now Sammy is about to leave. What could be wrong?"

Aunt Catharine's look of surprise turned to a glare during this little speech. When he was done, she waited for silence to fall, her eyes narrowed and she said softly, almost menacingly, "But you do have your health."

The two of them stared at each other for a tense few seconds, and then at the same moment they burst into laughter.

"Yes, I do," he said, his face red from laughing, tears streaming from his eyes. "I do have my health!"

*

After the dishes were cleared, Phebe and Sam decided to walk down the path toward the salt marshes along Narragansett Bay. Sam remembered her when she was a child as growing more talkative once she was out from under her mother's shadow, but tonight she remained quiet. They passed the dairy herd, all lying down and facing as precisely in the same direction as if they were people in church awaiting the sermon. The air, though cold, was still. A fingernail moon had climbed about a third of the way up the night sky. He wondered how to talk about what he wanted to talk about.

As they neared the beach, she began to ask him some questions in her soft, low voice. He had avoided talking about the war but suddenly, almost unwillingly, he found himself telling her about the dead and the severely wounded men who could no longer provide for their families.

They looked out at the ocean for a while in silence. "What *will* become of them?" Phebe asked at last.

"I saw Uncle Henry after the General Assembly adjourned and asked him about one family, the Shepherds. Tom was killed in the assault. He said the family would get a death payment. After it was gone, they would be put on the poor rolls of the town."

"How sad! He should have a better reward."

Sam nodded. He threw a small rock into the water of the ebbing tide. They walked slowly back toward the farm in another direction, past the sheep and the horses and the hens. He thought about how fresh and pretty Phebe looked, and how many days and months he had longed to have the chance to see her again. It was likely a girl of her age was being pursued in serious courtship, and he wanted to know if the path was blocked from his being considered. Yet now when they were alone and a chance to speak had at last presented itself, all he had spoken of was loss and helplessness.

They passed the graves of his mother and his sister Hannah, Hannah's still new enough to have a roundness of earth above where she lay. While he had been gone, his mother's plot had at last grown flat, as if she had finally surrendered. He looked at the ground. There, between earth and sky, ocean and land, war and the threat of war, he felt so many things, everything was suddenly a confusion to him. He wanted shelter but when he looked at Phebe, he wanted to offer shelter. He wanted to hold her breasts naked in his hands, and he wanted to lay his head on them and be held. *It may be easier,* he thought, *to march through a vast and uncharted wintry wilderness than to examine clearly what lies in a man's heart.*

"Can I see you when I return?" he asked.

She looked at him, puzzled. "Of course."

He regarded her steadily. "Can I see you in the way of courtship?"

Her dark blue eyes grew round. "Me?"

"Perhaps you are spoken for..."

"Nothing that serious," she said, looking down. "I am so... so surprised."

"If you have misgivings or your heart does not welcome it, Phebe, please say so now. I should not like to leave tomorrow under a cloud of misunderstanding."

"It is sudden."

Sam collected himself. To him, it was not sudden at all. He felt as he looked at her there under the stars that he could marry her in a second. He understood that she might not feel that herself at all. "We are discussing courtship, Phebe. Perhaps you or I will find on deeper acquaintance that we are ill-suited to be anything more than friends. If what I have suggested strikes you as futile, you would help me greatly by saying so now."

Slowly, her astonishment gave way to something else. "No, yes," she said, serious and smiling all at once. "Please."

He understood her tone better than her words. "Then I may come to see you on my return?"

Half a dozen feelings crossed her expressive face, the last of them with an edge of something like anger. "Yes," she said, for a brief moment sounding quite like her mother. "If you *do* return."

"I will try. Very hard."

He gravely took her hand, bent down, and kissed the back of it. Her face serious, she took his hand, raised it, and kissed him back just above the middle knuckle. Then, looking at him, she turned his hand over and slowly kissed his palm with her warm, soft mouth. He was astonished at the erotic jolt this gave him.

Of all the things he thought about from that evening in the days and weeks to come, it was this moment that came to his mind over and over again.

Chapter Twenty-Four

When he greeted Nat Greene this time at his Fort Lee headquarters in New Jersey, he was expected. Sam arrived about an hour after Nat and his staff had received intelligence that thousands of British troops were sailing south to fight under Lord Dunsmore in South Carolina. This reinforced Nat's conviction that Howe was about to settle into winter quarters and let the campaign be fought in the South. What he was hoping, however, was that General Howe would come out of the city and test their defensive works.

"If he engages us, we will give him another Bunker Hill," Nat said. "We repulsed him at Harlem Heights, and we will do it again. Our immediate concern is Fort Washington." He passed Sam a spyglass and invited him to look directly across the Hudson River. There, two hundred feet above the river, Sam saw a well-fortified encampment bristling with cannons.

"The fort is the only remaining area we hold on the entire island of Manhattan. Since I last saw you, we have been in repeated discussions about the wisdom of keeping it. I have argued and argued, with some success as of now, that we must keep it. At the very worst, if Howe was able to find some way to assault it in a determined fashion, we could evacuate. According to my estimate and the commander, Colonel Magaw's, we would be able to hold out six weeks against even a full assault. The longer we hold Fort Washington, the more it keeps cautious Howe from wandering far afield. We give their shipping a damned difficult time and pin them down, too."

"How?" Sam asked.

"You and I both know that it is against all the rules of warfare to leave an unreduced strongpoint behind your lines. Howe knows this, too. So Fort Washington remains the great obstacle to all their plans. General Washington has some misgivings, but this news of thousands of Howe's men heading south should secure the fort for a long time. And it is also news that should relieve some of the fears we have at home."

Sam took this moment to hand Nat the dispatches from the governor and General Assembly. Nat read through them as Sam resumed staring at Fort Washington through the spyglass. He could not make out individuals, but from this perspective, it looked like a small and isolated point. But with American soldiers at Fort Lee on one side and Fort Washington on the other, the British failed to control the great watery highway of the Hudson.

Nat finished reading the notes and promised to reply to them in writing this evening. "I do not think Rhode Island needs to fear an invasion," he said at last.

"No?"

Nat explained that though Newport was vulnerable to attack, Howe would not want to get bottled up in New England again, given his experience in Boston.

"Sammy, the truth of the war is this: our first task is to avoid losing. France and Spain are waiting to become our partners. One more Bunker Hill, and they will do it." He pointed out the window across the river. "And Fort Washington could be it."

"These strategic terms will not much console those living near Newport. They will strike many at home as, well, unkind. Pitiless, even."

"To those who do not know me, perhaps that is true. Lest *you* think my calculations are cold ones, I know I don't have to remind you that Caty and my son live near Newport."

"No, you need not remind me," Sam said. "But in your dispatches back home, I hope you will reassure people more directly. The greater their comfort, the more soldiers they will authorize to send here."

"Shrewd. What I will say is no more than the truth. The enemy is here. We need men here now. Rhode Island would do better to concentrate her forces in New York with us and stop the enemy where they are rather than withhold forces for some imagined mischance."

"Which," Sam said, "if it were to happen, we could not forestall with every militiaman in New England."

"Yes," Nat agreed soberly, "I'm afraid that is true, too. Though I will not be writing that in my letters. When you talk to your Uncle Henry on your return, explain that we need every available man. In fact, His Excellency has reinforced us at Fort Lee and will soon be here in person. Before he arrives, I need to inspect the progress of the works at Fort Washington." He briskly stacked the dispatches and letters Sam brought into a neat pile. "Why don't you accompany me? Your observations will be useful. Though you cannot yet rejoin us for the fight, you can offer advice."

Sam laughed. "Since when, General, have you ever taken advice from me?"

Nat got to his feet. "You are older now."

*

SAM, BILLY BLODGETT, AND Nat Greene made their way across the river in a packet rowed by a dozen strong men. The closer they came to the fort at the intersection of the Harlem and Hudson rivers, the more Sam could see how truly valuable a place it was. The heavy artillery on the fort's upper sides brought in range both rivers' central passageways. Howe could not send a large ship anywhere without risk. Though the waters were clear of British warships when they pushed off from shore, two heaved into view by the time they crossed the river.

It was a long climb up from the river to the first lines of defense, and a steep one, too. Sam had still not recovered from his imprisonment, and he found himself panting and light-headed when he reached the top.

In the outworks they found men Billy Blodgett identified as Colonel Magaw's Pennsylvania regulars as well as Virginia and Maryland riflemen and some black-shirted Rangers. In their size and toughness and with their long guns, they reminded Sam of Daniel Morgan's riflers. They knew Nat Greene, and all the riflemen not on direct guard stood at respectful attention when he passed. Just past the line of men with the rifles were hundreds of cheerful-looking pink-faced Pennsylvania militia. They were enlisted for one month, and though they would be likely to sign up again now that the harvest was over, they failed to respond to the major general who walked past them. A number of them lounged about, dozing.

Colonel Magaw, a tall lean man with a hawk-like face and watchful gray eyes, met them at the outworks and immediately took them on a tour to show General Greene the changes since his last visit. They had carted in tons of dirt to build breastworks and ramparts on the granite face of the fort, and they had developed them in a series of parallel lines up the slope, allowing for fallback and retreat by measured degrees, if necessary.

Nat added to Sam, "The British ships have been unable to elevate their cannon high enough to reach us from the river. So any attack against us will have to come by land, directly into these earthworks."

Colonel Magaw pointed northeast where, just at the horizon, they could see enemy soldiers digging in. "Some Waldecker and Hessian regulars have tested us already. They were light skirmishes but they suffered heavy casualties."

Sam, thinking of their return trip across the river, asked what was to prevent the British warships from cutting off the fort even if they could not strike at it directly. Colonel Magaw answered that the cannons of the two forts prevented the largest warships from plying the waters.

Inside the central flat area of the fort were huge heaps of ammunition, food, and supplies, and though they were unsorted, Sam judged there was enough to hold them over for many weeks. But he also noticed the central area was small. Small forts, Colonel Arnold had once explained, were easier to defend because you could man the perimeters thickly with men but harder to escape from if you had to.

Still, Sam was impressed with the level of preparedness. He could see why Bunker Hill occurred to Nat as a comparison—Americans in entrenched positions firing on an attacking enemy, though this time there were enough cartridges and cannons and powder and shot to outlast a dozen assaults.

Colonel Magaw led them toward the southern glacis to show them some newly arrived New Englanders. They approached their site from the rear, and though Sam could not make out any faces, there was something vaguely familiar about the men. He thought at first perhaps it was their accent or way of way of standing or their uniforms, but that was not it. They were quick to pass the word that the commanders were coming, "Colonel Magaw *and* General Greene," and they stiffened to attention as they passed. Some of them, though, began visibly to shrink back when they saw Sam, aghast, and it took him a full minute to understand it. He heard one of them whispering, "It's Captain Ward!"

These New Englanders were from Connecticut, many of them from Colonel Roger Enos's division, the men who had turned their backs during the march to Quebec. In a flash he remembered their carping and their whining, their slowness and faintness of heart, their disobedience of their officers' orders, their reneging on their agreement to provide food for those who continued.

"Is Enos here?" Sam asked, looking around, feeling an enormous pressure grow behind his eyes. His hands balled into fists. He stared at the men from Connecticut, hoping one of them would look at him wrong.

Billy Blodgett, who was suddenly uncomfortable, shook his head. Enos commanded militia in Danbury. Colonel Magaw, who could not miss the shocked looks on the faces of some of the Connecticut men, asked what was going on. Blodgett explained in a quiet voice that these men never expected to see Captain Ward alive.

"Why not?" the colonel asked.

"They were on the Quebec expedition."

Sam could see the understanding slowly dawn on Magaw's face. He looked at Sam as if seeing him for the first time.

"You are Captain Samuel Ward, then," he said.

"Yes," Sam replied.

Magaw gave Sam two slow respectful nods. None of the men in the Connecticut company would meet their eyes anymore.

Nat noted Magaw's own sudden new discomfort and said to him that men who have failed once are often braver when they had a second chance to redeem themselves. The colonel nodded again.

Sam was barely able to pay attention for the rest of the tour, though when he heard that Magaw's adjutant defected to the enemy two weeks ago, he could not shake a growing sense of foreboding. Defections happened all the time, he knew. And this was not Quebec where they needed to make a surprise attack. This was defense, and the men from Connecticut had no arduous march to complete. And Nat, for all his confidence, was also cautious by nature. He had two emergency evacuation plans, one by land and one by water, plans that he reviewed with the colonel as they walked.

As they rowed back to Fort Lee in the gathering dusk, Sam broke his silence to ask how they got water on a granite outcropping. The answer was ropes and buckets from the river. "What if there is a siege?"

"A long one would present a problem. But for a successful siege, Howe would have to amass twice the number of men we have in the fort. We do not know where he could possibly find six thousand men, hold his own territory, and prevent an attack from us."

*

A WEEK LATER, ON November 15, just as Sam was about to return to Westerly, the British, reinforced by a new arrival of troop ships from England and mercenaries from Central Europe, made a feint toward New Jersey. They sent several ships back to London, confused the entire Continental Army, and then surrounded Fort Washington with over eight thousand men.

*

SAM RODE AS FAST as he could to Fort Washington's headquarters and found the place in bedlam. Tom Paine explained that Nat and Major General Putnam had crossed the river under fire in order to consult with Colonel Magaw. General Washington and the main army arrived this morning, and his boat was crossing the river so he could assess the situation personally.

"Where are they now?"

Paine pointed to the river where two longboats, about two hundred yards off shore, had pulled together and locked sides.

"His Excellency is in one boat, Generals Greene and Putnam in the other."

"How long have they been consulting there?"

"A good ten minutes." He peered back out to the river. "Ah. They are both pulling this way."

Nat and General Putnam arrived back at headquarters both appearing confident. Nat issued general orders for full readiness, doubled the guards, and explained to Sam and Tom Paine that they had to persuade General Washington that it was not necessary to cross over himself. Sporadic cannonading had already begun, the sun was dropping low in the sky, and Colonel Magaw was ready.

The next morning the riflers fought murderously well, wounding or killing what appeared to be several hundred Hessians in their sector alone. But as they watched in mounting horror, first on one side and then on the other, the American defenses were overrun, their lines collapsing. The men were driven back into the redoubts of the small fort, an easy target for the cannon and mortars and grapeshot which had been wheeled up the slopes on all sides. Nat sent a message by Rhode Island Captain John Gooch—one he delivered by sneaking his little boat past men-of-war and making his way past lines of British soldiers—with a request to Magaw to hold out until nightfall. Nat planned to mount a rescue from the New Jersey shore.

Gooch made it back without a scratch. He said Magaw has already rejected one demand for surrender, but he reported that many of the militia and the New Englanders looked panic-stricken. Some of them begged him to take them back with him.

Magaw held on for another hour and then, after suffering one punishing round of cannon fire, capitulated.

Billy Blodgett looked like all the blood had drained from his body. He sat down and shook his head back and forth in shock. When he saw Sam looking at him in concern, he passed him a sheet of paper where he had marked the totals in an inventory he took of Fort Washington last week. Tom Paine looked at it with him.

They had lost 161 cannons; 8,000 cannon shot; 4,000 cannon shells; 2,800 muskets; 400,000 cartridges; 1,000 barrels of flour—and everyone knew how far beyond price such supplies were. Most costly of all, they had lost nearly three thousand men, one-quarter of General Washington's entire effective army.

Sam looked at the figures in disbelief. If their loss at Quebec had been excruciating, this loss was a flat-out disaster.

*

General Washington ordered them to abandon Fort Lee and to proceed in a general retreat south through New Jersey. Their duty now was to preserve what remained of their army from total destruction.

General Howe, smelling a chance for total victory, sent his army across the Hudson to complete the Americans' humiliation. Nat and Sam and every other officer were awake all night organizing a retreat, trying to leave as little behind as possible. They got word that British General Cornwallis was driving six thousand men toward them at a quick march. At the same time, a huge herd of several thousand mooing cattle arrived from Pennsylvania, having been sent to provision the entire American army.

At midmorning on November 20, Sam and Nat Greene and his entire staff watched the last trains of men and wagons they had available leave Fort Lee. Billy Blodgett said they still had two thousand barrels of corn, hundreds of tents, and thousands of the invaluable cattle that had just arrived from Pennsylvania to try to transport, but they had nothing and no one left to do it. Sam, light-headed from lack of sleep, worked on spiking one of the scores of remaining cannons that still dotted the walls.

Not a messenger but a Pennsylvania cavalry officer, together with his aides, galloped into the center of the fort. "General Greene!" he yelled. Nat waved a response. "Cornwallis is on our heels. You must leave now! He is less than five hundred yards behind us!"

Everyone in the fort grew still. They could hear the footfalls of the British army through the still fall air.

And so they were forced down the muddy, cold New Jersey roads, pressed hard by the enemy at their heels, all the way through Newark and Brunswick and Princeton, finally to Trenton. Sam, instead of heading north to Westerly, was driven south with the army, one that was ill-clad, badly sheltered, and undernourished without entrenching tools to help them make a stand. They traveled eighty miles almost without stopping, the militia dropping away in droves and even many Continental soldiers deserting along the way. Congress, they heard, had fled from Philadelphia in the wake of the disaster and was headed to Baltimore.

Nat Greene was so stricken by the losses, he could not speak of them. He tried instead to keep his attention on preventing the complete crumbling of Washington's army. Tom Paine was up every night writing by lamplight well into the small hours, writing right through the exhaustion and fear and growing despair around them. Sam looked at the first page of the stack one night on their retreat through New Jersey just as Paine was preparing his pen and ink again. It said *Crisis* in large letters with a thick slash underlining the word. *These are the times that try men's souls,* read the first sentence. *The summer soldiers and the sunshine patriot will, in this crisis, shrink from the service of their country.*

Just as Nat was making plans with General Washington to retreat still farther, across the Delaware and into Pennsylvania, they were given the word by local scouts of a safe way for individuals to get around Cornwallis's pursuing army. Nat told him to take it.

"Every man is needed here," Sam protested.

"Every man is needed here, and that is why we need you to get word back to Connecticut and Rhode Island that we require every available assistance. Urgently."

Sam was reluctant to go, but Nat reminded him that he was not yet exchanged and was under oath not to fight until he was. He insisted that they must get reinforcement and supplies. "If we do not, Sam..." His voice trailed off. "At this moment, you can serve your country best by going back."

*

BUT WHEN SAM MADE it back to New England on the first day of December, he found that the region would not be helping anyone anymore. Six thousand of the British and Hessians who departed New York under General Clinton had not gone back to London. They had landed, taking possession of Newport almost without resistance. All of southern New England lay wide open to assault.

Sam was barely home when he started to hear and read the criticisms of General Washington. He was indecisive, they said, too easily swayed by subordinates' opinions—especially Nathanael Greene's—and, though he looked good, he might be simply unfit for the job. Some, including General Washington's own staff, it was said, wanted General Lee to succeed him as commander in chief, and the sooner the better. Lee, went the reports and the whispers, had the confidence, the ambition, the decisiveness, and the discipline to command.

Just as these whispers and grumblings and editorial opinions were beginning to reach full-throat, within weeks after the fall of Fort Washington and the taking of Newport, came another thunder strike. On December 16, General Lee, continuing his habit of staying in comfortable quarters even if miles from the army he commanded, was surrounded at his tavern lodging. With two guards and a small staff and his brace of dogs, he was helpless before the detachment of British light cavalry. The guards overpowered, the exits sealed, he was captured in a snap of the fingers.

Sam soon heard men saying in Rhode Island that this loss was worse than Quebec or Newport or even Fort Washington, and not only was Lee's capture the greatest loss of the war, but the war itself was now probably over.

Chapter Twenty-Five

What Guy longed to do—he thought of it by day and dreamed of it by night—was to steal a boat and row with June to Newport. They said that any slaves who escaped and presented themselves there were immediately freed and hired to perform labor to support the British army and navy. Young John said that at least two slaves in southern Rhode Island had done it already.

June reminded him that the British would take only the slaves from rebel families. Slaves of loyalists were sent back. And in Newport, Simon Pease and Joseph Wanton would make dead sure any slave of John Hazzard's was returned on the next packet.

Guy thought for a moment. They could lie about what family they're from, but since both he and June had worked in the town, they would too easily be recognized. And even if they weren't, the Hazzards would post notices and rewards as soon as they ran off, and the lie would never stand. Even if Lucy insisted there was no freedom out there anyway—the British were white, weren't they?—and running away wouldn't work, it still did not keep Guy from dreaming about it. He didn't care which side he ended up on: he was on his and June's side.

Lucy. Last summer her back was torn up so badly and got infected enough to make her sick and useless for work for weeks. It was all she could do to nurse her baby boy, and she even had to stop that for a time because Jubah said she might make the baby sick, leaving Jubah to figure out how to give the baby goat's milk through the finger of a muslin glove. The black woman who helped deliver Lucy while she was following the army knew enough about letters to tell her the first letter of the name John was "J," and so that was what Lucy named the baby, Jay. He was about the color of a strong cup of tea, not Africa-black like Guy or Quamino or Jubah, and a shade lighter than either June or Lucy. When she got the nerve up, Lucy said she was going to tell Mistress Hazzard the truth—that this baby was her own grandson—and hope that kept her from selling him off from his mother.

Jubah said to keep her mouth good and shut—the shame of it might *make* her sell him off.

Oddly, though, the entire fall after the British takeover of Newport was their best time in years. The Hazzards suddenly grew more generous with food. And some of their clothes, which they had mended and re-mended, finally got passed on to the slaves in time for cold weather. If they had more work because Young John got sent off to be with the militia most of the time—Rhode Islanders worried that Newport was going to be a launching place for attacks—they also had less meddling without the boy snooping around them.

But then, not long after a quiet Christmas celebration and as the year began, the brief space of good times at the Hazzard place abruptly ended.

They felt the difference long before they learned the cause. The food grew poor and the portions shrank. Worn-out clothes had to be used in tatters, and they all lost weight fast enough that it grew hard to stay warm even when they were working. What had happened? Quamino heard in the house that rebel General Washington did a surprise crossing of the Delaware River at the end of the year, and then he won some surprise victories in places called Trenton and Princeton. The winter of 1777 was brutally cold, and Guy was not rented out anywhere for the first time he could remember. Master John complained that nobody had the money to rent him.

As bad as the winter was, the spring of '77 was worse.

In late April, there was an attack on a supply depot in a town in Connecticut named Danbury. The British looted the place and then destroyed the entire town. Meanwhile Rhode Island's economy ground to a halt. The British fleet at Newport sealed off all shipping. Insolvencies were being declared even by once-powerful people like the Wards, dragging others down with them. On top of it all, Rhode Island towns were given a quota based on their population of able-bodied men not already in service—they wanted a thousand men, and they wanted them now. But especially now, with the British a few miles off shore, men wanted to stay close to their families.

Two of Master John's loyalist friends had had enough. They leased their house and land for next to nothing, packed up their families, and headed to Nova Scotia. Some of the area farmers with large properties, like the Robinsons and the Stantons, began sending their least-able slaves to serve in their place, ignoring restrictions against permitting blacks in the army. Feeding a field hand had come to cost as much, or more, than the goods they could produce.

Master John had no intention of sending Guy. He offered them Quamino, and if he had not looked all of his seventy-odd years, they probably would have taken him. (Master John was surprised to see the militia captain actually look the ancient slave over carefully before shaking his head no.) Master John reminded town officials that his son was already in the service and his servant had already been to Boston and Quebec with the Continental army. Besides, Guy's carpentry skills had become even more valuable in the lean times. No one bought anything new anymore, so carriages and wagons and plows had to be fixed, and with so many men in the army, finding skilled help was nearly impossible. When spring came and tools and plows were needed, he was able to rent Guy out at last for a very attractive fee—to the very few who could afford him.

*

IN LATE JUNE, JUST as the crops were coming in well, and weeds right along with them, a white man and a black man rode up with a third riderless horse trailing behind them. Guy glanced up from the wood splitting pile and thought someone had come to hire him out yet again. Each week, a new place, sometimes two or three times a week. Master John had long ago stopped paying him anything for his troubles. His and the mistress's faces had both begun to look pinched, their eyes tight as their purses.

Both of the men on horseback looked familiar, but Guy had seen so many faces in this last year, he could no longer sort them all out. It took him a few seconds, but he finally recognized Jack Sisson and his master, William Barton, someone Young John said had become lieutenant colonel in the militia.

As Barton knocked on the front door of the main house, Sisson took the horses over for water and stumped about the yard on his muscular bandy little legs. He shaded his eyes and stared toward the woodpile. Guy raised a hand in greeting.

Sisson made his way over. "Guy Watson. How you feel 'bout comin' with us?"

Guy set the ax-head into the dirt and leaned onto the handle. "Where?"

"Need help for 'bout two-three weeks."

"Mastuh not let me go nowhere right in mid-season."

"Oh, I think maybe he will let you go," he said with a grin, his Sugar Islands accent strengthening.

"Have to pay him a whole heap."

"Colonel Barton pay him. But it won't be no heap."

"What you fixin' to do?"

"Can't tell you that. But come over with me to the horses."

"What for?"

He nodded toward the front door. "Colonel Barton can be real convincin' sometime."

The colonel, whom Guy guessed to be a few years younger than the master, had an oval face that looked round because of his round chin, large round eyes, and a straight blunt nose that was itself round on the end. His voice was quiet, but he had an air of great self-assurance. His dark hair, cut short, was unpowdered, and it fell carelessly across his forehead.

Master John was shaking his head no for about the fourth or fifth time. "I'm sorry, Colonel, but we are trying to eke out a living at the moment. Even a dairy maid would be a sacrifice. But with all the tools and outbuildings," he swept a hand about, "all of them needing repair, Guy is the last person I could part with."

"If the British make a raid in these parts," the colonel said in his soft voice, "as we hear they may, you and your neighbors could lose everything in a few short hours. I'm sure you've heard that the Hessians are not very careful about what civilians they attack or whose houses they burn. We would like to offer you the very best protection against such a terrible event, but in order to do that, we shall have to borrow your servant for a short time."

Master John's entire body stiffened but his voice remained unshaken. "I know there is a shortage of mechanics, but surely you can find someone else to assist you."

"Let me be plain with you, Mister Hazzard," Barton said so quietly Guy had to strain to hear him. "We have heard for some time now about meetings held on your grounds where matters were discussed that were unfriendly to the cause. We know, of course, about your son's participation in the militia, and while some have said his presence is not in support of our common goals but is done with an eye to advance some peculiar ones of your own, I prefer to be more positive."

"That is absolutely..." the master began to sputter.

Colonel Barton held up a hand. "There are others besides me who would hate to give these reports credit, but I cannot guess how people might respond if they heard that you refused a direct request from a command officer in the militia. A request, when all is said and done, for some brief assistance for which you will be offered a more-than-fair return."

"So in order to silence these defamatory rumors, I am supposed to lop off my arm in the middle of the planting season and give it to you."

"I mean only to describe the situation so you can be able to determine your own best course of conduct. I'd say, though, that we are not asking you to sever an arm so much as lend us a hand."

Ten minutes later, Guy was riding north on an army-issued horse. He was not given the time to say goodbye to June. He could not help being worried. He had twice been attached to the army before, and neither of them turned out to be brief. Jack Sisson, though, seemed about as cheerful as someone who was not drunk could be, and Colonel Barton did not himself seem in the least tense.

"Where we goin'?" Guy asked Jack.

"Place called Tiverton. Way round on the other side of the bay."

They rode on for a while before Guy asked his next question. "Why take me?"

"Colonel want somebody can help build and fix boats, who know the area round Newport, and can keep a secret. You can keep a secret, can't you?"

Guy shrugged. "What is it?"

Jack grinned. "Can't tell nobody a secret you don't know." Guy frowned. "Don't get all vexed up. I tell you, I tell you. Not now. When we get to Tiverton."

*

THE SECRET, HE LEARNED a few days later, was that Colonel Barton, Jack Sisson, and about thirty other white men were going to try to capture the hated British commanding officer at Newport, General Richard Prescott.

"*What?*" Guy said.

"You heard."

"How in this world you goin' do that?"

"Keep your voice down. Colonel Barton got a plan."

Guy shook his head. He did not want to know it.

Jack looked at him to see if he had calmed down. Then he explained. The colonel did not want any locals or slaves of locals from the Tiverton part of the state to be involved in getting boats ready. British spies were everywhere, and the last thing Colonel Barton wanted was anybody wondering why the first Rhode Island Brigade suddenly needed some boats. The colonel was down in South Kingston to consult with the General Assembly, and when they rode past the Stantons' place, Jack reminded the colonel they were near where Guy lived. The colonel had not forgotten the whipping Master Hazzard meted out to Lucy on the day they were all supposed to be celebrating independence, and the colonel agreed what an excellent thing it would be to bother Gambling John Hazzard and help themselves at the same time.

"Simple as that," Sisson concluded.

Guy did not see it or anything else as simple. But once the colonel set the two slaves up in the large barn out in the middle of nowhere to work on the six hidden whaleboats, he admitted he could see why having someone local might be risky.

Colonel Barton had been hearing for months about how much the Americans in Newport loathed General Prescott. The man who preceded Prescott, Lord Percy, had been civil, and he made efforts to keep in check the Hessians' plundering of houses, and even attempted to limit arrests of citizens to those who had actually done something wrong. With Prescott's arrival, though, the occupying soldiers' vandalism, attacks, arrests, thefts, and bullying resumed. It turned out this was not a matter of indifference to Richard Prescott. He approved of it heartily. He did not *like* Americans.

When Prescott moved into the large and elegant Banister House at the corner of Spring and Pelham a few months ago, he was annoyed to discover that mud from the spring thaw was being tracked into the house. So he ordered all the doorstones in the neighborhood removed from the front door of their houses and put down to make a path to his door. This left his neighbors with nothing between the mud of the streets and their homes. He also insisted on Newporters who passed him to bow and show signs of public respect, giving his servant standing orders to knock the hat off anyone they passed, including Quakers. After General Lee was kidnapped, patriots in Rhode Island began casting about for a reply. The more Barton heard about the arrogant General Prescott, the more he wanted him.

*

Caulking and rigging the whaleboats was familiar business for Guy. But there was one task he and Sisson had been charged with that he knew less well. The whaleboats, like the boats they rowed across the St. Lawrence to Quebec, were to be made silent. No creaking, no grinding oarlocks, not so much as a barnacle left clinging to the side to drag and hiss through the waters. It was while they were working on scraping the bottoms smooth that Colonel Barton gave Guy the bad news.

"Sisson. Watson. Work well. You both are coming with us. If we have a problem, you will have it, too. Am I clear?"

The two black men nodded and said, "Yessuh."

He was clear, all right. He glared at Jack Sisson, who rolled his eyes and shrugged. Guy felt like smashing something. It was not enough that he had to give his labor. Now he had to risk his life. Guy took a deep breath and turned back to the boat. In his head, he could hear Quamino's voice telling him not to fight what comes, but to try to use it like wind and current to get to a better place. But his experience was that the current sent him to worse places.

He ran his hand over the boat bottom and studied the problem of rigging for silence. He knew which wood would respond to soaking in water by swelling to become water-tight and which would risk the groaning of wood on wood. A single passenger shifting his weight on a creaky bench could make as much noise as a bad tholepin. They worked on the boats painstakingly, day and night, for six days.

As they neared the end of their refitting, Jack wanted to paint the hulls to reduce the drag of the water. Guy shook his head, saying that the paint would come off too easily in the salt waters.

"What you say, then?" he asked.

"Dye it. Then oil it, seal it all up good. Oil make less rubbin', too."

Jack checked with the colonel, who was there for his second visit of the day. His aide, the muscular and watchful John Hunt, had been to check on them as well. The colonel approved Guy's suggestion. First he asked Guy what color he wanted to dye it.

"Cross at night?" The colonel nodded. "Color oughtta be ocean color at night." Guy pointed to a charred log from the morning fire. "That color with some green it."

The colonel looked at him for a second in a way Guy was familiar with—it was the moment when some white person took in the fact he was smart. Guy never knew what would come out of that recognition. Some were annoyed, some just noted it and went back to treating him like an eight-year-old in an adult's body. "Well," the colonel finally said. "It's coming along." He looked at Jack Sisson. "You will have them done by noon tomorrow," he said for the eighth time in four days.

"Yessuh," Jack said. "Done tomorrow."

"Tomorrow *morning*."

"We go tomorrow night?"

The colonel gave a thin smile. "July fourth should be a good day."

Jack grinned. "Still…I sure hate goin' right into Newport with all those Hessians."

The colonel looked at him in silence for a moment, apparently weighing whether to respond. The only other person they had seen in a week was the colonel's trusted aide. "We are not going to Newport."

"No?" Jack said. "I thought we was goin' after General Prescott."

"We are. He spends these hot summer nights out of the city."

Jack heaved a visible sigh of relief. Then he suddenly looked worriedly at the skies. "We better hope the weather don' get cool then."

The colonel said that fresh air was not the only thing drawing Richard Prescott away from Newport in the evenings. "Time to stain and oil the boats. I will be back before dark. Do you need anything?"

Guy shook his head no. They had the oil and the dye pigments. After the colonel left and they started daubing on the greenish black stain, Jack said, "This all work out, the colonel give you a good reward."

Guy thought that the reward he wanted was not in the colonel's power to give.

Chapter Twenty-Six

At sunset on July 4, Colonel Barton, John Hunt, and almost forty other men, all dressed in dark clothes, tested the whaleboats. They picked the five best among them and then, one boat at a time, headed off for Bristol by water. The boats were tight as drums and made barely a whisper as they rowed across the bay. It was a good thing, too—for they came within an easy musket shot of two men-of-war and a patrol boat.

They laid over in Bristol for one hot day and another airless night while waiting for a final load of supplies and for confirmation of Richard Prescott's nightly whereabouts. On July 6, they rowed to Warwick Neck, the colonel wanting to head straight from there to attempt the capture. They all knew the British had their spies, too, and if word got to Newport that forty men were rowing about under cover of darkness, they could all look to spend their next years in one of the foul, disease-ridden prison boats that floated offshore of Aquidneck Island.

"Not years," the colonel corrected himself. "Most die there in a few months." Though the heat was stifling, Barton ordered no one to leave the remote area where they were beached. By afternoon, welcome clouds rolled in, but then they thickened and darkened ominously. By dusk, the wind drove in on them from the northeast and the rain came down in torrents. The colonel thought about going anyway, but the visibility was so poor and the wind so strong, he concluded it was impossible.

The rain and wind continued unabated all the next day. A scattered few people in the area began to notice their presence, despite all their precautions. The men grew more anxious with each passing hour. The wind continued to be so strong, everyone recognized it would take them all night to row to their destination, and even if they could complete their capture, they would be rowing home in broad daylight. If an alarm was sounded in Newport, they would not have a chance.

His usually serene face lined with worry, Colonel Barton delayed the mission.

This waiting reminded Guy of what the soldiers in Quebec had to do before they began their New Year assault. He tried unsuccessfully not to think about how that turned out.

The waiting took its toll. The men became edgy, their tempers short. Those who could manage to sleep woke up mosquito-bitten to a milky sky and a hot, humid day. They waited for the long hours until nightfall to crawl by. Their eyes nervously scanned the horizon; their damp forefingers checked the wind direction.

Finally, as the light slowly drained from the sky, just after nine o'clock, the colonel ordered them to load the boats. As they worked, he and John Hunt told them the final details of the plan. They were going to row along Prudence and Patience Islands and make for the shore at Portsmouth, the little town ten miles north of Newport. Hunt, who grew up in Portsmouth and knew the area well, would be in the first boat. He would lead them ashore and to Overing Farm.

"You see, men," Barton said in a voice just loud enough for them all to hear, "General Prescott spends his nights there with his mistress. Cool weather or hot, he has been there almost every night for the past month."

The men laughed in a loud gust, quickly silenced themselves, and exchanged winks. Guy was not happy about the word "almost."

"And because Prescott does not want his activity widely known," the colonel continued, "he brings no troop of guards. There will be one aide-de-camp and one sentinel. Think we can handle it?"

The men muttered "aye!" and kept themselves from yelling once again. "What do we do with his whore?" one of them asked.

"We will be taking back only what soldiers we find."

There were groans of mock dismay. Finally, the colonel gathered them around him in a tight circle and went over their deployment after they arrived at the farm. Once they landed, he reminded them, he wanted no talking. Then he asked them all to blacken their faces and hands with wood ash and charcoal. Hunt told Guy and Jack they needn't bother. A couple of the men sniggered. Hunt silenced them with a glance.

Guy said, "We do our face anyway? Get rid of the shine?"

Hunt looked at him in the failing light and nodded.

Jack and the colonel and Hunt were in the first boat. Guy was in the last.

A sliver of moon slipped in and out of slow-moving clouds. The air, thick with heat, was still and the water in the bay was as calm as a mill pond. Guy judged it to be nearly midnight by the time his boat pushed off.

*

AS THEY NEARED THE first British frigate, they could hear a bored voice from the quarterdeck calling out through the still night, "All is well."

Guy and the other rowers were ordered to ship their oars and switch seats with the four rested men. By the time they exchanged seats, they had drifted so close to the frigate that Guy could smell the shit and piss where the sailors had dumped their slop jars over the side. The new rowers were having trouble finding a rhythm, one or another of them splashing clumsily and two of them in their anxiety even thudding their oars against the side. Guy's mouth grew dry as dust. They drifted steadily closer to the warship. A lantern sat upon the closest rail, the kind that was blocked off with tin behind and shined light only in one direction. Ahead of him he noticed the eerie green phosphorescent glowing of disturbed summer ocean waters—the wake of the whaleboat ahead. They passed so close to the frigate that the path of the lantern's yellow light passed over their heads, falling three or four oar lengths beyond them. This, he knew, was a piece of luck. It could just as easily have lit them all up.

Just as they cleared the frigate, a second bulked ahead, a dark shape in the night. The rowers found their rhythm, and they sped swiftly and noiselessly past, powered by fear.

They rowed on in silence across the night waters. Less than an hour later, John Hunt directed the boats onto a strip of deserted shoreline. As planned, they jumped from the whaleboats, dragged them ashore, and then carried them across the beach to hide them among some thick bushes. One man from each boat ripped down a tree branch and raked away their footprints in the sand. Then they formed in five squads. The men were issued pistols and muskets for defense. Jack had explained to Guy to expect to be permitted only a knife, but Colonel Barton handed him a loaded pistol. Whatever his reason, he felt a flush of pleasure at being trusted. He touched the knife in his belt for reassurance. If he had to use a weapon, he was glad to have the chance to use a silent one.

Following the lead of the soldiers ahead, they moved at a half run from tree to tree, bayberry bush to bayberry bush. Guy worried less about being seen than about the noise the men made. Barefoot, he was able to keep his step almost soundless. The man in front of him crashed through the undergrowth in heavy shoes and, not hearing Guy, kept checking behind him to see if he were still there.

Within a mile, they could see a farm. It was at least as large as the Hazzards', and it had several outbuildings. Colonel Barton stopped the five squads on the far side of the road and reminded the leaders of each squad's assignment. Squad one was to go to the front door of the main house, squad two was to remain behind to guard the road. Squad three was to go in the side and squad four would guard the outside of the house to keep anyone from leaving. Squad five, with Guy, was to break in the back door.

Their first task was to remove the sentinel who was supposed to be at the front door. Guy peered through the darkness. He did not see a sentinel.

The white man next to Guy muttered to his friend, "No sentinel means Prescott's not there! We've made the Goddamned trip for nothing!"

Barton told the men to be quiet. He waited patiently at the front of the group, apparently calm. A minute passed, and he no longer looked so calm. He had his hand on Hunt's shoulder, about to send him forward to examine the grounds, when a soldier in a bright red British regimental uniform stepped from behind the house finishing buttoning his breeches. They were going to have their chance.

"On your lives," Colonel Barton whispered, "quiet now."

And then, to everyone's astonishment, John Hunt and Jack Sisson simply walked out of the woods and headed up the road toward the house. Hunt's face and hands had been washed clean. Guy watched them, dumbstruck.

"This isn't the house," Hunt said, his voice clearly audible to the waiting men. And to the sentinel.

"Don't know, Mastuh," Jack said. "Could be. Could jus' be!"

They stopped and looked around, Hunt with his hands on his hips. He scratched his head. "Doesn't look right."

The British guard took a few steps from the front of the house toward them. "What's wrong here," he said in a low voice, apparently not wanting to wake his general. Hunt and Sisson flinched as if in surprise.

"Who's that?" Hunt said loudly.

The guard said, "Not so loud, sir. People are sleeping here."

"Sorry," Hunt replied and took a few casual steps toward the sentinel. "My servant says his wife did not come home this evening. She was working at the Coddingtons'. Is this the Coddingtons'?"

"Next farm over. About a quarter of a mile."

"Ah. Which way is that?" Hunt asked.

The sentinel walked helpfully with them toward the road, still speaking in a low voice. He pointed north up the road. "Just up there on the right."

Jack grabbed the guard's rifle with both hands and at the same moment Hunt took the man by the head and pulled him down. He grunted as his back hit the packed dirt. Hunt pulled his pistol and set it between the man's eyes. "Not a sound," he said.

Colonel Barton gave the signal. The first squad came out of the woods and even before Guy's squad had risen to their feet, they had bound and gagged the guard. A kerchief tightly through his teeth, he was left behind with the second squad. The other four quickly deployed themselves, each according to their assignment.

They were given exactly one minute to post themselves at the proper sites. As Guy rounded the corner of the house, he saw Jack Sisson tapping the front door to assess its thickness. He was setting himself up to butt headfirst through it as soon as Colonel Barton gave him the go-ahead. Guy's squad, panting outside the rear door, waited for the sound of the front door crashing in.

There was a loud splintering thump and then the sound of a door banging against a wall. Two men smashed open the back door and Guy and his squad, as ordered, fanned out through the lower rooms to make sure no one escaped. Within seconds, they encountered the squad who made their way through the kitchen at the side. Not a single soul was downstairs. They waited in tense silence to see who Colonel Barton's squad found upstairs. They could hear several doors above them bang open and then some unintelligible shouting.

Out of the corner of his eye, Guy's saw something move at the window. He looked, saw nothing. Just to make sure, he moved closer to the divided panes and looked out. Immediately below him was a man in a white nightshirt trying to struggle to his feet. The squad at the front of the house was all looking upstairs and had missed seeing this man at the side. Guy threw open the casement and called, "Heah! Over heah!" The man was seized even before the shouting upstairs stopped.

A few painfully long minutes later, a tall man completely naked except for a dark greatcoat thrown over his shoulders, was led at gunpoint down the stairs. His face was as white as the man outside's nightshirt; his hands were shaking. John Hunt came down behind him carrying a bundle of clothes.

The last man came down and reported to Barton. "She is tied tight to the bed, sir."

The four squads made their way out at a half-run to rejoin the fifth squad across the road in the woods. It was Jack Sisson and Guy who thought to look at the other outbuildings as they left. Sure enough, several slaves were peering toward them from the edge of a cabin. Sisson broke in on the colonel to tell him the news. They all knew the slaves would sooner or later release the woman who would then raise an alarm.

Colonel Barton weighed what to do for a moment and then said, "We will have to make greater speed. Let's go." Before they made their way to the boat, the man in the nightshirt—who identified himself as Prescott's aide-de-camp Major William Barrington—was ordered to wear dark breeches and a dark overcoat for the return journey. General Prescott, still naked under the greatcoat, was placed in the first boat, the sentinel in the middle boat, and Major Barrington in Guy's boat.

They were less than a quarter of a mile offshore when the sky over Newport began to light up with orange and yellow rocket fire. The alarms were being sounded. Prescott's capture was already known.

Chapter Twenty-Seven

The news of Colonel Barton's expedition reached the Hazzards long before Guy returned. And it helped the master and Betsy make a painful decision. Master John found a slave dealer in Connecticut who could get him good money for his slaves, and get it now before they changed the laws. A loyalist family from New Haven was selling everything and planned to move to a friendlier town in the Maine territory. With three small children and another on the way, they needed a cook and midwife. A wealthy old New Britain couple wanted a gentleman's servant, theirs having died. And in the Carolinas, with their long growing season and the squeezing off of the slave trade by the war, a young black woman with a baby was less a burden than a demonstrated good breeder and an investment in the future of some vast tobacco and cotton plantation. Despite the trader's steep commission and the scars on Lucy's back, they could get close to top dollar.

The Hazzards assessed their financial plight over three days and nights. By the time they were done, it was clear, unpleasantly clear. Betsy could cook, if less well than Jubah, at least tolerably. Lucy's work had been of the poorest quality since she returned, and, with her baby, she cost far more than she produced. Quamino's loss would be especially painful for Master John who enjoyed the high social standing of which Quamino was a sign, particularly since Guy would have far too many duties to replace him as a body servant. But in the end, they all would have to make sacrifices. June knew some medicine and midwifery and was required in the dairy, and Guy would have to do something of everything. But who knew the mysterious ways of Providence? The Hazzards hoped they might be more prosperous in the end than ever.

*

Though not a word of this was breathed where a slave could ever hope to overhear it, Quamino immediately sensed something was happening. He did not know what it was, but he could feel it in how the master and mistress's eyes slid over them like oil, lingering on him and Jubah long past the usual time, but never meeting their eyes. He could see it in their tightened mouths and the drawn skin around their eyes, hear it like a faint humming underneath their voices.

He asked Jubah if she noticed something different about them.

"Do, now that you say it. Nervous as cats."

For the first time in a long time, that night he turned his clothes inside out and, by himself, carrying his prayer stick, made his way all the way to the crossing point. He drew the ritual circle, lit the old stub of a tallow candle, and sifted the sacred herbs and grave dust into a clamshell. He sprinkled them over the flame and inhaled the smoke of their burning. He chanted, "*bisimbi!*," "*mpati!*" and chewed on the herbs. He shuffled his aching old legs in the ancient dance and his cracked voice grew louder in the chant. Rounding the circle three times, he stopped, grew silent, and stepped solemnly onto the crossing point. He raised his prayer stick to the darkened skies. In a swift moment, but clear and unmistakable as daylight, he saw what he saw.

"No," he said aloud a few quiet minutes later. "Not that way."

He thought for a while, breathing the thick air in and out. Then he walked out past the strip of trees and across the thin line of beach and into the almost warm waters of the July ocean, taking his prayer stick with him. Water and life, God and the Dead. It was all one, and it was his time to become part of it.

*

AND SO IT WAS when Guy returned that Quamino, Lucy, baby Jay, and Jubah were gone without a trace, one dead and three sold.

June, her eyes swollen and her face frozen in a mask of sadness, was so stricken that she could not speak of any of them without weeping. "Gone," was all she could choke out to Guy when he asked where everyone was. Rising and sleeping and every meal and every break were agonizing reminders of who she no longer had. Convinced that Guy might also be sold, or even be dead, she put together some plants and berries she knew would kill her. The mistress assured her Guy would be back and explained over and over that if they had not sold the others, everything and everyone would have to go. It was tragic about Quamino, but they believed he was sick and had not told the others. The doctor said it might have been a brain seizure, for why else would he be walking to the beach in the middle of the night? At least this way, she insisted, with the sale of Lucy and Jubah, she and Guy could still be together. Until Guy's return, June thought every night about taking the fatal medicines.

Guy was stunned. In a sense, the vanished slaves were all dead. He knew how far Maine was. He had been there. The Carolinas were even farther. In the way he knew the world to work, he believed he would never see Jubah, Lucy, or Jay again in this world. No more of Lucy's beautiful singing; no more of Jubah's cooking and medicine and reassuring touch when someone was sick. And, most painful of all for him, no more advice from Quamino. He felt alone in a way he never had before, and he felt congealing in the cold pit of his stomach the desolation he saw on June's face.

*

THE MASTER CALLED HIM into his study. Master Hazzard seated himself and crossed his legs comfortably at the knee. Guy stood before him, his fingers working on each other, wondering if he was going to sell him off. Or June.

"So," he said. "You helped William Barton capture General Prescott."

Guy nodded, then added, "Yessuh. I was ordered to."

The master nodded back. "In Newport."

"In Po'tsmouth, outside Newport."

"He was with his whore, as the papers say?" Guy nodded again. "And a negro smashed in the front door? Was that you?"

Guy shook his head. "Jack Sisson."

"But you helped fix up the boats they used."

"Yessuh."

Master John put both feet on the floor. "That bastard Barton forcibly takes you away right when you are needed most, and then he uses you for…for *this!*" He slammed his hand on a newspaper on his desk and got up, beginning to pace behind his desk. "He'll be sorry, by God. He won't get away with this."

"He pay you like he promise?"

The master shrugged. "Not enough." He looked at him sharply. "And the general. Did they hurt him?"

"Nossuh. They send him in a coach to Providence."

"Anyone else taken?"

"An aide and a guard."

"They raised an alarm and still Barton was not spotted?"

"We was in small boats. Hard to see, I guess."

"*Bastards…*" he muttered again and resumed his pacing. In a gesture Guy had never seen before, he stopped and bit his knuckle, lost in thought. He looked up, appearing almost surprised to see Guy still standing there. "You have heard we had to sell Jubah and Lucy."

"Yes," Guy managed to say.

"And poor Quamino. Terrible loss." He sighed and looked down. Then he looked up again. "Harvest will begin in a month or so. It will be a hard time. I know you will miss them. So will we all. June will remain in the dairy. Both Young John and I will be working this season out in the field, too, and we'll hire some help. We will get by." He cleared his throat and said with a heartiness that did not show on his face, "With a change of luck and a good crop, who knows. Maybe we can go back to the old ways."

A change of luck could go either way, Guy thought. Bad as something might be, it could also get worse.

✷

GUY WANTED TO MAKE June feel better, but he found he had nothing to say. He could not say that they perhaps will see Jubah and Lucy again. He could not say at least they were safe, because she knew as well as he that they were not. Tears sprang to her eyes as soon as she heard "Jubah," "Lucy," or "Quamino." He left it to her to bring them up, and as the days passed, once in a while she was able to. Mostly, though, she was withdrawn and silent. Something Jack Sisson said to him one day when they were fitting the whaleboats occurred to him, but he did not know how much credit to give it. But it was hard for him to see her suffer, and he wished to do something, anything, to bring back the light of hope in her eyes. "Jack Sisson, he say lot of people in Rhode Island beginnin' to turn 'gainst ownin' slaves. He say change is comin'."

"He say lot of things, Jack Sisson."

Guy had to nod at that. But he had been giving the matter some thought. "Hazzards probly have to sell everyone off because change comin'." June didn't respond to this. "Maybe we be all right."

"What you mean?"

"That crack of daylight Quamino used to talk about. Could happen."

"How?"

"Don' know," he admitted. "But look how even *they* got to work now. Don' think they make it without you or me. Have to hire somebody do our work, an' they say they don' have the money do that."

She shrugged. "Maybe they won't make it at all. Like the Wards."

He looked out at the trees, unhappy at the direction of their conversation. They had reached the dreaded point where their interests and the Hazzards' had become identical, and it felt like a trap closing. There was no room left to maneuver. He looked at June's distressed face. There was nothing left to say.

*

EAVESDROPPING ON THE HAZZARDS had become hard. Without Jubah to serve their meals or Quamino to prepare their rooms, there was no opportunity to do it. June and Guy tried when they could, but they were rarely in the house anymore, and when the Hazzards were out in the field or working in the outbuildings, they had grown careful of what they said. Guy did hear Young John get casually scolded by his father for his "treatment" of Lucy, and June heard the mistress complain to a neighbor that Young John was under watch in the militia. Otherwise, nothing.

One August afternoon Guy was called in to repoint the bricks in the chimney throat in the kitchen. Everyone knew a cracked brick or some loose mortar could start a fire in the wooden walls behind, so the Hazzards were vigilant about it. He had just last week scraped out the cracked clay, replaced the bricks and cured the wet mortar in the parlor, so he had all the materials at hand. The mistress was working in the root cellar. He had refitted the bricks and just started a small fire to check for air leaks when he heard voices in the dining room. He lowered his tools and listened quietly. He knew that if he could hear them, they could hear him.

"So it's next week," the master said.

He heard Young John give a murmur of assent.

"At last!" said Master John. "I'd been beginning to wonder why they came to Newport at all!"

"They have plans. But they had to wait for Prescott's replacement."

"Pigot has arrived, then?"

"Last week. They say he is a fighter."

"He will have to be," the master said. "Spencer is making no secret of wanting an invasion in the fall. The fool. Well, this will let the damned assembly know there's a price to be paid for kidnapping."

"We've mapped out the farms and livestock for them. Only rebels will feel the hard blows." He recited a list of names. "And when they're done, our goods will be worth double what they are now. More!"

"Correct, son. But with Narragansett so close, how are you going to avoid being pulled into fight?"

"I've volunteered for camp duty all week in East Greenwich."

"Good." There was a brief silence in which Guy heard his own breath moving in and out like a moving sawblade. He quieted himself. "What if," Master John continued in a musing voice, "on the evening of the raid, you warn your commanding officer about receiving intelligence that an attack is planned on South County. By the time the information is sent on to higher officers and an alert called, the attack will be underway or over in any case."

"And I get credit for my patriotic warning…"

"The danger is if the raid is somehow delayed."

"I'll get word to them that they must mount their assault as planned."

"Excellent." Guy could hear the master's smile even if he could not see it. "But wait until you get word back from Pigot before you breathe anything to a militia officer." His legs ached from keeping them locked in one position. Guy did not move until a few minutes later when he heard the front door open and close.

*

After he told her what he had heard, June asked if they should find a way to get word to someone like the Wards or Jack Sisson. He knew of no way to do it. He reminded her that the way matters stood, anything that helped the master helped them.

She shook her head, and he saw a spark of anger in her eyes for the first time since his return. "Selling the others off help us?"

"The Hazzards go under..." He shook his head and did not finish the sentence.

"I want them to suffer like Lucy goin' suffer."

"She goin' be with her baby and lots of other slaves. Maybe she have to work harvest-hard most of the year but she won't have to work to keep warm in winter."

"Jubah by herself. Among strangers, too."

He nodded, and though he was reminded hourly how painfully he missed them himself, he said, "Be surprise what you can get use to."

*

The next morning, June's stomach turned at the thought of breakfast. She checked herself for fever and thought that last night's dinner with the pig entrails might have made her sick. She forced herself to eat some plain bread and drink some water. She felt a little better at midday and was almost herself at dinner. The next morning she threw up a half hour after breakfast and burst into sobs. Jubah had told her about it often, and she had seen it twice with Lucy.

She was bigged up.

She did not tell Guy, and she struggled through the next days praying she was wrong and hoping against hope the feelings would pass. Every time she even thought about the possibility, she was terrified. Perhaps there would never be a time in her life when pregnancy was going to be a good idea. She knew, even if that were true, it could not have come at a worse time.

Guy noticed her not eating in the mornings, but when he asked, she shrugged and said it's just the heat or that she ate too much last night.

A week later, the British attack on Narragansett came. Alarm riders tore through the countryside, minutemen were called. The discharge of cannons was close enough for them to hear them on the Hazzard place and Master Hazzard even made a show of taking down his fowling piece and riding off with some other landowners to defend the road leading to their properties.

The British burned scores of fields and carried off hundreds of cattle, sheep, pigs, horses, and cartloads of supplies. While several men were killed and a number of others wounded on both sides, the Rhode Island militia—despite a warning from John Hazzard—was not able to respond swiftly enough. The newspapers reported that the British were "driven off." The Hazzards knew, though, that the raid was carried out precisely as planned.

*

WHILE PRICES FOR THEIR produce and animals and dairy products steadily began to rise, and Master John took delivery on goods he had ordered before the raid knowing he could resell them more dearly afterwards, Guy noticed June's lower stomach rounding out under her shift.

He was afraid to ask, sickened at the idea of a yes for an answer. He heard Jubah's voice—he thought he heard hers and Quamino's words in his head more often now that they were gone than when they were here—saying to him, "Hidin' your face in a blanket don' make the sun go away." That night he ran his hand over June's stomach, and she grabbed his wrist to make him stop, rolling over to hug him.

"You sneakin' cheese out there in the dairy?"

"What you mean?"

"You gettin' bigger."

She was silent and stiffened ever-so-slightly in his arms. "Think so?"

"Mm." When she said nothing for a while but did not relax toward sleep, he asked, "Somethin' goin' on?" He felt her grow still, her body tense. His stomach knotted. "Sweet God," he said softly. "What we goin' do?"

She wept softly for a while. Finally she said, "Lot of women lose it long before it get a chance to get born. Or it die like Lucy's first. Or she die."

"Don' say that."

"What *are* we goin' do?" she asked.

They both knew that if she cost more to the Hazzards to care for than her work brought in, they would sell her. Who knew what they could do with a baby. If there was one and it lived, South was the only place to sell her. *South.* Despite what he'd said about Lucy, they had heard about the South in the way they had heard about hell in Sunday sermons. He made himself think the times were a little better. Tell the Hazzards now? No, that just gave them more time to make a plan to sell.

"Stay quiet," he said. She nodded. "We need work harder than we ever work before. Keep them from gettin' ideas."

"And then what?"

"Pray."

After she was asleep, he got out all his money from where it was hidden and looked at it. They were all coins, and some of them were worthless. Some of them, like the two gold Portuguese half Joes, were worth a lot. He could not count well enough to add their sums and did not know how much a slave sold for even if he could. He only knew that he did not have enough. When the time came, he was prepared to offer all of it, every last Jo, sou, penny, and farthing, if they wouldn't sell her away. If it came to it, he was prepared to kill anyone who tried to take her.

*

GUY WAS RENTED OUT for the afternoon to the neighbors when Young John came home on leave. He was not off his horse for an hour when he came sniffing June out in the dairy. He talked to her about this and that for a while, and she knew in ten seconds what he was there for. He had not talked to her about the weather or the harvest since they were children, and with a quick glance she could see the bulge in his breeches had persuaded him he could work something out with her just like he did Lucy. Money, a favor, some worthless trinket or pretty piece of ribbon. June thought for half a second about what she might get that could save her and the baby, if there was anything, and she was instantly ashamed for considering it. There was nothing he could do anyway, though she knew he would offer almost anything. She continued milking the cow and put her foot over the sharp bone-handled knife she used for a hundred different things, cutting twine to cutting chicken heads. Jubah always told her to keep herself clean, her clothes mended, and her knife sharp.

"You must miss Lucy," he said.

Against her own wishes, she felt a stab of pain. "Oh, yes," she said, continuing making steady long splashing squirts into the bucket of milk.

"I do, too," he said in an insinuating tone she knew was supposed to make her turn and look at him, even if only in anger.

She kept milking. He stepped closer, so close that she could hear him breathe.

"If she was still here, I could have made her happy," he said.

She kept milking, and it was now clear to them both she was ignoring him. She wondered if he thought she was afraid. He did not have the slightest sense how much she had changed. She was as far from fear at the moment as she was from laughter.

"I can make you happy," he said. Then he put his hand on her shoulder.

She stopped milking and in single unhurried movement reached down, took up the knife from under her foot, and rose to turn toward him as if in an embrace. She held the front of his shirt with one hand and faster than he could react lay the flat of the blade along his neck and cheek. He didn't move and neither did she. She spoke softly. "I knowed you since we was little. An' I don' want hurt you if I can help it."

"Put the knife down," he said, his voice one of anger and command.

She could tell that he expected her to cower. He started to reach up to grab her wrist. She turned the blade so he could feel the point of it just under his ear. "Don' you touch me. Not ever."

"Put. It. Down."

"Want you to understand me first. I'm not Lucy. I'm not even June anymore." She did not know what she meant by this, it just came out, but she could see from his face that in some important way it was true, and he knew it. She could feel his anger and surprise begin to turn toward something else. "I cut you, for what they do to me later, I might just as well kill you. You try and touch me again, I will." She looked deep into his eyes to see what she could find there. His breath smelled of malt beer. She saw a flicker of disbelief. She knew this was not healthy for either of them. She had gutted hogs and steers and chickens with this knife, and she knew where the body was soft and where it had bones that resisted a plunging blade, and she knew for a fact she was now capable of slitting his throat if he touched her. She did not know how to convince him of this, but she knew if they both wanted to go on living, she must.

His shirt was open where she held it in her fist. She brought the knife blade there and sliced open his skin about half the length of her little finger. He looked down in shock. She knew the cut would not hurt for another minute but it welled with bright red blood almost instantly. When he looked back up at her, she saw in his eyes just what she wanted—full belief. Then she let him go.

He stared at her, panting, his frightened face pale.

"Put some cobwebs on it, it stop bleedin' in a minute. Slice of onion make it heal. But don' you touch me ever again."

Clutching his chest, he glared at her and backed out of the barn.

She went back to milking, astonished at how calm she felt. She knew right away, though, that she could not tell Guy what happened. No telling what he might do.

Chapter Twenty-Eight

The creditors could not be held off. Before the spring of 1777 was out, the Wards had to sell everything—livestock, land, house, outbuildings and all their contents—everything except some personal effects and the little plot of land where their mother and sister were buried. A birthplace, a livelihood, a land of memories, and the enchanted country of the Wards' childhoods all vanished with the single signing of a pen. Only one thing made the sale bearable. The purchasers were Nat Greene and his brothers, their Hope foundry being one of the few businesses to prosper in this time of war, making desperately needed cannon and shot and digging tools. The price the Greenes paid was more than fair. And since one of Nat's brothers was married to one of Sam's sisters—pretty Catharine—the farm and its lands had not entirely left the family. But one way of life had ended for all of them forever. If they ever returned to their place in Westerly, it would be as guests. Sam and his brothers and sisters now would have to make their way in the world on their own, no home or farm or store to fall back on. His older brother, Charles, was, they said, a sergeant somewhere in the ranks of the Massachusetts army and had not been heard from in many months. His brother-in-law Ethan Clarke would be joining the army as a captain of artillery, and Nancy would be moving in with sister Catharine and her new baby.

Sam, at last exchanged for a British prisoner and freed from parole, had been promoted to major, a rank that came with a new uniform and a salary nearly twice that of a captain. But he had no other personal money, and he immediately sent half of what he got to Nancy to distribute among the youngest impoverished Wards. He was now among the poorest of all the New England officers, and yet he found himself in the absurd position of having, of all things, a personal servant. Old Cujoe, his limbs stiff with rheumatism, came with him when he reported for duty in the Hudson highlands in New York.

When they sold all their property, they had to face the uncomfortable question of what to do with their slaves. With the estate's debts cleared, the slaves, Cujoe, Violet, and Toby, were all safe from being seized as payment. It was illegal to sell them out of state, the Greenes had slaves of their own, and, like many patriots, they were growing uneasy about fighting for freedom while perpetuating human bondage at home. If they simply let the slaves go, the freed blacks would not be able to live on their own with no money, no shelter, nor anyone to employ them. In the flattened state economy, no farmers or merchants were doing any hiring anyway. Cujoe and Violet said they were too old to care if they were free or not free—they simply wanted to continue with life as they had always lived it. In the end, Violet went to work for Catharine, and the Greenes agreed to hire out Toby in exchange for food and shelter, but no one could find a place for Cujoe. The entire family urged Sam to take him as his manservant. The army would feed and lodge him, Sam could pay for other necessities out of his own pay, and Cujoe would not have to be thrown to the meager mercy of the town's poor rolls. And so the three former slaves, who were told they might strike out on their own any time they wished, continued life much as they always had. And Sam, his family pauperized, still arrived at the army with a servant, a lean gray-haired African-born man who looked tough and dour on the outside, his face lined with chronic pain, yet who was actually one of the sweetest-natured people Sam had ever met.

Sam arrived at Peekskill in early summer with a haversack full of the carefully sewn, newly adopted Stars and Stripes. The air was soft, and the green, giant-treed landscape unfolded before him like a gorgeous dream. The forests on the way were full of wild game, the streams ran clear and cold down from Canada, and here and there, popping up almost by surprise, they saw houses as grand as any in Boston or Newport, but standing all by themselves surrounded by vast lawns and landscaped grounds. As he and Cujoe entered the fecund Hudson Valley, they got a hundred ever-shifting vantages of the blue-gray stripe of the broad shining river and the surrounding lush green hills, high enough almost to be mountains. Though the flavor of the soft air did not have the salty tang of the ocean breezes of Westerly, the sun in the valley was filtered by so many dense trees that even a hot day did not seem unpleasant. In the evening, cool air slid down out of the darkening sky behind the hills like a benediction.

Despite having to bid a painful farewell to Phebe, to his family, and to his former way of life, despite the pale faces of the dead who appeared to him almost nightly, and despite his recurring horror at the thought of captivity, Sam was relieved to have a role to fill once again. He had no place in Rhode Island to be or to live, no vocation to pursue, and he knew, whatever else happened, that here in the soldiery he was needed. In the wake of the calamitous loss at Fort Washington, the Continental army had barely managed to survive. Sam was told that half the men he saw during his visit to the fort with Nat Greene just before it fell were now dead of disease and malnutrition, and the rest were suffering in the deepening heat of summer aboard the pestilential holds below decks of the prison ships. Howe and his army remained in New York, a powerful crouched animal. In the north, they heard that British General Burgoyne was defeating the Americans in encounter after encounter. And if Howe and Burgoyne's two armies joined each other, the newborn country would be sliced in half. The grand Hudson River was the watery highway that could permit them to join. Everyone who could read a map said the river's protection from British domination was crucial, foremost among them General Washington, and he had once again placed the Rhode Island brigades at the heart of its defense.

And so, under a hot sun, Sam reported to Peekskill, across the river from Fort Montgomery, a place named after the ill-fated general who died leading their attack on Quebec. Sam made his way to present himself to serve in General James Varnum's Rhode Island brigade under now full-Colonel Christopher Greene. In the brigade's other regiment was Major Simeon Thayer. And he found excellent new captains—or at least new to him—including his cousin Eben Flagg and his old friend and former lieutenant whom he had not seen since he marched off north from Boston, Elijah Lewis. And there was his friend and neighbor, Tom Arnold, and young Oliver Clarke who, in his impatience and ardor to serve, reminded Sam of himself when he first joined the army. Serving under Major Thayer was another old lieutenant and his friend from the journey to Quebec, Sylvanus Shaw, who, when he returned from the prison ship off New York, found his family fled and his Newport home garrisoned by British soldiers. Sam could tell from the heartiness of their welcome that they were as glad to see him as he to see them. Experienced, tested, smart, and resourceful, these tough officers were ones he was willing to stake his life on.

Soon after his arrival, however, he made the discovery that the Rhode Island brigade had become notorious as the worst-supplied men in a badly supplied army.

Rhode Island and Connecticut had pooled their states' supplies for the Continental army in a huge depot at Danbury, and when the British landed troops, attacked, and rampaged through the Connecticut town for two full days, the army lost virtually everything. General Benedict Arnold arrived all the way from Providence to finally offer opposition. Arnold went at them fiercely in attack after attack. His own horse was killed under him, but still he attacked on.

His second horse got wounded and Arnold would not leave the field until he finally succeeded in driving the British back to their ships. But the damage done in Danbury was irreversible. Crops could not be regrown, clothes remade, or animals replaced without the ripening of time. While the Rhode Island brigade had its veterans from Boston and Quebec, it also had a huge supply of fresh recruits who signed up on the promise of a twenty-dollar bounty and a new full uniform, from boots to breeches. As of July, most of them had received nothing.

The encampment offered Sam a sight that was painfully familiar. Soldiers were in clothes that were filthy and patched, eating bad food, when they could get any. Measles and smallpox abounded. They could not even get vinegar to treat the camp itch that raged through the ranks. There were no enemy troops anywhere in sight, nothing to maintain the tension that made discipline natural. The men were bored, their tempers short, and they were being flogged at the rate of three and four a day for ignoring orders. Desertions began. For the first week he was there, conditions got worse each day.

When they got the bad news that Fort Ticonderoga had surrendered to Burgoyne without a fight, discipline immediately improved. An invasion by Howe from the south or a drive down by Burgoyne from the north now seemed inevitable, and the Rhode Islanders knew that they were the only obstacle remaining between the two hostile armies and the last defense of their own homes. Only when they heard of Colonel Barton's amazing kidnapping of General Prescott did their morale lift. Sam was especially happy to learn of the Colonel's inspired borrowing of the Hazzard's slave Guy Watson to employ in his task.

But the supply problems continued. The state tried to provide materiel, but wagonloads were lost in British raids and even more disappeared through cheating, pilfering, bribery, theft, and plain misdelivery. The men grew increasingly ragged and filthy, and by August, half of them were unfit for duty. Nonetheless, they were suddenly marched halfway to Morristown to join the main army, and then just as suddenly recalled to Peekskill, leaving many of them with bare cut and blistered feet. And then Howe, who had done little for most of the year, loaded thousands upon thousands of his men aboard ships, mystifying everyone as to his intentions. No one like Sam or any of the Quebec veterans who had been below decks in midsummer heat doubted that Howe had a plan in mind. But what?

There were three possibilities: an attack on Philadelphia, a landing somewhere on the coast of New England, or a drive up the Hudson River right into the highlands past Peekskill. General Washington was convinced that the Hudson must be Howe's goal. He ordered three full divisions north to reinforce the Rhode Islanders, Nat Greene's among them. But then Howe's ships suddenly disappeared off the Atlantic coast heading south. The three divisions were frantically recalled. Then reports came in that Howe's ships were circling northward. The divisions were ordered to stop where they were and "hold themselves in readiness to march."

The Rhode Islanders were ferried across the river to prepare Fort Montgomery for an assault. They immediately fell to digging. They then strung thick cables and heavy chains across the river to stop the passage of ships. It was all hot, hard, and dirty labor, but the men also knew they might yet prove to be the last bulwark against a British stranglehold. And if their clothes were just as tattered, their feet just as bare, and their bodies just as tormented by lice as they were a month ago, the urgency of their work kept their minds off it. Perhaps it all still *would* have been all right if, when the worst of the backbreaking work was over, the command had not sent in the regiment made up of British and Hessian deserters to man the lines.

The deserters were fully clothed. The deserters were well-fed, their pink faces and pink hands scrubbed clean. The deserters were paid fully, as they had been promised. The deserters had not been eating wormy meat and moldy bread. Disloyal to their own side, they had left to join the Americans not out of sympathy for the cause.

They were not protecting their honors, their families, or their sacred rights. The deserters were there because they did not like how they had been treated. Some could barely speak a word of English and had already shot, bayoneted, and mercilessly killed American soldiers in earlier fights, but what they really wanted was better food, better clothing, better pay, and lighter duty. Did these traitors and butchers get what they wanted? Yes, they did.

So when the Rhode Islanders heard about a British raid on Narragansett right near their homes, and then learned that the value of their still-unpaid enlistment bounty was worth less than two-thirds what it was when they signed up, they were boiling mad. Finally, though, they got word that the British Gentleman Johnny Burgoyne had been stopped at Bennington up north, and perhaps all their sacrifice *wasn't* so important after all, they were furious. The weather, hot in the day, was starting to get cold at night. Yet their clothes, coats, and blankets had still not arrived. On August 22, after a month at sea, when General Howe's fleet finally made landfall, it turned out to be in the Chesapeake Bay. As his army began to move on Philadelphia, it became clear that all the Rhode Islanders' backbreaking preparations were in fact for nothing. Washington marched his army through the streets of Philadelphia, but the Rhode Islanders were not offered the honor to join him. And then on August 27, after a cold night without tents or blankets—amid a cloud of rumors that General Spencer was planning an invasion of Newport that they also would not be sent to join—they had had it. They broke into open riot, firing their guns in the air, burning the breastworks, torching the Hessians' and the British deserters' tents, rampaging and screaming through the encampment, an armed mob, ragged, barefoot, filthy, and enraged.

Sam, Colonel Greene, Lieutenant Colonel Olney, and all their captains and field lieutenants tried to calm the men. They ordered them to put down their weapons and not waste precious powder and shot. The men ignored them and raged on, shouting, "Food! Money!

Clothes! Boots! We want what we've been promised!" While half the men did not participate in the riot, they also would not follow their captains' orders to arrest the rioters. Colonel Greene, unable to quiet the men and worried that the disaffection would spread, sent two of his aides to General Varnum's with a request for assistance. He and several companies of guards did not arrive for two full hours. By then, most of the rioters' fury was spent and they could not find anyone to shoot or anything to destroy that would help their cause. From horseback, General Varnum pledged on the strength of his own word and personal fortune that the state's commitments would be honored. The yelling and screaming began to subside. Confronted by guards who appeared prepared to shoot and having gotten attention at the highest levels, the rioters finally lay down their arms.

Sam sat on the court-martial board that tried them. While he and the other officers, Varnum, Greene, Thayer, Olney, and Angell, were sympathetic to the men's grievances—and they shared most of them themselves—they knew they could not let the riot go unpunished. The privates, they decided, could be let off with a stern warning, a cut-off of all spirits, and a week's duty digging privies. But the sergeants and corporals were a different matter. The ones who ignored orders of a superior officer and participated in the riot would have to suffer a penalty. An army that did not comply with commands was not an army. Nine sergeants and three corporals were convicted of disorderly conduct, suspended from their rank without pay, and were warned that any future infraction on their part, however slight, would send them to prison. If in the weeks ahead they could conduct themselves "in a manner befitting the authority with which they had been entrusted," Colonel Greene would reinstate them.

*

As September began, money, food, and blankets began to trickle in. Discipline improved, but morale, which everyone thought could not be lower, continued to sink. They all had been hoping to have the honor to be called to join the main army in the fight to save Philadelphia. America had already lost Boston, Newport, and New York to the enemy, and now the country's largest and, many said, most beautiful city was imperiled, the seat of Congress, the capital of the country. A decisive blow was about to fall, history was to be made, and they were trapped on the Hudson. Each day they heard a new rumor. They'd lost! They'd won! The city was in flames! Howe was coming to attack! Washington was captured, the war was over with thousands slain! Sam began to drop in at headquarters three and four times a day to see if General Varnum had received any official dispatches from the main army.

It is not until September 15, four endless days after the battle at the Brandywine was over, that they got word about what happened. They lost the field and suffered twice as many losses as the British. They appeared to be not so much out-fought as out-smarted—Howe, aided by loyalists who had not evacuated Philadelphia at his approach, was better informed about American territory than the Americans. There were interesting sub-stories to the main one—Nat Greene's brigades of Virginians rescuing General Sullivan and preventing a rout; one old French general, Preudhomme de Borre, panicking and fleeing in battle, then resigning from the army rather than facing charges of cowardice, being balanced by one new French one, nineteen-year-old Marie-Joseph Paul Yves Roch Gilbert du Motier, the Marquis de Lafayette, holding fast against British bayonets and having to be helped from the field, blood pouring down his leg with a musket ball in his thigh. But the question for Sam was whether they would at last be called to join Washington's army.

Instead, all they heard was more bad news, none of it rumor. Howe edged toward Philadelphia and happened across an obscure place called Valley Forge where he was able to plunder an unguarded American depot of enormous supplies laid in reserve for the coming cold weather. To the deprived Rhode Islanders, this sounded like a horrifying loss until a few days later they heard news that made the loss at Valley Forge pale. Men under General Wayne, men who had fought bravely against the Hessians at Brandywine, were sleeping in their encampment at a tiny place called Paoli. A large force of British troops, flints removed from their guns to ensure silence and permit no muzzle flashes, attacked and slaughtered them in their beds. Wayne's division had as many hundreds dead in a few minutes as the entire Continental army suffered in the day-long battle at the Brandywine. The British had six men killed.

And then a few days after this, to the cheers of thousands of loyalist inhabitants, Howe effortlessly and without opposition took possession of Philadelphia. Congress fled to Baltimore.

Sam knew it was just his father's earthly remains, and they were safe from desecration in the ground, but he was still sickened to think his father was buried in a city the British now controlled. He had hoped to be part of the force that protected the city of his father's grave, or at least fought to do so. Instead, the greatest challenge he had faced was maintaining order in his own mutinous brigade. He knew that there had been talk for months of America making an alliance with the Spanish or the French—once they could be persuaded that the Americans might hope to win. But General Washington had not won an engagement since his crossing of the Delaware.

Sam had been back with the army for three months and still he had not seen Nat Greene. He decided it was time.

*

As he checked his saddle cinch for tightness to make the ride to Nat's headquarters, Sam felt the coolness of the late September air and found, as each day passed, he was thinking more and more of Phebe. He thanked Cujoe for his help and asked him to be sure to assist Colonels Greene and Olney while he was gone. He checked his haversack for the messages from General Varnum and then began his journey south, the soft clop of his horse's hoof immediately reminding him of the iron clang they had made on the frozen earth of the Post Road when, last winter, he had gone on another ride, this one to visit his Aunt and Uncle Greene and Phebe in East Greenwich. As he rode, the memories of his visit came back to him as clearly as if he had just experienced them.

He had, back then, already passed their house three times while arranging for the unpaid wages of his men who were imprisoned in Quebec to be granted, consulting with the General Assembly on new officers, settling his father's last debts, and helping recruit new soldiers for the army. Finally, in the early dark of one of the coldest nights of the winter, he made his way to their house on Main Street. A fat January moon bathed the snow-covered ground in bluish light.

He'd thought what a long time had passed and how much had happened since he first marched past their house on his way to Boston, a new recruit marching through the cheering townspeople and past the girls who offered their brightest smiles and warmest waves. As Sam rode up to their house, he could see their fear and vigilance had not passed, even in the dead of January. The Greenes had a horse and carriage standing ready at all times to take them inland if word came from the harbor about enemy ships. Staying with them now were Newporters cast out of their homes and, as usual, the place thronged all day with family visitors. Phebe, to his disappointment, was busy supervising and cooking in the kitchen, having begun the day at dawn spinning, weaving, sewing, and seeing that the fires in half a dozen fireplaces were properly stoked. She looked different to him dressed in her thick layers of winter garb, and she barely had enough time to fulfill the requirements of politeness. That only a few months before she had kissed his hand with her warm mouth seemed to him like a distant cherished dream. They had written each other half a dozen times since, but both of them were shy to put in written words what they felt—at least Sam knew he was. She drew the back of her hand wearily across her brow to push back some stray hairs and smiled at him, but soon she had to excuse herself to help with dinner.

At dinner he sat at yelling distance from her at the far end of a long, crowded table while people talked of war and money and politics, topics he could barely pay attention to. He had a question he wished to ask her, not about marriage but very close to it, and he needed a private moment in which to address her. Such a moment had not been possible since the second he arrived. When the food, spare and plain and nothing like the bounty before the war, was done being consumed and hot cider was offered to accompany the bread pudding dessert, he managed to ask Phebe if she might join him for a walk after the dishes were cleared. He had seen the water in the harbor smoking with cold when he rode up, but there was no privacy possible inside the Greene house this night.

When he asked Phebe to join him, he could feel his aunt's and uncle's watchful glances fall upon him, just as they had all evening when he spoke. It was friendly watchfulness, but to Sam it felt like having feathers constantly tickling his cheek. Phebe turned to her mother with an inquisitive look, and Aunt Catharine rolled her eyes and nodded. "But in this weather, don't be gone long," she warned.

"In this weather, no one could be gone long without freezing to death!" said one of the guests to the hilarity of the table. Through an act of pure will, Sam smiled.

"Wear your heavy coat," Uncle William said to Phebe.

"Of course, Dada," she said and kissed him solemnly on the brow. As they left, she picked up her hand muff near the door. "I like the cold," she said to Sam.

He did, too, but the truth was that even months after his release, he had not yet been able to gain enough weight to make himself feel winter hardy. Some days the cold seemed to drop out of the air straight into his bones. Their breaths issued from their mouths in vaporous plumes. They walked carefully on the snow-covered path.

"You are going back to the army this spring, Father says."

"I am, as soon as I am properly exchanged and we settle affairs in Westerly."

Phebe nodded, her face sad. In the light of the coach lantern, tiny shadows of her lashes fell onto the arch of her cheeks. Sam thought how much he loved her face, even when it was sad. They walked in silence while Sam weighed how to word his question, and he suddenly remembered Nat Greene's ashen face when Sam's sister Nancy refused his hand. Sam's right eye, stung with cold, teared fluently. "I have enjoyed your letters," she said.

A hundred words suddenly crowded his mouth, and then they vanished. He said plainly what he felt. "I have thought of almost nothing except our last time together."

She looked at him, her blue eyes serious, and she removed one hand from her muff, passed it through his arm, and returned it to the muff again. "I think of it, too."

"I had thought to ask your parents' permission for us to bundle tonight." He glanced at her and she at him. Her eyes widened. Though songs and bawdy poems joked about it, this winter act of courtship was serious, and in respectable families occurred only when a couple was certain to marry. "But first I need to ask yours."

Phebe nodded. Sam felt a grin spreading across his face. "Are you sure?" he asked.

"I am sure."

*

It was Phebe's suggestion that he ask her father while she asked her mother. "I think," she said with musing look, "that that will offer our best chance of success."

His pulse raced and his groin stirred.

After the guests left and the others retired, he found his Uncle William in his study going over some law cases. Sam's father had been chief justice of the Supreme Court, too, but there the resemblance between them ended. Where Samuel was smooth, articulate, and worldly, Uncle William was blunt, plainspoken, and resolutely old-fashioned. When court was held in Providence, this strict Quaker farmer would walk the dozen miles there and the dozen miles back, just as he had to for meetings of the General Assembly where they kept electing him as representative.

"Excuse me, sir," Sam said.

Phebe's father looked up over the rims of his half-lensed reading glasses, his brow pinched in concentration. "Major Ward," he said. He took off his glasses and rubbed his eyes. "I cannot continue reading much longer this evening in any case. Sit down."

Sam nodded and sat on the wooden chair next to the desk. "Phebe and I have had a talk together this evening. She and I would like—with your permission, sir—to bundle this night."

William Greene's thick eyebrows rose. "Bundle...?"

"Yes, sir."

"I see." His brow pinched again. "What does Mrs. Greene say?"

"Phebe said she wished to talk to her about the matter herself."

He steepled his thick fingers together. "You plan to be married, then."

"That is my hope, sir."

He looked at Sam steadily for a while in silence. "You are a fine young man, but I want you both to remember the constraints of virtue. We are in the midst of a war whose length remains uncertain—

though I do not doubt we will prevail in the end. Still, it is a time when young people may especially mistake the feelings of a moment for something more lasting."

"Speaking for myself, sir, these are feelings which have taken root and grown over many months."

Phebe's father rose and stirred the embers in the fireplace. "Assuming Mrs. Greene agrees, and I have reason to think she will, thou hast my permission." Sam knew his uncle chose the times he used "thee" and "thou" with great care. In effect, he had just given Sam his blessing. The older man looked out the frosted window. "Certainly it is a very cold night."

*

SOME FAMILIES USED A bundling rod suspended between the couple as reminder of "the constraints of virtue." The Greenes simply used Phebe's youngest sister who was left to sleep in another bed in the same room. On a night as cold as this one, couples went to bed with all their clothes on and hugged one another for warmth. Sam and Phebe, tented among hanging woolen blankets and buried under quilts, were not warm at all for the first half hour in their frigid room. In the half-light of the window, they could see their breath turn to steam. Phebe trembled with cold or excitement or both over this unfamiliar sleeping arrangement. They embraced and whispered quietly, one or the other of them sometimes bursting into muffled laughter at the oddness of their circumstance. A half hour after that, with Phebe's slumbering little sister at a distance that to them could better have been measured in miles rather than feet, they grew warmer. Phebe loosened the kerchief at her neck. A few minutes later, she opened her jacket. Their clothes and bedsheets and quilts had at last been suffused with heat. Sam unbuttoned the collar of his shirt and removed his woolen waistcoat, noticing that the rope webbing that supported Phebe's mattress was far quieter than his creaking old wood-framed bed would have been.

They held each other again, and this time Sam could feel Phebe's body distinctly against his. He knew she could feel the long lump at his middle as well, and he wondered whether she felt attraction or repulsion, curiosity or longing in the way he saw and heard his sisters waver in their feelings about the subject of sex. He tried to keep from pressing himself against her too ardently. Phebe took off her ribboned cap and untied the string at the top of her bodice. "Aren't you hot?" she asked in a whisper.

He said he was. "Should I remove the quilt?"

"Yes!" She put his hand on her neck where it met her shoulder. It was damp. "See?"

He saw. He removed her kerchief and used it to blot up her perspiration, checking afterwards with his lips to see if her skin were dry. He soon found that there was a large area that required these attentions. He opened the neck of her bodice farther and farther. She smelled of good soap and faintly of lavender. He found with a few licks of his tongue that her skin tasted deliciously salty. He blew softly on the tenderest areas of her skin. She squirmed and made tiny muffled sounds as he kissed her, somewhere between passion and laughter. He forgot completely about removing the quilt. He kissed her for a long while until her breasts were almost completely exposed. She reached under his shirt to press her hands against his back, showing him, she said, that her hands, at least, were still cool. He reached down, intending to touch her knee at the juncture where her stockings ended and her underskirts began, to show her that his hands were warm, very warm. He felt some soft, smooth skin, but it was much higher than her knee. Her skirts, he noticed, had ridden up a great distance since they first had gotten beneath the covers.

He meant to say something, but the small shuddering he felt under his hand and Phebe's fast breathing silenced him. She pressed her cool hands harder against his back and, her breath unsteady in his ear, she rolled from her side to her back. Her skirt rode up further and his hand followed. Sam, beginning to be a bit dizzy, kissed farther down the slopes of her breasts, finding more sweet saltiness to taste as he progressed. His hand slowly, over many minutes, made its way farther and farther up her thigh until he found his way under the layers of skirts and petticoat and undershift to a wet and soft place he gently and slowly explored. She grew still. He could hear only her ragged breathing. He waited for her to say stop. Instead, her hands reached for the top button of his breeches. Pressed taut, he knew he would have to assist with the other buttons.

"Yes?" he whispered, thinking of the constraints of virtue. Her hands went to the next button and soon the constraints of virtue were a small leaf in a great wind. Life was too full of cruel chances, he had learned, not to take advantage of the sweet ones. He tried his best to be gentle the first time, and he seemed to succeed. The second and especially the third time, his and her main concern was to try not to wake Phebe's little sister. They succeeded in that, too, though they had to interrupt their fourth joining when she began to stretch and yawn. At dawn, when the rest of the house began to stir, they had not slept a wink, and at breakfast, judging by the others' faces, not a soul but themselves seemed to know about what happened during their first night of bundling.

But ever after, when Sam thought of "home," he did not think of the lost Ward place in Westerly. He thought of a rope bed tented with blankets in which, every night, slept someone he loved. This made it harder for him to return to the army, though, because it brought him face-to-face with elemental concerns, in one sense easier. He had not just something, but someone, he wanted to fight for, to live for, and, if necessary, to die for. He only hoped that his desire to live did not master the requirement to fight.

*

In the early fall days it took Sam to find his way to Nat Greene, a great deal happened, some of which he heard about on his way. Good news and bad. The good news was very good. In mid-September at Saratoga to the north, New York's General Gates—aided by Benedict Arnold, Daniel Morgan, Henry Dearborn, and hundreds of Sam's Quebec veterans—stopped Burgoyne cold. The bad news was that as October opened, General Washington launched a full-scale attack on Howe at Germantown, a little place just outside Philadelphia. After a series of small and large snarls and miscues, the Americans lost the field, suffering losses twice that of the British. The disorderly retreat to Morristown made finding Nat that much more difficult, since he was part of an army that was now doing its best not to be found.

But after his own miscues, including one narrow miss at being captured by a British scouting party on horseback, he was able to find Nat just outside Morristown working in some improvised field headquarters. The closer Sam got to headquarters, the more surprised he was to discover that the recently defeated army did not look or sound defeated. He decided it must be worse to hear about these losses, as they had for weeks back at Fort Montgomery, than actually to be involved in them. He read in a New Jersey paper Washington's words in the general orders before the battle, trying to kindle in them envy of General Gates's triumph to the north: "Covet! My countrymen and fellow soldiers! Covet a share of the glory due heroic deeds! Let it never be said that in a day of action, you turned your backs on the foe; let the enemy no longer triumph!"

Well, the enemy did triumph, but you wouldn't know that from looking at the American army or at Major General Nathanael Greene, who looked up from a portable desk in a large field tent and said to Sam, as if it had been hours instead of many months since he had last seen him, "You got here quickly enough."

Since he had gotten lost half a dozen times and had to go long paths around whole towns to avoid accidental encounters with British patrols, this came as a surprise to Sam.

Nat looked at Sam for a moment before asking, "Is the rest of the Rhode Island brigade with you?"

"No, general. I left them at Fort Montgomery almost a week ago. But I have some letters and dispatches for you from Colonels Greene and Angell, and from your brothers at home." Sam put a bundle of correspondence on the corner of the desk.

"Ah. Well, your brigade will be joining us here very soon. I would guess that about a day after you left, they were ordered to join us here in New Jersey. General Washington has another important piece of work for you."

Sam was surprised and relieved to hear this news. "They will be glad to join the main army. And glad to leave. The problems of supply have created problems of morale and discipline that would be hard to exaggerate."

Nat frowned. "I have read and I have heard. Was it better when you left?"

"Better. But worse would have been almost impossible."

"Despite it all, your brigade still has a reputation as one of the most able in the army, and that is why General Washington called for you. Your assignment is one of the most important we have." He reached under a pile of papers and pulled out a small map of the area. He pointed to the bending lines of the Delaware River. "The Rhode Island brigade will be defending Fort Mercer at Red Bank here in the New Jersey shore." He dragged a forefinger an inch downstream to an island. "Fort Mercer, along with Fort Mifflin right here on Mud Island, are the keys to our strategy. Howe has control of Philadelphia, but while our main army keeps him bottled up by land, these two forts on the Delaware can cut off all his water transports.

If we hold them, it will be impossible for Howe to remain in the city. Once out, he will be ripe for attack."

"So we will not be with the main army yet."

"In terms of supply and proximity, yes. But it is a delicate business of balance. To succeed, His Excellency needs to use as few men as possible to hold the two forts. If the main army was weakened and divided for the purpose, it would itself become vulnerable. That is why we *need* the Rhode Island regiments."

"Good. I am confident we can acquit ourselves well. Our situation at Fort Montgomery is becoming irreversibly bad, and that is why I came to see you. But I see my travel was unnecessary."

Nat smiled. "'Tis good to see you, anyway, Sammy. And consider it this way. Your ride here saves you the inconvenience of a return."

Nat lent himself a few minutes to talk about affairs and people in Rhode Island, including about Nat and Caty's new daughter, Martha Washington Greene, and about the purchase of Ward Hall and the Westerly farm. When he said Caty reported that Phebe followed the war with a keener interest than she had ever seen a person suddenly show, Sam was too embarrassed to let the topic stand. He asked about the battle of Germantown.

Nat's jaw clenched. "An excellent plan, but star-crossed. Sullivan's men crashed into Howe's army, drove them running from the field, and I was supposed to join him after an all-night march. A local scout got us lost in the fog, we then ran into surprise early resistance, and so we arrived later than scheduled. In the meantime, at daylight the fog thickened, one of my brigadier generals, General Stephen, got stumbling drunk, ignored orders, and, without informing me, headed off my right wing and marched directly into General Wayne's men, and they proceeded to shoot *each other* in the fog. This let Howe concentrate his fire on my division, who were tired enough from our twenty-mile march, and we had to give back our gains. Stephen has already been cashiered from the army and is lucky if he does not suffer worse. But no one in Sullivan's division will forget the sight of seeing Howe's men break and run like frightened children. With a tiny bit better luck, this all would have been a different story. And our soldiers know it. They feel more cheated than they do defeated."

"So I saw. How fares His Excellency?"

Nat lowered his voice. "Some members of his own staff have mewed that our general is indecisive, which is a complete misunderstanding of his care and caution, and we hear rumors that some members of Congress would like to see him replaced. And there are a few generals who are seeking to advance themselves on the hopes of His Excellency's ruin. All I can say is, not only is my admiration undimmed for General Washington, but it grows every day."

"What about these rivals?"

"Their little hopes are smaller than the little men themselves."

Sam knew that Nat blustered and overstated only when he was nervous. "A victory would silence them."

"It would. Which is why we need you to hold these forts." His finger pointed back at the map. "They are the key to our plans."

Chapter Twenty-Nine

Sam was able to tour the fort at Red Bank the day before the Rhode Island regiments arrived. It was large, clearly made to be defended by at least two thousand men. With a handful from the first Virginia regiment and all the Rhode Islanders, Sam judged they would have scarcely more than five hundred. Fort Mifflin down on Mud Island was already taking artillery fire from British batteries, and it, too, was badly undermanned. The two forts were the only land-based points of defense in shutting down the Delaware. Just upriver from the sharpened logs they imbedded in the river bottom, the Americans had a motley collection of floating vessels: Sam counted a brig, a schooner, several galleys and half-galleys, four sloops, three xebeques, six rafts, and four half-ruinous crafts that could be used only as fire boats—sent into an enemy fleet to torch their ships. That was the American flotilla that proposed to take on the world's most powerful navy.

Sam worried about their small force trying to defend such a large fort. If they strung their men thinly enough to try to defend everything, they would effectively be defending nothing. They could be punched through at any point like paper. But he knew that the main army could spare not another man, and Fort Mifflin was already being defended by what scattering of local New Jersey militia they had been able to muster. Within a day, General Washington personally wrote Colonel Greene to request volunteers to reinforce Fort Mifflin. Tough old Major Thayer growled he'd go. When men from Angell's regiment heard Thayer would be leading the detachment and that, though pounded by artillery shells, they had lots of fresh food, within a day, 150 men volunteered to join him.

Colonel Greene did a nose count. All told, they were down to four hundred men defending Fort Mercer.

General Washington sent a talented young French engineer and artillerist, the Chevalier du Plessis, to study and prepare the fort. He took a tour of the outworks, muttering to himself in French, made a quick survey of the men, and shook his head.

"Impossible," he said in heavily accented English. He made a large circle with his arms and then constricted it. "We must make it more small, the fort."

Colonel Greene nodded but suggested leaving the farthest works right where they were. "The enemy doesn't know how many men we have in here. We post a few sentinels on the wall, build a few campfires near the perimeter each night, and we may keep them from attacking at all."

Du Plessis nodded but said they must bring in materials to build new breastworks. He drew a picture showing a fort within the fort, reducing the area to defend to about half its present size. And the French engineer soon proved to be skillful at using the terrain and whatever materials the army could provide. But Sam was still uneasy, though this time about the steady flow of local suppliers and day laborers who came in and out of the fort. They could not fool the British for long about the size of their garrison. One of Nat Greene's bitterest complaints was that the British intelligence sources appeared to be better than the Americans, and everyone knew the area was lousy with loyalists. He raised the matter with Colonels Angell and Greene, and discovered that they had been wrestling with the question themselves.

Angell pointed out if they were to complete their reconstruction in any reasonable time, they *had* to use local labor. "We would not be done before winter on our own."

"The size of our garrison is already known," Sam said, "but we can keep how we plan to defend ourselves from getting out."

"Go on," Colonel Greene said, looking at him with sudden interest.

"The suppliers could be instructed to leave the building materials outside the main walls and we can cart them in ourselves. We can require the men to wash and mend their own clothes or, if necessary, send the clothes outside the fort."

"You mean close the gates to all but our own soldiers."

"Precisely."

To Sam's relief, the plan was implemented before the morning was out. The words "Fort Washington" still haunted him. There, a force ten times the size of what they now had was dug in behind elaborate earthworks, mountainously supplied and fully prepared for a siege. Fort Washington was supposed to bottle up Howe in New York just as their Fort Mercer was supposed to do now to Howe in Philadelphia. Yet he watched Fort Washington, despite Nat's best plans and careful review, be smashed like dropped crockery. They had heard more from British deserters about what became of the men taken prisoner there. The thought of all those men, some of them riflers just like the ones from the first Virginia, dying in the airless, black, and stinking holds of a prison ship horrified him. He felt a twinge of guilt, too. He had fervently wished Colonel Enos's men baked in hell for turning back on the march to Quebec. Since many of the men captured at Fort Washington were Enos's men, his wish had come true.

He threw himself into the work, joining his eight captains in doing physical labor—the more backs and more hands, the faster they would be done. It kept him from brooding and sent him to bed at night weary and ready for sleep, blunting some of the bad dreams and distancing some of the imploring faces that still assailed him in the night. Morning and afternoon, rain or shine, weekday or sabbath, they worked. In the middle of October, they were raising the palisades of the inner fort when a piece of astonishing information arrived. Colonel Greene read the official news: Colonel Morgan and Generals Arnold and Gates had caused British General Bourgoyne to *surrender his entire army*. While Arnold was wounded once again, the Americans suffered few casualties and achieved the first total victory of the war.

The men burst into a spontaneous gust of cheers and the colonel permitted them the remarkable luxury of a battalion-wide *feu de joie*, firing powder from unloaded muskets and thirteen cannons, one for each state. They could spare the powder now, but never the lead balls. The men were issued an extra gill of rum, and for the first time they were permitted an afternoon without work.

Within the hour, Sam began to hear the first rumbles of jealousy, and he felt them himself. Why was it only their army in the north who won glory and enjoyed success after success? (Sam heard one of Angell's lieutenants say, "Is it Bourgoyne who is so poor up there, or is it Washington down here?" "Maybe," replied another, "it's Gates who is so good…") Sam could imagine this news was having a similar effect in the main army, at General Washington's headquarters, and in Congress.

Meanwhile, the shelling of Fort Mifflin continued day and night, and Major Thayer sent word that they would soon need relief. Most of the New Jersey militia had passed the point of military usefulness, going sleepless most nights, cowering in holes, and ignoring their duties. Desertions began, some men plunging in the river and swimming off the island to get away.

While it was far quieter where they worked at Fort Mercer, Sam began to be more and more convinced that it was they who would become the target when the time came. He had not seen the British mount a full siege yet, and, since mounting an attack on an island was difficult, a siege would be their likeliest way to take Fort Mifflin. If Fort Mercer were to fall, Fort Mifflin on Mud Island would have to be deserted without a siege. When the energy of his captains flagged, he reminded them of his analysis. He did not foresee, though, that the attack would come immediately.

At midmorning on October 22, a day that had been like every other day at Fort Mercer, without even a rumor of troop movements reaching them, they suddenly discovered a great massing of the enemy in the woods outside the fort. Most of them were wearing the blue coats of the Hessians, though here and there they could see without field glasses coats of bright red dotting the deploying columns. Looking at them, Sam could hear a familiar, almost inaudibly high keening sound in his head. He knew the symptom. His captains looked at him for advice. He tried hard not to pant.

Colonel Greene ordered the gates closed and called the command officers together at his hilltop headquarters. He seemed undisturbed, though the failure of scouts and area intelligence was almost complete. The only splinter of information in their total ignorance was something one returning sentinel reported. "There are approximately two thousand Hessians under Count von Donop."

"Von Donop!" Lieutenant Colonel Olney exclaimed. "He's the one General Washington routed after he crossed the Delaware."

"He has now crossed back," Colonel Greene observed. "Looking to avenge his humiliation. I have sent a courier to General Washington to tell him the enemy has appeared in substantial numbers. I did not state a specific figure. More," he added grimly, "may yet appear."

As it was, they were outnumbered five to one. A siege, Sam remembered from Nat's old analysis, required two soldiers outside for every one inside. An attack was certain, probably soon. Washington's army was on the far side of the river, his attention centered on General Howe. If they were to get help from the main army, it would not come for some time.

It was just like the disaster at Fort Washington, though this time the odds were much worse.

Colonel Greene issued the general orders for battle. Lieutenant Colonel Olney joined Colonel Angell to prepare his division. Sam called together his eight captains and their lieutenants. He repeated the general orders. Still, while he knew that some of his men were experienced veterans, most had never seen an enemy solider up close or heard the sound of an incoming shell or the weird whistle and buzz of a musket ball passing by. "Your first task," he told his captains, "is to keep your men steady and their confidence high. By your example, by your voice, by your words." Taking his own advice, he stood straight and spoke clearly. "With your resolve, and our men's good shooting, by the grace of Almighty God, we will have the honor of holding this fort." His own heart was beating hard. He knew he would never allow himself be taken prisoner to go aboard a prison ship with Enos's men. He knew that neither would Colonel Greene. They would die first.

"Could they be starting a siege?" asked the youngest captain, Oliver Clarke, his cheeks pink with excitement.

"It is possible," Sam said, "but we must remain ready for an attack. Remind your men that a disciplined group of soldiers holding a strong point can fight off forces many times larger than their own. As we can. As we *will*, by the grace of God."

"Where will you be, Major?" Clarke asked, his voice unsteady.

"I will be with you." He knew from his own experience that it was in the moments before a fight that a captain established himself with his troops, and it was also when he most needed to. In a battle's final preparations, the captain was the real general, and it was Sam's view that this was not the time to have majors or colonels getting in the way.

He looked through his field glass at the sunlit woods to the north. The Hessians, their bayonets and mitred bronze helmets gleaming in the sunlight, were unlimbering their closest artillery—a good dozen field pieces and several howitzers.

Colonel Greene gave the order to deploy the men. They stopped their gaping, dropped their digging tools, and took up arms, their captains organizing them into squads. Du Plessis and an aide took a swift run along the embankments of the inner walls, picking up tools left behind and looking for flaws that might still be repaired.

And as the soldiers checked and loaded their weapons, Sam saw a boatload of Rhode Islanders arrive from Mud Island—Simeon Thayer, Sylvanus Shaw, and about a hundred other men who knew where they wanted to be in case of a fight. His heart surged with a kind of joy at seeing them. They needed every man they could get, and he knew these were some of the best anywhere in the world.

By coincidence, the sergeants and corporals who had been court-martialed and suspended for their rioting back in August had been reinstated that very morning, and Colonel Angell reported they were damned grateful about it. And while there were some rough areas in the defensive works, they were as ready as they ever would be. At least that was what Sam told himself.

As he and Colonel Greene and Colonel Olney watched, the Hessians began rapidly to deploy themselves, concentrating their forces at the northern and southern ends of the fort. Sam saw they wanted to split the small garrison in half in order to prevent any concentration of their defensive fire.

He glanced at Colonel Greene. Cool as he was under pressure, he had nonetheless forgotten that they had planned to keep the outside walls manned as a ruse so the enemy would be convinced they were spreading themselves thin. "Colonel?" Sam said. "How many men shall we keep at the outer wall?"

"The…?" he said and stopped. "Yes, of course. We need more than sentinels. Send two companies. Their orders if there is an attack are to fire *once* and retire to their present positions. We want no one taking any risks."

As Sam headed over to his unit's position at the inner walls, he considered whom to send. Veteran or not? He quickly decided it was best to give this first exposure to the inexperienced. The encounter would build their confidence and take some of the edge off the excruciating waiting. He called Captains Tom Arnold and Oliver Clarke over to him. "Understand," Sam said, after repeating

Colonel Greene's orders, "if an attack comes, we want them to think you have panicked. Fire when they get within range, and then turn your backs and run!" He turned to the enlisted men of their two companies who were listening to these new orders. He raised a hand and pointed at them. He raised his voice to bellow, "And you, men. You listen to your captain's orders as if he is the voice of God."

Sam went with the two companies to oversee their placement at the perimeter walls. He was there only a few minutes at the northern end when a private appeared at breathless run. "Major! Colonel Greene would like to see you, sir! Right away!"

Sam trotted across the distance between the outer wall and the inner, and mentally he put himself in the position of an attacking Hessian. He would not see until the last moment du Plessis's clever defenses: deep ditches at the base of the slope that lead to the topmost revetments. Before that, he would make out the abatis that ringed the top of the walls, a barrier of fallen trees bristling with sharpened branches. The southern gate at the other side he knew had a row of palisades and high parapets for the Virginia riflers. If they kept their internal defense from British intelligence, the Hessians would not know that once inside the outer walls, they were going to be funneled directly into the path of American artillery and into a small area where the outnumbered Rhode Islanders and Virginians would be able to concentrate their fire.

Sam made his way to headquarters and found the entire field command gathered in a worried knot.

"All set on the outside wall," Sam said, trying to catch his breath.

"My thanks, Major," Colonel Greene said, his face showing some new tension. "We have just received through the southern gate a communication from Count von Donop under a flag of truce. I should like you and Colonel Olney to do the courtesy of making our reply. His message is in English and so will be my reply. But Colonel Olney tells me you have some stock of French and German at your command if translation is needed."

"Some, sir. What is in von Donop's message?"

Colonel Angell replied, his usually good-humored face tight. "He says he will put every man in the garrison to death if we do not surrender. Immediately."

Sam could see from the officers' reactions that this threat had an effect even on repetition. "And our reply, sir?" he asked Colonel Greene.

Greene's eyes narrowed. "No surrender. No quarter expected. If they cannot follow the English or my handwriting, tell them what I have written in whatever language you have to—that we will defend this fort to the last drop of blood."

He handed the written reply, folded and sealed with a cheerful red wax, to Colonel Olney, and then he ordered two horses saddled.

Cujoe was there to help Sam mount the horse, holding the bridle as he climbed up. "Luck, suh," he said.

Sam thanked him, thinking, *La derniere goutte de sang. Bis zum letzten Blutstropfen.*

He and Lieutenant Colonel Olney rode out from the north gate under a white flag. Oliver Clarke saluted them from the parapet of the outer walls as they passed.

They were met by a square-jawed, ruddy-faced English officer who identified himself as Lieutenant Colonel Alexander Stewart. Though shorter than either Sam or Jeremiah Olney, he managed to convey the impression of looking down his strong beak of a nose at them. Since neither French nor German was required, Olney did the talking, introducing himself and Sam. Stewart sighed impatiently and confidently broke the seal with the look of a man going through a wearisome ritual. He read the message to himself and then said to his aide, "Their commanding officer writes, 'With these brave fellows, this fort will be my tomb.'" He looked at Sam and Jeremiah Olney with a quick, derisive glance. "Too bad." Without another word, he turned his horse and headed back to the English and Hessian lines.

Sam and Lieutenant Colonel Olney barely had the gates of the fort closed behind them when the artillery barrage began. Sam's horse reared in fright, his front hooves pawing the air.

The men from Captain Clarke's and Captain Arnold's companies ducked the whistling volleys of grapeshot. Sam saw one man from Clarke's company topple from off the top of the wall. He jumped off his horse to see to him and discovered he was unconscious. Sam surveyed his head and clothes and found he was unwounded. A sergeant yelled down that a cannonball hit the wall just where he had huddled. "Must have been the concussion," he said. Sam and Colonel Olney threw him over Sam's horse and carried him off to the inner fort. The barrage continued. They began to lob the frightening exploding shells of howitzers, but they landed harmlessly in the vacant area between the inner and outer fort. After ten frightening minutes, as abruptly as it began, the cannonade stopped. Sam felt every man in the inner fort stiffen in the silence. His throat tightened and the high-pitched keening in his head grew.

They all knew that if the attackers were going to mount a siege, the artillery barrage would be continuing. Sam looked out to the woods to the north. The sky, a brilliant October blue, was dotted with white puffy clouds that slid silently overhead. And then they heard the rattle of drums and the almost jolly piping sound of fifes. This could be a parade of the Kentish guards but for one thing. They heard a strange, unearthly sound, a kind of buzzing that Sam had been told about but had never heard before. It was the sound of thousands of Hessian throats starting their yells of "huzzah!" as they marched forward.

He and Colonels Angell and Olney had to remind their captains to tell the curious men to keep their heads down and only their musket barrels resting on top of the walls.

The buzzing huzzahs of the attackers swelled louder and louder—a thousand pointed insects heading straight at them.

A man from Arnold's company at the front wall yelled, "They're coming!"

Sam gazed out beyond the far wall. It had been a long time. He had not seen an enemy attack since the battle at Bunker Hill a lifetime ago.

It was an awesome sight. Blue and gold pennants furling in the breeze, the careful formations marched toward the gates at either end of the fort, their ranks dressed to knife-edge sharpness. They passed over obstacles and around bushes, pausing only to reform their lines and move on. The high polish of their brass helmets gleamed in the afternoon sun, the metallic thrum and beat of their drums grew louder as they marched. As they drew closer and reached flat open ground, their implacable march accelerated, the front columns breaking into a run but somehow still maintaining their knife-edge precision, their bayonets bristling before them. Next to Sam, his old friend Captain Elijah Lewis croaked in a quavering voice, "Great God…" Blue coats and white breeches approached in waves. Sam, dry-mouthed, scanned the far woods. Von Donop seemed to be sending his entire force on them, no units held in reserve.

In back of them all, Colonel Greene walked along the lines and in a reassuring voice said, "Stay calm, lads. Keep down. Hold fire until you get the order. And don't forget—aim for the buckles on their belts." He repeated these words over and over. Sam could see men all up and down the inner ramparts murmuring prayers, checking their powder and cartridge pouches, praying again.

As they had drilled all spring and summer and into the fall, they were in two lines, the right heel of the man in front touching the left toe of the man behind. The front line was to fire, step back, and reload. The second line then took their place and, on command, was to fire as well. After that they were to fire and reload as fast as possible. Only one out of four of them had bayonets, and many of these men had never been trained on how to use them. Old Cujoe, who had taught Sam how to handle a musket, was preparing to fire his rifle in the second line of Eben Flagg's company.

The Hessians approached the front walls and then disappeared from view beneath the brow of the works. Arnold's and Clarke's companies stiffened and sighted their muskets against their cheeks. Sam gritted his teeth, thinking, *Why don't they fire?*

The men waited in their single thin lines, with no one to relieve them. Sam held his breath. At last he could hear Arnold and Clarke call out their order. A row of ragged plumes of smoke puffed out into the bright fall air and a half-second later the crackling sound of musket fire reached his ears. The men turned and made their swift and orderly retreat from the far walls. Behind them the huzzahs grew louder.

Sam could see the Virginia riflers nervously preparing themselves up in the parapets, longing for their chance to fire. They were under orders to wait until the first enemy soldiers breached the outer walls. They did not have to wait long.

Swarms of Hessians came over the far walls with a deafening shriek, their bayonets fixed, their faces full of triumph. Sam and all the colonels now spoke to their captains the same words, "Steady now, men. Stay low. Hold your fire. Hold it. Aim for their belt buckles, their belt buckles."

Above their heads and behind, du Plessis readied their artillery.

Chapter Thirty

The Hessians dropped from the walls and, with barely a pause, stormed forward, apparently thinking the day was theirs. Avoiding the formidable-looking gates to the inner walls, they funneled themselves toward the center of lines, just as the Americans had planned. As the first of them reached the ditches at the base of the long slope leading up to the breastworks, Sam noticed Colonel Greene draw his sword and glance back at the artillery. Still, he waited in silence as more and more Hessians pounded their way across the ground toward them. The attack from the north side was reaching them first. Only when the first line of the enemy had crossed the ditches and begun toiling their way up the slope did Colonel Greene raise his long arm to its fullest length, his officer's sword gripped tightly in his hand. When the second lines of Hessians reached the ditch, he lowered his arm to his side in a single long sweep.

Eight charges of grapeshot blasted, whistled, buzzed, and sliced over their heads. Ears ringing with the thunderous sound of the discharge, Sam's heart sank. Nothing happened. Had they missed them entirely? And then virtually the entire vanguard of the Hessians dropped where they stood. The few unwounded soldiers at the front looked around themselves in shock and bewilderment. They tried to find their officers and then began to drop back and help pull away some of the wounded, waving the second lines forward. The Virginia riflers opened up and more men toppled.

The second wave of Hessians came forward, their screams of attack filled with rage and fear at what they had seen happen to their friends, but secure in their belief that the Americans had expended most, or even all, of their small artillery force. They knew they needed to reach the top before the cannons were reloaded. At close range, the grapeshot would hit the defenders, and then they could use their dreaded bayonets. On the south side to the right, where Colonel Angell and Major Thayer commanded, the Virginians were able to shoot from high parapets eight men at a time with almost no chance of suffering return fire. From their quarter Sam heard another volley of grapeshot. A hundred yards to his right, he saw a group of Hessians wearing huge fur-outlined helmets drop in their tracks.

Colonel Greene called, "Firelocks ready!"

Sam heard the clicking of hammers all up and down the lines. The enemy drew steadily nearer, some of them almost to the protective ring of abatis, close enough to begin to pour their own fire in on the Americans. Sam and Jeremiah Olney stood upright, steadying their captains, trying to ignore the terrifying buzz and whistle of lead balls slicing past their ears.

"First line, ready!" Colonel Greene called.

Sam and Colonel Olney repeated the order. Their men, two hundred of them, rose and set themselves at the wall.

"Take aim!"

The Hessians were now within forty yards, close enough to see their faces and hear their panting. Thirty-five yards. Thirty. Some of them were working their hands around the sharpened branches of the abatis, hoping to clear a path directly to the top. Sam noted with satisfaction that, despite the fear and the screams and the tumult and the enormous temptation, not a single Rhode Islander had yet pulled a trigger.

Colonel Greene raised his arm once again, sword held high. Once again, he brought it down.

"*Fire!*"

"*Fire!*" the other officers, colonels, captains, and lieutenants called out.

The rush of the oncoming Hessians slowed, stopped. Scores of them fell, many of them backward into men trying to make their way up the slope.

"*Second line ready!*"

"*Second line ready!*"

The first rank stepped back, crouched down and began to ramrod new cartridges down their barrels. The second line silently stepped forward to the wall. Blue-gray smoke from the first volley hung in the air and burned everyone's eyes and throat. They could hear cries of the wounded mix in the oncoming huzzahs of fresh attackers.

"*Take aim!*"

"*Take aim!*"

Some of the blue-coated enemy had scrambled over the spiked abatis or had crawled forward over the bodies of the dead and wounded. Sam readied his pistol.

"*Fire!*"

"*Fire!*"

The second volley was fired almost point-blank into the oncoming Hessians. It was more deadly than the first. As Sam braced for the enemy's arrival, four new charges of grapeshot blasted over their heads, shredding the lines of new troops making their way up the slope from the ditches.

Sam could see the entire attack, like a great wave, teeter and hold still. He waited for it to break forward or roll back, but the great wave remained fixed. In the brief silence he could hear Thayer's voice giving the order to fire on the south side.

A dozen Hessians roared up over the walls and were fighting the Americans hand-to-hand, furiously trying to use their famous bayonet skills. Sam headed straight to the areas of the greatest fighting—Oliver Clarke's men, having fired their first volley at the wall, had been unable to position and reload in a second line, and more of the enemy were able to break through at this point. Clarke's men were swinging their muskets like clubs. Sam saw one of Clarke's sergeants, a man who had not lost his rank from rioting, get run through sickeningly by a bayonet, half its bloody length appearing out the screaming man's back. Before the triumphant Hessian could pull his rifle from the sergeant's spasming hands, Sam fired his pistol into the killer's face. Sam's hand jumped with the discharge, a puff of smoke appeared, and the man dropped as if axed. To his right, Sam saw a blur of blue and found a Hessian driving straight for him, bayonet first. Sam drew his sword and prepared to meet him when Jeremiah Olney stepped past him and fired his pistol into the man's chest. He clutched his shoulder and lost hold of his weapon. A second later, he was surrounded by Clarke's defending soldiers. Captain Clarke was so outraged at what he had seen happen to some of his men, he went headlong over the wall swinging his rifle butt at the suddenly retreating heads of the Hessians.

Sam screamed at Clarke's lieutenant to go get his captain back. The man paused, not wanting to leave the revetment. "That is an order!" Sam yelled. The lieutenant disappeared over the wall.

Sam glanced down at the man he shot. A flap of his skull over the left side of his forehead was peeled back like an orange. His fixed eyes were open and he still clutched his bayoneted rifle. Facing him on the ground was the American sergeant, his mouth open, his ragged breath growing shallower every second. A corporal crouched next to him, speaking softly to him.

The entire slope of the glacis was covered with wounded, dead, and dying enemy soldiers. Another charge was mounted by the men nearest the top. Du Plessis had a horrible surprise for them. They expected he could not safely fire grapeshot, and they were right. Instead he used a two-foot iron bar held on each end by a half cannonball. The bar spun in a wild, noisy, and totally unpredictable course, making an unearthly sound and smashing anyone it came into contact with. Sam saw half a dozen Hessians at the top of the hill explode into an appalling shower of bloody pieces. Some of their unit behind them were splashed with so much blood, they believed they themselves were wounded.

By this time, most of the first lines had reloaded and set themselves back at the walls of the inner fort. Colonel Greene called out for everyone to fire at will. The Hessian wave, which had slowed and wavered and stopped, remained dead still for a long and strangely quiet moment. And then, as more men dropped to the ground around them, finally, it broke. The men turned and went headlong down the slope toward the ditch. Sam and the other officers had to scream for the men not to pursue them. Their own men could shoot them in a disorderly charge.

The second line, now reloaded, fired at the fleeing enemy.

The Hessians tried for a brief time to regroup just inside the far walls to try another charge, but the Virginians' rifles and du Plessis's artillery made their position untenable in a matter of minutes. As they retreated over the far wall, the Americans rose to their feet, cheering wildly. Colonel Greene ordered the surgeons to see to the wounded Americans. When someone asked him about the wounded Hessians, he said, "They will have to wait until it is clear we cannot expect another attack."

He, Sam, Olney, Thayer, and Angell walked along the lines and congratulated the men, ordering them first to reload before they celebrated. If another attack was mounted, this time their defensive arrangements would not be a surprise.

They surveyed the field from abatis to wall. Colonel Angell estimated there had to be four hundred Hessians on the ground, with who knew how many more dead and wounded who were carried off.

The captains were ordered to do returns on their own companies.

Sam, numb and yet full of a kind of terrible joy at being alive and unhurt, learned that Captain Clarke was nowhere to be found.

The lieutenant who tried to retrieve him found him struggling with several Hessian soldiers with more on the way and feared he had been either killed or taken prisoner.

When the totals were brought in, they were astonishing. Twelve dead, twenty-five wounded, and one missing.

Simeon Thayer said his regiment's casualties were light, but they lost one captain. Sam could guess, from looking at Thayer's stricken face and the uneasy glance he gave Sam, who it was. "Sylvanus Shaw," Thayer said. "Shot through the throat."

Sam's felt his own throat catch. Sylvanus Shaw. He survived the march to Quebec, their deadly attack on the city, their long imprisonment, and in the midst of this extraordinary triumph, a stray shot at the very end during the Hessian retreat, said Thayer, brought him down.

Colonel Greene asked Sam to be the one to write and personally deliver the report of the battle to General Washington with a copy to go to General Greene. "First, though," the colonel said, "we must wait to see if the day is concluded." Their chaplain, Ebeneezer David, putting down his musket and wiping some of the powder stains off his face, called them together for a prayer.

Within two hours, as the sun set into the river behind them, they knew they were safe from another assault, at least for now. One of Thayer's men who remained behind at Fort Mifflin came to tell them there were enemy troops stirring on the Pennsylvania side and British warships appeared to be making their way upriver.

A siege would be next. Thayer said they had food and water enough at Mifflin for a week to ten days at the most. Here at Fort Mercer, their ammunition needed replenishment, and with all the dead bodies so close by, sickness and putridity were sure to follow soon.

As night fell, two of Sam's companies were given the task of providing comfort to the Hessian wounded and of collecting their rifles, bayonets, and cartridge pouches. It was a melancholy task, and, as Sam wrote the battle report, he could hear out in the field moaning and sobbing, sometimes in German, sometimes in the universal groan of human suffering.

He had not quite finished his account when they heard that Count von Donop himself was among the wounded left in the field. They brought him to Colonel Greene's headquarters, in agony, his white breeches red to his boots. Dr. Turner, the brigade's chief surgeon, examined his wound. Von Donop's hip had been smashed by a piece of shrapnel. Dark-haired, handsome, and slim, he was well spoken in English when he could overcome the waves of pain well enough to speak.

When they began to probe the wound with his permission, von Donop began to turn white with the agony. Then he yelled; then he screamed. Sam excused himself to get some air. A few minutes later, to everyone's relief, von Donop passed out. Dr. Turner came out to report to Sam and Colonel Angell that von Donop had a chance. "But if he told us to leave the metal in there, he would have bled to death by morning. Now he has to avoid a fever."

*

As Sam prepared to leave the next morning, the men were hard at work digging two huge mass graves for the Hessian dead. In the field of the corpses, they had been grateful for a sudden snap of chilly weather. Just as their chaplain began to read prayers over the bodies and on behalf of the souls of the dead enemy, cannon fire suddenly boomed out over the river.

An attack on Fort Mifflin had begun. Simeon Thayer and his men dropped their shovels and were back aboard boats to return to their posts. The motley American flotilla positioned its various strange craft to take on the enormous British warships that were heading for Mud Island. Within an hour, the men-of-war began pulling up to the fort and firing broadsides point-blank into its works. Several hundred redcoats assembled across from Fort Mifflin, apparently readying for a landing. All of this was easily visible to Sam and the others at Fort Mercer, including the British hoisting a blood-drenched flag that announced the fort would receive no quarter. The cannonading went on for hours, and though Sam was ready to leave, he knew his report would be incomplete if he did not know the fate of Mud Island.

The huge sixty-four-gun British ship, *Augusta*, was trying to avoid one of the blazing firecrafts the Americans had floated down into the British fleet, and it ran aground. The nimble American flotilla bore down on it, pouring what fire it could into the man-of-war before it could work its way off the sand bar. The British ship caught fire at its stern, and while they watched and cheered from Fort Mercer's headquarters, there was suddenly an enormous explosion. Even at a mile's distance, they could feel the thump of the concussion. The plates on the table and the inkwell on the Colonel's desk jumped as if they had been hit with an earthquake. The men looked at each other in astonishment. The exploding magazine created the greatest volume of sound any of them had ever heard in their lives. Every man in the fort broke into cheers. Within minutes, the twenty-two-gun British ship *Merlin* ran aground and promptly suffered the same fate as the *Augusta*.

Amid the smoke and confusion, the British ships and soldiers began to withdraw. Colonel Angell called for the officers at headquarters to be silent. "Listen!" Across the distance, they could hear the high, thin sound of the men at Fort Mifflin cheering.

Before Sam left to make his careful crossing of the Delaware to deliver the report, he checked with Dr. Turner on Count von Donop's condition. Turner sighed and shook his head. "He's grown feverish. I am not optimistic."

Colonel Greene warned Sam to be vigilant on his travel to General Washington's headquarters near Whitemarsh. "The enemy has parties roaming all up and down the countryside. Our sentinels are jumpy, so you must watch out for them, too. We do not want you to survive a battle only to lose you now."

"I will be careful, Colonel. If only so I can add my own praise of your command to this dry report."

Greene, whose humility had always impressed Sam, actually blushed.

*

HE COULD SEE AS he headed toward Whitemarsh that the main army was in poor condition. He had heard that under orders—and through panic—the main army left most of their supplies and baggage behind in the headlong retreat after Brandywine. Washington and his staff, setting an example, left their own personal belongings behind when Cornwallis and Howe came driving at their heels. The newsprints reported that the commander in chief and his staff had but one knife and one fork and one tin plate to their names. And once he arrived, Sam saw nothing in the white farmhouse Washington had made into his headquarters that suggested there had been any change since. It was clear through their haggard faces, though, that the main army was beginning to suffer the bite of deprivation.

When Sam announced himself at headquarters amid a large and busy staff, he was directed toward a young, brisk, energetic dark-haired man of about his own age. He introduced himself as Lieutenant Colonel Alexander Hamilton, and he was the first to read Sam's account. Though he had scarcely heard of Hamilton, there was something in his assurance and self-possession that told Sam he was important in the workings of this headquarters. Colonel Hamilton congratulated him warmly on their achievement at the forts and excused himself to consult with two other officers on Washington's staff. And it was Hamilton, with Sam's written account in his hand, who went into the commander in chief's office after a brisk knock, scarcely waiting for permission to enter before opening the door.

Almost five minutes passed before Hamilton reemerged. This was time enough for Sam to discover his sense of awe had remained since he last saw General Washington at the siege of Boston. As he stood in this dining room, fragrant with wood-smoke, he was aware how much had changed in those two years. The heroic stories his father imagined for himself and for his family had been blunted by chance and fate: Samuel, retired from state politics, had become one of the most important members of the First and Second Continental Congress, voting for General Washington as commander in chief and working successfully to persuade others that the country needed to be free. But the smallpox took him before he had the chance to sign the Declaration of Independence, an act he predicted and had supported for ten years before it came to pass. He was buried far from home, though only a few miles from this farm, in a place now completely under the control of British soldiers. His farm and property were gone, his family scattered. Samuel had hoped to be remembered by the larger world after his death, but his son saw that could not happen.

If they should lose this war, and Sam was forced to admit that such a possibility was far from remote, no one would remember the Declaration of Independence or the impressive man brooding in the next room, either. He understood that only the future revealed the importance of the present, or of the past. You can do the impossible and march to Quebec through hundreds of miles of trackless wilderness, mount an attack, and end up not in glory or remembered in fable and song, but in prison. *There are,* he thought, *stories and guesses we make about the future.* And while Sam had found there were no certainties, he had seen many of the irreducible realities—Gus Mumford, Sylvanus Shaw, Tom Shepherd, Mrs. Warner, and a man whose forehead could be opened like the top half of a barn door.

He dusted off his uniform, preparing himself to tell His Excellency the bracing stories of Fort Mercer at Red Bank and Fort Mifflin at Mud Island.

Hamilton stepped out and nodded to Sam.

Sam was taken aback to find how much the man had aged. Until he straightened up from writing something at his desk, Sam thought perhaps he was someone else. His once-brownish hair, though unpowdered at the moment, had grown almost entirely gray. His face was drawn and deeply lined, and he had grown much thinner, as if someone had stretched his long frame on a rack. His lips were pressed into a tight slash.

Hamilton introduced him, and General Washington got to his feet in order to greet him. He extended his large hand for Sam to shake, and he said it was good to see him again after all this time.

"You have been through much since I last saw you, Major."

"You are kind, sir, to remember me. We all have been through much." The grip of the general's large hand, warm and dry, remained firm.

"How I wish your father were still with us and in the Congress at this hour." Sam noticed a sardonic look briefly cross Hamilton's face at these words. "His counsel and wisdom are much missed."

"He would know, as we all do, sir, that the army could not be in better hands."

General Washington seemed to weigh replying to this remark for a moment, but instead he deflected it. "I have read your excellent report about our New Jersey forts. Tell me about what is not written there."

Sam described the sudden arrival of the Hessians, the demand for surrender and Colonel Greene's reply, and then he explained the inner and outer walls and how their force of scarcely five hundred men could withstand the determined assault of over two thousand. He was careful to insist on the skill of du Plessis's engineering, the bravery and spirit of Major Thayer, and especially the calm, inspiring command of Colonel Greene. Hamilton and General Washington drank in his narrative, rapt.

He readied himself to answer questions, but Washington wished only to know the state of the fort on Mud Island and Count von Donop's condition when Sam left. Those questions answered, he gave a brief satisfied smile and said, "Thank you, Major Ward. My congratulations to your regiments and to Colonel Greene for this brave action. All honors and laurels will be bestowed on each of you. But this action is far from over." His soft voice took on a metallic edge. "Tell Colonel Greene we will try to provide you with every means of support. These forts *must* be defended to the last extremity."

Sam could see that this interview was at an end. The general turned to Hamilton and instructed him to provide some refreshment. He congratulated Sam once again and, stiffly, lowered himself back to his seat. As Sam left, though, he could see the weary commander in chief hungrily rereading his report on Red Bank, an unmistakable look of satisfaction on his face.

As Sam was preparing to leave, he discovered that Colonel Hamilton was preparing his own horse as well. Sam invited him to ride with him, if they were heading in the same direction.

"No, alas, Major, I cannot have that pleasure. I am heading north to see the new great hero, General Gates."

Hamilton's tone could not be missed. "His victory was not so great as the reports of it, then?"

"Perhaps it is, but the general has chosen not to communicate officially with his commander in chief about it or anything else. His Excellency finally was informed by Congress about it weeks after the event."

"On what meat has Gates fed that he is grown so great?"

"Excellent question. I am being sent to study his diet. And to find out why he is withholding twenty regiments he has been ordered to send to join the main army—or rejoin it, in most cases. We could not afford their departure when we sent them to assist General Gates in defeating Bourgoyne, and with the Delaware hanging in the balance, we cannot afford them being withheld on some point of personal vanity. The truth is, Gate's army greatly outnumbered Bourgoyne's by the end. And there are some who have not been present with the main army and do not appreciate the difficulties under which we have labored. They are critical of General Washington for not having performed miracles."

"Congress?"

Hamilton nodded, and Sam now understood his earlier sardonic scowl. "Given our situation, we *have* performed miracles."

"General Washington looks beleaguered."

"I tell you, Major, he bears responsibilities any several of which would have crushed most men. He is tired at the moment because, against the advice of most his staff and most of his generals, he has been trying to find an avenue—any avenue—to attack Howe. We are outnumbered and need supplies badly, yet our quartermaster has become more interested in his own future than keeping our army alive."

"General Mifflin? He was a member of Congress with my father."

"General Mifflin. You should talk about him with General Greene. He has a full and nuanced understanding of the man." Hamilton glanced at the sky. "I must get some miles north before dark if I am to pass along a few letters to General Gates." He patted a leather case he had strapped to his saddle. "These will clarify his understanding on a few points in a manner he will not mistake."

"Good luck, Colonel."

He gave a small, tight smile. "Oh, I will have luck. It is you, Major, who is about the work we all support with our prayers. Godspeed."

*

"Thomas Mifflin," Nat said with a sigh, putting his boots up on the corner of the desk and slumping down into his chair. Sam had reached Nat's headquarters just before dark, and he decided it was best to spend the night there. "An intelligent man, a brilliant speaker, revered here in Pennsylvania—which is why we have a fort named after him that you and Major Thayer have been defending. And he has an excellent head for business, his own and the army's."

"Not so good from what Colonel Hamilton says."

"What would you call resigning from the job with no notice and making no effort to arrange for a replacement?"

"I would call it…unconscionable."

"It is bad now, but it is nothing to what we will pay when winter comes."

"Why did he resign?"

"He wishes to have a greater military role, an object for which he has no talent and no experience. I have been with him in the field, Sam. The sound of even distant gunfire unnerves him. Congress has begged him to stay on as a major general and gave him a new post even more influential than quartermaster. He is a member of the new Board of War. And although General Washington thinks of Mifflin as an old and trusted friend, he has been promoting the belief far and wide that His Excellency has made poor military decisions because his ear has been captured by one man, a man Mifflin says is neither wise nor brave nor patriotic. This devil figure has so hypnotized General Washington that he cannot be trusted to make his own judgments anymore."

He paused, and Sam took the cue. "And this satanic figure…?"

Nat offered a smile that was somewhere between a grin and a wince. "Me."

This was not the answer Sam was prepared for. "You?"

"Less amusing is Mifflin's expansion of the War Board's authority. It will not be long before he and his allies will be giving General Washington orders."

It was Sam's turn to sigh. As with his father's old stories about Rhode Island politics, he sometimes thought he was happier not knowing what happened in the councils of command. But he also knew from experience that ignorance was the father of disaster. "How did this rage toward you start?" he asked.

"He blames me for the loss of Philadelphia. I was among those who said that we should leave our army poised at the middle of Howe's possible goals—the Hudson highlands and Philadelphia—until he showed his hand. His abrupt resignation and disappearance have made it impossible to raise men or supplies here in Pennsylvania where he is so idolized."

"And he has allies?"

"Oh, yes."

"And General Gates?"

Nat nodded and lowered his booted feet to the floor. "And one here, an Irish-born French general named Thomas Conway. Unlike Mifflin, he does have a small military gift, though mostly for discipline rather than in any sense of enterprise. But a vainer, more arrogant, more meanly ambitious man you will never know. He threatens every week to resign unless Congress satisfies his every whim and bottomless vanity."

"And what does General Washington think of him?"

Nat snorted. "Conway's sneering has inspired our general to a kind of loathing of which I had never thought him capable. But because he is loyal to men who have been his friends, I am not at all sure he appreciates how much Mifflin is now his enemy. Nor can I be the one to warn him."

"Because Mifflin has made you his special target."

"I tell you, Sammy, with all that we have had to endure and the sacrifices men have had to make, these intrigues sicken me. We have an enemy to fight and a cause to win, and these fools Mifflin and Conway belong with Cornwallis, not with us." He wiped his mouth with the back of his hand and leaned forward in his chair. "How did His Excellency seem when you saw him?"

"Weary."

"The world expects a victory from him, and he expects one from himself. I know, though, that your news of the triumph at Red Bank has brought him great comfort. And I think it will also strengthen his determination not to buy a victory at the risk of the ruin of our cause. We need to continue to survive. Then we will prevail."

Sam believed this, and had always believed it, but who knew how *hard* it was going to be simply to survive? "Any news to report these last days from home?"

Nat frowned. "I was saving this until later, but it will not be happy to hear anytime. General Spencer's planned invasion of Newport has failed."

Sam, who thought he was beginning to become used to shocks, felt his spirits plummet. "Are many dead?"

Nat shook his head. "It never got properly launched. Everything was ready on October nineteenth, including the weather, but it was a Sunday so Spencer decided to delay. The weather turned bad and the militia lost confidence. In a few days, half the men had gone home."

"But all our friends and family are safe?"

"Safe enough." He looked anew at Sam. "And what did General Washington say about the Delaware forts?"

"To defend them until the last extremity."

Chapter Thirty-One

At a remote place that was not in a valley and whose ironworks was destroyed back in the fall by the British—a place that some of the men took to calling "not-Valley no-Forge"—Sam spent some long winter days at the end of 1777 thinking about how hard they had tried to preserve the Delaware forts. He returned to Fort Mercer back in October with a head full of information, General Washington's compliments, and his orders to defend the forts. He arrived just in time for two hangings and a funeral. He had never seen a hanging before, and though the two New Jersey men, Dick Ellis and John Mucklewain, deserved it, their final strangulated cries, the kicking of their spasming legs, their purpled faces, and their horribly elongated necks and tongues were sights he wished he could have missed. But they had not only given intelligence to the enemy about the fort after the Rhode Island regiments arrived, they had personally guided the British and Hessian troops through the New Jersey countryside right up to the gates. The funeral, which came a few hours later with full military honors, was for Count von Donop. Among his final words was his expression of regret for having ever participated in this war.

That long day came to a close with the arrival of General Varnum and over a thousand men under orders to protect the New Jersey shore and the downstream approaches to Fort Mercer. Not long after Varnum's defensive works were established three miles to the south, it became clear that it was Fort Mifflin that was the actual target. British artillery batteries opened up on the place followed by a merciless cannonading by ships. Almost every place of shelter was destroyed. The commander, Maryland Lieutenant Colonel Smith, was wounded and his replacement got violently sick. The excellent captain of the artillery and his principal lieutenant were both killed. A torrential rain turned Mud Island into its own blood-spattered namesake, and, when things grew darkest, again Simeon Thayer volunteered his services. General Varnum put him in command of the fort. The British promptly turned the little fort on the little island into the outskirts of hell.

They cannonaded night and day. The rains had so raised the river that when the tide was right, British ships could sail right over the sharpened logs buried in the river bottom and put themselves at pointblank range of Fort Mifflin's ruined walls. Coming as close as twenty yards, the men-of-war poured every kind of ordnance known into the place: sailors threw hand grenades, artillery raked it with grapeshot, mortars launched bombs, and they drew so close even picking off American soldiers with musket fire was no hard task. The fort's artillery was soon completely destroyed.

Thayer held a council of war and came out insisting that despite it all, he would hold the fort.

General Varnum and Colonel Greene assessed the situation. The American flotilla had become useless, there were two thousand enemy troops a few miles to the south, the main army would not be coming to their aid, and no other reinforcements were possible. Without artillery, the fort could no longer serve its basic function, which was to stop shipping in and out of Philadelphia. Finally, Varnum knew he could not protect both Fort Mercer on the New Jersey side of the river and Fort Mifflin on the Pennsylvania side. He passed all this information along to Simeon Thayer.

Reluctantly, Thayer ordered to abandon the place. After dark, late on the night of November 15, he personally oversaw the burning of the ruins and the loading of supplies and wounded onto transports. He was the last man to leave the fort, a smoldering heap of mud and debris. And while General Washington and eventually even Congress had nothing but praise for their defense, half the Delaware was now open to British shipping.

Five days later, at nine o'clock at night, they received word at Fort Mercer from General Varnum that a force of nearly eight thousand men under Cornwallis was bearing down on them. The main army was many miles away, on the wrong side of the river, and Washington's men could not intercept him if they tried.

Colonel Greene called the fort's officers together. Their conversation was brief. Ammunition was low and they would be outnumbered by more than ten to one. With the fall of Fort Mifflin, shipping was already getting in and out of Philadelphia, and while no one said it outright, they knew their remaining would not only result in their certain destruction, but it no longer served any military purpose.

The vote was unanimous. Less than half an hour later, they were loading the wagons with tents and supplies and were setting the kegs of powder to blow up du Plessis's artfully constructed fort.

They had fought so long and so well there, it was painful to do, but after the last wagons pulled out and Colonel Greene struck the colors, Colonel Olney blew up the headquarters and Colonel Angell spiked all the cannons that could not be removed. Sam then lit the fuse to the south gate while Major Thayer, who had just been through this at Fort Mifflin, blew up the parapets and towers to the north.

Before he left, amid the dull boom of the last detonations, Sam made his way back through acrid clouds of smoke to Sylvanus Shaw's grave to make sure his wooden marker survived the blasts. He straightened its steep tilt and stood over the fresh mound of earth. Twenty-five years old with a wife and two small children, Sylvanus Shaw wrote letters home every day. No more. Sam murmured a prayer for the repose of his soul. Cujoe was waiting for him outside the smoking ruins of the gate with their horses.

By the time their brigade joined the main army on the other side of the river at Whitemarsh, with Cornwallis's huge force on their heels the whole way, Howe had brought out most of his army. Despite the icy December weather, he appeared to be preparing for a full-scale attack. Washington's army, reinforced at last by Daniel Morgan and some other regiments Horatio Gates had held back, took up defensive positions, ready to beat Howe this time. As they waited, extraordinary northern lights appeared, turning half the night sky to curtains of red velvet. It was hard not to be convinced that a great battle portended. But if it did, Howe must not have liked the signs. He retreated into winter quarters in Philadelphia, and the Americans decided to canton themselves, after a march through slush to the west side of the Schuylkill, on a high flat area surrounded by a few ridges someone had named a valley.

*

"Remember how back on the Hudson the men were clamoring to join the main army?" Simeon Thayer said, sitting by a nearly heatless green wood fire that hissed and belched more steam than smoke. "Remember?"

Now in late December, a week into their winter encampment, what Nat Greene had said about Thomas Mifflin abandoning his job as quartermaster came home to roost like a flock of vultures. Washington's entire army was in as bad a state as Sam's brigade was when it rioted. The Rhode Islanders discovered that, in one respect, they were better off than the rest of the army—because they had marched less, their shoes and boots were still intact. The men they saw from Massachusetts, North Carolina, Virginia, and Connecticut were not so lucky. Sam estimated that one out of four of them, maybe more, were barefoot, and their march along rutted, frozen roads had further taken its toll. Many of the men were sick, most so ragged they had no way to protect themselves from the icy winds, and a few of them had begun to suffer the terrifying and dreaded signs of frostbite.

Just outside the camp, the entire brigade walked past a man from North Carolina sitting at the side of the road waiting for the hospital wagon. Men who barely flinched watching two hangings at Fort Mercer averted their eyes in horror from his blackened, bloody feet. The old bitter joke that most Americans would rather be shot in the head than wounded in the legs was truly not a joke. If the soldier from North Carolina lived, a farmer like most of them—both legs hacked off at the knee—he would spend much of the rest of his life wondering why.

When Sam went with three of his captains to check on their sentinels the first night in camp, they found them standing on their hats, determined to avoid the North Carolinian's fate.

Sam took a bite of their fourteenth straight meal of a paste of flour and water grilled over green wood that everyone called firecake. Those who weren't too sick, but not clothed enough to work outside in the cold, had spent the day trying to build shelters, excavate wells, and dig privy vaults. The general orders called for shelters to be sixteen feet by fourteen feet, but when General Washington offered a reward to the first company who finished their huts—eighteen dollars, a huge sum even to the scattering of men who had actually been paid in the last few months—and with no sawmills around to help make doors or roofs, a strange village of quarters began to emerge. Some roofs were made of evergreen boughs and still others, before orders could be issued against it, from deconstructed tents, valuable material many fought over for clothes and shoes. The evergreens let in the air and the sleet but had the advantage of letting out the smoke that billowed into the huts at night instead of up the rough new chimneys.

Dr. Turner reported smallpox, dysentery, putrid fever, typhus, and typhoid as well as scabies and lice. There was no soap, though without a change of clothes, soap wasn't of much use in any case. Since their third day, no morsel of fish, pork, beef, chicken, or mutton remained in the entire camp. Sam bedded down that night in his tent to angry cries of "no meat!" from every quarter.

"How many horses died today?" Sam asked. He had been out with a squad in the countryside looking to buy food and clothing. They traveled over thirty miles and came back with five turnips and a sack of brown potatoes.

Colonel Olney stopped chewing his firecake to say, "Two in our brigade."

"Are they buried?"

Olney nodded. Sam noticed the bloated and rotting corpses of at least half a dozen horses near the Virginia division. They had ignored orders to bury them, since the ground was frozen and all their efforts were spent finding food and fuel and building shelters.

The Rhode Island officers looked out at the surrounding hills and ridges where, already half denuded of their tree cover, a cold wind sliced down on them with nothing to break it. There was no fodder, and the horses that had survived were so weak, it was hard for foraging parties to travel far and, if they were lucky enough to find anything, to be able to bring back anything that weighed much.

"Any desertions?" Sam asked.

"Not from here," replied Colonel Angell. "But remember that British and Hessian regiment of deserters encamped next to ours?" Sam nodded. How could he forget? They were one of the main causes of his brigade's riot at Fort Montgomery. "They deserted in the first place because of poor conditions. They're doing it again."

"What worries me," Thayer said, "is the camp followers have started to leave."

"Don't want to do your own laundry, Major?" Olney said.

Thayer looked at him for a second before replying, "'Tis the sewing I'm worried about. Needles are sharp."

Sam grinned but he and Thayer had already discussed the fact that most of the camp followers were soldiers' wives. And when they started to leave, their husbands would not be far behind. He noticed as he chewed on his firecake that one of his teeth was loose. He remembered his spongy flesh and ugly bruises and the bleeding gums and lost teeth from scurvy when they were in Quebec. Dr. Turner told him before he left this morning to ask the local farmers about a winter vegetable the Pennsylvanians ate. "Tastes terrible," he said. "But they say it's a powerful antiscorbutic."

He brought out a large jar of shredded gray stuff and told officers what he had gotten. Simeon Thayer and Colonel Greene, who both remembered scurvy in prison with the same loathing as Sam, said to give them some, *please*.

"What's it called?" Colonel Angell asked.

"Sauerkraut."

They all took a bite, and grimaced. Sour was right. Colonels Olney and Angell stopped after one bite. Quebec veterans Ward, Thayer, and Greene kept eating.

✷

THEY HEARD LOTS OF cursing from men all over the encampment, but rarely about General Washington, who chose from the first day they arrived not to move into the comforts of a nearby farmhouse but to sleep just as his army slept, in a tent. When the huts neared completion at the end of the first week, he moved not into some nearby palatial home but into a hut. They all knew he had sent out calls for assistance from Congress and the Pennsylvania legislature—and Sam heard he had written that the army would soon starve, dissolve, or disperse if aid were not forthcoming. Sam got the sense that as their situation grew worse daily, many of the men's affection and admiration for their commander grew.

Colonel Greene noted this, too, and he arranged for himself and all the Rhode Island officers to follow in Washington's footsteps. Though one was offered, they would take no farmhouse barracks.

Sam supported the plan, but he asked Colonel Greene not to site their huts close to the enlisted soldiers so both groups could talk freely. He also urged they take their meals in plain sight so the soldiers would know the deprivation was shared. All this worked well enough that they did not anticipate another riot, or at least not in their brigade.

On Christmas Day, there was half a foot of snow on the ground, making the slow arrival of their trickle of supplies stop completely. There were not enough spirits for men or officers to have the customary gill of holiday rum, and it was especially hard for the men from the South. Unlike most New Englanders, they were used to celebrating the twenty-fifth day of December as Jesus's birthday. The winds now sliced down from everywhere without obstruction. Housing eleven thousand men and stoking fires day and night had stripped the area of trees as far as the eye could see.

But the number eleven thousand was sinking fast. Even officers had begun to disappear, either resigning first or simply heading home without leave. Most of them had been unpaid for months and had families who depended on them for survival. Given that the poor conditions showed no sign of improving, it was hard to blame some of them for packing up. The Rhode Island officers remained, but their men began to vanish in large numbers like they did in other brigades.

Still, Howe had never shown an interest in a winter campaign, and they hoped, with luck, many might return with the spring.

At least that is what Nat Greene said at the Christmas gathering he had for the Rhode Island officers. He unearthed some salt beef, dried apples, and hot cider with a suspicion of rum in it, and while none of them were convinced the Bible told them this was a day to celebrate the birth of Christ, with something to eat other than firecakes, it certainly felt like a holiday. "The largest group of departures," Nat said, "have been made up of men from Virginia. This stings His Excellency more than far worse matters."

Their conditions were too poor for any of them to feel merry, but the usually confident Nat looked disturbed. “Far worse matters?” Sam repeated, and Varnum, Thayer, Olney, Greene, and Angell grew silent.

“Thomas Mifflin, may he suffer a season in hell, is not content just to let the department of the quartermaster fall into ruin. He’s arranged a new chairman to join him on the Board of War. General Horatio Gates. And at the end of last month, this board appointed a new inspector general with vast new powers. He is able, in principle, to give orders to General Washington.”

Sam had told the others about Mifflin and Gates, and he could see their already-thin holiday mood vanish with this news.

“Who?” Colonel Greene asked.

“The man His Excellency detests most in the entire army: Thomas Conway.”

“I forgot to tell them about Conway,” Sam said.

“He is insolent and vain and makes enemies like this sky makes snow. But despite General Washington’s impassioned request not to, Congress has promoted him to major general over many who are senior to him.”

Brigadier General James Varnum nodded. “I know men who would rather have a case of bloody flux than spend ten minutes with Conway.”

Nat lowered his voice, compressing his anger into something quieter but hotter. “His Excellency has just discovered that Mifflin, Conway, and Gates, whom he had believed to be his enemies individually, have been in correspondence together for months. They are, we believe, working with some men in Congress to remove General Washington altogether. To replace him with Gates.”

Sam and the others were thunderstruck. The army without Washington was unthinkable! Without him it would fall apart in days.

Varnum said, “Mutiny would be a certainty.”

Nat nodded. "The plotters, even blind with ambition as they are, know this. Their best hope is to get His Excellency to resign."

Sam could feel his heart sink into his stomach. "Will he?"

"I do not think so. Conway has been sending letters to His Excellency full of such contempt that he cannot go long without an answer in gunpowder."

"Does Congress know of this?" Varnum asked.

"They are just now being acquainted with Conway's letters. His French colleagues, including the Marquis de Lafayette, have deserted him."

Sam, who knew from Rhode Island politics how these matters played out, said, "Then they are isolated."

"It does not look promising for Conway. He and his confederates have unmasked their batteries too soon."

Sam noticed the others still looked as outraged as he felt. It was enough that General Washington had to worry about the survival of the army. It was absurd that he must also worry about the security of his own position. If Sam's father were still alive and in Congress, he knew their commander would have had less to worry about.

"But what about the spring?" Jimmy Varnum asked. "I hear we are far behind in enlistments. And to get men to fight in the Continental service, and be paid—if they are paid—in a currency worth a third of its stated value, and then march two hundred miles from home while the British remain in Newport..." He shook his head.

"We talk about this subject all the time," Colonel Olney said. "We have no prospect of meeting our responsibilities. When even the British deserters have begun to desert, and when word of conditions here gets back to the states, what can we do?"

They all looked at Nat Greene. He sighed and raised a leather tankard of cider. "To better times, gentleman. To better times."

*

Late on the evening of January 1, Sam and all the Rhode Island officers dined with General Varnum at brigade headquarters. There was not much to eat, but unlike at their officers' huts, it was warm enough not to have to wear a coat indoors. After spending what had become a required half hour of cursing Conway, Mifflin, and Gates, General Varnum asked Colonel Greene to tell him more about their remarkable defense at Red Bank.

Christopher Greene did not love talking, and he liked least talking about himself. He took a while before replying, "We tried to get use out of everything we had."

Jeremiah Olney said he had his own servant armed and fighting. Sam added that he had old Cujoe do the same. As Major Thayer was talking about the sound of the fife and drums the Hessians played before their assault, General Varnum's servant, Cato, came in to clear the trenchers. Sam and Colonel Olney looked at Cato, a lithe and powerfully built young man in his twenties, and then glanced at one another. They had already talked about their idea with Colonels Greene and Angell, and they all agreed it was worth raising with General Varnum.

"General," Colonel Olney said. "We have a notion we would like to raise with you." He stopped himself. "More than a notion, sir."

To everyone's surprise, Varnum agreed with it almost immediately. After another hour's discussion, he took out a pen and inkwell and in his own hand wrote out a draft of the letter he would deliver to General Washington first thing in the morning.

To His Excellency, Gen'l Washington—

The two battalions from the State of Rhode Island being small, and there being a necessity of the State's furnishing an additional number to make up their proportion in the Continental army, the field officers have represented to me the propriety of making one temporary battalion from the two, so that one entire corps of officers may repair to Rhode Island in order to receive and prepare the recruits for the field. It is imagined that a battalion of negroes can be easily raised there. Should that measure be adopted, or recruits obtained upon any other principle, the service will be advanced.

Their idea of an all-black regiment, while endorsed by General Varnum, they knew depended on two matters, both of them possibly fatal obstacles. As Colonel Olney put it, "Do you think that General Washington, coming from a hearty slave-owning state and himself the largest slave owner in the country, will give approval?"

"We can ask, Colonel. It is an idea worth advancing, rejected or not."

One brief day after Varnum sent the letter, they received their reply from General Washington. It came in the form of a letter to be given to Governor Nicholas Cooke of Rhode Island. Attached to a copy of General Varnum's letter was a personally signed statement expressing Washington's "desire that you will give the officers employed in this business all the assistance in your power."

Since most slaves lived in southern Rhode Island, Colonel Greene, Sam, and Colonel Olney decided they should be the ones to try to raise the new regiment, and that Colonel Angell should take over the remnants of their old one. They also knew that since they must persuade the General Assembly to pass the enabling legislation to raise such a regiment, Sam and his family connections would be useful.

But the real question, and the remaining threat to be overcome, was how Rhode Islanders would feel about the idea. After all, as soldiers they had seen scores of blacks serving in Massachusetts and Connecticut regiments since the beginning of the war and did not find the idea needed getting used to, but only one or two blacks had ever been in the Rhode Island regiments. It would be a totally novel idea at home, and one whose support would be uncertain.

Chapter Thirty-Two

June was helping the mistress prepare a spare Christmas celebration for the Hazzards' few friends who remained in the area, the mistress sighing about the sweets and delicacies they would have to forgo, when June's back—aching from repeated bending and the pull of her heavy belly—made her forget herself. Putting her hands at the small of her back, she straightened her spine. The mistress happened to turn from the fireplace at just that moment and glanced at her. Then she stared. Her mouth dropped open, closed. "June," she asked sharply. "Are you with child?"

Too late, she resumed a stooped posture. Her heart raced painfully in her chest. She told herself the news would have had to come out soon, but she was still frightened. She glanced at her mistress's face and, biting her lip nervously, nodded.

"Oh, dear heavens. How soon?"

"'Bout two months, ma'am." The corners of her mistress's mouth turned down. "But I will be all ready fo' planting time. And a baby don't eat much. I work harder than anyone ever work in their life! I swear it. You'll see!" She had carefully rehearsed this speech for months, but it still did not come out as she hoped. Her mistress was absorbed in worried thought and scarcely seemed to hear her.

"Another mouth to feed," she said, speaking just the words June dreaded to hear. If they could sell off Lucy and Jubah and try to sell Quamino, they could sell anyone. Suddenly dizzy, June put her hand on the cutting table to steady herself.

The mistress went back to her food preparations, taking up a heavy knife and chopping the dried apples angrily. June made herself go back to stirring the cake batter. Many minutes passed before Mistress Hazzard spoke to her.

"We need potatoes from the root cellar," she said, her voice as flat as it was before she suspected a thing. As June hurried out the door, she had the uneasy feeling that this flatness was the worst of all possible reactions.

*

AS THE NEW YEAR opened, she and Guy struggled to keep their spirits from sinking. He worried constantly, looking at her with his sad unblinking dark eyes. They knew the Hazzards could not sell June at a favorable price while she was pregnant, and no one in Rhode Island wanted a slave with a baby. But if the Hazzards went broke, there was no telling what might happen. June thought that if they could hold on until spring with new food and new dairy milk coming in, and she could prove she could still work hard enough to be worth keeping even with a baby, maybe they could make it.

Guy looked at her silently for a while. He said spring was a long way off.

And then in early February they heard the Hazzards talking about a new law the General Assembly was going to vote on that has something to do with slaves. And suddenly, but with the finality of a heavy door swinging shut, the Hazzards went back to whispering or growing quiet whenever June and Guy were in earshot. The master went to a flurry of meetings, some of them held late at night at his own house.

Guy decided the time had come for them to plan running away.

"*Now?*" June said. Guy nodded. "Baby be born soon."

"If they make a change the master don' like," Guy said, "you know he goin' figure a way around it. Sell us or trade us. Move us down to the Carolinas. Somethin'."

"Maybe we be together," June offered.

"He split us up like a piece of kindling. Did Lucy or Jubah go the same place?" June shook her head. "You think they was goin' send Quamino with 'em?"

She shook her head again. "It a *bad* time." She asked him to get on his knees and pray with her.

Guy put his hand on her arm and squeezed. "It always a bad time." Slowly, he explained what they needed to do. Steal food from the root cellar and hide it. Get their clothes packed in a bundle they could grab and run with. If they had to run in daytime, he would set fire to the barn to keep them busy. June had trouble getting her breath when he said this. Men were hanged for setting fires.

"A fire? What about the horses and cows?"

"Leave the doors open. We have to take two horses anyway."

Her hand flew to her mouth. "Steal horses!"

"Got to have them to get away. You think we get anywhere walkin'?"

"Oh, Guy, they'll kill us..."

He nodded, his mouth a grim slash. "If they catch us."

"*Kill* us."

He put his hand on her belly. "Rather be dead than not with you."

She looked at his grave face and nodded. "Where we go?"

"I was thinkin'. Thinkin' Maine territory. Big country, lot of space. Went right through it on the way to Quebec. Won' look for us there, won' find us if they try."

June heard in her head the mistress's flat voice telling her to go to the root cellar. She felt her stomach knot up at the memory. The next morning they started to steal small amounts of food to put by.

Suddenly, though, the meetings and the Hazzards' whisperings stopped. A full week passed, and though the Hazzards summoned their son Young John home from the militia, they began to wonder if the problem had all blown over.

June, exhausted by her worry and hard work and the drain of her final weeks of her pregnancy, fell into bed and into deep sleep within seconds. Guy, jumpy and unsettled, could barely sleep at all anymore. He knew that if they waited too long to run away, even by an hour, it would be too late.

They awakened to a chilly gray day, six days short of a full moon, carrying with it the smell of snow but promising nothing else remarkable. He knew it was Thursday, and June, who could count better than he and kept closer track of these things, knew it was the nineteenth day of February. He would come to know this last bit of information before the morning was out, however, because it would be written on a piece of paper with what they said was his name next to it.

Three uniformed white men and a wiry black man appeared at the main house not long after breakfast. He recognized the one-time slave and part-time spy Jack Sisson, though he had not seen the tall rangy blond man since he marched at the head of a column of men into the teeth of a blizzard and toward the walls of Quebec. Samuel Ward looked like a boy no more, his face lean and grave, his alert eyes serious.

The master, face puffy from lack of sleep, and Young John came outside to meet them in the yard. After Guy took their horses, the master told him to get to work on the barn gate and for June to get to the dairy. When they lingered, the master broke into a near-scream that astonished them all: "*I said get to work! Now!*"

June, flinching as if at the report of a gun, scurried off as quickly as her large belly permitted. Guy's work left him in easy earshot.

Master John worked to control his temper and suddenly looked as if he were squinting, though the light was too gray to require him to do so. "I want you to know, Major, that this family has lent very important assistance to our state's defense, and it should not be called on to do so again in such irreversible terms."

"I see," the major said, "that you have guessed the purpose of our visit. You must also already know that the new legislation permits us to reward you handsomely."

"For what? For taking a man's property and livelihood?" When the major shook his head but said nothing to this, Master John said, "Isn't it enough that my son is in the militia?"

"Having the governor of the slaves of Rhode Island will offer a reassuring presence and assist our recruitment."

He saw a flash of hatred cross Master John's face. "I think governors are often greatly overestimated. Don't you, Major Ward?"

Astonished, Guy's pulse began to race. He lowered his head and pretended to work on his task. They were talking about *him*! He glanced up in time to see the major's blue eyes frost to gunmetal gray. "Bring the man forward."

"He must seek to enlist first."

"You are well acquainted with the new law. Then you will know that all we require is a willingness on the part of the slave to enlist. We do not require the permission of the master."

"You cannot simply confiscate a man's property, sir!"

"As I said, you will be amply reimbursed." The master glared at him and said nothing. "It was our hope to compose this matter with you in a friendly way. But compose it we will." Guy could see slowly dawning on the master's face the awareness that the Ward boy was a boy no longer. He blinked nervously even before Major Ward said to him in a voice full of command, "Call the man. Call him *now*."

For the first time, the master's eyes darted toward Guy. "All right. But I wish to talk to him in private. I will not be told on my own land to whom I can speak."

"No one has said nay, Mister Hazzard. You will do us the courtesy of first letting us explain to him what enlistment requires."

Master John gestured toward the barn. "There he is."

"Captain Lewis? Please read from the authorizing act."

The captain unfolded a piece of paper and started to read in a slow and halting voice. Guy gathered he had not yet read this passage often, and actually he was grateful for the slow pace. "'Every able-bodied Negro,'" Lewis read, "'mulatto or Indian man slave in this State may enlist in the Continental Army in Rhode Island to serve during the continuance of the war with Great Britain. Every slave so enlisting shall, upon passing muster before the Colonel, be immediately discharged from the service of his master or mistress and be absolutely FREE.'" Guy could follow the man's finger on the paper as he read. He noticed that the last word, *free*, was printed all in big letters.

"Free?" Guy asked Major Ward.

"Forever," he replied.

His heart raced and his eyes stung with the start of tears. The crack of daylight at last. It was almost too much for him to take in. The dream of his entire life—free! Then he thought, *June*. The froth of his elation settled, vanished. *How could he leave her?*

Master John called him aside and behind the corner of the barn. Young John came along.

"You do not have to do this, Guy. And I do not want you to do it. You must remain here with us. This is not the great and grand offer you think it is. If you go and the rebels lose—and I am certain they will—the British will punish you as a traitor. They could even hang you. And in any event, win or lose, you will be compelled to fight in the army not just for one year as others do, or even for two or three years, but until this war comes to an end. Wars in Europe have lasted thirty years at a time. More! You may never quit. You may never leave." The master stared intently in Guy's eyes to see how his arguments were working. Guy listened closely. "You will no longer be a servant to me and Mistress Hazzard but you will be a slave to military service. Even the rebels admit that their soldiers are now risking starvation at

Valley Forge. You will be in an army of whites, and I know you are too wise to believe that you will ever have anything but the poorest food and the worst and most dangerous kind of duty. You can and almost certainly will be killed as easily as *this.*" The master raised his hand in front of Guy's eyes and snapped his fingers with a loud pop.

Guy nodded and hung his head. He guessed that everything the master said was likely true, but none of it would stop him for a second.

"Just tell the men no."

"Can't say no, can't say yes."

"Do you think they would be signing up Negroes if their war plans were going well? They are on the edge of ruin and are about to fall into disaster, man!" When Guy said nothing, the master paused. Then he spoke more softly. "What about June?" Guy's head snapped up. "Your wife, ready to give birth any day. You can't leave her."

"Maybe I buy her."

The master snorted. "Not on a private's salary. No, Guy. You stay here. I will reinstate your wages, share any cash you make working on other's farms. We will work out your and June's freedom over time. Soon, too, I promise you."

When Guy said nothing, Young John began to say through clenched teeth how mulish and ungrateful he was. His father silenced him with a look.

"We are offering you food and clothing and shelter and a doctor's care when you need it. We are offering to keep you and June and your baby together, safe and at home." Guy nodded, beginning to feel the force of the master's persuasive powers. "You understand, Guy, how hard things have become, our having to sell off Jubah and Lucy and losing Quamino, and they have become hard again. If we lose you now and lose the value of your work, I honestly do not know how we will get by. This is not a threat. I am just explaining to you how things are. If we cannot get by, there is no way on earth of telling what will happen to June and your baby. Everything is auctioned off, sold to whoever makes a bid. Is that what you want? Is it?"

"No, Mastuh."

"Then tell the men no." Master John folded his arms across his chest and waited for an answer.

From where they were standing, Guy could see into the open door of the dairy. June was preparing the cheese press, and she pushed back a damp strand of hair from her forehead with the back of her hand. Guy could see in every gesture and every movement how worried she was. She turned and saw him and the master and Young John and her hand flew to her mouth.

"I say no," Guy said, his voice hoarse.

The master nodded in satisfaction. "Good. You won't be sorry."

The three of them returned to the yard in front of the main house.

Major Ward raised his hand. "Before you say anything, we need to tell you two things. I am told you have a wife here." Guy nodded. "I just wanted to assure you that there are laws that prevent your master from selling her out of state." Guy looked at him impassively, thinking he didn't know Gambling John Hazzard. The major then turned to the master and said, "These are laws which you have violated twice already when you sold two of your slaves last year. We know this," he held up several pieces of paper, "and have the documents to confirm it. Attorney General Marchant has informed me, however, that he does not intend to prosecute unless you should attempt to violate the law again."

Young John blurted, "And what we if are forced into insolvency?" His father glared at him as if he didn't want this question raised.

Major Ward continued to look steadily at Young John. "In case of insolvency, your servants are freed to do as they wish." He turned to Guy. "Do you have any questions before we proceed?"

"Can I speak to my wife, suh?"

Ward nodded. Guy did not dare look at the master or his son as he walked off, but he could feel their glares upon him like knives.

June waited at the dairy's entrance, her face full of anxiety and impatience. "What? What?"

He explained the offer made to him and her eyes grew wide. "This is it, Guy. This is what Quamino told us would come. You *got* to take it."

"But it only for men. No cooks, no washerwomen."

"This is your chance, it ain' never goin' come again."

"What about you?"

Her eyes grew fierce and brimmed with tears. She seized the lapels of his jacket and began to hit him. "You got to go! Fo' both of us, fo' the baby. You *got* to *go*!"

He tried to embrace her, but she batted his arms away. He tried again and she pushed him back, hard.

She glared at him, breathing hard, her hands doubled into fists. "I mean it, Guy Watson. You stay here, I never goin' forgive you."

"What if they make you stay a slave forever?"

"'If'? Things happenin' so fast now, no one know what happen tomorrow, never mind forever. This my best chance, havin' you out there free. You think runnin' away was goin' work? Don' be a fool. They catch us sure as Sunday. You stay, an we never get away. Then you goin' hate me for makin' you lose your chance to be free. I goin' hate you for bein' the biggest fool in the world. You hear me, Guy Watson? Don't be a fool!"

He nodded once, slowly. June grew still and her breathing slowed. "You know where I keep all my money?"

"I know."

They hurried to their cabin. He took a gold half Jo for himself and left her all the rest, warning her to keep it hidden well. He took a little piece of cloth from his mother's death dress, and the tiny box of dirt from his father's grave, and added them to his pouch of charms. He stepped outside and with Quamino's old prayer stick and made a cross on the ground outside the entrance. He held June, and they stood together on the crossing point, and with his face pointing up to the gray February skies he called on the spirits of the living and the dead, and of the sky and of the earth, to surround and protect them all the days of their lives.

He heard Jack Sisson calling his name. He embraced June hard in his arms, feeling her pregnant belly against him, inhaling her warm coppery smell, and then he turned to leave, fighting with all his might the impulse to turn around. Sisson called again.

He presented himself before Major Ward and said, "I wan' enlist."

Master John swore bitterly and the mask of confidence Young John wore cracked, curdled, and fell away in shock.

"I insist on the maximum sum for this man," the master said, jabbing a finger toward Guy. "One hundred and twenty pounds, in cash!"

"Your acquaintance with the new measure is excellent, Mister Hazzard, but imperfect. One hundred and twenty pounds is the highest figure, yes, but not paid in cash. The money is expected by the end of March," Samuel Ward said. "And I do not doubt this man will be valued at the highest price. Captain Lewis will write down my recommendation to that effect and leave you with a receipt." He nodded at the father and then the son. "Mister Hazzard. Lieutenant Hazzard. If there are any goods you wish to send with Private Watson or anything you would like to say to him…"

Master John shook his head in disgust, then stopped himself. He leveled his gaze like a gun. "Don't say I didn't warn you, Guy. You're leaving a good long life for a short bad one, mark my words."

Guy, still deep in his lifelong habit, nodded and said, "Yessuh."

He looked for June. She was nowhere to be seen. Jack went to get the horses and pulled Guy up to ride behind him. As they reached the boundary of the Hazzard property, all the while letting Jack's chatter wash over him, Guy looked up at the vast sweep of sky. He had always wondered what it would feel like to be free. It seemed very solemn to him, not at all what he expected, and as the Hazzard place disappeared from view behind him, he suddenly felt a cold wave of loneliness.

He wondered if June would have a boy or a girl. He wondered whether he would ever see them again. Even when the place and all its outbuildings were out of sight, he found himself still turning around.

*

THAT NIGHT, FOR THE first time ever, the Hazzards shackled June to the walls of her cabin.

Chapter Thirty-Three

Guy, Jack Sisson, and the white officers traveled throughout southern Rhode Island to find slaves to become soldiers. Guy was surprised at how easily recruitment went. No one argued the way Master Hazzard did, at least not once they heard how much money the army was offering. Captain Lewis explained that all the men in the General Assembly who were against the measure had insisted on a very high sum to be paid to the owners for their slaves. They believed the high cost would force others to vote against it. When the measure passed the General Assembly anyway, masters, no matter what their political views, found it hard to resist. Everyone needed the money.

Loyalists got a large chunk of income, avoided becoming the target of some local committee of safety, shed themselves of another mouth to feed and body to clothe, and when they found that even men like Gambling John Hazzard had surrendered a slave, it seemed pointless to resist. They knew true organized resistance would require loyalists to pay slave owners at least as much to keep their slaves as the General Assembly had offered them to sell, and no one could afford *that*. Patriots, on the other hand, were happy because they could contribute to the cause, be well paid for their sacrifice, ease their conscience about being a slave owner, and know it meant fewer local white men would be forced to fight far away with the Continental army, all while leaving more of them to protect Rhode Islanders at home. And if their town filled their recruitment requirement—

white or black, a soldier is a soldier—their tax bill would be lower. Getting money now and saving some later. That was hard to oppose.

Suddenly money was on Guy's mind. It never had been before, at least not this way. All he knew was he was supposed to be paid every month for being a soldier, and if he got enough money, he could buy out June's time from the Hazzards. The thought began to seize him like a fever. He could never figure out what moved the men and women he saw being whipped every year on 'Lecture Day for stealing money or silver or jewelry. Food or clothing, yes, he could understand. Revenge by breaking something valuable or dropping it down the well he could appreciate. But why steal something you could never use? But now in every home he entered among the great plantations of southern Rhode Island, all he could think about was stealing. Candelabras, salt cellars, silverware, bowls, and pewter tankards all seemed to lean toward him when looked at them—and the houses he visited were full of them. As soon as he stepped in the door, his palms began to itch. He had seen white people in Newport pay huge sums of money for these gleaming metal objects. One or two good pieces might even be enough, and some of these masters would scarcely notice they were missing. It gnawed at him with sharp teeth like some small hungry animal. Finally, at the Gardiners' house, Guy put a silver shiny candlestick holder from a sideboard in his hand, the cool metal warming under his touch. He looked around the quiet room and then he heard in his head Quamino's voice speaking an old saying from Africa times. "Not hard to steal the king's trumpet. But where you able play it?"

If he stole the candlestick holder, he would have to find someone to sell it to. And if he got caught, he would be whipped and jailed and get no soldier's pay.

But how, he wondered, *how* would he ever get June out? Unbending his grasping claw of a hand took all his effort. He put the candlestick back on the sideboard. He felt light-headed with the strain.

He wanted to talk it over with Jack Sisson, but Jack was leaving and would not be a member of the First Rhode Island Regiment. Not yet. Colonel Barton wanted him to do more spying for him, and Jack said that a spy who was also a soldier and who got caught would hang. A civilian, if he were caught, was far less likely to suffer death. So Jack's enlistment had to wait.

In a matter of days, even without Sisson, there was a list of black men far higher than Guy could count, and every morning Sergeant Spink called the roll: there were Guy's old neighbors, York and July Champlin; his cousin, Jack Watson, who was kindly but not very smart; lots of men he had seen on 'Lection Day every year, Cuff Cheeseborough and the Narragansett Indian, Quam Tanner; the preacher's old servant, James Clarke; Caesar Wheaton and Rutter Gardiner of the wealthy Gardiners; Primus Babcock, the doctor's old servant; a boy of fifteen, Peter Leavitt, someone they wanted to make the company's fife player. And there were men he had never seen before, a huge number of them named Greene—Cato, William, Thomas—two Princes and two Newports, and a great number of one-z and two-z Hazzards, Dick and Peter and Sampson and Baccus. And there was William Frank and Hercules Thompson and Major Ward's favorite addition, Ichabod Northrup, the slave of one of the men in the General Assembly who voted against the measure to raise the regiment in the first place. And there was even the forbidding Mingo Rodman, still muscular and mean, who was immediately made the drummer of the company because he administered whippings as well as led the men in their march.

All of these men, and more, came to join them in the cold spring of 1778.

In fact, the group was soon big enough that they had to split it into two units, one of them made of men like Guy who had had some training, and a new one who needed to learn everything.

And there was a lot to learn, some of it hard even if you were not slow like Guy's cousin, Jack Watson. Some things they all were able to learn right away, like marching in step to the rhythmic thrum of a drum. And all of them could see how practical this was. When they marched somewhere in single file, they no longer bumped into each other but went forward together. But other commands, like "file right" and "file left" were hard, and "line front" and "line rear" were harder still. And hardest of all was learning how to carry, present, load, shoot, reload, and clean a musket, a weapon only a few of them had ever been permitted to touch. At first, none of them were permitted to use real powder and lead, so it was hard to know if they could aim enough to hit the wide side of a barn. Every once in a while, they had a good day and began to feel like real soldiers. Then some new recruits arrived and turned right instead of left or in file when they should form a line, and the entire regiment was milling about in confusion.

The officers were in a hurry to train them so they could report to Valley Forge. They worried that the British were ready to come out of their winter quarters in Philadelphia and begin attacking. Encamped in East Greenwich while they completed their training, the officers yelled and cursed at the men, constantly giving orders on everything from what to wear and how to stand to when they could sleep and where they could urinate. As two weeks passed, Guy learned to follow orders well enough to avoid being singled out for discipline. But as more days passed, he kept thinking that he was less than a day's march from the Hazzard place, but he did not know if June had had their child, nor did know what plans the Hazzards had for her now.

He steeled himself to ask Captain Lewis if he could see Major Ward.

"What for?" the captain asked.

"To aks fo' a day's leave."

Lewis snorted. "Leave?!"

"The major, he…"

"The major is off getting married. And even he gets no leave. In three days he is heading for Valley Forge to deliver supplies. Hard to say when we'll see him next. You don't see officers leaving, do you?"

Guy shook his head. "That's right. No leaves for nobody." The captain walked off, muttering in a mincing voice, "'I wants a leave…'"

Guy looked up at the pale half-moon, easily visible even in the full light of afternoon sky. He thought he might as well be perched up there on the moon as in East Greenwich.

The days of drilling began to blend together. Free or not free, his life began to seem the same as it ever was. He started to wonder if he had been a fool to have left the Hazzards. He had less control over the minutes of his life than he ever did, and though they were supposed to be paid every month, they were not—though neither, he learned, were the white officers. They had to wait for the payroll. How long? No one knew. In the meantime, more drills, more marching. For more than a few of them, it was the first time they had ever worn shoes, and while their soles were tough, the soft and tender tops of their feet blistered. Without real powder and shot, most of them began to feel like children, marching about in costume with harmless weapons and pretending to be serious.

*

ONE MORNING NEAR THE end of April as the weather softened, Guy stopped his work on digging a new vault for their wastes when he heard the sound of piping fifes and laughter and cheering. He hurried back into camp to find the white officers embracing one another and pounding each other's backs. One of them, tough old Sergeant Spink, was actually weeping. The youngest drummer thrummed out the call for assembly. Colonel Greene himself stepped forward to give the announcement of the news that had filled them with such a great spirit of celebration.

"I have the pleasure to tell you," he said, his face wreathed in a rare smile, "that the French have joined the war. And I order that every man here be given a half-gill of rum to celebrate!"

The offer of rum caused a shout of approval to rise from the men, but Guy knew that none of them, including him, really understood why the officers were so gleeful. Primus Babcock, the doctor's old house servant, said the French were great enemies to the English, and for most of the men, this was a start. James Clarke, the Baptist preacher's former slave, said the French were a big and wealthy country not far from England—Primus corrected him to say the country was called "France," not "French"—but no one cared about this. Finally, Lieutenant Thompson said, "'Tis great news we've heard! The French, you see, are going to send men and clothes and guns and powder. We shall win now, you see. We cannot lose!"

"Is the war over?" Jack Watson asked.

"No, private. But with France on our side, you see, we know how it will end!"

"There be more fightin'?" Guy heard himself ask. He usually tried to keep his mouth shut, but this time he could not.

Elias Thompson nodded.

Then, he thought, whether they won or not, they could still get killed. And while the officers and the men drank the rum and celebrated—and he could tell from watching the hugely happy whites that they felt this was one of the best and most important things to have happened in their lives—Guy thought that they should save their celebrating for when the war was over.

*

MAJOR THAYER ARRIVED FROM Valley Forge with a whole new series of drills he and the army there had just learned from some German general named von Steuben. They were just getting into the habit of these new commands a few weeks later, when Major Ward himself returned from Valley Forge with a wagonload of copies of a new weapon, burning with the conviction that they needed to learn how to use it. It was called a bayonet.

Captain Lewis described to them what it was like to have a large group of enemy soldiers running at you with long honed knives fixed to the ends of their rifles and muskets, how helpless you felt if your gun has been fired but you did not have time to reload, how horrifying it was to see your friends and fellow soldiers run through with a shiny length of sharpened steel, how painful was their death, and how quickly that same bayonet might be pulled from a bleeding body and driven into someone else's. "Like your own," Captain Lewis concluded.

Guy had seen distant combat at the Boston siege and dealt with wounded men at the field hospital. He had helped prepare Sam Ward's company for its assault on Quebec, and these last weeks he had been practicing shooting his musket at targets. But it was securing the silvery blue, sharpened bayonet to the barrel of his weapon that made it become gruesomely real. Shooting was familiar. Most of them had been permitted to use a pistol or fowling piece to hunt small game or defend hen coops from foxes and weasels. Shooting was a distant act. Plunging a bayonet into someone in the center of the chest just below cage of their ribs—as they practiced doing to red-uniformed bags of beach sand—felt different. Personal. It took no special act of imagination to picture a face a few feet from your own, a knife coming out his back.

Major Ward said the Hessians and the British had killed hundreds, maybe thousands, of Americans in this horrible way, and if they encountered the First Rhode Island Regiment, they would do it again. "No American lines have ever stood up to a full bayonet charge," said the major. "It is time for that to change."

Amid the recurring alarms and continued attacks by the British upon the coast, amid their all-night marches to terrified towns where the fighting and ransacking were always over by the time they arrived, the sentinel duty and the drills continued. They did not feel like toy soldiers anymore.

*

WHEN JULY ARRIVED, BAD news came with it. General Washington attacked Howe in Monmouth, New Jersey, but instead of a great victory, there was a huge mass of confusion. Rhode Islanders there fought bravely, but many were killed and wounded, and Major Thayer himself lost an eye. And the overall commander for the Rhode Island sector, the famous and recently released General Lee, the ugly Englishman with the ugly dogs who some thought the best general in the American army, behaved so badly on the field of battle, he was arrested. Paralyzed by fear and indecision, he refused to follow General Washington's direct order to attack. He was under guard waiting for a court-martial. And most dramatic bad news of all was the word of the arrival of an entire fleet of new British transports in Newport, doubling the size of the enemy force. Colonel Greene said the entire Rhode Island militia and First Rhode Island Regiment put together were now outnumbered more than five to one.

It appeared, according to the officers, that the British had decided to bring the fight to New England, and Providence was their next target.

Two days later, most of the men and all the officers were given uniforms. They were ordered to wash themselves and clean their firearms. At dawn, they were to march north to Providence. Amid the preparation, officers congratulated themselves for having ended up in the right place in one regard. Major Ward's new father-in-law, Judge Greene, had just become governor of the state, and as long as they stayed local, they likely were not going to have to suffer like the soldiers at Valley Forge.

But mostly, Lieutenant Thompson said with a narrow squint, it looked as if the First Rhode Island would not have to march far to have its first battle.

And on the very same hot July afternoon when they reached Providence, they were told the French allies had arrived in a vast fleet and bottled up the British forces in New York. General Washington was now sending thousands of regulars under the command of General Lafayette and General Greene to Rhode Island.

A great battle was planned. And by the way things were taking shape, it appeared the First Rhode Island Regiment would be in the middle of it.

*

FOR THE FIRST TIME in his life, Sam Ward wished he did not know so much. He had never believed that ignorance was bliss, and much of his life had taught him the opposite. But as the Americans and the French gathered in Rhode Island for the jointly planned assault on the British and Hessians holding Newport, everything he knew made him wish that he knew less.

The enormous French fleet under Count d'Estaing arrived off Point Judith impatient for action. And for good reason. The rumor was that a large British fleet was on its way to reinforce the garrison at Newport. The count and his men had been aboard their ships for almost four months, many had scurvy, needed fresh water and fresh food, and the Rhode Islanders were only able to feebly respond. And last of all, the longer they waited, the better the British general in Newport, Robert Pigot, would be able to prepare to defend himself. So the French wanted swift action.

General Washington, trying to avoid jealousies, left General Sullivan in overall command and sent the Marquis de Lafayette to help coordinate plans with the French as well as Nat Greene. Nat wrote Sam that it was also probably a gesture of gratitude for his having agreed in the wake of the near starvation and disaster at Valley Forge to take over the post of Quartermaster General. Nat had also not been home in over three years and Washington knew that he did not want to give up his command of soldiers in the lines. "Who," Nat observed dryly, "has ever heard in history about a Quartermaster General?" But jealousy and conflict began immediately, and it was caused by the man who was sent to prevent it.

The Marquis de Lafayette—who seemed determined to be heard of in history—decided he wanted to be the first ever to lead a joint force of American and French soldiers. This was not what General Sullivan had planned. Under orders from General Washington to mix Continental soldiers in among the militia and volunteers in order to increase the new recruits' confidence, Sullivan opposed Lafayette's scheme since it required siphoning off many of the most experienced Americans. The marquis, however, in what Nat called "a great thirst for glory," pressed Count d'Estaing to support his proposal, arguing that in Sullivan's plan the French would appear to be under cover of American fire and the pride of their nation would suffer in such a humiliatingly secondary role.

Sullivan explained his objections to the count. The count agreed with Sullivan—for one day. Then he thought better of it, and two days before the planned assault insisted the marquis lead a joint force or the entire French-American alliance would fall apart. Since Sullivan's main order from General Washington was "to make harmony your first object," Sullivan gave in. He also asked for the invasion to be put off to Monday, August 10, so he could complete the difficult task of organizing all the newly arriving soldiers.

Despite the maneuverings, everyone was growing optimistic about their chances of success. With a huge continuing stream of reinforcements, Sullivan's army now outnumbered the British in Newport by two to one. John Hancock, swept up in the wave of confidence, decided at the last moment to come command the Massachusetts militia himself. The French ships, some armed with an incredible eighty-four guns, looked like it could make short work of the British ships in the bay.

And, remarkably, for a while things went just as planned. On the morning of August 8, the French fleet sailed up and down both sides of the narrow ten-mile long island, with Newport sitting on the southernmost tip, a drop of wax running down a long candle. The French gunboats blasted away at ships and batteries and especially the redoubts and barracks on the hillsides at the northern end of the island. The plan was to land a force behind the northernmost redoubts, attack them from front and rear, slicing Pigot's army in two. And then they would concentrate all their forces for the assault southward on Newport itself.

Sam thought it was an excellent plan. Early on the foggy morning the day before the invasion, he reported to the Tiverton headquarters of Fort Barton, a fort named after the man who made the daring midnight capture of British General Prescott. A month ago, poor Colonel Barton caught a musket ball in the thigh while leading a militia defense against a Hessian assault. The last word Sam got on his condition was that Barton was delirious with fever, and no one knew whether he would live or die. But he arrived at Barton's fort just in time to be told that General Sullivan, hearing that the British had withdrawn from the northernmost forts, had seized the unexpected opening and sent Sam's old friend from Quebec, now–militia Colonel John Topham, to land a force. Topham was to hold the redoubts until the rest of the army could arrive.

When the sun was fully up and the fog was slowly burning off, Sam learned that an outraged Count d'Estaing got word of Topham's landing exactly one hour after he had gotten a message from General Sullivan repeating his intention not to attack until the next day. As noon drew near, the French count, angry at being misinformed, decided to come to land to talk with Sullivan directly. Before he could make it to land, the last of the fog over the bay evaporated to reveal a huge British fleet of thirty-six sails at the southern horizon.

Without a single word from American intelligence, the British fleet from New York had arrived just offshore. General Sullivan at first insisted that such an arrival was impossible and he urged the Count to pursue their plans for the capture of Newport. Count d'Estaing sent out a ship to verify the arrival of the enemy ships and, when he got it, immediately decided his first task must be to sail out and attempt to destroy the British fleet. His huge ships were difficult to maneuver in little Narragansett Bay, and if rumors of a reinforcing fleet from England proved true, this might be his last, best chance to destroy the British navy.

In the meantime, as he gave orders to his French fleet to hoist sail and prepare for battle, the American army continued its landings.

The French-American alliance was not off to a smooth start.

*

WHEN THE WAR FIRST began and Guy was at the lines outside Boston, he had seen many men in one place. But he had never seen this much confusion. Men arrived without having any idea where they were supposed to go. Wagons, cannons, and howitzers rolled about. Horses trotted past and heaps of supplies were dumped here and there with no one to dispense them. Because the state had called out every man in its militia for battle, many slave owners who wanted to stay home suddenly decided to sell more men to the First Rhode Island. Dozens of new recruits arrived who knew nothing about drilling, marching, bayonets, or handling a gun.

When the veteran Continental soldiers arrived, it was easy to tell them from the militia. The gray-faced regular soldiers looked both tired and determined; the new men looked around themselves in awe, their necks loose and their pink faces bright with surprise. Guy was busy instructing for the third time the most recent regiment arrival how to load his musket when a filthy black man appeared dressed in an old and ragged flour sack. He stood at the recruit's elbow. Guy sighed, thinking it was pretty clear they would take just about anybody now. He glanced at the tattered figure's face for a second and found him grinning right at him. It was Jack Sisson.

"What happened to *you*?" Guy asked.

Jack looked Guy up and down in his new uniform with the blue coat and white breeches. "Same thing happen to you, 'cept I actually get paid fo' it." Guy looked at him in silence, knowing an explanation would be coming. “Colonel Barton come out of his fever and say he got one last spyin’ job fo’ me.”

“You done it?”

“I done it. Been to Newport the last couple of days.”

“What you find out?”

“Find out they are plenty scared, don’t have much in the way of food, and they been raidin’ farms all up the island and burning every house near their lines in so we won’t have no place to hide when we get there. Almos’ didn’t get out of there myself.”

“Why not?”

“Gener’l Pigot, he put out a call to all the island’s blacks offering them money an’ food if they join the fight for the English. When no one came, he jus’ round ’em all up and force them behind his lines and into work. Jus’ missed roundin’ me up with ’em. Meantime, they put their cannon up on hills over the fields. Gettin’ ready as they can. But now I’m back an’ ready to put me on one them uniforms. Where Sergeant Spink? Need get out of this beggar’s outfit.” He shifted his shoulders uncomfortably. “Itches.”

Guy pointed over to the fort’s far side.

Sisson was about to turn away when he offered, “Heard June had a baby.”

Guy stiffened. “What? When?”

“I heard yesterday. She had the baby back in the spring. You didn’ know?”

“They all right?”

“They both fine.”

Guy felt his face stretch into a grin. “Boy?”

Jack shrugged. “Don’ know. Didn’ aks.”

“Aks who?”

“Young John Hazzard. He wit’ the militia. You haven’t seen him?”

Guy shook his head.

Chapter Thirty-Four

Guy looked for Young John amid the Rhode Island militia, but the brigade was overrun by volunteers—apothecaries, shopkeepers, tailors, farmers, and coopers, all still dressed in the clothes of their trade. And they all were being funneled to flatboats at Howland's Ferry to make the crossing. The veterans looked serious as they headed for the boats. Colonel Greene said if the British were smart, and they often were, the best time for them to attack would be now, striking while the Americans were still landing and before the whole army could be brought to the island. Rhode Islanders—militia, volunteers, and regulars—had been chosen to be in the first wave to land. And it was their task to hold their positions at all costs.

Many of the men in Guy's regiment had never been on a boat before. Half of them, including rock-hard Mingo Rodman, got sick during the crossing, some from nervousness and smelling others' vomit as much as from the roll of the ocean waves. Guy stood downwind at the far rail, breathing in shallow sips through his mouth and thinking about being a father. As the flatboats started to reach shore, they listened through the still summer air for the sound of cannon and musket fire, but except for the sound of their unloading, all was quiet. Colonel Topham was waiting there to direct them, and, squinting in the sunlight, he said his scouts could find no evidence of any imminent attack. Still, they wasted no time in shifting to the task of setting up camp and placing men in the lines of the enemy's abandoned redoubts.

Major Ward came to the revetments and examined the artillery emplacements. Shading his eyes, he surveyed the low-lying ground where his regiment had begun to pitch their tents. His mouth tightening into a thin line, he ordered the officers to have the men stop what they were doing. "Move the tents," he said, pointing to an area farther behind the lines and on the upper reaches of a nearby slope.

"Move the tents?" Lieutenant Thompson asked.

"Yes, Lieutenant. Whole brigades will be moving in here soon, and if the weather changes... You do not want to be downhill of other men's latrines."

The next day turned gray and cool, with a breeze coming in from the north.

*

THE AMERICAN ARMY CONTINUED to arrive in larger and larger numbers. As more supplies were brought up, Guy noticed that whatever dirty or unpleasant task needed to be done, his regiment was told to do it. They dug vaults for latrines, extended trenches, cut trees, and hauled water from an inland stream. Next to them, white men from a Connecticut company sat around, wrote letters, drank, diced, and sang.

"What we think?" muttered Primus Babcock as he hauled leather pails of water to dump in a cistern. "Just because we suppose be free, they ain' white?"

Late in the afternoon, Lieutenant Thompson kept staring through his spyglass. French ships on both coasts had begun to sail south. "They're to land men on the western shore," he said.

Captain Lewis shrugged. "Maybe it's to fool the British."

Rumors began to bubble up in the units on either side of theirs. The French were attacking. The enemy was trying to escape by sea. New enemy reinforcements had arrived and were trying to land at

Newport. Finally, at four in the afternoon, the entire army was instructed to muster. The officers were going to read to each regiment General Sullivan's orders of the day. All questions would be answered then.

Guy's throat was dry from steady working and his brain felt light from lack of sleep. He forced himself to concentrate as Colonel Greene read in his deep but soft voice. The wind began to gust so strongly, he missed some of his words. The wind was warm and damp, and carried with it a tropical smell.

Right away they learned the French had left, but they would be back soon. The entire army was ordered to march toward Newport at six o'clock the next morning. "So we work ourself all day on a camp we goin' leave," muttered Ichabod Northrup. "Is that stupid, or..." Mingo Rodman turned and Northrup grew silent.

The wind gusted louder and the language grew a bit thick for a while, but Guy made out that General Sullivan was happy to find himself the head of an army that now outnumbered the enemy, and now they must do everything to press on to victory. At the end, the colonel's voice grew strong even through the wind. "'The expectation of the country,'" he read, "'the safety of our land, the protection of our property, and, in short, everything which animates men to fight and conquer call aloud upon us to act the part of freemen and become the character of Americans!'" Colonel Greene paused before he read the last words, making certain everyone was listening. "'Engaged in so just a cause, we must conquer, we must win the laurels that await us, and return in triumph to the arms of a grateful country!'"

"Hope so," said Primus Babcock. He held up a tattered shirt. "Specially wan' protect my property."

*

HAVING SLEPT LITTLE THE last few days, and despite the sound of rain pelting his tent, Guy fell asleep before midnight. Two hours later, he awakened to one of the loudest sustained noises he had ever heard. The wind was no longer gusting. It was roaring. He wondered for a moment if he were asleep dreaming of being back on the march to Quebec and the terrifying river flood. The next thing he knew his tent was gone and he was being drenched in a downpour. His tent, half on the leeward side of the slope, must have been one of the last to go. Everywhere in the black night, tents were blown about like rags. Men slipped on the mud-slick ground. Lightning veined the black sky in huge jagged white bolts and thunder boomed in long clamorous explosions.

Guy wiped the streaming water from his face and peered through the thick air. The wind was swirling and driving the rain at them from all directions. Trenches were filling with water. Here and there, one or two of the biggest campfires flickered on in the darkness, but they had only a few minutes' life left in them. Men were yelling, but their voices whirled away in nature's great uproar. Guy could make out Major Ward and Colonel Greene leaning into the wind, yelling orders. Finally, the officers and their sergeants and corporals had to move among the men, standing directly next to them to make their orders heard.

"Protect your powder!" Sergeant Spink yelled in his ear. "Stay on high ground!" Guy could see now how wise Major Ward was to have gotten them to move their tents. The Massachusetts company who bedded themselves on the lower ground were wading in a stinking swamp of overflowing privies and floating debris.

Everyone thought that a storm so ferocious could not last long. But it blew unabated all night. And though the roaring of the wind let up from time to time, the rain continued pouring all night and the next day as well. They were, it was now clear, in the savage middle of a rare New England event: a hurricane. The Africa-born wind whirled up again at nightfall, and it rained all that night, too. The great storm did not begin to relent until the early hours of the next day. By the time it was over, their stores had been destroyed, their powder ruined, and their cartridges made unusable. Two horses from the Massachusetts regiment below them drowned in the night.

Thousands of the militia picked up and went home. Hundreds of others scraped together money and carefully dried their sodden currency to hire pilots in high-sided boats to take them ashore. The army that remained was cold and hungry. No one had been able to cook any food or heat any water for three days.

At dawn, Guy stood on a small hill and surveyed their decimated ranks. Though the officers put on a determined front, no one needed to tell the army the truth of their situation. They could see it plainly. Before the great storm, they were poised to begin the seizing of Newport. Now, with the hurricane over, everything was different. Not only could they no longer attack, but they could scarcely defend themselves. The British had houses during the downpour in which to take shelter—they and their powder were dry. All the Americans had to defend themselves were bayonets, and only a few Continental soldiers in Sullivan's army had been trained to use them. In three days, they had gone from almost certain victory to staring disaster in the face. If they stayed, they risked being attacked where they were. If they left, they would be sitting ducks in the open bay—and the wind-tossed gray-green waters were still too rough for flatboats.

Retreating was impossible. Staying was worse.

The French fleet was nowhere to be seen. Everyone wondered how they could possibly have survived so ferocious a storm.

Guy's regiment was ordered to find and re-pitch their mud-soaked tents.

*

THE HIGH-SIDED BOATS THAT took the militia back to the mainland returned with fresh powder and wagonloads of new stores. The remaining men struggled to make themselves into an army once again. They built new fires and dug new trenches in the mud. As the weather continued to clear and the sun began to dry them out, gradually but steadily, a flow of new soldiers arrived. Nervous sentinels reported every hour: no enemy movements.

They were ordered to be ready the next morning to march on Newport.

With the sun barely up at the eastern shore, General Sullivan, surrounded by two hundred horsemen, led the army himself through a light ground fog on its southward march. Because Colonel Greene had been asked to command a brigade at the center, Guy's regiment learned that Major Ward would be at the head of the First Rhode Island. Less than an hour after the thousands of men began their march, Sam Ward, his webbing whitened and uniform finally dry, led them down a split in the road to the right, bringing them down the western side of the island. The other half of the army continued to the left down the eastern road. Though there were some tree branches down and the road was flooded in spots, they made good progress, their supply wagons rolling behind them. By midafternoon they reached a place Captain Lewis called Honeyman's Hill where, at last, they halted.

Lieutenant Thompson raised his spyglass and pointed to a row of hills in the distance. "There they are," he said.

As Guy peered toward the green hills, suddenly the ground a few hundred yards in front of their lines kicked up in a muddy splash. A few seconds later, they heard the distant booms of the British cannons.

The Americans unlimbered their cannons and the men were ordered to dig in.

The cannon firing went on all day and then all night. The next morning they were ordered to move one hundred yards closer to the British lines and to dig new trenches. The morning after that, they got the same order again. One hundred yards and new trenches. No one was happy about being exposed to cannon fire. Guy was not the only one who had seen what happened to a man who was hit by an iron ball or sliced open by fragments from a bomb. Least happy were the Connecticut militia on their left who had to work shoulder to shoulder with a black regiment. Why, they grumbled, did they have to do the same labor as men who, until a few weeks ago, were slaves?

As the days wore on and the cannonballs landed closer, tempers grew short. The Connecticut men began to give orders to the black Rhode Islanders, and when most of them turned deaf ears, they made bitter jokes, grew angry, and hurled insults. Guy tried to ignore it all, and he and the others edged away from the Connecticut regiment, working nearby only when their white officers who were on hand ordered them to do so. Captain Lewis and Sergeant Spink had just left to inspect the middle of the lines when a Connecticut man turned to Mingo Rodman and told him to move the damned rock he had just unearthed out of their way. Rodman ignored him.

The man touched Rodman on the back. "You listen when someone talks to you. You understand English, don't you?" Rodman kept on digging. "Hey. Monkey man. I'm *talking* to *you*!" When Rodman still ignored him, he shoved him on the shoulder.

Rodman straightened, his eyes narrowed into slits. He lifted his shovel and was about to smash the man in the face when two black corporals struggled to stop him. Whites from the Connecticut regiment made a general rush toward them man, and soon Guy and everyone else had raised their shovels. Sergeants Spink and Smith came at a run, Captains Lewis and Dexter just behind. Amid yelling and shoving, the two units were separated. In the brief quiet that followed order being restored, the Colonel in command of the militia arrived and demanded that Rodman be taken off and whipped. There was a surge of yelling and approval from his men.

Major Ward arrived. Guy listened in as the captains explained what happened. The major listened quietly, glanced around at the tensely gathered men, and then ordered his regiment back to digging. He walked up to the Connecticut colonel, introduced himself, and apologized for the uproar. The colonel made no effort to send his men back to work, and they gathered in knots to listen to the officers' conversation. Guy and those in the black regiment close enough to Major Ward listened, too, but they went about their work at the same time. Guy didn't really care if Mingo Rodman got into trouble—he had never liked him—but to his surprise he felt his stomach tighten, as if something truly bad was about to happen. The Connecticut officer again demanded in a loud voice that Rodman be whipped.

"Well, Colonel," Ward said, "I understand your soldier struck the first blow."

"He did *not* strike the man." Murmurs of assent and nods came from his regiment.

"No blows were struck, then?"

"I understand he may have pushed the Negro for his insolence. But your private here tried to dash his brains out!"

Major Ward nodded. "A serious matter." Their conversation was interrupted for a few moments when the British fired cannons in their direction. The balls fell short, thudding into the soft ground and then rolling to within thirty yards of their lines. The colonel seemed jumpy about the cannon fire. Major Ward barely blinked. He continued, "But we have a common enemy from whom we should not be distracted."

"Exactly," the militia colonel said, tearing his eyes away from the closest spent cannonball. "Without discipline, the army will founder. The man must be flogged."

"Your man or mine?" the major asked politely.

The colonel's voice tightened. "What is your point, sir?"

Major Ward looked him squarely in the eye and said, "I will have my private punished to same extent and degree as you will have your own. No more and no less. If that is not satisfactory to you, Colonel, you can take the matter before General Varnum or General Greene and request a court-martial."

“It is absurd to punish a man for…pushing.” Murmurs of assent from his men.

Ward nodded. “I understand, sir. And it is hard for me to punish my man for a blow that didn’t fall. For my part, I would be content to let the matter drop. Our generals are busy with the concerns required for army’s success, and I imagine they will be grateful not to be troubled with this.” He nodded toward Mingo Rodman.

The colonel frowned, another British cannon coughed, and, as he glanced nervously in its direction, said he would discuss the matter further with him in private this evening. The Connecticut men muttered in disappointment and straggled back to their trenches. Once they were gone, the major walked over to Mingo Rodman and said, “If I hear any more trouble about you, you will be whipped. And when that is done, I will send you out to pick up every spent cannonball between here and the enemy lines. Understood?”

“Yes, suh,” said Mingo Rodman.

After the major left, Rodman gave a faint hint of a satisfied smile and returned to digging. And whatever it was that caused Guy’s stomach to clench into knots eased.

*

THAT NIGHT GUY WAS put on all-night sentry duty. The army’s password was “Revere,” after a famous man from Massachusetts, now a militia officer, who had just arrived to join the fight. But the big question about arrival on everyone’s mind was still this: where were the French? If the Americans kept inching toward the British at this rate, they wouldn’t reach Newport before winter.

But inch they did. And as the days passed, still no sign of the French fleet.

In the heat and idleness, the men began to get dysentery and putrid fever. Two new arrivals in Guy’s regiment fell ill with smallpox.

Once again, volunteers started to head home in shoals while others were sent to the mainland hospital. The numbers began to shift in favor of the British and Hessians.

The French fleet suddenly appeared on the horizon off Brenton's Point.

✷

THE AMERICAN ARMY WAS electrified at the news. All old gripes and conflicts were forgotten. Companies began to huzzah and cannons fired up and down the American lines. They knew fortune had now shifted powerfully back to their side. The time had come at last to do what they came for—take Newport.

✷

ON THE MORNING OF August 20, Sam Ward heard the cheering and cannon fire all the way at General Varnum's farmhouse headquarters a mile away. He and the other officers had done their own cheering when the news of the French arrival reached them an hour before. Since then, though, the news had turned less exultant. While all the French ships had miraculously survived their encounter with the British and the great storm, Count D'Estaing's own command ship, the *Languedoc*, had been dismasted and lost her colors. The officers assured themselves, though, that if the French could sail well enough to make it back, they were more than able to do the little that was required now. With their guns and their army on sea, joined with the Americans' on the ground, nothing but another cataclysmic storm could save the British now. The northern army under Gates, Arnold, and Morgan would not be the only victorious group! And the French-American alliance will be off to a glorious start. A successful stroke here, and it was not hard to think that the British would start to consider giving up the entire war.

And so when he was back at the lines the next morning, spirits high, ordering extra food to be cooked and all cartridges checked, Sam was astonished to hear the news brought by the Count de Cambis on behalf of Admiral D'Estaing.

The French fleet would come no closer to Rhode Island. It was on its way to Boston for repairs.

Two days later, at midnight, despite reasoned appeals from Phebe's father Governor Greene offering to repair the fleet in Providence, despite repeated impassioned appeals from General Sullivan, and despite patriotic appeals from the Marquis de Lafayettte for them to remain, the French fleet raised anchor and sailed off to the north to Boston, taking every ship, even the three frigates that had been left behind to guard the American soldiers' crossing.

By midmorning, every man in the army knew about the French departure. The volunteers and militia needed no further prompting. By the thousands, they took what the remaining American officers called, in disgust, "French leave."

When the next day's general orders from General Sullivan said "the General cannot help lamenting the sudden and unexpected departure of the French fleet," Sam had to join Nat Greene at headquarters to help him persuade the outraged the Marquis de Lafayette not to challenge Sullivan to a duel. When they succeeded in that, Sam left Nat to the task of persuading the marquis not to quit and head home to France. This task was not complete two hours later when they got more news: the British had sent a large number of ships from New York to reinforce their besieged soldiers in Newport.

Sullivan still wanted to attack, and he searched for any means to do so, sending urgent appeals for more reinforcements and weighing trying secret landings behind British lines. Every day he rode to the lines in person to cheer the men. Every day, he sent posts to Boston imploring the French fleet to make hasty repairs and return. Every day, Sam could see it all slipping away. The small but steady flow of British and Hessian deserters over the last two weeks stopped and began to flow the other way. Some Continental troops caught an American sneaking his way to the British lines, and the man was hanged the next morning.

Sam was not surprised when the order came to move back to the northern lines. When three British frigates arrived with reinforcements, no word came from the French at Boston, and General Sullivan's latest returns on the army discovered it badly shrunk, he ordered a council of war with all his generals.

They decided, reluctantly, that a secret nighttime retreat was required.

At eight in the evening, at first full dark, the army broke camp. Sam's regiment, some pickets, and a rear guard were left to stoke all the abandoned campfires. By nine o'clock, the artillery and the reserves began their muffled march back to the northern lines. An hour or so later, Sam and the rest of the rear guard pulled in the pickets and began their own march north. By three in the morning, what remained of the army was encamped in the very same lines John Topham had been sent so urgently to seize early in the month. Sam Ward and his men were ordered to man the posts across from Turkey Hill not far from the western road. Under the command of Nat Greene, they were to anchor the right wing of the army.

In Sam's pocket was the fifth letter he had written to Phebe since they landed. He sat on a rock near a new campfire and in its flickering light attempted to finish the letter. He knew what tomorrow would bring, and he did not know when he would get another chance to complete it. He had learned never to underestimate the British ability to seize an opening. This was a big one.

*

Guy awakened with a start and lifted his cheek from his musket stock. He had dozed off for a moment, something he had done half a dozen times fitfully in the night. There was a crackling sound up ahead, and it was becoming steadily more distinct. He smelled, faintly at first then unmistakably, the acrid smell of burned gunpowder.

They were coming.

He licked his dry lips. He and the men had not eaten in a day nor slept in a day and a half. He looked along the breastworks. In the reddish orange of dawn, everyone—privates and officers alike—was staring across the muddy stream at two low gray stone fences, and a cornfield over at the slope of Turkey Hill. The cornfield, still green, had not a single ear left on its spindly stalks. To their right a few hundred yards off were the beginning reaches of the beach.

Sergeant Spink told him on the march last night that General Prescott—the very man Guy and Jack Sisson had helped capture in his nightclothes from his mistress's bedroom just one summer ago—was back in command of the British forces. And the man Prescott had been released in exchange for—the ugly man with the dogs Guy had seen early in the war, who everyone marked as a great hero—was now under arrest by order of General Washington for failing to obey orders while under fire.

Maybe Master John was right, he thought. *Maybe he had been freed in order to die.* He tried to shake off the thought. He thought of June and their child, and focused on the idea that they were alive somewhere in the world, and then considered his regiment's position. Major Ward had placed them carefully in a well-made redoubt. If they were a bit in advance of the rest of the extended lines, they were also solidly entrenched, unlike the men in improvised works of the regiments hidden among trees and bushes to their right and left. Not only was their defensive ground higher, but there were bunches of sharpened branches tied together and set into the approaches of their slope. Major Ward knew what he was doing.

They waited. Ichabod Northrup looked up and down their lines and said at least they were in a good place. Primus Babcock gave his head a small shake and said that strongest points were just where the enemy would want to attack. "Break it, and ever'thin' around it go, too."

The officers passed among them, Spink and Thompson and Lewis and the rest, repeating that they must stay where they were until they were ordered to retreat—or to charge. And they repeated what they should expect to see in the course of the morning. An attack on them would probably come from their left near the western road. Colonel Laurens and his light corps were up there with orders to resist and retire, resist and retire. If the enemy was just scouting them out, Laurens would stop them. If it were a real attack, Laurens and his men would come, probably at a run, for the lines. Some of them might be wounded and bleeding, most would look scared. This, the officers said, was all right. It was to be expected. But, they repeated over and over, as if instructing small children, it was the First Rhode Island's job to stay right where they were. They were to let the Americans pass. Then, when they were ordered, they must open fire on the pursuing British and Hessian troops and reload as fast as they were able.

The sound of musket fire grew louder, its distant pops sharpening now into loud cracks. It appeared that Colonel Laurens was doing more resisting than retreating. Though the morning air was cool at first, the sun had risen above the tops of the trees. Guy felt sweat trickle down his back. His fingers tightened on his musket.

All of a sudden, from behind them a large crowd of American militia and regulars came running. They passed right through and over the First Rhode Island's defensive lines and headed toward the gunfire. Within two minutes, they had disappeared over the breast of Turkey Hill. There was a lull of comparative silence, and from behind him Guy could hear Major Ward talking to the captains. He explained that because the firing had gone on for so long, General Greene and General Sullivan had sent reinforcements to the advance guard.

"They are under the same order as Laurens," Ward explained. "Resist and retire. Make sure if they retreat this way that the men let them through."

Guy rehearsed in his mind the orders they were going be given: *First rank, ready! Fire!* And then he would have to step back, kneel, prime, and reload, just as they had practiced a thousand times. He touched his cartridge pouch, feeling the reassuring bulk of his thirty carefully prepared cartridges.

Captain Lewis paced behind them, telling them to examine their bayonets and make sure they were properly sharpened and securely fastened. He then began to say, over and over as he passed behind them, that they were to stay calm, steady, not fire until ordered, to be sure if the enemy came up the hill at them to fire low, between their knees and their belts, no higher. "And remember, tighten your finger on the trigger. Squeeze, don't yank."

Behind them, on a hill higher than their own, men in black artillery uniforms and leather skull caps readied their cannons. The sun's raking light had grown yellow.

Soon men would appear. Men he had never seen before, and they would be trying with every fiber of their being to kill him. This seemed at once unimaginably strange and perfectly familiar, as if something long hidden was going to, at last, make itself known. The musket fire was growing louder.

The man on his left, Caesar Wells, and the man on his right, Walley Allen, both stiffened. And all at once, at the top of Turkey Hill, the Americans were retreating down the slope. A few turned and fired, but none of them stopped to reload. They came at a steady trot—and some of them in a panicked run—straight back to the lines. As they passed on either side of the First Rhode Island's redoubt, panting, Guy recognized some faces from the Connecticut militia positioned on their flank. Maybe they complained about having to "work like niggers," but unlike thousands of other soldiers who had picked up and gone home, they at least were still there. And if they were militia, and the militia usually didn't fight well, at least they had done something. His life depended on theirs, and, in a few moments, their lives would depend on his. Captain Lewis called to the men, "Let them pass!"

The men of Laurens' corps did not continue their retreat through the lines as the Connecticut militia had. They took up new positions along the stone fences and in the thickets and gullies near the brook. One of them, a man in blue and buff on a big roan horse, pulled a sword and held it high, galloping along the newly formed lines and shouting orders and encouragement. Lieutenant Thompson said, his gruff voice full of approval, "That's Laurens himself. A great man." Laurens sent a whole detachment of men into the cornfield down to Guy's right. They disappeared into its neat rows like water into sand. Occasionally Guy could see the thin line of a tamping rod lift into the air as the men reloaded. Colonel Laurens hid himself and his horse. Then, all at once, it was silent. A squirrel behind them chirred and chittered. Guy could hear Caesar Wells and Walley Allen breathing.

And then they appeared at the brow of the hill, men in blue and gold coats, white breeches, black boots, their faces darkened with gunpowder from their own musket fire. Some of them had on huge helmets that gleamed brassily in the morning light. Drums in the distance began a steady metallic flamming.

"Hessians," Captain Lewis said. "Anspachers."

They began to march down the hill.

Guy could see them clear as day, their thick uniforms, wigs, webbed belts, and helmets. They marched leadenly, one of them carrying a blue flag with a gold lion on it, its fabric luffing gently in the offshore breeze. It occurred to Guy they must be tired. These men had marched all the way from Newport that morning, and then fought continuously for the last hour under an August sun. Their wave of gold, blue, and white came steadily on. Suddenly, to their left appeared men in green coats carrying long rifles, and still farther to their left a small knot of men in red coats. When these last men came into view, the officers began to curse, hatred thickening their voices. Sergeant Spink said those red-coated bastards were Fanning's Loyalists, American men from Newport who had chosen to fight with the British.

To their right yet another group of blue uniformed Hessians appeared, most of them on horseback. They were galloping down the slope, the horses' hooves tearing up the turf beneath. Behind them, their foot soldiers were coming at a run. They headed right toward the cornfield, veering off only at the last moment. Lieutenant Thompson said, "Watch the chasseurs. Look! They're going right past the cornfield."

The horses and men came so close to the field and extended along it so far, Guy wondered if Laurens and his soldiers had secretly withdrawn. But they hadn't. There was a rattle of loud pops, and then another. Puffs of smoke appeared above the green stalks. Hessian horses reared and shrieked, blue-coated soldiers toppled. The infantry who had been marching steadily down Turkey Hill stopped, bunching themselves, rapidly deployed into groups of three tight ranks. The first crouched low, the second knelt, the third stood behind. They prepared to fire but could not find a target.

Behind him, Guy felt, then heard, the American artillery boom. Balls whistled over their heads. It was hard not to duck behind the earthworks, but he made himself remain where he was. He watched for the landing of the balls. Finally, they splashed dirt and rocks all along the brow of the hill, some of their fragments just missing the bunched ranks of the Hessians. Firing at random and fanning out into a line, the Hessians began slowly to back up the hill.

Within five minutes, the enemy was nowhere to be seen. The cavalry at the cornfield had gathered its dead and wounded, leaving only a dead horse behind as evidence they were ever there.

The New England troops all cheered their approval of Colonel Laurens and his men. Laurens appeared on horseback, gave new orders to his men, and sent three soldiers back to get more powder and shot. He still would not retreat to the lines.

"Is it ovah?" Walley Allen asked, his voice hoarse.

In the silence they could hear cannon fire and muskets crackling from the direction of the east road.

Major Ward ordered the men to stay ready. "If they come now, they will come hard," he said. Though it was only nine in the morning, he ordered a gill of rum mixed with water to be issued to every man, officers as well.

"Liquid bravery," Captain Lewis said, and cheerfully drained his cup.

In a half hour, the Hessians would not be so tired, nor would they be surprised. They knew now exactly where the lines and artillery emplacements were.

Guy looked at the men to his right and left. He heard no nervous laughter or joking. Some of the men were shaking, others were drenched in sweat. Toney Ross, a boy of seventeen, was a new recruit and he was so frightened, his eyes threatened to roll back into his head every time he blinked.

He glanced at the officers and noticed Major Ward standing alone on the slope behind them. He was standing very straight and still, his arms folded across his chest, and he was studying the men carefully, his eye stopping on one, pausing, and then moving slowly on to the next. The set of his face was determined. When he saw Guy looking at him, he nodded, and then his eyes moved on.

The sun grew higher and the dew on the grass dried. As the shadows were pulling themselves in under the summer light, voices started to call from the direction of the beach. Captain Lewis backed up the hill and raised his spyglass.

"British ships," he said. "One…two…three. Four. Gunports open."

Within minutes the men-of-war opened fire, aiming straight for the Rhode Islanders' redoubt. Primus Babcock was right. If you wanted to take a house down, you take out its strongest supports. Though the balls fell short, they could feel their concussion as they thudded into the earth. The batteries had not yet found the range. As their hands tightened on their muskets, they all began to hear it: drums rattling and pipes sounding almost merry from the far side of Turkey Hill.

Then they heard a long, strange, loud buzzing, like a thousand giant wasps boiling out of a nest, and then enraged and triumphant voices screaming together as if from a single lung, their banshee sound raising the hackles on the back of Guy's neck. The screaming Hessians came at a trot over the hill and straight toward them.

He could see Colonel Laurens' thin string of defenders sight their weapons along the stone fences and from the gullies and thickets where they had moved from the cornfield. They fired, and though a few of the enemy toppled, the rest came headlong at them in a huge crowd. The Hessian chasseurs rode right into the cornfield this time, their swords swinging and thrashing. Soon they could see Laurens' detachment withdrawing from the back of the field and running toward the lines. Some of his men waited too long and were caught in hand-to-hand fighting, others getting overrun before they had a chance to flee. Hessian bayonets flashed in the sun, some of them raised high in the air before they came down on the fallen Americans. Guy watched one of them stamp his boot hard on a man's chest in order to pull out the blade.

Guy felt a jolt of pure fear. It was not the hold-your-breath anxiety he felt rowing past the British man-of-war with Colonel Barton and Jack Sisson, nor the mouth-drying nervousness when he saw the white puff of a cannon aimed in his direction. As the Hessians came and came and came toward him, he was seized by a cold fist of dread that squeezed all his life and force into his eyes. He looked at them, transfixed. A second passed. Then another. The fist loosened. He could breathe, blink. Walley Allen was shaking and crying. There was an acrid ammonia smell in the air. Someone nearby had wet his pants. Guy wondered if he himself had done so.

The artillery behind them fired. A moment later it struck soldiers still coming over the crest of the hill. The ones who had reached the brook and the gully below them remained untouched and drove on, faster, straight toward them.

"Let the Americans through," Captain Lewis said behind him in a firm voice. "Don't shoot until you hear my order. Be ready now. Be ready."

More British cannons fired from the ocean. The drums and the screaming grew louder. "Steady," Captain Lewis said. "First rank! Take your positions," he called.

Guy settled himself at the breastworks. He checked his bayonet and firing pan for the tenth time, leveled his musket. The Hessian huzzahs had grown so loud, it was hard to hear the officers.

"Second rank! Prepare!" He could feel the men behind him locking in.

It had looked all this time as if the Hessians were heading straight for their position, but as they reached the bottom of the slope, a group of green-coated jaegers knelt and leveled their rifles. "*Both ranks! Heads down!*" the captain called. Guy did as he was told. A second later there was a crash of rifles. Guy could hear the zipping buzz of bullets pass just over his trench. Most of the command officers had not ducked, and Guy was looking at Captain Lewis as he began swearing. He held his hand in the air. There was a bloody hole between his left thumb and forefinger. He dug into his pocket and wrapped a cloth around it, tied it with his teeth, and then was back telling the men to remain steady. "Your chance to prove yourselves is almost here, men."

Major Ward, his face stony, called for the first rank to ready. The captains echoed him all up and down the line. Guy could hear the flintlocks cocking back and locking. The first rows of the loyalist units and the Hessian infantry began to fire. Musket balls, bigger, louder, and slower than the rifle bullets, buzzed overhead. Right in front of him, two puffs of dust kicked up where balls slugged themselves into the earth, the dust close enough to spray his face. The first rows of Hessians took two steps forward, knelt to reload, and those behind them opened fire.

A man two people to his left, Philo Phillips, screamed in pain. His musket clattered to the ground. Between his clutching fingers, blood poured from his shoulder. Guy was panting with fear and excitement, his finger tightening on the trigger. He wanted to shoot. Why wasn't the major saying fire yet? Guy aimed his weapon where the blue coats and brass helmets were densest. They were coming on faster now, their guttural yells swelling in their throats. The warships in the bay fired again, and he steeled himself for the impact of the cannonballs. Moments later, the ground thudded under him. The balls had fallen short.

At last he heard the major's voice over the din. "*First rank, FIRE!*" he called. Captain Lewis did not even have time to repeat the words when the first hammers dropped. Flame shot out the long barrels and Guy felt his musket jump in his hands. Suddenly, smoke was everywhere so densely he could not see if he had brought anyone down. They could not linger to see. Just as they had drilled over and over and over, he and the rest of the first rank dropped back two paces and began to reload.

"*Second rank, ready!*" the major called. Guy was working to clean out his warm, smoking barrel with the ramrod and a bunched rag. He did not look up. "*Second rank, FIRE!*" Guy heard the crackling of massed fire above him and fumbled for a new cartridge to push down the mouth of the musket. Time, which had passed so unbearably slowly as he waited to pull the trigger, now torrented past like a waterfall. No matter how he urged them, he could not make his hands perform their tasks fast enough. Above him, he pictured the helmeted Hessians drawing nearer and nearer.

"*First rank, ready!*" Major Ward said.

He primed his musket, pricked the powder in the firing pan, and cleared the flint. Captain Lewis repeated the major's order. Guy threw himself back into the breastworks. He sighted his musket and found, to his surprise, that the Hessians had barely advanced at all. A number of them lay sprawled on the ground. The American regiments to their left and right opened fire. He took aim at a tall man in a green and gold coat who had just finished firing his rifle.

"*First rank, FIRE!*"

He squeezed the trigger and his musket jumped again. The man in green knelt down and began to reload, undisturbed. Guy realized he had missed. Just before he dropped to reload, he saw the Hessians begin to back slowly toward the brook, helping their wounded off with them. Guy and his entire regiment, under orders, fired twice more. Though the enemy was soon out of range, Lieutenant Thompson says it wasn't bad to practice. Though the Hessians had withdrawn, Captain Lewis pointed out with his bloodied hand that they were reforming their lines at the top of Turkey Hill.

"It is not over yet," he called. "All of you, ready your weapons! First line, prepare to take positions."

In the ensuing silence as they worked, Guy could clearly hear Major Ward cursing at Toney Ross and two other of their newest recruits. They had fired their muskets and then cowered behind the breastworks without even attempting to reload. One of them had even attempted to run off. The major struck him with the flat of his sword and told him to act like a man. He pointed at the grimacing but silent Philo Phillips who was being looked at by a surgeon's assistant. "Like him," Major Ward said angrily. He swept his sword along their entire lines. "Like everyone else here."

The Hessian drums began once again to clatter and roll, again their throats swelled with terrible cries, and again they marched forward. The British ships boomed their cannons once more, this time striking men in the regiment in the lines to their right. Their cries of agony were even louder than the Hessians' cry to battle.

Guy looked out over the brook toward Turkey Hill. The enemy was massing to attack directly upon their redoubt, aimed at them like an arrow. The Hessians' trot broke into a flat run toward them, and with a great series of blasts, the American artillery opened fire. Guy stared in disbelief as the right shoulder and chest of a green-coated jaeger simply disappeared. Gaps appeared in their lines as men were flattened by grape and ball. Still, the others came on, remorseless as an ocean wave.

Something like silence fell over the tense American lines. Neither side was in effective range. Peering down their muskets and rifles, they awaited their orders. To Guy the sun suddenly seemed brighter, colors sharper, smells more intense. He was less afraid this time. They stopped them once. If they could do it once, they could do it again. He sighted his barrel on a man in a high brass helmet and blue coat at the center of the wave. Captain Lewis told them to hold steady. The first rank of Hessians dropped to their knees and opened fire. Dust kicked up all around them and lead bees buzzed overhead. The second rank of the enemy fired, then the third.

Major Ward was letting them get too close this time, he thought. He could see their powder-blackened features and sweat glistening on their faces. Some of them reached the first bundles of branches at the bottom of their redoubt. Guy's fingers tightened around the trigger. Why weren't they being told to fire? He wondered if the major had been shot. The Hessians worked closer, and he kept his weapon sighted on the tall man. They were so close now, he could hear their panting between their yells. Finally, he heard Ward's voice, loud and firm: "*First rank, fire!*"

Some opened fire without waiting for Captain Lewis to repeat the order. Guy waited, though, and in that moment the man at whom he had been aiming fell. Quickly, he pivoted the barrel to another man and pulled the trigger. The helmeted Hessian flinched, his rifle dropped, and he grabbed his upper arm, his teeth showing whitely from behind his lips. Guy felt the second rank pressing in behind to take their places at the breastworks. He dropped back to reload.

The Hessians had reached high up on slope of the redoubt. As he reloaded, Guy felt Ichabod Northrup, the man to his left, unbend himself to prepare to fire for the second time. Guy hurried his cartridge down the barrel, and then he felt Ichabod shuddering violently. He looked up to see that a musket ball had entered at the bridge of his nose and come out the back of his head. Bluish-white, blood-covered brain matter spattered on Guy's arm. His gorge rising into his throat, Guy forced himself back to the line. Aiming at the first white crossed belt he saw, he waited for the major's command. Behind him, a surgeon's assistant dragged Northrup's body away.

They fired again, and the lines were so densely covered in acrid, eye-burning smoke, it was hard to see if their musket balls reached their target. He reloaded and fired, reloaded and fired in an almost mechanical sequence. He heard screams from men nearby and from the enemy who came steadily on toward their breastworks. The regiment to their left was having to fight hand to hand against the Hessians and face their terrible bayonets. In fascination and horror, the men found it a spectacle, hard not to watch. The officers began to yell at them to reload and prepare to fire yet again.

When he threw himself to the line, he saw the Hessians were withdrawing, slowly, on all fronts. They only took the wounded they could reach without coming under point-blank fire.

This time there was no cheering from the American lines. They were too numbed even to consider it. Most of them were praying it was over. The Rhode Island regiment knew how very close the enemy had come to their lines. Sergeant Spink said another thirty feet and they would have been in the redoubt.

Guy wondered what the Hessians made of the fact that almost every man in this forward area of the right flank was black.

They had been close enough now to look right in their faces and see it confirmed. He would not be surprised at all, if they thought that black soldiers would not defend their position strongly, though it was also possible the last two failed charges could persuade them otherwise. A deerfly buzzed above his head and then settled on his sleeve where the bloody remains of Ichabod Northrup were smeared.

Chapter Thirty-Five

Major Ward ordered a barrel of plain water to be wheeled in. No rum this time. With his mouth and throat dry and thickened with burned gunpowder, Guy thought he had never tasted anything so good in his life—sweet, cool, clear water.

As they drank and cleaned and reloaded their weapons, they could see that General Greene had ordered cannons toward the beach to reply to the British ships, and a large number of reinforcements to the lines to their right and left began to arrive. Guy checked his cartridge and powder supplies. They were half gone. Time lost its shape in the quiet, and he found it difficult to make his mind attend to anything for more than a few seconds at a time. Fragments of pictures of what had already passed came in splinters into his head, a sound, a look, a smell, but nothing came into focus.

Nothing until they saw new British batteries unlimbering on Turkey and Quaker Hills directly across from them.

The day was not over.

Guy noticed that their reinforcements were almost entirely militia. He looked for Young John in the ranks but could not find him.

In the early afternoon, as the sun's heat gathered in dense waves around them, the British artillery opened fire.

*

Over and over again, Sergeant Spink insisted the Hessians were just showing them what they would be in for if they attempted to counterattack. "You needn't worry," he said. "They're only trying to frighten us." He said this to the men and to the officers. Everyone wanted to believe him, and many did, all the way up to the moment they heard the drums roll once more. Spink peered out over the edge of the redoubt in disbelief. "Great God in heaven," he said quietly. "They are coming again."

For the third time that day they heard the long guttural howling buzz of Hessian huzzahs. This time, they were louder than ever before. Guy looked at the Massachusetts and Connecticut men on their right flank and saw they were ready. He looked at the Rhode Islanders on their left and found himself looking right at the sweating, miserable, pallid face of Young John Hazzard. He was not much farther away than the first Hessian he had sent a musket ball toward. The boy's terrified face made his own unease deepen.

"Present as first rank!" Captain Lewis called.

Guy threw himself into the breastwork and leveled his musket. He soon saw why the enemy's yelling was so much louder. There were two, maybe three times more of them than ever before. The slope of Turkey Hill could scarcely be seen through the blue and gold coats, bristling bayonets, and high gold helmets.

In reserve on the flank were the group of red-coated Newport Americans who had chosen to fight with the British. Onward the Hessians marched, and this time their stiffened legs kicked out rather than lifted, as if they were on parade.

There were so many, Guy wondered how they could possibly stop them this time.

The enemy made its disciplined way down the slope, over stone walls, past the empty cornfield, across the brook. The American cannons fired with a whump, and a few Hessians went over like tipped bottles, but the rest came on, faster now in a headlong mass up the slope. The green-coated jaegers stopped and aimed their long rifles at the redoubt. Major Ward ordered them to keep their heads down. The bullets zinged overhead, though this time they appeared to be aimed at the cannons behind them. Guy, huddled behind the earthworks, glanced behind and noticed two artillerymen go down.

"*First rank, ready!*" the major called over the Hessians' blood-curdling cries.

Guy threw himself against the walls, leveled his weapon, and waited for the order to fire. At the bottom of the slope that rose to their position, the attackers suddenly began to divide to the left and right like a swarm of ants filing around a puddle and began to drive toward the regiments on either side. A smaller force at the rear of the Hessian assault continued on straight at them. Again, Major Ward waited, waited, waited. There were shouts and screams and guns firing from the men on their left and right, but still Major Ward waited. The Hessians, in fresh uniforms and their faces unstained with burned powder, came up the slope faster than any had in the previous charges. Guy watched them come, feeling as if he were in the midst of a terrible dream out of which he could not wake. He sighted his long barrel on a huge man coming straight at him. He waited the unbearable interval for an order to fire, the man looming before him like a monster in the dark.

Finally, the order came.

The flintlock fell and his musket jumped in his hands. He was certain he hit the man, yet the Hessian kept coming up the hill as if he had been bitten by a deerfly and not struck by a musket ball large as the end of a man's thumb.

Guy hurried to reload but he could not keep himself from looking at the Rhode Island militia to their left. He saw Young John, slack-faced and panic-stricken. His regiment had fired twice and was struggling to reload as the Hessians drew closer. Young John, his widened eyes darting wildly around, began to back away from the lines. His captain yelled something to him, but he backpedaled as if he had not heard a word. As Guy watched, it looked like a sand bar collapsing: others in the boy's area seemed to catch his panic. First one, then another, then an entire mass began to back away with him, streaming around their screaming captain. By the time Young John turned to his heels and ran, two-thirds of his regiment was following behind.

He saw Major Ward draw his pistol and raise his sword, calling for the ranks to be ready. For the first time that day, Guy lost his rhythm and fell behind in his loading. By the time he joined his rank at the breastworks he had no time to do more than point and pull the trigger. A boy, no more than seventeen, his helmet fallen off, his light brown hair tousled in the offshore breeze, was hit. The boy, looking proud and excited at having come so far, dropped his weapon and clutched his throat with both hands. He fell. Guy could hear him gagging. Feeling sick at what he had done, Guy crouched to reload and was shocked that the American lines to their left and right were in full, headlong retreat, with the biggest hole created right where Young John had fled.

In a few moments, the redoubt would be surrounded.

Some of the privates who had seen the retreats all around them began to panic, and a few of them stood up to flee. Major Ward raised his sword and began to curse at them, driving them back to the lines and threatening to kill the first man who tried to leave. He leveled his pistol at Toney Ross, the major's blue eyes blazing with rage, and said, "Pick up your musket, Private. Now, Goddamn it, or I will pull the trigger."

Ross was more frightened at the usually mild major's fierceness than he was of the oncoming Hessians. He threw himself back into the lines and fumbled to reload.

"*Look to your bayonets!*" the major called. "*Remember your training!*"

The officers rallied the men. Guy saw he would not have time to reload.

"*First and second rank! Present as one rank!*"

Everyone pressed themselves into the breastworks, corporals, sergeants and lieutenants with them. Guy wondered how many more seconds they would live.

The first Hessians appeared at the brow of the redoubt in a crouch, shrieking in triumph, their bayonets poised to plunge.

They had practiced two responses with the bayonet—parrying and thrusting or, if they were in a trench, to come straight up under an attacking man's defense before he could jump in. The Hessians at the top appear confused, as if they had expected the First Rhode Island to run like the rest. The corporals, sergeants, and lieutenants opened fire and shot half a dozen. Guy saw out of the corner of his eye Mingo Rodman throwing an attacker back like a sack of flour. In a blur of movement a Hessian came from nowhere, remarkable in so large a man, and his bayonet was through Walley Allen's shoulder before Guy even knew what had happened. The next instant, Guy was falling over backward and his bayonet was coming out the Hessian's back. Walley was screaming in pain, and the bleeding, sour-smelling German was groaning. Guy could not pull his musket free. Over the blue uniform of the heavy man's shoulder, he could see to the left and right of them Hessians pouring toward them in a great rush. Guy felt the hope drain out of him like water pouring out of a blown barrel. He had seen how they bayoneted even unarmed men who were trying to surrender. They were dead, all of them.

*

Sam could not believe he had misjudged Nat Greene. Convinced that his regiment was safer in a strong defensive position than in a retreat, he held the redoubt at all costs. He knew that American resistance had crumbled on all sides of them. He knew that there were no prearranged fallback positions. If they left, the entire wing would collapse. Men would lose contact with each other and their officers.

Chaos would reign and the retreat would become a rout, the army caught helplessly between the Hessians and the sea.

Nat knew, as all the officers knew, that the militia could never stand up to a bayonet charge. Nat promised to hold a reserve for a counterattack, but where was it? The Hessians were not only coming at them from the sides but from the rear—they could not even hope to file off toward the beach, his only retreat plan. It stunned him to think that his men, who had fought so well and so bravely, repelling three determined assaults by some of the best soldiers in the world, were going to be abandoned at the day's end by Nathanael Greene, his oldest friend.

And then he saw the oncoming Hessians' faces. They were double-time marching, but not in good order for a final assault. Seconds later they were running for their lives, their faces masks of fear and panic. And finally they could hear the American fifing and drumming, the bright yells and triumphant hollering of Continental and militia soldiers alike. They were coming from the woods in swarms, Nat having released the reserve at last like a coiled spring.

The retreating Hessians ran pell mell in all directions around their redoubt like a creek flowing around a rock. They did not slow down for their wounded nor to help a fallen comrade. The spectacle was so exhilirating Sam forgot for a moment that he had to give orders and, instead, just found himself watching the wonderful sight of the enemy running for their lives. Behind them a few moments later came Colonel Angell's Second Rhode Island, Colonel Livingston's Light Corps, and General Lovell's Massachusetts militia, all running after the panicked Hessians.

"*Prime and load!*" Sam called out. As the first wave of the pursuing American soldiers passed, Sam raised his sword high in the air and spoke the words he had waited this entire long war to give: "*Prepare to charge!*"

*

As dark began to fall, they made their way back to the lines. Their ammunition was low and they had not eaten or slept for two days. Tomorrow would bring more challenges, and they had to be ready.

His throat raw from yelling and breathing in the thick smoke of burned gunpowder, Sam congratulated his officers. With a few exceptions, like Toney Ross among the newest recruits, the men fought remarkably well. If he could have, he would have ordered double food and rum portions for them all. Instead, he saw they were properly tented and made his way to headquarters to report the returns and tell General Nathanael Greene that, next time, please commit the reserves just a few minutes earlier.

He could not find Nat, but an aide he didn't know clapped him on the shoulder and told him he was sorry he had such a hard time of it. Sam shrugged. They had two dead, nine wounded, and eleven missing—superb numbers considering what they had been through. He got some vinegar to splash himself with for the camp itch and returned to the lines to try to doze for a while.

The next morning he found that Nat's aide and some others at headquarters had been left with the impression that Sam was unhappy with his regiment's conduct under fire. He was told as he waited outside headquarters that General Sullivan had been up all night exploring the possibilities of pursuing an attack on Newport. Morning brought news that the French would not be leaving Boston for weeks, and the British fleet of a hundred sail was bearing down on them. The Americans were going to have to retreat to the mainland.

Sam was called into a meeting with Colonel Topham, General Varnum, Nat Greene, and General Sullivan himself. Though they were all as exhausted as he, he was surprised to find a tense atmosphere. He had assumed that he and Colonel Greene were going to be given orders for the retreat. Instead, all eyes turned to Sam.

"We wanted to raise this with you directly, Major," General Sullivan said, his usually florid face pale and his bright eyes dulled with fatigue. "We hear that you were highly dissatisfied with your regiment's conduct."

"No, sir," he said firmly. "That is not correct. My officers were excellent and the privates and corporals did extremely well for men who had never seen fighting before."

Sullivan's eyebrows lifted. "This is most puzzling. We have received half a dozen reports that you encountered censurable and even mutinous behavior in your ranks."

"Reports? From whom, general?"

The commanding general moved aside a few papers on his field desk and said, "The Connecticut militia reported serious discipline problems."

"We did have some conflict with them two days before the battle. Perhaps they are referring to that."

"They speak of actions during the fight."

Colonel Topham, his old friend from the march to Quebec, said, "A Rhode Island lieutenant attached to one of my companies reported that during the assault he heard you cursing and having to threaten some of your men with sword and pistol."

Sam had to think for a moment even to recall the incident. "A private or two did appear to quail under fire from time to time, and I did have to speak harshly to them. To be honest, I can scarcely recall what I might have said in the heat of them moment. But I did not want a single one of them to fail at his duty lest the others took it in their heads to follow. I am happy to say they did not."

The officers seemed to relax at hearing Sam's explanation.

"Who is this lieutenant?" Sam asked John Topham.

"Someone who turned and ran against the express orders of his captain. He insisted afterwards that when he saw and heard cowardly and mutinous conduct so widespread among your men, he knew their position was lost. He's trying to save his own skin. We may have to open a court-martial for him."

"You must do as you think best," Nat said, "but first I suggest we must get ourselves off the island safely. Open recrimination will only make that task harder."

"Speaking of which, sir," Sam said, "I should appreciate it if you would personally put a stop to the rumor of misconduct among my men."

"Major?"

Sam was thinking how unhappy his men would be, after all they had been through, to find themselves accused of cowardice. He also knew sentiment alone would not be enough to persuade General Sullivan to write officially on the matter. He racked his fatigued brain for another reason, and one came swiftly to mind. "General, there are a lot of local slave owners who are looking for an excuse to attack the General Assembly for their actions in raising this regiment."

General Sullivan blinked, and Sam could see he was remembering that in addition to being an officer, Sam was the governor of Rhode Island's son-in-law. He nodded.

That afternoon, he received a copy of the general orders for August 30, 1778. He mustered his regiment and read them the orders himself, knowing that each regiment and brigade in the army was hearing exactly the same words. He read aloud its final paragraph with special care. He wanted them all to know that the conduct of a company could be judged by its worst as often as by its best.

"'It having been represented by some persons,'" he read, "'that the conduct of Colonel Commandant Greene's Regiment was not in the action equal to what ought to have been expected, and also that Major Ward who commanded the Regiment was much dissatisfied with their conduct, the General assures the officers and soldiers of the Regiment that no person has undertaken to censure their conduct to him and that upon inquiry from Major Ward and sundry other officers who were with them in this action, there is not the least foundation for censure. By the best information, the commander in chief thinks that the Regiment is entitled to a proper share of the Honors of the Day.—John Sullivan, Major General.'"

His officers nodded but the men looked down at their feet or off into the distance with down-turned mouths. They had not heard about the rumors until now, and now they knew that the rest of the army had not been giving them credit for fighting well during three attacks over a long day.

Sam did not give them time to dwell on it. He ordered them to dig new trenches and cut wood for large campfires. He knew after dark they would be leaving the trenches and striking their tents. They would be igniting the campfires only to abandon them. Their withdrawal, the most perilous part of any island operation, was to be secret. The First Rhode Island would be the very last to leave.

As night fell, the army began to steal away. Sam's regiment remained in the lines putting up a brave front while, all around them, men and horses and equipment were quietly heading toward the harbor and General Glover's flatboats.

When they finally left the lines in the small hours of the cool night, all orders and instructions were whispered. They marched north with muffled tread. Behind them, their abandoned campfires burned at full blaze, stoked with thick logs and destroyed wagons. When their turn came at last, they climbed aboard the flatboats in the harbor, listening for the British frigates that floated not far offshore. They were careful not to utter a single word. As they headed toward Tiverton, Guy could hear only the lapping sounds of the water against the sides. There was a scent of fall in the air. He and the other men of his regiment sat, exhausted, staring into the blue night, wondering if they would live to fight again, or have to fight in order to live.

Chapter Thirty-Six

SAM HAD FOLLOWED THE court-martial carefully. It was not until he saw that John Hazzard had brought a ragged-looking Ebeneezer Tolman all the way down from Massachusetts and found the Connecticut militia colonel whose men nearly got into a brawl with the soldiers of the First Rhode Island that he began to worry. Giving Young John a regimental court-martial had been suggested by his own militia captain to deliver an embarrassing swat on the rump. Requiring five officers and, at most, a morning's deliberation, it promised to be an open-and-shut case that the militia officers felt would conclude in a well-deserved reduction in rank. By the time Young John's father was through, however, he had turned it into a general court-martial requiring thirteen officers and a judge, and instead of deliberating on Young John's offense, it turned into a blistering trial of the character of Guy Watson.

The infamous name of Dr. Church had gotten everyone's anger and attention, and when Church's bespectacled assistant testified that Guy Watson was his regular informant, Sam could feel the sentiment shift in the room like a powerful weather front blowing through.

A trial of Guy Watson was a trial of the new First Rhode Island Regiment. And a trial of the First Rhode Island was a trial of its field commander, Major Samuel Ward. Besmirch one, and you can besmirch them all. Sam knew that Hazzard's main aim was to exculpate his son, just as inflicting these other damages to Sam's honor and reputation was a highly gratifying reward along the way.

Guy Watson was not the only witness against Young John, but he was the first. At least two of the lieutenant's own militia company were prepared to testify about his cowardly behavior under fire. Or, at least, they had been prepared. Sam saw now that it was Master John's intention to show how thoroughly he could discredit anyone who planned to testify against his son, and Guy was his first gaudy illustration. Reports of the trial had filtered out to the other witnesses, and they had already begun to grow less emphatic about what they may or may not have seen Young John do. They had even begun to suggest that perhaps they could not absolutely swear the boy had been the first to run off in panic. There might have been others…it was a confused and difficult time…in the end, they ran, too… And what if John Hazzard decided to put *them* on trial?

And this was why Sam finally asked an old friend and political ally of his father's, Gideon West, Esquire, to step in. At first Attorney West had been reluctant to commit himself, less because of a lack of interest than because of being unwell in recent months. He had, he said, a thick lump in his abdomen that wouldn't go away, and he had lost weight in the last few weeks, though he believed he ate as much as ever. In the end, the old man could not resist the opportunity to set foot back in a courtroom.

*

Sam is shocked at how haggard Gideon looks, his skin faintly yellow, with deep hollows under his cheekbones and his skin hanging on him almost as loosely as his clothes. Still, under his thick gray upswept eyebrows, his dark eyes are bright. What Gideon is looking forward to most, he says, rubbing his bony hands together to generate some warmth this chilly fall morning, is the chance to question John Hazzard's witnesses.

"Had a brief chat with Private Watson," he says. "And I learned some interesting things, when I could make out what he was saying through that accent of his. He's generally truthful, you think?"

"Yes," Sam replies. "That has been my experience."

The old man nods. "I cannot promise much," he says in a gravelly voice. "But I can promise that the Hazzards are no longer going to have it all their way."

*

"GIDEON WEST, IT PLEASES the court, appearing as counsel for Private Guy Watson."

"So noted," says General Varnum from the front table. He turns to Master John. "Proceed, sir."

"I request the court call Sergeant Ebeneezer Tolman."

Guy has not seen Tolman since the march to Quebec, and he is not sure he will recognize him. Clean-shaven, his clothes new, his hair tied back in queue, he looks, today at least, like some prosperous shopkeeper. Guy wonders if Master John has dressed and rehearsed him for the day.

Tolman is sworn in and seats himself comfortably in the witness chair, one leg crossed at the knee and his hands folded, one over the other, neatly in his lap.

"Tell us, Sergeant, when you first encountered the defendant."

"Fort Western, sir, September of seventy-five."

"And why were you there?"

"I was attached to Captain Samuel Ward's company, and so was Guy Watson. We were beginning a march to Quebec under Colonel Arnold."

"Was Guy Watson a soldier?"

"No sir, he was not. He was a servant to the captain."

"What was he doing when you first saw him?"

"Picking out boats for the trip. And in my opinion, and a lot of others, he picked out the worst ones. He was supposed to be good with wood, so we found that strange."

"Anything else?"

"He kept having secret meetings with this man from Colonel Enos's division, some doctor's assistant."

"Ah. The court has already heard testimony about that from the man himself, Enoch Flinter."

Tolman shrugs. "Never knew his name."

"Anything else about the defendant that struck you as odd?"

"He was always off wandering in the woods, digging up roots and lighting candles and mumbling some sort of chants. I think he was trying to put a curse on us. And judging by how things turned out, he damn well succeeded."

Master John frowns for a second at this profane language and shoots a glance of disapproval at the witness, but he quickly moves on. "And when was the last time you saw Guy Watson?"

"Last time I saw him was in the snowstorm we marched through to attack the city of Quebec. He stayed behind, safe and sound and warm as toast."

"And what became of this attack?"

"Everybody knows that. Men were killed and wounded and the rest of us got captured. I was there in that stinking nunnery-turned-jail for eight long months." He turned to the table with the thirteen Rhode Island officers sitting in judgment. "Wasn't I, Colonel Greene? Every word the truth. You can ask him…"

"That won't be necessary, Sergeant. We have your word on it already." With a satisfied smile, Master John returns to his seat.

Gideon West gets up slowly from his chair and glances at some hastily scribbled notes. "Sergeant Tolman, all of us have heard and read about the remarkable journey you, Colonel Greene, Colonel Topham, Major Thayer, and others made through the wilderness, and I just want to say before I ask you a few questions that I have the greatest respect for your extraordinary efforts and heroism in undertaking that fateful march. Our young country owes you a debt that can never be repaid."

Eb Tolman looks as grateful as a hungry cat being offered a bowl of cream. But he shrugs and lifts his eyebrows, as if it was all nothing, really…

"I just had a couple of short questions. I don't want to take up your time. You've traveled a long way to give this testimony, and I imagine you have a long trip back." Tolman nodded gravely. "Did Mister Hazzard give you any money for your inconvenience?"

Tolman stiffens and starts to stutter, "Well…" Master John leaps to his feet and objects to Attorney West bringing up irrelevant questions.

General Varnum reflects for a moment and then asks Ebeneezer Tolman to answer Mr. West's question. "He did give me some money for my troubles."

"Is that all?"

"And he gave me these clothes to wear."

"Very nice clothes they are," says Gideon West in an admiring tone. "How much money did he give you, if I may ask?"

Master John is on his feet again. "General Varnum, if he is implying Sergeant Ebeneezer Tolman is lying under oath, then he should just go ahead and say so!"

"That is not what I mean at all," old man West says mildly, and he turns to Eb Tolman and says, "And I hope you don't think that for a second, Sergeant. I am only curious about the arrangements. There were a good twenty or thirty other Rhode Islanders in Samuel Ward's company, and I found it odd that Mister Hazzard had to go all the way to Weymouth, Massachusetts, to get the testimony he needed. I imagine he could have paid a lot less for someone's inconvenience if he lived closer."

"You've made your point, Mister West," General Varnum says. "Please proceed to your next area of concern."

"Yes, your honor. I'll do that." He turns back to Eb Tolman. "Just a couple of questions. You say you think Guy Watson intentionally picked out bad boats for your company."

"Yessir, I do."

"Correct me if I am wrong on this, but I remember reading that there were just enough boats to go around. Is that right?"

"That's right."

"So even if Guy Watson had not picked bad boats for the trip, another company would have had to use the bad ones anyway."

He glances nervously at Master John. "I suppose so."

"And as you say, your company made it all the way to Quebec, bad boats or no." Tolman nods. "I am not sure the court officers could see you, Sergeant. Are you nodding yes?"

"Yes," he mutters.

"Thank you, Sergeant. Now about these secret meetings Guy Watson was supposed to be having with Enoch Flinter, Dr. Church's former assistant."

Eb Tolman pulls himself up in his seat and brightens. "Yes…"

"How many would you say he had?"

"At least three I know of."

"So they weren't very secret, were they?"

"What?"

"These meetings. If you saw them, they had to be pretty open."

"Well, I didn't trust him one little bit, so I kept a close eye on him."

"You don't know what they were talking about when you saw them together?"

"No."

"Do you have any idea what good any information would be passed from one man in the wilderness to another man in the wilderness?"

"No."

"But I suppose you knew that just after you left on your march, Dr. Church was in jail, under guard and accused of treason."

"No, we didn't hear about Church until we reached Quebec."

"But you do know that this man was from Colonel Enos's division."

"I knew that, all right."

"But Colonel Enos's division turned back when you were about half way to Quebec, did it not?"

"They did, the bastards." Guy sees the veterans Topham, Thayer, and Greene smile humorlessly. "Excuse me for the word, sirs…"

"So from that point on there could be no more secret meetings, could there?"

"I don't follow your meaning."

Gideon West suddenly speaks slowly, as if to a not-very-bright child. "If Enoch Flinter turned back with Colonel Enos, Guy Watson could not have any more meetings with him, could he?"

"Well, the damage was done! Watson probably told him something that made them want to turn back."

The old lawyer snorts. "I see. A slave who can neither read nor write, who is not privy to any of Colonel Arnold's plans until they are announced to the rest of the army, and who spends most of his time hauling bateaux and carrying wood for fires, is going to have information that, when passed to some physician's assistant, will discourage an entire division? Is that what you are telling this court?"

"Could be. Why not? He probably performed some spell."

Gideon West looks silently at Tolman for so long, Guy begins to wonder if the old man is at a loss. Finally, though, it is Tolman who shifts uncomfortably in his chair. West says, "If I understand you, Sergeant Tolman, you are here today to testify that Guy Watson somehow undermined your company's legendary march to Quebec. But as far as I can tell, even if the boats were bad and there were 'secret meetings,' as you call them, or even if evil spells were performed, your company got there even when others did not. Yes or no?"

"We might have gotten there a lot faster with decent boats."

"And Guy Watson could not participate in the assault on the city because he was not then a soldier. When you marched off into that snowstorm, he was not 'warm as toast' before some fire. He was ordered to wait below the Heights in a howling blizzard with half a dozen soldiers and a dozen boats, preparing to help men cross the river in case a retreat was required. I'm sure Colonel Greene can confirm that."

Christopher Greene nods.

"I have no more questions, Sergeant."

*

At a break in the proceedings, Sam asks Gideon West how the trial feels to him. "You mean can I get Watson acquitted? That's a difficult question, Major. The surest way to establish what truly happened is to call Enoch Flinter back. But what if Mister Flinter has damning things to report about what Watson told him? I have had a preliminary interview with him, and the man is slippery as a snake. He claims he thought Dr. Church was gathering intelligence only in his capacity as surgeon general of the army, and he says he never dreamt the man was in communication all the while with the enemy. I fear that once under oath, he may offer information that will make Watson's life more difficult."

"Why do you believe that?"

"According to what I read in the secretary's notes, Flinter's earlier testimony suggests he is very friendly with the Hazzards. If we do not call him back, though, his earlier testimony stands unchallenged."

Sam sighs. "What if the court were asked to drop the whole proceeding against Lieutenant Hazzard? Just let the two cases vanish..."

"From everything you tell me, I suspect that John Hazzard would then insist on following through his pursuit of Private Watson. And with nothing to distract him and the boy no longer on the defensive, he could go after him with a vengeance—say, calling the boy himself to the stand to offer incriminating testimony against Watson."

"What do you suggest?"

"Defend Watson vigorously, get him acquitted if we can, and then consider getting the court to drop the case against Lieutenant Hazzard."

Sam shakes his head ruefully and then nods. "Thank you, Mister West, for your help and counsel. They are much appreciated. And badly needed."

He puts a liver-spotted hand on Sam's shoulder. "Glad to be of service, son. I fear, though, given the situation, you are unfortunately correct. I—or someone like me—*is* badly needed."

*

THAT AFTERNOON, THE HAZZARDS call a witness Guy does not remember ever having seen before. A white woman in her middle thirties named Priscilla Anders had testified under Master John's questioning that these days she works as a midwife. Guy and the rest of the courtroom looks at her, suddenly curious about what she could have to say.

"Where were you working in the summer and fall of seventeen seventy-five?" Master John asks.

"I was working for Dr. Church in his field hospital at the Boston lines."

"And have you ever seen the defendant?" Master John points directly at Guy, still seated at his scarred table.

"I have."

"When was that?"

"He would come by once a week or so to talk to Enoch Flinter, Dr. Benjamin Church's aide-de-camp."

"And why is it you remember it?"

"I thought it was odd seeing this black man, a slave, show up at the hospital and have these nervous, quiet talks with Dr. Church's assistant. And after Dr. Church was convicted of treason, I've often thought back on it."

"Did you ever overhear their conversations?"

"Only twice, and then just little pieces."

"What did you hear?"

"Once it was about the Rhode Island men's powder supply..." Guy sees the hearing officers stiffen in their chairs and two or three of them exchange glances. "And the other time it was about a march to Canada. That would have been in late August. I remember it because Dr. Church was arrested just a few weeks later."

"Thank you, Mrs. Anders. No more questions."

Guy looks at Gideon West. He is rubbing his forehead. He gets up and slowly straightens himself, as if it is painful to do. "Mrs. Anders," he says. "I know you are not a soldier and probably not an expert in such matters, but didn't Dr. Church travel all over the Boston lines and see for himself how well the men were supplied?"

"I believe he did."

Master John rises. "This is all secondhand."

General Varnum nods. "Hearsay," he says.

"Pardon me," Gideon West says. "Did Enoch Flinter not march to Quebec?"

"Yes, he did," Mrs. Anders replies.

"And so did Guy Watson. So what would be so odd about their discussing it?"

"I found out later it was supposed to be a big secret."

"Well, it was not a secret to the men who went, was it?"

"Obviously not. It's just that this conversation happened almost a month before the men left on the march."

The old man frowns. "We all know military planning takes a long time. No further questions."

Master John rises. "Begging the officers' indulgence, we have no more witnesses for the court at this time on the matter of Guy Watson."

✷

GUY IS THERE FOR the conversation Attorney West has with Major Ward when the court session is dismissed.

"I don't like it," Mr. West says. "Hazzard is laying a trap."

"What?" Major Ward asks.

"He is *forcing* us to call Enoch Flinter back to testify. And he knows it. And that means he knows that what Flinter is going to have to say will not be good."

"What if you don't call Flinter back?"

"I can put Watson on the stand, and he will tell them he was just doing what he was told to do by John Hazzard." Guy nods, but neither man seems to be paying him much attention. "And that means we have to put the Hazzards on trial, both of them. But I think the father is ready for that, too. What is his nickname?"

"Gambling John."

"Precisely. And I don't like the odds to the game he is setting up. If we do not play—that is, do not call Flinter to testify—I believe we will lose. If we do play—put John Hazzard on trial as a loyalist—I suspect we may lose there, too. His son is in the militia, his former slave is in the First Rhode Island..." He shakes his head. "Frankly, it looks bad."

"What do you think we should do?"

West's hand goes to his abdomen, and he gives a small wince. "I think we have to call Flinter and see what unfolds. But I do not like the smell of it. Not at all. You know the two militia soldiers who were going to testify against Lieutenant Hazzard?"

"Yes," Major Ward says.

"They have withdrawn their testimony. John Hazzard has been questioning their friends and family and neighbors, and they want no part of it anymore. They flatly refuse to appear. Even his captain has grown shaky."

"So there is no case against him anymore?"

"Just the word of his former servant. From another regiment who happened to see him thirty yards away and in the heat of battle. Can you imagine Hazzard's summation? 'Embittered traitorous former slave trying to get revenge on his old master,' et cetera..."

"It's hopeless, then?"

"We can make the case that whatever information Watson passed along was, in the great arc of things, insignificant, and that he had no idea any of his information was going to the enemy. Or we have to see what Flinter has to say and hope we can somehow outsmart him."

*

IN JAIL THAT NIGHT, alone, Guy draws two lines in the dirt, stands at the point where they cross, and looks out the narrow barred window opening to the night skies. He chants and prays, and feels for the sacred pouch he has tied around his waist, forgetting once again that they have taken it away from him. No water. No trees. He cannot even see the ground outside. A single star hangs in the great dark of the sky. *Mpati!*

He hears nothing, sees nothing. There is the spiced scent of fall in the air.

Chapter Thirty-Seven

"Sergeant Flinter," Gideon West begins. "Before I ask you some specific questions, let me establish a few facts with you. Remember, you are under oath."

Flinter's eyes glint behind his glasses and his birthmark is a faint, dull red at his temple. "I would not forget that, sir. I just took my hand off the Bible."

"Good. First, did you have any idea that Dr. Church was using his position to pass intelligence to the enemy?"

"No, sir, I did not. When I heard the news, I was shocked to the boots."

Guy looks at him, hard. He is almost certain Flinter is lying about this, but he seems so cool and self-possessed, he begins to wonder. "You testified a few days ago that Dr. Church asked you to get Guy Watson employment serving in the officers' dining area. Was this an unusual request?"

"Unusual? What do you mean?"

"Did he ever ask you about employment of servants and low-ranking soldiers?"

"Yes, he did. He liked to see everyone busy, high or low. He had his fingers in many pies."

"Was it unusual that he asked you to meet with Guy Watson from time to time to see what information he could offer about the state of the soldiery?"

"Dr. Church loved to get information from as many sources as he could. I thought it was to help him understand the army's health and general readiness of spirit."

"That was Dr. Church's task, wasn't it?"

"Well, looking back, I would say his job properly would have been to see to the health of the men's bodies and not snoop into their military plans."

"But as surgeon general of the army, he would need to know as much as possible, would he not?"

He turns his long, narrow face directly toward Gideon West. "I was his assistant. I don't feel able to say what a surgeon general of the army ought to do."

Mr. West pauses and looks at Enoch Flinter as if he cannot quite get him into focus. "Did it strike you as suspicious that Dr. Church wanted to know the state of the army's powder supplies?"

"Not at the time. As I say, he wanted to know everything. I got used to it."

"Why would he want to know about the planned march to Canada?"

"I never questioned why he wanted to know something. He was a general. I was still a corporal. He asked me to do something, I did it."

"So you were a bit like a servant."

"Sir?"

"When you had Guy Watson serving the officers their evening meal and reporting to you about what he heard, do you think it was his idea?"

"I don't know what was his idea or not his idea."

"Are you suggesting that Guy Watson was telling Dr. Church what to do?"

"No, sir, not if you put it that way. It was under Dr. Church's orders."

"But why, then, did you have meetings with Guy Watson during the march to Quebec?"

"Well, Dr. Church asked me to send back reports on our progress from time to time. And Watson was in another regiment and knew things I did not."

"Did you do this on your own initiative or at the suggestion of Dr. Church?"

"He said I should check with Watson to make sure my reports were complete."

"Did you know that Dr. Church was under arrest while you were marching north?"

"No, sir! None of us heard until we returned to Cambridge with Colonel Enos."

"Do you know what became of your reports?"

"I only had the chance to send one back with the sick. By the time it arrived, Dr. Church was in jail."

"All right. Let me see if I understand, Sergeant. You are saying you had no idea the information you were passing to Dr. Church might also be passed to the enemy."

"Correct."

"And that, as far as you know, Guy Watson did what he did because, through you, the surgeon general ordered him to."

"Yes, sir."

"And, finally, nothing Watson told you during the march ever reached Church."

"That is true."

Guy can tell the old attorney is pleased with how the questioning has gone. "I have no further questions. Except this. Did you ever meet John Hazzard Sr. or John Hazzard Jr. before this trial?"

"No, sir. Not until Mister Hazzard got in touch with me a week or so back."

Guy remembers clear as day the afternoon many months ago when Enoch Flinter rode onto the Hazzard place and walked right in the door to meet with Master John. Nor will he ever forget Flinter's asking him at the Boston encampments about June Harris. As Master John rises from his chair to take his turn asking questions, Guy knows that the outcome will be bad.

*

"Sergeant Flinter," Master John begins. "Did Guy Watson ever meet directly with Dr. Church?"

"Yes, three times that I know of."

"I see. And were you present for those meetings?"

"No, sir. They happened in the late evening all three times and Dr. Church ordered me out and shut the door."

Guy shakes his head and says, "No! He lie!"

General Varnum bangs a gavel down on the wide hearing table and the sound of it cracks throughout the room. "Silence, Private Watson. Mr. West, would you have your client observe decorum, please?"

The old man mutters that Guy needs to be quiet. He can only speak when he is on the stand.

"But he lie!"

Gideon West nods but raises a bony finger to his lips. "Shh."

Master John waits with a half smile on his face for Guy to settle down. Then he turns back to Flinter. "So you have no idea what was said in those meetings?"

"Well, I did find it curious. I never knew the doctor to meet with a slave before. And I know I shouldn't have, but one time I stood at the door for a minute to listen."

"When was this?"

"A few days before we left to march to Newburyport. Which is where we started our journey to Canada."

"And what did you hear on this occasion?"

"What was odd was that Watson was doing most of the talking. He was talking about having worked for a Simeon Pease in Newport, and that Pease owned ships that sailed to Canada, and that was a way to send messages."

"Anything else?"

"That was it. I never thought about it again until I came here to testify."

"Do you know who Simeon Pease is?"

"I have no idea."

"He is a Newport merchant and a loyalist presently held under arrest in Providence. And indeed he owns ships that have sailed up the Atlantic and then down the St. Laurence to Quebec. Thank you, Sergeant." Master Hazzard turns to the table of officers. "We will be producing witnesses who will testify that Mr. Pease did precisely that."

*

No one needs to tell Guy Watson how terrible it looks for him now. The dejected expression on Gideon West's face belies all the reassurances he gives.

*

This night as he sits on the floor of his cell, his back against the wall, gazing out the barred window, he lacks the spirit to invoke the spirits of his ancestors. Still, he settles himself on the crossing point, hoping to summon the force and focus to use it soon. As he waits, his mind jumps from thought to thought, and splinters of memories and half-formed ideas drift through his consciousness. He thinks of the Hazzard place, the vanished slaves, June and their baby, the smell of the sea, chores he has done for the Hazzards over the years of his life, including the intentionally ill-made privy, and suddenly he remembers making the special compartment under the master's bed and its carefully fitted panel with no handle. Outside he can hear old man West's rumble of a voice. Aiming his own voice at the window, he begins to yell for Mister West as loudly as he can.

*

JUNE MOVED THE MAPLE rocker closer to the warmth of the brick hearth and held the hungry baby to her breast. She crooned to him, wishing she could sing half as well as Lucy. He found her nipple and, with one of his perfect tiny hands resting on her breast, nuzzled in against her intently, his large dark eyes blurring with relief. How much she loved this little creature startled her almost every hour of every day. She knew with every strand of her being there was nothing she would not do for him, nothing. She rocked, slowly. Though it was still September, the air in the daytime was spicy and cold in a way that made her think of November in Rhode Island.

She and the master and mistress had been at Gardinerstown in the Maine territory for over a week now, staying at the large house of one of the Hazzards' friends who had also fled Rhode Island. When they had packed and left under a steady rain in the middle of the night, the Hazzards had given no reason for leaving, only that it was urgent. She had never seen the master so agitated nor the mistress so frightened, and affected by their distress, her hands trembling and heart pounding, June had helped fill the crates and load the carriage with every ounce of strength and speed she could muster. It had been a frantic departure, but she could tell when they packed the dishes and the silverware that they did not expect to be back soon.

She looked up at the night's rain clouds and starless sky and thought for one long moment about running away—this might be her and the baby's own crack of daylight. But where in the world would she go? With Guy in the army, or, worse still, in jail, and a tiny child to raise, who would shelter her this night or any of the nights ahead? The law was still the law, and she still belonged to the Hazzards.

*

Only in the last few days had she been able to piece together some of what happened. One piece of it the Hazzards would never know.

Two days before the Hazzards' panicked departure, Jack Sisson and a young white officer appeared in the middle of the day. Master Hazzard was, as usual, in court in East Greenwich, and this time the mistress had gone with him to visit Young John who they said was to begin his trial that very morning. Ever since June's baby was born, they grew less and less anxious that she would run off, and it was not unusual for them to leave her at the house unsupervised for whole days at a time. On this day, Jack Sisson asked if he and the man with him, Captain Lewis, could enter the house.

"Why?" she asked.

His eyes darted around nervously, and his sped-up voice was that of a man in a hurry. "Guy in trouble at court. Bad trouble."

This was the first she had heard of Guy being in court, though she had heard a great deal from the Hazzards about Young John's plight. "What happen to Guy?" she asked in alarm.

"Master John trying to make him out a spy."

"A *spy*?"

Jack nodded. "He think it goin' get his son off."

She was deeply shocked at this news but, at the same time, convinced the report must be true. Some odd looks and strange, coded expressions between the master and mistress in the last weeks suddenly made sense to her. They had been talking for days with obvious satisfaction about "doing someone in," and that it therefore looked good for Young John. She felt a surge of rage against them.

"What can we do?"

"Guy think something in the Hazzard secret keeping place help."

June looked at him sharply. She was cautious and mistrustful of everyone now. "What place?"

"The place in their bed."

She knew, then, that Guy truly had sent them and, wiping her hands on her apron front, she brought them straight to the bedroom. Captain Lewis had come with him, Jack explained as they mounted the stairs, because the captain could read. Guy had told them the Hazzards kept papers in the secret place, and the captain wanted to take only as few as possible in order not to tip them off that something was missing.

She lifted the heavy gray bedclothes and pushed down the bed apron. There, almost invisible because Guy had matched the grain so well and fitted the door so closely, was a thin rectangular line making a shape not much bigger than a loaf of bread. Jack Sisson carefully set his knife blade in one of the cracks and, moving it to each of the four sides, slowly pried off the panel. Inside, tied in a pale yellow ribbon, was a thick stack of letters and papers and a small ledger book. Captain Lewis took them over to the window to look at them in the full light. First he studied how the ribbon was tied, and then undid it, delicately as a woman might untie a bonnet. Jack kept an anxious watch out the window. She stared at the captain as he unfolded the papers and his eyes began to move swiftly across the page. In less than ten minutes, he was done. His face was grim and angry. He folded and handed three different pieces of paper to Jack Sisson, and then carefully retied the yellow ribbon. They replaced the papers and the ledger, reset the panel, and were ready to leave before she had even straightened the bed apron and smoothed the sheets and blankets.

Before they left the room, though, she asked how Guy was.

The captain turned to her and spoke to her for the first and last time. "He will be a lot better now." He lifted a finger to his lips. "Not a word about this to anyone." Jack Sisson nodded.

*

What she had pieced together since then was this: Master Hazzard, who had a friend among the officers hearing the case against his son, found out the court had gotten hold of some letters that were about to be submitted in evidence. An arrest warrant for the master was being prepared. She heard the name Dr. Church and something about the British commander at Newport. Though she did not understand the references, they were enough to send the Hazzards packing. And now, these many days on, she had also begun to understand what their flight meant.

For the first time in her life, she had seen the Hazzards weep, both of them, sometimes quietly, sometimes stormily, often several times a day. Gone were Master John's bravado and confidence. Gone was the sparkle in Mistress Hazzard's eyes. It was not just their house, land, and livestock they had left behind, leased to a friend for a pittance in the slim hope that their property wouldn't be confiscated. What truly gave them agony was that they had to leave their son behind. When the Hazzards fled, his legal defense fell apart. Staying would have been no help. And from what they had heard by post in the days since, he had been sentenced to jail for many years.

She felt pain and sadness for her master and mistress in a way she could never have done before having her own child. Whatever he was like, Young John once, too, was a baby, their first and in the end their only, and the Hazzards no doubt had felt the same fierce tenderness for him that she now felt for her own. But she had also begun to understand with unspeakable regret that she had left Guy Watson behind, if not to jail then to a life where she could not imagine a way to be able to join him. In this new place in the north, just a few wagon lengths from the front door, the woods were thick and dark. She had seen during their flight up here that there were no towns or even farms for miles, no paths through the woods, and the terrain was rocky and hilly and latticed with fast rivers and streams. Even if she were on her own, she would be afraid of walking out into such a trackless wilderness. But with a baby whose fate depended on hers—the baby the Hazzards forbade her to call Guy, a name she still whispered to him all the times she was alone with him—running away was beyond what she was able to do.

And now the Hazzards had begun to speak of moving to a place in Canada where others like them had fled and begun new lives. June knew from Guy's account of his long and exhausting march that Canada was a vast distance off. Still, she knew what a determined man Guy Watson was, and she was convinced that if he was able to survive to the end of this war, a free man, he would come to look for her.

As her son began to doze at her breast, she looked at him and thought the Hazzards had lost a son, but he was still alive in the world, and they still had each other. She had lost a husband but he, too, was alive on the earth, and she still had their baby. It was not everything, and not what she and Guy had dreamed of and hoped for. But it was something. Until that day when he came, she would have to find a way to live with it. She rocked slowly. Her son, warm against her lap, sighed and his trusting eyes drifted shut. She glanced up and saw out the window that some of the trees had already begun here and there to blaze with color.

Afterword

In January of 1781, after the First Rhode Island Regiment was combined with the Second Rhode Island, Samuel Ward retired from the army with the rank of Lieutenant Colonel. Four months later, while guarding the Pines Bridge on the Croton River in Westchester County, New York, the regiment's command was surprised in a nighttime attack on their quarters by soldiers from DeLancey's Loyalists, Americans fighting on behalf of the British. Colonel Christopher Greene and thirteen other Rhode Islanders, most of them black, were killed in hand-to-hand fighting. Greene's body was mutilated by castration, dismembered, and dragged over a mile off into the woods.

In the fall of 1780, after a series of inept appointments by Congress, Washington personally chose Nathanael Greene to become his second in command and head up the war in the South. Greene evaluated the situation and brilliantly pursued the opportunistic strategy of what he called a "fugitive war," or what we might now call guerrilla tactics. Over the following several years, his campaign—which is still studied today by military students and historians—drove the British out of the deep South. Three years after the war ended, Nathanael Greene died of an apparent stroke on his plantation in Savannah, Georgia. He was forty-four.

Former slave governor Guy Watson, though wounded more than once, served in the First Rhode Island regiment to the conclusion of the Revolutionary War in 1783. Thirty-five years later, after being described by witnesses in court records as "a good soldier" and partly disabled from his wounds, he was granted a veteran's pension. According to the journal of Daniel Stedman, a local farmer, Guy Watson's widely-attended funeral took place in Kingston, Rhode Island in 1837, fifty-nine years after his battle with the Hessians.

Samuel Ward and Phebe Greene were married for fifty years. They had ten children and sixteen grandchildren, one of whom, Julia Ward Howe, wrote "The Battle Hymn of the Republic." Samuel died in his home three months before his seventy-sixth birthday.

Acknowledgments

SINCE THIS NOVEL IS based on recent scholarship as well as on books, letters, papers, and diaries of the period, I have some sources I take pleasure in having the opportunity to thank. Especially helpful were Lorenzo Greene's pioneering work *The Negro in Colonial New England*, J. L. Dillard's linguistic study *Black English: Its History and Usage in the United States*, William D. Piersen's *Black Yankees*, David Lovejoy's scholarly inquiry *Rhode Island Politics and the American Revolution*, Robert Middlekauff's engaging overview *The Glorious Cause*, Gordon Wood's elegant distillation *The American Revolution*, Joseph Ellis's absorbing and persuasive *His Excellency: George Washington*, Sylvia Frey's *Water from the Rock*, Lawrence Levine's thoughtful *Black Culture and Black Consciousness*, Ira Berlin's sweeping *Many Thousands Gone*, Philip Foner's survey *Blacks in the American Revolution*, Sidney Kaplan's *The Black Presence in the Era of the Revolution*, James and Lois Horton's vivid *Slavery and the Making of America*, Paul F. Dearden's detailed *The Rhode Island Campaign of 1778*, Justin H. Smith's meticulous *Arnold's March*, and Kenneth Roberts' carefully edited diaries of the men who undertook that remarkable journey to Canada as well as his entertaining novels about the era.

I would also like to thank the Newport Historical Society for extending their hospitality and the Rhode Island Historical Society for generously making available to me their collection of the Ward Papers. And I would especially like to thank my friend, historian Ellen K. Rothman, who helped me keep my sources to the hundreds instead of the thousands and who introduced me to the work of Nancy Cott, Mary Beth Norton, Jacqueline Jones, Linda Kerber, and Laurel Thatcher Ulrich, as well as to her own excellent book on the history of courtship, *Hands and Hearts.*

To the late C. Vann Woodward who read an early draft, to Ray DiPasquale for approving the sabbaticals that permitted me to write, and to those friends whose meals and many conversations have enriched both life and work: Maggie and James Burke, Randy Chinnock, Isabelle de Courtivron, Tom and Cheryl Creeden, Paula Derrow, Ana Flores, Gus Freedman, Liz Gelfand, David Halloran, Fi and Bob Herbert, Annette Kolodny, John Marron, Peter and Trudy O'Connell, Dan Peters, Alya Reeve, Jackie Sand, Ed and Elaine Shoben, Vic Strasburger, Jerry Sundheimer, Gabe Warren, Antonia Woods, Jane Ulman, and Michael West, all thanks. And to Lisa and Dan, as always, love.

DUFFIELD BRANCH LIBRARY
2507 WEST GRAND BOULEVARD
DETROIT, MICHIGAN 48208
(313) 481-1712